AND

NIGHT

DESCENDS

The Third Book of the Small Gods

by

Bruce Blake

Also by Bruce Blake

The Books of the Small Gods:

When Shadows Fall
The Darkness Comes
And Night Descends
When Ravens Call
The Twilight FadesAnd Kingdoms End

Khirro's Journey epic fantasy:

Blood of the King
Spirit of the King
Heart of the King

The Icarus Fell urban fantasy series:

On Unfaithful Wings
All Who Wander Are Lost
Secrets of the Hanged Man

Prologue

Long ago, blood and anger colored his dreams red every night until the night she came to him.

In his sleep, steel glinted through the haze of crimson, pain flashed. A coppery scent stirred him in his bed, rank bile soured his tongue, and Trenan woke with sweat on his brow and agony tearing through him from an arm no longer there. Every time he awakened, he reached out with a phantom hand, expecting—hoping—for fingers to brush the rough wool blanket or touch his face. But they found nothing because they remained attached to an arm rotting in the bottom of a ditch with the rest of the dead.

"At least the rest of you isn't down there," Erral had said with a chuckle one day as he sat beside his bunk, struggling to articulate his appreciation.

Trenan thought lying in the ditch with the dead might be better than losing the arm meant to wield his sword.

What good is a soldier with no hand to hold his weapon?

The one-armed swordsman stared up at the dark ceiling, the muscles in his jaw clenched hard against the throb in his shoulder and the knot clogging his throat. Since the days of his childhood, his life had been based on what that arm could do with a sword. It performed feats others couldn't, moved in ways and with speed beyond the abilities of but a few men. It took lives, saved lives, helped to put down a rebellion.

But no more. Off it came, a sacrifice to save the king from a blow meant to separate his royal head from his regal body. A more than fair trade in the kingdom's mind, but a bitter mouthful to a master swordsman left with the wrong arm.

Trenan closed his eyes and inhaled through his nose, filling his lungs to capacity and using the air to squash regret from his chest. Sacrificing himself for the king was expected of him and an honor. But it wasn't he who'd been sacrificed but his arm, with the rest of him left behind to cope without it.

I'd rather have died.

And they knew it; it was the reason his chambers were devoid of sharp weapons.

"Trenan?"

The whispered word didn't startle him, but he was surprised by the timbre of the voice speaking it. The doctor assigned to his bedside like a hairy-chested wet nurse would return soon to touch his forehead to gauge his temperature, or give him more of the acrid herbs to hide a pain that would never leave, but the man charged with caring for him didn't speak with a woman's voice.

Trenan dragged his lids open, cocked his head. The woman perched on the chair set beside his bunk was the last person he'd have expected to find.

Her hair, which he'd only ever seen her wear up, hung loose past her shoulders in waves the color of honey tinted with a few drops of blood. Her eyes sparkled with the dim light of the taper flickering in the far corner of the swordsman's chamber, worry plain in their set. Concern tilted the corners of the full lips of her exquisite mouth.

"My queen."

Trenan scrambled to push himself up on his elbows, forgot he had but one, and tumbled onto his side on the mattress, jarring his wound. He gritted his teeth and pressed his lips together to keep from crying out, but when he found the queen's hand upon him, he forgot the pain.

"Are you all right?"

He looked into the eyes of the young woman who'd seen the seasons turn eighteen times since her birth and once since she'd become wife to the king. The knot of despair that had choked him dissipated, the pain in his shoulder faded. He nodded.

"Yes, my queen."

"Ishla," she said and brushed his cheek with the backs of her fingers. "You poor man."

She settled back on the edge of the chair, removing her touch from his face, but the feel of it remained with him. He struggled himself up to sitting, the wool blanket falling from his bare chest as he stretched to see past the wife of his friend. Behind her, the chamber lay empty.

"Where is Gollard?" He looked to her face, found her still gazing at him, so diverted his eyes. "Where is the doctor?"

"Do you need him?"

She stood, took a half-step toward the door and stopped, awaiting his reply. He'd have answered at once but, when she stood, he saw she'd chosen not to wear one of the elaborate dresses he'd seen her wear every other time he'd been in her presence. Instead, she wore white bed clothes with sleeve cuffs that clung to her wrists and a hem that brushed her ankles.

"N...no. I'm fine, just wondering where he'd gone."

Ishla clasped her hands in front of her, lowered her chin to regard her intertwined fingers.

"I had him called away."

Trenan stared at the young woman. Now her eyes weren't upon him, he let his gaze linger, saw that the taper burning behind her cast her outline in the fine cloth. Trenan swallowed hard.

"Called away? For what?"

She raised her head, making him slip his gaze back to her face, then gestured toward the side of the bed.

"May I?"

Trenan looked from her to the bed and back, uncertain what she meant, at first. He cleared his throat and nodded.

"Of course, my quee...Ishla."

She alighted on the edge of the mattress close enough Trenan felt her warmth. Her perfume filled his nose—not a cologne she'd put on, but the smell of her hair, the scent of her skin. Apprehension stirred in the swordsman's chest, excitement, confusion.

Why is she here?

"I've come to thank you for saving the king, Trenan."

It might have surprised him that she read his thoughts, but what else might he have been thinking? Trenan shifted away, trying to quell his excited discomfort.

"There's no need. The king has conveyed his appreciation with the best surgeons the kingdom can offer and his promise to take care of me as long as I need."

The words were Erral's, but this marked the first time Trenan had spoken them aloud. They tasted of vinegar on his tongue, but the queen's sweetness was enough to overpower the bitter morsel.

Ishla wiggled nearer, closing the distance he'd created, her lithe body making little impression on the mattress. His eyes strayed from hers, fell to her curves beneath the bed clothes before returning to find a smile beginning on her lips.

"That is Erral's way of thanking you, not mine. And I suspect his method may be more hurtful than fulfilling."

She lifted a hand and touched her palm to his cheek. Trenan nearly jerked away out of sense of duty to king and kingdom but didn't for fear of offending the queen. And because he liked the way her warm flesh felt against his.

Ishla moved closer and leaned in, leaving a hand's-breadth between the tips of their noses. Her breath touched his lips, her gaze found its way inside him.

"It is my thanks I bring tonight."

"And Gollard?"

"Won't be back until morning."

"Who else knows you had him called away?"

She shook her head. "A queen can be discreet."

Trenan licked his lips, resisted the urge to close the space between them. A plethora of furtive smiles returned to his memory. From the first time he'd seen his friend's wife—the queen of the kingdom—they'd been there, finding their way to her lips whenever their eyes met. As much as he wanted them to be for him, about him, he'd convinced himself her nature and her youth brought them forth, convinced himself the tingle-inspiring smiles and gentle blushes weren't meant for him.

Now he didn't know if he should be elated he'd been wrong, or fearful.

His gaze slipped form her eyes to her mouth. He imagined his lips pressing against hers, their tongues finding each other, until the king's angry visage intruded on his thoughts.

"Erral—"

"Is your friend," she finished for him. "And my husband, but he isn't here. There is you and me, and no one else knows I'm here."

Her hand left his face, fell to rest on his upper chest. The tight thrill swirling beneath his ribs expanded, flowing into his stomach, lower, stirring other things. Ishla held his gaze but moved no more, staring into his eyes with her lips parted, her head tilted.

This is wrong.

Trenan's mind continued to resist even as he leaned forward and their mouths came together.

***

Ishla ran the tip of her finger along the swordsman's breastbone, tracing a line through the cooling perspiration. The ache in Trenan's shoulder he'd forgotten as the queen expressed her appreciation crept back as though someone pressed the tip of a stick into his wound.

The queen peered at him and he held her gaze. Though neither spoke, words swam through his mind— things to say, plans never to be executed, the vision of an impossible life. He thought he saw the same shining in her eyes, hidden behind a mix of nurturing care and sadness.

After a moment, the breathtaking young woman climbed off him, her weight lifting from his hips as another palpable one settled into his chest.

"I must go before I am missed," she said, one corner of her mouth lifting in a lopsided smile.

She bent and retrieved her nightgown from the floor. Trenan watched as she shook it out, revelling in the way her muscles moved beneath her porcelain skin, the tremor shaking her breasts. She stretched her arms toward the ceiling and slipped her hands into the sleeves, let the nightshirt fall around her like the curtain falling at the end of a masterful play.

A performance Trenan never wanted to end.

The gown fell into place and she smoothed the front with her palms. The swordsman reached out, a jolt of pain shooting along the right side of his chest, and grasped her wrist, coaxed her back toward the bed.

"When will I see you again?"

She looked at him, the smile still on her face, but he watched the sliver of sadness in her eyes overtake it. The queen said nothing in response; she didn't need to. He'd already known the answer before his lips spoke the words—this was a dangerous game they shouldn't play again.

Dangerous, but worth the risk.

Ishla leaned over and put her lips to his, the passion and longing of their earlier kisses usurped by regret, mourning. The touch lingered, and he thought to grab her, pull her to him, but the moment passed and she moved away. Trenan released his hold on her wrist and watched her stride across the room to the chamber door.

She let herself out without a backward glance.

***

"I've seen the seasons pass nearly fifteen times," Dansil mumbled under his breath as he stalked through the castle halls. "I'll be a man soon enough; bitch can't tell me what to do."

His cheek still stung in precisely the shape of his mother's hand, but her punishments didn't hurt like they did in his youth. Then, they'd caused him more than physical pain; it was as though she'd struck his soul.

But if something gets beaten enough times, it toughens.

He came to a corner and slowed his pace, peeked around before continuing. Getting caught wandering the halls wouldn't get him killed, but none of the king's men would be impressed should they discover him. Even with the red haze of anger at his mother hanging around him, he knew better than to be careless—he'd crept these halls enough times.

Dansil followed the hall and went up the next staircase, avoiding the routes the guards followed when patrolling in the evening. At the top of the stairs, he paused a second time, checking both ways along the corridor. Thick carpet in a shade of deep red covered the floor in both directions; portraits of people he neither recognized nor cared to recognize lined the walls.

On a whim, he took a right and maintained a slow but steady pace, the muscles in his thighs tight and ready to hie him away should one of the many doors lining the hall open and a visiting noble step out. He figured none would this late at night, but better ready than caught.

The end of the hall intersected another; here he stopped again and found himself rewarded for his care. Halfway along the corridor, a door opened. A woman clothed in white bedclothes emerged, the wall sconces behind her illuminating the outline of her body through the cloth.

Dansil sucked a sharp breath at the sight and his hand darted to his groin. The woman stood for a short time, hand on the door's handle, her head hung. Her long hair caressed her arms and shoulders, the light highlighted the shape of her breasts, the curve at the small of her back. After a moment, she raised her head, glanced along the hall away from where Dansil peered around the corner, then swivelled her head toward him. The young man faded back from the corner before she saw him, a silent curse on his lips.

He waited, breath held, resisting the urge to peep around the corner again. If he did, and she was walking away, the wall sconce's light might shine between her legs, outlining the most secret of places. But if she headed toward him, he'd be discovered.

The whisper of footsteps padding on the rug interrupted his thought.

She's coming this way.

No time to hurry back the way he'd come; if he tried, she'd see him, even if she didn't turn his direction. Lips squeezed hard together, he pressed himself against the wall and hoped she'd continue straight along the corridor.

A moment later, she passed by and Dansil saw her face. His eyes widened and his grip on his half-swollen man thing released.

The queen!

As she hurried down the corridor, Dansil stepped out

from his hiding spot to watch her go, forgetting the possibility she might glance back and see him. She didn't and, instead of admiring the swing of her hips, the shape of her body hidden beneath the bedclothes, the young man wondered why she'd be out alone at this time of night. When she disappeared around the far corner, he peered back toward the door she'd exited.

The curiosity was too much for Dansil. He crept along the corridor in the direction from which the queen had come, his hand extended and fingertips dragging along the rough stone wall. Every door appeared the same as the others, but he'd noted the one from which she'd emerged: the third on the left. A moment later, he stood in front of the plain wood slab, staring at the handle. After a quick survey of the empty hall, he leaned close, pressed his ear to the door, but heard no sounds within.

Excited saliva filled his mouth. He swallowed hard, raised his hand and rapped his knuckles against the wood.

The knock garnered no immediate response so Dansil assumed the chamber empty until a man's voice spoke a single word.

"Ishla?"

The curiosity burning in his brain tingled into his chest and along his limbs. The hand he still held raised after knocking fell to the door handle, gripped it. He didn't recognize the voice or know who might reside within, but was aware he shouldn't enter any room in the castle without invitation. He also knew no invitation would come if he waited for one, and he'd never discover who the door concealed.

Dansil set his jaw and pushed the door open.

A musky odor filled the air in the room, one he recognized from the occasions when his mother came home with a man and sent him off to his chambers. The furnishings were sparse and a man lay upon a bed to the left, one shoulder wrapped with a pink-tinged bandage where his arm was missing. The tender expression on his face went stony when he spied the lad.

"Who are you? What are you doing here?"

"Beg your pardon, m'lord swordsman. Wrong chamber."

Dansil backed out of the room and closed the door behind him, a wicked grin creeping onto his lips as he went. The door clicked shut; he hurried away along the hall lest the man rise and come after him.

Trenan and the queen. The king's friend and his wife. Together.

He rounded the corner and hastened to the staircase, the path of his future falling into view.

Sometimes, one unexpected turn of events can change a boy's life.

I Teryk - Stowaway

Afraid to swallow for fear the tip of the saber brushing his throat might slice him, Teryk's mouth filled with saliva, threatened to spill out between his lips. The sailor holding the broad-bladed sword glared at him, one brow raised, sun gleaming on the wax holding his moustache in its curls. A bead of nervous, fearful sweat on the prince's forehead rolled between his eyebrows and along the bridge of his nose.

"Well?" the blade wielder asked as his patience waned. "Do you think you're deservin' of feedin' the God of the Deep? Don't know if'n he likes the flavor of stowaway or not. Only one way to find out."

Whispers and chuckles washed through the other men gathered, passing from one to another like a bottle of hooch to be enjoyed by all. The man with the sword leaned closer, forcing Teryk to lean away or be skewered on the end of his saber. The wale pressed hard against his lower back as it bent until his head hung out over the sea.

"Please," the prince whispered, lips barely moving.

The fellow laughed, but the others gathered behind him went silent as another sound rose in place of their joyous encouragement. *Clomp-thump. Clomp-thump.* When the sailor holding the sword heard it, he leaned back a little, allowing Teryk to stand almost straight, but the blade's tip remained at his throat.

"Cap'n on deck," a hoarse voice cried.

Clomp-thump. Clomp-thump.

"What's going on here?"

The words rumbled across the deck, dripping with the sound of authority and of a man used to being heeded. Teryk's mustachioed captor's eyes flickered toward the voice and back to the prince.

"A stowaway, Cap'n. We be deciding what's the best way to deal with him."

"The last I checked, such decisions belong to the captain. Were you proclaimed captain while I slept, Digred?"

The man shook his head, the waxed ends of his moustache not so much as quivering with the movement. "Not as I recall, Cap'n."

"Then lower your blade and let's treat this fellow like a real person until we learn his intent. We're sailors of the king, not heathen pirates of the Water Kingdom."

With a final scowl and a flash of yellowed teeth, the saber's tip left Teryk's throat and its wielder stepped away. The prince immediately swallowed hard and brought his hand to his neck to check for blood; he found none.

After heaving two relieved but still frightened

breaths, he raised his head to peer upon the face of the man who'd spared him.

So far.

He wore his graying hair cut short and tidy, unlike most of the crew gathered around, and his salt-and-pepper beard matched his coif. His clothes appeared cleaner and in better repair than those of the other men, but none of this meant a thing once Teryk's gaze reached the captain's footwear.

A polished leather boot with a modest heel and a gold buckle on the side covered his right foot, but where the left should have been was naught but a block of wood. Whatever doctor or artisan affixed it in place hadn't bothered to shape it to resemble a foot or boot—a block of unfinished wood instead.

Teryk had seen that unusual foot once before, when seasons past he'd gone for a ride on the Devil of the Deep's maiden voyage. He gulped again but said nothing, waiting for the skipper to speak.

"I'm Captain Bryder. You must forgive Digred for his lack of diplomacy; he's just protecting His Majesty's ship."

The prince nodded and realized he'd been rubbing the spot on his throat where the point of Digred's saber had kept him at bay. He made himself stop and glanced past the captain at the mustachioed man. He'd stored his sword back in its scabbard but continued scowling as he twisted the end of his curled moustache between his thumb and first finger.

"Well, don't be rude, lad. I've told you my name, and you've probably guessed my purpose for being aboard His Majesty's Ship Whalebone. How about you enlighten us with your moniker and reason for finding your way onto my deck?"

Teryk's gaze flitted from one sailor to the next before returning to the captain. He recognized none of the others, wouldn't have recognized the captain if not for his unusual foot. But did Bryder or any of the other sailors recognize him? It didn't seem so.

If I tell them the truth, they'll turn the ship about and take me back. Going back to Draekfarren will be the end of my part of the prophecy.

"T...Taylor. My name is Taylor." He heard the hesitation in his own voice and hoped they'd assume fear of being thrown over the side caused it rather than a struggle to find a lie.

Captain Bryder nodded. "All right, T-Taylor. Now we know who you are, what brings you aboard my ship?"

Teryk paused again, licked his lips; they tasted of salt and the sea.

"I'm running away."

Before the captain could respond, Digred barked a harsh laugh. "Runnin' away, be ya?" he said. "And what be ya runnin' from?"

"None of your damned business," Teryk replied with a curl to his lip. The response surprised him; it had come from him before he had the chance to consider an answer. Digred tensed and his hand dropped from twiddling his moustache to find the hilt of his saber.

"Well, you look the part, lad," Bryder said, surveying Teryk up and down. "Stand down, Digred."

Teryk watched the man look to the captain. His expression shifted as though he might say something, perhaps to plead for the opportunity to dispose of the scoundrel who'd stowed away on their ship, but then he released his grip on the sword. His hand found its way back to the end of his moustache and a smile spread across his lips.

"As ye say, Cap'n."

"If we were closer to port," his gaze swept across the crew gathered behind him, "if my lazy crew had done their jobs and cleaned the ship before we got this far from land, I'd put you ashore. Alas, I'm not of a mind to be turning the Whalebone around."

Relief flooded through Teryk and he felt the tension in his shoulders ease. A murmur spread through the sailors and the captain waited for it to pass, as though he'd expected it. When it didn't die away, he faced his crew.

"Any of you got something to say?"

"One more mouth to feed," a man with a shiny bald head called out.

"Ain't no space," said another missing his two front teeth.

"We've got plenty of food in the stores," the captain pointed out, "and if he came out of the hold, then he can go back into it to make his bunk, too."

The murmuring continued, but no one else spoke until Digred took a step toward his captain. The way he acted suggested to Teryk that he held higher standing on the ship than the rest of the crew. He hooked both his thumbs in his sword belt, smile gone from his lips, and glared at Teryk for a moment before returning his attention to Bryder.

"If'n you let one stowaway aboard your boat," he said, his voice no louder than if he engaged in a regular conversation, "then others'll surely follow. Don't want no one thinkin' ye be soft, do ye, Cap'n?"

The prince couldn't see the captain's face, but his tone suggested he pressed his teeth tight together, that he thought Digred had spoken out of turn.

"He's a runaway. No one but us on this ship know of his presence. Which of you will tell so other stowaways try their luck, too?"

The murmurs ceased and a palpable tension fell across the crew. Digred's smug look eased and he shook his head slightly, indicating it wouldn't be him. To

Teryk, it was obvious the men respected their captain, perhaps feared him despite his seemingly calm and fair demeanor.

"Right, then." Bryder spun on his wooden foot, the grain of it grinding against the deck. "No one rides for free, lad. You'll be pitching in and doing your part or Digred gets his wish. Understand?"

Teryk nodded enthusiastically, the fear and dread at being put overboard or taken back to the wrath of his father dissipating and the hope to fulfill the prophecy returning. Captain Bryder nodded, too.

"We have an agreement. Ash."

Behind the captain, the crew dispersed, heading back to their duties. As the crowd parted, a boy Teryk hadn't seen amongst them made his way to the captain's side. He looked to have seen no more than twelve or thirteen turns of the seasons, and his diminutive stature explained why the prince hadn't noticed him before.

"Taylor, this is Ash, my cabin boy. Seems the two of you might have somewhat in common."

Teryk nodded toward the boy. "Hello, Ash."

He took a step to his left, half hiding himself behind the captain.

"Don't worry, he'll get used to you quick enough." Bryder put his hand on the cabin boy's shoulder and Ash looked up at him. "You'll be showing our guest around the boat, Ash. Get him some bedding and clothes and find him some jobs so the boys don't get riled by him being here."

Ash nodded and took two tentative steps forward, reached out and grabbed Teryk by the wrist. The captain spoke again before the cabin boy led him away.

"Before you do all that, take the poor lad to the galley and get him some food. Looks like he hasn't eaten in a long while."

Wood scraped wood as Bryder spun on the block of a

foot and strode away across the deck. *Clomp-thump. Clomp-thump.*

Teryk tilted his head back, gazing skyward and filling his lungs with salty air. Ash tugged at his arm, but he stayed put for a moment, enjoying the sun on his face and noticing a bird circling in the cloudless blue high above. It wasn't a gull like he'd have expected, but a black bird with wide wings and a long, blunt beak. He watched it until his stomach gurgled, confirming what the captain had noted but what, in his excitement and then fear, he hadn't realized until now.

He looked away from the raven, rubbed his belly, and allowed Ash to lead him away.

II Trenan – A Familiar Voice

Godsbane's hilt felt foreign in Trenan's hand as he gripped it tight. The man called Stirk knelt before him, forced to his knees by Dansil. Jeers and cheers rose from the crowd, each taunt and holler grating on the swordsman's ears, disgusting him that the mob so enjoyed watching the deaths of others. He took no joy in death, no matter what the reason or how deserved; any soldier would tell you the same.

What must be, must be.

He raised the crownsword, his face pulled into a frown, and the rabble gathered in front of the platform fell into relative silence. Stirk shifted, staring at the wooden boards, and Dansil tightened his grip on the man.

"Trenan! No!"

The words reached him clear and loud, spoken in the

princess' voice as though she stood beside him. Trenan jerked his head away from the task at hand, blade still held aloft, and for an instant the crowd parted. He glimpsed two figures—one clad in the drab green smock and wooden mask of the Goddess, the other in red—then they disappeared. The mob's noise rose in angry tones calling for blood, but the master swordsman ignored their pleas.

Trenan leaped from the platform and waded into the sea of onlookers, its members doing their best to move aside and avoid Godsbane's sharp edge, but their mass impeded him. He shouldered his way through, growling in his throat, and finally burst out the far side into the open.

The lanes beyond lay empty.

Three of them opened into the square. In his haste to pursue the voice that sounded like the princess, he hadn't seen which one they'd followed. He stared first down one, then the next and the next, hoping to spy a green smock, a flash of red, but saw nothing. With no other reason than a feeling in his gut, he took a step toward the lane to his right, halting at the touch of a hand on his shoulder. Trenan wheeled, sword poised ready to defend himself, but held up when he found Osis standing behind him, arms raised defensively. The sword master lowered his weapon and spun on his heel to continue his survey of the lanes.

"It was Danya who called out. I'm sure of it," Trenan growled.

"Then we must inform the king," Osis said.

Trenan clenched his teeth and breathed heavily through his nostrils. His friend was right. Any news of the princess or prince should be relayed back to the king and queen as expediently as possible, but the master swordsman couldn't bear the thought of returning to Ishla with news and nothing more. The next time he saw her, he intended to have both her children with him.

Finally, Trenan nodded and faced Osis.

"You return to the king. I'll keep after the princess while the trail is warm."

The clatter of armor caused both of the men to spin around and stare back toward the square where the execution took place. They found Dansil and Strylor heading toward them at double time. The sight of them tightened Trenan's chest with anger.

"What are you doing? Where is the prisoner?"

A vision of Dansil's axe falling across the big man's neck, completing the job they'd intended, came to Trenan. His grip tightened on Godsbane's hilt; it wasn't the soldier's place to execute a man without a direct order. Doing so was murder, not justice.

Maybe this is how I'll be rid of him.

"Bastard escaped," Dansil said as the two of them pulled up short of where Trenan and Osis stood.

"Escaped? How could you let—"

"We ain't to blame. He slipped away in the ruckus you caused jumping off the platform instead of finishing the job you was supposed to do."

"A kneeling man escaped," Trenan grated between clenched teeth. "All you had to do was keep him there."

Dansil shrugged. "He was quicker than we thought and Strylor's feet got caught up in the woman's body when he went to go after him, didn't they, Stry?"

The other man glanced sideways at the big soldier but said nothing. He replied with a quick, curt nod.

"He headed toward Waterside, though, makin' for the docks. He can't have gotten too far."

"Forget him," Trenan said.

"Forget him? Has it left your mind what the bastard and his mother did to the prince?"

"No, it hasn't," he snapped. "But that was the princess who called out my name. If there's a chance we can recover her and return her to the queen, that takes priority."

Dansil raised an eyebrow. "You mean return her to the queen and king, don't you?"

"Yes, of course." Trenan glanced at Osis; he remained beside him but stayed out of the conversation. The man was a good soldier, willing to do anything to support his friend; anything except turn against his king.

The master swordsman drew a long breath, hating the stink of the city streets that found its way into his lungs. He looked from Osis to Strylor, who wore a derisive grin Trenan wanted to knock from his face with the butt of his sword, and then to Dansil. Every fiber of his being wanted to return the two of them to the castle with the latest news, allowing him to be free of them, but he didn't trust Dansil and, by association, Strylor.

"We'll find the man, Stirk, another time to administer the king's justice. Now we must do everything we can to locate the princess while she is so close."

Dansil nodded but refused to speak his agreement. The grin on Strylor's visage continued unhindered. Each passing moment as they remained there doing nothing tugged at the back of Trenan's mind as he pictured Danya's footsteps carrying her away from being found.

What is she doing? Where does she think she's going?

"Osis will return to Draekfarren and pass news of the princess on to the king and queen," Trenan said.

"And Strylor will go along with him so I know nothing ain't amiss."

Trenan bit back a curt response. Another time, he'd have called out the soldier for his insubordinate words and tone, but the press of time kept him from doing so. In addition, he'd have less to worry about with Dansil's compatriot safely out of the way with Osis, whom he knew as trustworthy. Still, the thought of being alone with Dansil brought a curl to his upper lip.

"Fine," Trenan agreed at last. He turned his attention to Osis. "Take Strylor with you, sergeant. The king will decide whether you two should return to us on your own or with reinforcements."

"Reinforcements?" Dansil scoffed. "Against one novice of the Goddess cult?" He devolved into laughter.

Once again, Trenan bit back his response. He held his gaze on Osis, knowing the sergeant could see the flame of dislike burning in his eyes. The opportunity would come for Dansil to answer for his ways but, for now, he had to concentrate on the princess. If they found Danya, perhaps she could lead them to the prince, though he had no love for spending his time alone with Dansil.

"Be off," he said to Osis, returning Godsbane to its sheath. "And take Strylor with you."

Osis nodded, glanced sideways at Dansil then back at Trenan, as if to ask if the two would survive each other. He then turned his attention to Strylor who, in the master swordsman's estimation, resembled a grinning fool.

"Come," Osis gestured for Strylor to follow and started along the lane that led most quickly back to the walls around Draekfarren.

Dansil slapped his companion on the shoulder with the thump of leather gauntlet against armor. "Keep an eye on that one," he said. "And I'll keep mine on this one."

He nodded toward Trenan, ensuring he caught the master swordsman's eye. Strylor continued grinning and took off after Osis, armor rattling.

For a moment after the two of them left, Trenan and Dansil remained facing each other in the middle of the lane, gazes locked. In that time, Trenan realized that, if he still held the crownsword in his hand, he'd have struggled to keep from wetting it with Dansil's blood.

Perhaps Osis is right to wonder if both of us will

survive.

The lopsided smile on Dansil's face suggested the same thought had occurred to him.

III Stirk - Escape

The big soldier who'd lopped off Elishbieta's head clapped one hand on Stirk's shoulder while the other gripped the axe tinted with his mother's blood. Stirk considered glaring at him, fighting back against his fate, but the sight of his mother's lifeless body lying near his feet drained fight and defiance from him.

The soldier—he'd heard the one-armed man call him Dansil—exerted downward pressure, directing Stirk to his knees in front of the block of wood stained with Bieta's lifeblood. He did his best to make it difficult, but his legs didn't have the energy to resist. Fresh blood on the boards of the platform soaked the knees of his breeches, its wetness bringing tears to his eyes, blurring the faces in the crowd barely more than an arm's length away.

With his face near the stump, the odor of cedar and the coppery stink of his mother's death penetrated his nostrils, clogging his already constricted throat with the threat of nausea. He swallowed hard and Dansil pushed him forward. Stirk turned his head, his cheek pressing against the blood-dampened wood, eyes finding his mother's slack, dead face; he immediately wished he'd chosen to face the other direction.

Trenan, the one-armed sword master, stood to the right, the tip of the crown blade destined to end Stirk's life dangling above the platform's floorboards. His tears transformed the sunlight shining on the blade into shimmering stars, dazzling him. The sword tip disappeared from his view, raised above his line of sight. He chose not to follow its path, knowing what it meant.

Dansil pressed hard against his back, holding him in place so Trenan could end his life with one killing blow. The buzz of the crowd diminished and Stirk closed his eyes. Never had he wondered what became of a man at the end of his days. People sometimes talked of new lives, or a different world; with the stench of blood in his nose and the sweat of fear on his brow, he was less convinced than ever such might be the case.

But if it's true, will I see mother again?

The thought didn't ease his tension.

The crowd fell silent and Stirk imagined how Trenan must look with Godsbane raised skyward, pausing before administering Stirk's punishment for imprisoning the prince and planning to ransom him. A smile would curl the sword master's lips, the way one had tilted Dansil's when his axe separated Bieta's head from her neck. Stirk parted his lips to explain he hadn't realized who the boy was, to blame his mother for the idea, but the time for pleading and excuses had passed. If they didn't work before, they'd do him no good now.

Sweat rolled along Stirk's temple and down his nose. In the breath-held silence, he imagined he heard the droplet trace its path along his flesh and his mother's blood drying in the sun. He thought—

"Trenan! No!"

The words broke the hush like the blast of a trumpet and Stirk's lids snapped open.

I'm still alive.

He saw the one-armed swordsman's feet shift as he faced the crowd, searching for the owner of the voice who'd called out, and Stirk knew he'd continue living at least a moment longer. He blinked to clear the grief and fear from his eyes.

Godsbane's tip returned to his view and Stirk's heart

thumped in his chest. The blade dangled for a second, catching the sunlight, nearly blinding him, then Trenan's feet shuffled and he jumped from the platform. The crowd came back to life with a mixture of worried murmurs and shocked gasps that combined and grew to a dull roar. Someone shouted for blood, others took up the chorus.

"Trenan," Dansil called after the sword master. He must have straightened to get a look where his companion went, for the pressure on Stirk's back eased. Air came easier to his lungs. "Trenan!"

The weight on him lessened again and Stirk gulped a coppery breath. This would be his one chance for life to continue.

He jerked back, using his size and weight and surprise to catch Dansil off guard. It worked and the man stumbled away a step, releasing his hold. Stirk leaped to his feet and bounded over his mother's corpse then dove into the crowd. People parted before him, scared of getting in his way.

"Hey!" Dansil roared.

The clomp of a boot on the wooden platform reached his ears, followed by a louder thump. He glanced back over his shoulder to see the king's soldier had slipped in a puddle of Bieta's blood, his feet going out from under him and throwing him to his ass. Stirk longed to stop and laugh at the man's misfortune, enjoy the elation of escape, but he caught sight of his mother's head lying on the boards. Her wide eye stared at him, her mouth frozen open as though it might yell at him to stop gawking and run.

Stirk turned, lowered his face, and did just that.

＊＊＊

The stitch in Stirk's side from running felt how he imagined it must be if someone inserted the tip of a pike between his ribs.

27

He stopped and bent at the waist, one hand and one stump planted on his knees as he gasped whooping breaths into his chest to satisfy his aching lungs. The first few didn't make it in, the pain in his side squelching them, but after a struggle, some air made it through.

It tasted of salt and creosote, of bird shit baking in the sun. He fought to keep it from bringing nausea to his throat and making it more difficult to breathe.

I'm near the docks.

He raised his head, sweat and tears streaming down his cheeks. He wiped an arm across his stinging eyes, shaded them from the blinding sunlight with a hand at his brow.

I dropped the whelp off somewhere close to here.

Thinking of the prince made him grind his back teeth. He lowered his gaze to the stump at the end of his left arm, created in payment to save the fucker so he and Bieta might ransom him, profit from his misfortune. It hadn't turned out well—he'd ended up short the prince to be ransomed, one hand, and a mother, too.

"Mother."

He straightened and strode forward three paces, ignoring the now-bearable pain in his side. Gripping the edges of crates to steady himself, he continued on to where he'd left their captive, to where he'd brought Trenan and the others to find the young man gone.

If he'd been there, would my mother be dead? If they'd seen we made sure he stayed alive, what might have happened?

His teeth pressed together tighter, biting hard enough his jaw ached. His belly clenched along with it, his sweat-beaded brow creased.

"If you weren't gone, mother'd be alive."

He kicked a crate hard enough to splinter the wood and make himself wince at the pain it caused his toe, then booted it again anyway. A gull crawked at him

28

from its perch atop a nearby building, tilted its head like it didn't know why he'd do such a thing. Stirk picked up a piece of wood broken from the crate and heaved it at the shithawk, missing by a wide margin but sending the bird squawking into the sky.

The big man breathed hard in and out through his nose, nostrils flaring at the briny stink of the sea and the tang of his own sweat. Hauling the salty air into his lungs made him angrier. He balled his hand into a fist, fingernails digging into the fleshy part of his palm. He imagined feeling the same sensation at the end of his left arm where his other hand used to be not so long ago.

Anger boiled over into rage.

"You killed my mother," he said aloud between his clenched teeth. "If we didn't help you, she'd be alive."

Stirk grabbed the edge of the crate he'd kicked and pushed it hard. It rattled back and crashed into another behind it, sending more chunks of wood tumbling to the ground. He held his other hand up in front of his face, glaring at the smooth skin at the end of his wrist.

"Mother'd be alive and I'd have both hands."

He bit his lower lip hard enough to draw blood, spat the bitter flavor from his tongue, then titled his head back and roared at the sky. The sound contained no words, only rage and grief. Another gull squawked at him, as though chastising him for the noise, then took off from its perch, winging its way toward the sea. Stirk watched it go.

"I'll kill him," he said after the bird like he imagined it cared to hear his plans. "I'll find the prince and kill him for what they did to my mother."

Saying it out loud, he realized how difficult fulfilling the promise might be. He didn't know what happened to the prince, where he'd gone. Had he woken from his prolonged swoon and walked away, headed for home? Did someone find him and return him to the castle? In either case, he'd soon be back behind fortified walls, gone forever from Stirk's reach, protected from his revenge. But if he'd gone in such manner, he'd have left signs of his passing.

Stirk cast his eyes to the ground, searching through dirt and pieces of packing straw, splatters of bird shit and streaks of grime. He was no tracker, having spent his entire life in the Horseshoe, so the hodgepodge of scattered bits and streaked splotches all looked the same to him—possibly footprints, more likely something else. He located no clues on the ground around his feet.

Because the prince was gone didn't mean he'd been rescued. The soldiers'd been fired up about finding him when Stirk brought them here and found the lad gone, their interest turning to severing necks instead of finding the heir to the throne. Did they see something he didn't? He bent at the waist, squinted, but the dirt and rocks and bird shit continued telling him nothing.

Another idea occurred to him as he straightened again: Perhaps a denizen of the docks came upon the prince and hatched the same plan he and Bieta failed at so miserably. If so, they may have the lad hidden nearby.

Stirk surveyed the buildings lining both sides of the street leading to the pier. Not a door stood open and most of the structures, being warehouses and the like, had no windows. They stretched before him and behind; each block to his right and left looked the same. It would take a great amount of time to check them all—time he didn't have. The men he'd escaped from would find him long before he finished searching.

An ache formed at the bottom of Stirk's gut, clawed up into his chest, brought nausea into his throat. It soon made its way to his head, causing it to throb and making him see his plan for vengeance dying before it started. The man responsible for his mother's death couldn't be found; he'd go on living while Bieta was no more.

Stirk's knees went watery and he stumbled forward a step, catching the edge of a crate with his hand to steady himself. The rage that had consumed him, tightening his muscles and knotting his jaw, melted way, leaving grief behind to wrap itself around him. It weighed on his shoulders, pushing on him until he crumpled and sank to the ground.

He sat with his back against a crate, face buried in his arms. His body shook with sobs. As long ago as he remembered, he'd never been alone—not for long, at least. Bieta had always taken care for him, guided him, told him what to do. Many times he'd resented the way she treated him, as if she considered him a child trapped in the body of a man, but now he didn't know how he'd live without her wisdom and guidance. Who'd feed him? Who'd comfort him and give him pleasure?

Who would be his mother?

Eyes closed tight, he pictured Elishbieta's face smiling at him, her tongue prodding the space between her front teeth as it so often did. The vision of her calmed him, and the sobs faded. He snuffled snot back into his nose and wiped his face with his sleeve.

"Mama," he whispered.

Her expression in his imagination changed. Her smile disappeared and her eyelids widened to a stare filled with fear. From out of nowhere, an axe sliced the air, and then her neck. His mother's head flew up, tumbling end over end until it hit the ground with a dull thump, bounced once, and settled. Blood gushed out of her neck and her corpse leaned and toppled revealing the one-armed man standing behind her, laughing and brandishing the axe.

Stirk's eyes snapped open and his body spasmed once, a massive shudder shaking him as if a malevolent spirit had passed through him. He shook his head to clear the vision and wrapped his arms around himself to stop the shiver quaking him despite the hot day. The grisly apparition of his mother disappeared from his mind, but the laughing sword master remained, blood dripping from the edge of the axe blade.

The big man's breath caught in his throat and his eyes narrowed. How had it eluded him before?

The prince was gone; he knew he wouldn't find the man responsible for setting in motion the events leading to his mother's execution. But Teryk wasn't the only one on whom responsibility for her death should fall. There was also the soldier who'd wielded the axe, and the one who gave him the order to take her life.

Stirk pushed himself to his feet, wiped his face on his sleeve. No more time for grief; there'd be no more whimpering and crying. He curled his hand into a fist and set his jaw, ready to undertake the work that lay ahead.

Trenan and Dansil must die.

IV Horace - Floatin'

Blue sky.

It hung o'er ol' Horace, stretchin' up and up and up with no more but it for him to see. A gull flew by once, its gray wings flappin'; considerin' the luck he were havin', he more'n half expected the damned thing to shit in his eye, but it didn't.

Cold sea water washed around him, sometimes splashin' up onto his cheeks or into his mouth. He didn't swallow any because he couldn't swallow any more'n he might've blinked or stroked his way to the shore. Limbs, mouth, eyelids, all refused to move. Eventually the salty water spilled back outta his mouth and o'er his chin to rejoin the rest o' the ocean.

After a short while, he paid no attention to the waves carryin' him away or the sun creepin' across the endless sky. His mind turned to Thorn and the two men what'd carried him off.

He didn't know what the big gray feller and the one what'd tried to drown him wanted with the Small God, but he s'pposed it might be easy to guess: he were a Small God from outta the Green, after all. That little man had magic in him and maybe they knew how to get it out.

Should've found a way to stop them.

The thought bounced around his head, but ev'rytime the guilt got its teeth into him, he recalled the tip o' the big gray feller's finger brushing his chest and endin' him up floatin' 'round like a chunk o' driftwood. Truly, he couldn't've done nothin' to stop them.

Sorry, Thorn.

His heart ached, his throat tightened, restrictin' his breathin'—the only thing he were capable of. He wished to close his eyes and cease starin' at the sky and the way it encouraged him into considerin' there might be a way out o' his predicament. But he were afraid that, if he closed them, he'd see Thorn's face, or that o' his son Rilum what Thorn'd turned into when they snuck up on the town o' Haven. Other'n when it showed up as the Small God's disguise, Horace hadn't pictured Rilum's face in a long, long while.

Instead o' blinkin'—which he couldn't do—or thinkin' o' his son—which he didn't want to do—Horace continued starin' at the vast blue emptiness above him. If nothin' else, doin' so kept him from imaginin' what might be swimmin' past in the green depths below. Wouldn't be no God o' the Deep—he were sure he hadn't bobbed his way so far from the shore—but a lot o' other creatures in the sea might wanna make a meal outta one gristly ol' sailor.

The sky o'erhead went misty and blurred, and Horace thought his eyes might've been stingin' if he were able to feel anythin'. Might've been from the salty water splashin' up into them, might've been tears what he didn't even know he'd cried. Either way, nothin' for him to do to clear the new, murky nature o' his sight, so he continued starin' at the smudgy heavens.

A larger wave washed against him, tiltin' him onto his side. Horace stopped his breathin' to keep from suckin' the ocean into his lungs. While doin' so, he glimpsed a smear o' another color off to his starboard, but then his floatin' body righted itself and nothin' but sky filled his vision again.

The shore!

His heart beat faster, hammerin' against his ribs. One o' them might've still hurt from when Thorn fell outta nowhere on top o' him, but his current condition kept him from knowin'.

I ain't floated so far as I figured.

Realizin' it stirred remnants o' hope in his chest, but it didn't last. Didn't matter how close he were to the shore if he couldn't find his way onto the beach. And even if he did, what would he do when he arrived? Lay on the sand until seaweed attached itself to him, the sun bleached him white, and crabs made homes underneath him, just like all the other driftwood? No, the time'd come for the ol' sailor to recognize his life were near its end. The only question left to answer were how long until his final demise.

His view o' the sky went even more blurry and this time Horace knew no waves was washin' into his eyes. The blurriness came from regret.

Salty tears sat on top o' his unblinkin' eyes. His ears heard the swish o' water rinsin' in and outta them; his nose sniffed the briny scent o' the deep what he'd come to hate durin' near thirty-five turns o' the seasons knockin' boot heels on one deck or another. When Dunal'd knocked him o'er the side o' the Devil o' the Deep, he'd conceded his life'd end in the ocean, but he came out alive somehow. Wouldn't happen twice.

Weren't that much luck left in his world. If there were, Thorn'd still be with him.

His vision cleared a little as the sun dried his tears, stickin' the leftov'r salt to his eyeballs. Another gull passed by, then a second. A minute later, a third flew o'er, but the bird did somethin' funny.

It stopped midair as though it'd flown into an obstruction, but there weren't nothin' for it to fly into.

Had he been able to raise a brow or crinkle up his forehead, Horace would've done so, but even that sort o' movement were beyond him. He owned no ability but to breathe and to stare where the gull'd flown into before turnin' 'round and takin' off the other direction. His hazy vision showed him nothin' but sky.

Nothin' to see.

He bobbed and bobbed, gaze fixed on the spot. Once upon a time, he wouldn't've entertained the notion o' somethin' invisible in the air, but that were before two towns named Haven and Demise seemed like they must've grown legs and moved 'round just to confuse him. And before a small gray man fell outta the sky and turned ev'rythin' he believed and knew inside out.

Ten breaths entered and left his lungs. A wave tilted him and he lost track o' the place the bird'd hit. His air caught in his throat as he stared, ev'ry handspan o' air above him lookin' same as the others. A feelin' like his heart sinkin' into his stomach came o'er him, crushin' the sliver o' hope seein' the shore'd brought as it did. The moment the last o' it disappeared and the ol' sailor'd settled himself back into the idea o' dyin' in the ocean, another strange thing happened.

The sky shimmered emerald.

It lasted for the space o' a heartbeat or two, but no more. The shimmerin' made Horace stop his breathin' and, after it vanished, he doubted he'd seen it at all. Must've been a trick played on his tired eyes, a result o' the sun and water and salt. He started his breath again and blinked to clear the mist from his eyes.

Blinked.

Horace's heart skittered like an excited child, but he refused to trust what his peepers'd seen, so he blinked again. His eyes hurt as the lids dragged across their surface gratin' salt o'er them. He blinked again and again and, when the hurtin' didn't stop, he raised a hand to his face and rubbed at them with a knuckle.

The unexpected action stopped him, the knuckle pressed against his eye. Horace flapped his other arm in the water, the movement propelling him forward. He tilted his head starboard, sucked seawater into his mouth and coughed it out in a splatter o' salty spit. When he'd cleared the offendin' brine from his throat, he opened his eyes and spied the beach, noted it were farther away now'n it'd been before.

Horace took his knuckle outta his eye and, with a great effort from his now-aching body, rolled himself onto his front and began swimmin' for the shore.

As a sailor, Horace'd always been a competent swimmer—he took care makin' sure he were strong enough to tread water a long time or swim a considerable distance, because you never knew when a slow-witted swabby might knock you o'erboard or a livin' statue might set you driftin' out to sea. Felt good to be swimmin', but it were also the most difficult strokin' he'd done in his life.

His arms and legs ached as though he'd spent all the time he'd been floatin' in the ocean workin' hard rather'n bobbin' 'bout in the manner o' a dead thing. His eyes refused to see the way they should—the result o' bein' stuck open so long. His lungs seemed like they'd shrunk, his mouth were dry as sand, his head threatened to burst open.

But his weary arms and burnin' legs carried him steadily, if slowly, toward the shore.

Ev'ry few strokes, he pulled his face outta the water and looked at where he were goin', saw the land gettin' closer, and his near-their-end limbs found a little more energy to carry on. If he made his goal o' the sandy beach, it didn't just mean his life'd go on once more when he thought it'd surely end, but he also might have a chance to find the little gray feller. Maybe he could rescue him.

For what could've been half the day, Horace forced his legs to keep kickin', his arms to keep strokin'. Sometimes he suspected they didn't do no more'n splash water about his head.

Stroke, stroke, stroke, raise his face. Stroke, stroke, stroke, raise his face.

After a while, he stopped lookin'. His progress were so slow, seein' the shore became a deterrent to continuin' rather'n a reason to go on. The kickin' o' his feet slowed. He twisted his body to throw an arm up o'er his head, his shoulder screamin' with pain. The next stroke, his arm didn't find enough energy to come outta the water and he knew that, after survivin' the God o' the Deep, a Small God fallin' on him, and two towns what wasn't wantin' to let him go, he'd prob'bly drown a few boat-lengths from salvation.

He heaved his arm forward one more time. It splooshed into the ocean, pulled him forward, and his fingers brushed against grainy sand.

With an effort, Horace raised his head outta the sea to find the beach close enough he might've been able to spit on it had he the means to brew up a mouthful o' saliva. Since he didn't, he scrambled forward instead and collapsed with his cheek pressed in the sand.

***

The ol' sailor raised his head and blinked. He weren't sure how much'd gone, but time'd passed while he lay with his face on the beach and the surf gurglin' 'round his legs. It all seemed too familiar, like he'd been here before—mostly because he had, though the other time'd been somewhere else. Washin' up on unknown beaches were becomin' a habit for Horace Seaman; fine by him, seein' as it were a better habit'n drownin' or gettin' ate by sea creatures or angry gods.

He peered along the sandy beach at the scatterin' o' rocks and driftwood littered across it like any other bit o' shore. It didn't appear no different than the last beach he'd washed up upon.

Maybe it were a dream. Maybe this be the same patch o' shore.

The thought gave him both relief and disappointment together at once. If the bunch o' sunrises since his last beachin' had been a dream, it meant there weren't no magical villages, no man made o' clay, and chances'd be good he weren't where he suspected he might be. Course, if he'd dreamed ev'rythin', it meant the little gray feller weren't real, neither.

He wanted Thorn to've been real.

Horace dragged his tongue o'er his lips then spit out the sand it'd collected off them. He pushed himself up onto his elbows and wiped more grit and pebbles away what stuck to his cheek where he'd been restin' it on the beach. In the distance, he spied the bright ball o' the sun sittin' on the horizon as if it might roll off should someone give it a push. Above it, the sky flared orange and pink and red. The ol' sailor'd seen enough sunrises and sunsets to know this were the end o' the day he were watchin', which meant night and the darkness was comin' soon.

Despite the protestation o' ev'ry muscle and joint he possessed, Horace clambered to his feet. Sand and seaweed clung to the front o' his damp clothes, a briny ocean scent forcin' its way up his nose but not turnin' his stomach like it did floatin' in the salty water for so long. He didn't bother brushin' it off as he dragged his gaze away from the sun creepin' downward into the ocean.

His gaze swept o'er a wide swath o' sand bordered by stacks o' driftwood and wayward branches what looked like someone'd placed them just so on purpose rather'n bein' washed up by the tides. Beyond that, tangled brush led to tall trees with broad trunks towerin' skyward, ev'rythin' underneath them already hidden in gatherin' shadow.

Horace weren't no lover o' a dark forest at night, but what lay behind him from whence he came demanded his attention. He completed his hesitant turn and what he saw choked his breath off in his throat.

The emerald wall shimmered and glowed, undulatin' and flowin' as though a reflection o' the sea. Only the wall weren't just in the sea, but continued on across the beach and into the forest, gleamin' and waverin' all the way.

The ol' sailor opened his mouth in the manner o' a man what had somethin' to say, but he didn't have no intention o' speakin'. If he'd tried, he didn't suspect nothin' more'n a squeak'd find its way out, and he had no one to talk to, besides. No, the openin' o' his gob expressed the awe grippin' him at what he were seein'.

And the fear at knowin' what it meant.

Horace stumbled forward on wobbly legs, not particul'rly wantin' to get closer to the thing Thorn'd called the veil, but feelin' like the settin' sun pushed him into doin' it. His feet squelched inside the soggy boots what were too tight on his toes as he dragged them through the sand. No more'n twenty paces separated him from the green partition keepin' one world out or the other one in, but it seemed to Horace he had to move his legs a lot more times'n that to get close enough to touch it.

He stopped, exhausted arms hangin' at his sides, breath what'd started again wheezin' in and outta his chest. His teeth grated, his lips pressed together tight, and he tilted his head back, starin' up the side o' the emerald curtain shimmerin' high into the sky.

His brain told his hand to touch the thing, but his arm refused to do what were needed to obey. He reasoned that, since he'd passed through it on his floatin' journey here, he'd be able to do the same goin' the other way despite Thorn's story o' needin' the giant raven to carry him o'er the top.

Its magic only works to keep folk like the little gray feller in.

He lowered his gaze to stare straight ahead, his own mind not believin' what it'd come up with. Beyond the translucent green wall, Horace made out the shoreline on the other side, the darkness o' night creepin' across the sand. He shivered and finally convinced his arm to move.

Shakin' and tremblin', his hand crossed the space between him and the shimmery thing, pausin' the width o' a hair away. He licked his lips again, this time findin' only dry skin and no grit, then moved forward the last bit.

Bright green lightnin' shot out from where Horace touched, runnin' across the surface o' the wall.

"Ahhh!"

He shrieked and fell back, his buttocks strikin' the beach with a thump what jarred his molars. The emerald surface smoothed, the jagged lines disappearin' as quick as they'd come. Horace stared for the space o' three regular heart beats—about ten o' his currently accelerated ones—before raisin' his hand to stare at his fingertips.

They didn't look no different, nor did they hurt or tingle or sting. The ol' sailor gulped a mouthful o' fearful spit and climbed up offa his ass. He rubbed his palms on the front o' his wet shirt, knockin' sand and seaweed off without noticin' as he stared at the shimmerin' veil.

He reached out again, hand stretched open and palm flat, sand still clingin' to his skin. The first time he touched it, it'd startled him, but caused him no pain. This time, he didn't hesitate before layin' his hand flat against it.

The bright green lightnin' flickered, shootin' out from his hand in a rough circle, but Horace didn't pull away. Instead, he pushed.

He might as well've been pushin' against a cliff made outta stone.

It were real: Thorn, the clay man, the veil. Ev'rythin'.

The ol' sailor let his hand fall and the green wall returned to its gentle shimmerin'. With a shudder what shook along his spine and through his shoulders, Horace shuffled his feet, spinnin' himself about to peer back toward sunset.

The sun'd sunk halfway below the distant horizon, the sky darkenin' to the red o' fresh blood. Had he been aship, Horace'd've been glad to see the sky bleedin' this way—it signified good weather and a calm sea for the night. But his too-small boots wasn't standin' on the deck o' the Devil o' the Deep or any o' the others of the king's ships and merchants he'd spent so many seasons upon.

Instead, he stood on a sandy beach behind what a Small God'd called the veil, on the shores o' the Green.

To port lay a land known to man only through legend and stories told at taverns along the coast, and none o' them he'd ever heard involved happy endin's or tales o' riches. Horror, creatures, and death were the stuff o' them stories.

Horace dragged his gaze away from the settin' sun and a breeze rustled through the leaves o' the brush leadin' to the forest. He squinted, starin' hard to see what might be hidden within its foliage. He spied nothin' but shapes what might've been stumps and bushes, or beasts he couldn't even imagine.

Skin goin' clammy, Horace stumbled back a step. His shoulders touched the shimmerin' veil and lightnin' shot along its surface, castin' green light on the beach what illuminated driftwood and rocks in a witchy glow.

The ol' sailor's legs gave up on him and he sank to the sand, his back draggin' along the emerald wall. He pulled his knees up tight against his chest and buried his face in his crossed arms, prayin' to any god what might listen—small or otherwise—that he'd make it through the night without discoverin' if the stories told at taverns along the coast was true.

V Stirk - The Horse Doctor

Stirk found himself halfway home before realizing what an ill-informed idea it might be returning to the place they'd found him. Could be he'd discover more of the king's men awaiting him, plus they'd taken the door off, anyway. Even he realized a place without a door provided a poor hideout.

He stopped shy of the border between Sunset and Riverside to consider his options, of which he saw few. Bieta knew people—too many people, Stirk would have said—but not him. He'd recognize most of them because he was usually around when his mother brought her work home. She'd send him away most times, but he often returned before they finished. Stirk hadn't learned to figure out the time by looking at either sun or hourglass, so he frequently showed up earlier than he intended or she wanted. The men never acted happy at his arrival, so he thought they'd be less than good choices to enlist for help in his quest for revenge. Beyond them, only Flenge the tanner came to mind. He doubted he'd want to offer aid, what with the broken door and all.

The big man raised his left arm, intending to wipe sweat from his head with his hand, forgetting a stump held the spot where it used to be. The smooth skin left by the healer brushed against his forehead and Stirk jerked away from the touch. He stared at it a second, anger that Enin even suggested such a thing brewing in his chest.

"Enin," he said and nodded to himself. "The horse doctor owes me for this. He'll help."

One corner of Stirk's mouth tilted up in a smile as he held the stump in front of his face a moment longer. Setting out, he amended his path to carry him straight toward the river. There, he'd cross the bridge to the other side, then find his way to the horse doctor's.

If Enin wasn't willing to help of his own accord, Stirk decided he'd make him.

***

Stirk waited at the end of the block, biding his time and watching the horse doctor's door from around the corner. Nobody came or went and he wondered whether or not he'd find Enin within.

As he leaned against the wall out of view of the door, he peered toward the sky. The sun had dipped low enough to touch the roofs of the surrounding structures;

even without the ability to estimate time, Stirk knew night wasn't far off.

And with night came the darkness.

He shivered at the prospect. Not knowing what might hide unseen in the dark always caused unease in the big man—one thing Bieta had made better for him. Most times, she'd made sure he didn't stay alone at night. But she wouldn't be around for him tonight, or any other night.

A nervous breath rattled into his lungs. He held it for a few heartbeats, attempting to calm himself but finding no success, then let it out with a huff.

I don't need to be alone in the night.

Stirk peeked around the corner again; the horse doctor's door remained closed. Despite the lack of movement or visitors, a surety crept into him he'd find Enin inside, probably hiding from Stirk himself. The thought angered him, pushed him to action. He narrowed his eyes, balled his fist, and set out toward the door.

Broken cobblestones grated beneath the sole of his boot. His toe struck a piece and sent it skittering across the street and into the wall of the building beside the horse doctor's. He ignored it, intent on his destination. When he reached it, Stirk hesitated, hand raised in preparation to grasp the handle and fling the door open. As he stood there, it occurred to him it could've been Enin who sent the one-armed man and his soldiers to find him and Bieta. Maybe as much responsibility for her death rested with him as with the fellow who dropped the axe on her neck.

The muscles in Stirk's jaw flexed and released, flexed and released as he fought the anger building inside him. As much as he might want to make him pay like the others, he needed the horse doctor's help.

Punishing him would have to wait.

Stirk sucked a deep breath through his nose, inhaling

the scent of hay and manure wafting from the doctor's place. He wondered briefly how someone lived in such conditions, forgetting the stink of the tanner's back room. He let out the chest full of air and laid his hand on the door handle, gave it a push.

It didn't budge.

He's barred it because he knew I'd come for him.

He tried it again with the same result, so he released the handle. His brow furrowed as he considered what to do next. Wait for Enin to emerge? Leave and let him be?

No, his patience had worn thin. He needed both the horse doctor's help and the satisfaction of seeing him beg for forgiveness when the time came to punish him for his part in Bieta's death. Leaving wasn't a choice.

But what, then?

He spun on his heel, intending to return to his hiding place around the corner, when an idea came to him. He returned to the door and rapped his knuckles sharply on the wood. A moment passed with no sounds from within. Rather than assume it meant the horse doctor wasn't home, he knocked again.

"Who's there?"

The door's thickness muffled the words, but Stirk recognized Enin's voice. He coughed into his fist and raised the tone of his own voice when he replied in an attempt to disguise it.

"I need your help, horse doctor. M'horse is...sick."

A pause. Worried goosebumps crawled along Stirk's arm. Did Enin recognize him?

"I'm closed. Come back on the morrow."

"But poor..." he almost said Bieta, but caught himself. "Poor Nellie is so sick. I don't think she'll make it through the night."

Another pause, then Stirk thought he heard the faint sound of a sigh through the door.

"Do you have the horse with you?"

Stirk hesitated. Would someone bring their sick horse to the horse doctor or expect the horse doctor to go to the sick horse? If he answered wrong, he worried it might expose his ruse.

"She's here."

He pressed his lips together, waiting to see if he'd chosen the correct response. A few heartbeats passed and he considered knocking again, perhaps even changing his answer, but the sound of wood rubbing against wood stopped him. Hinges creaked, the door opened a crack, and Enin's face appeared in the space.

For an instant, seeing the horse doctor froze Stirk. Imagining him part of the machinations leading to his mother's death had transformed the man into a monster in his mind, yet here he stood, gaunt-faced and sallow-cheeked as ever. In the same instant, Enin recognized Stirk—someone he obviously did not expect to see ever again. His eyes went wide with surprise, then the door swung shut.

The bang of door contacting lintel jarred Stirk to action. He grabbed the handle and pushed, but found it resistant—Enin must have put his shoulder against it as he tried to wrestle the bar back into place. If he succeeded, Stirk stood little chance of finding his way in.

The big man took two steps away and coiled himself. From within, something solid thumped against the door—the bar being lifted back into place.

He sprang forward, body angled to the left to aim his right shoulder at the wooden barricade. With his teeth clenched, his entire body tensed as he prepared to meet an immovable object. Instead, the door flew open with little resistance. Behind it, Enin had fumbled the bar and dropped it, leaning over to retrieve it at the precise instant Stirk burst through.

The edge of the door struck the horse doctor on the

top of the head, sending him flying backward. Stirk stumbled across the threshold, arms pinwheeling to keep his legs under him, feet skidding on the dirt floor as he slid to a stop. When he saw Enin laid out on the ground in front of him, a smile crept onto his lips.

He closed the door and sat cross-legged, waiting for the horse doctor to wake.

It didn't take long, a fact which relieved Stirk of a good deal of apprehension. Watching over an unconscious person reminded him too much of the time he'd spent babysitting the prince, which in turn brought his dead mother's face to mind.

The horse doctor's pained groan sent it from his thoughts.

Enin's eyes opened and darted back and forth around the room, groggy and unfocused. His gaze fell on Stirk but, dazed, he didn't appear to recognize his sometime lover's son at first. He shook his head, groaned again, then blinked hard twice before comprehension dawned on his face.

He sat up suddenly, face contorting with pain, and scrabbled away across the floor, heels digging into the dirt to propel him. Stirk didn't bother following— nowhere for him to go.

"Hello, Enin."

The horse doctor stopped trying to flee when his back contacted the bench set against the far wall.

"Stirk," he said with no note of pleasure in his voice. "What are you...? How did...?"

"Wondering how I'm still alive, I'm bettin'. Not sure how myself, but I am."

Enin moved his gaze from Stirk, glanced around the room as if he expected he might find some other object of more interest. When he didn't, his eyes met the big man's again.

"Is Bieta with you?"

Stirk pursed his lips, swallowed a hard lump that sprang to his throat. "She's dead."

Enin offered no condolence for the loss of his mother, nor did he break into sobs or swear revenge. Instead, he nodded in the manner of someone unsurprised by the revelation. His reaction brought Stirk to his feet, fist clenched. The horse doctor shrank back against the bench, hands held in front of him.

"Don't hurt me. It's not my fault."

"You tell the one-armed man about us?"

He hesitated for an instant, making Stirk wonder if the shaking of his head that followed was the truth. Rage brought heat to the big man's cheeks, but he fought to calm himself, realizing he didn't have the ability to track the sword master on his own. He didn't know for sure Enin could help, but he had nowhere else to go.

"Prove you didn't give us up."

Enin stared at him for a bit before shaking his head again. "I didn't. How can I prove it?"

"By helping me."

Sensing no imminent violence, the horse doctor lowered his arms and rested his elbows on the bench behind him, using them to pull himself up off the dirt floor. He sat his narrow ass on the seat and raised an eyebrow.

"Help you? In what way?"

"The sword master's gotta pay for what he done. Trenan and the other fella, the one who took my mother's head off with his axe."

Enin's eyes went wide and he came to his feet.

"No. I can't do that."

"You have to."

"You being here will bring me bad luck enough. Going after the master swordsman assuredly means death."

Stirk's lips pulled tight across his teeth and his

fingernails settled into the furrows they'd already dug in his palm. He stepped forward and the other man cowered back but found nowhere to go.

"Bad luck be standing right in front of you, horse doctor, and death is waitin' its turn if you ain't gonna help."

He raised his fist and took another short step toward Enin, who raised his arms defensively again. The expression on the man's long and narrow face lengthened, his features drawing down like tallow running from a lit taper. Stirk thought if he took one more pace toward the man, he might break into tears and sobs. He lifted his foot, threatening to take that step. Enin closed his eyes and bent his head away.

"All...all right. I'll help you."

Stirk kept his fist raised, but advanced no farther, waiting for the horse doctor to say more. After the space of a dozen heartbeats, his mother's gaunt lover cracked one eyelid open. When he saw his aggressor hadn't moved any closer, he opened his other eye and faced the big man, arms relaxing but not dropping.

"I can't do anything for you, but I can take you to someone who can."

Stirk lowered his arm and the horse doctor did the same. "Who?"

"I'll take you to the healer."

"The healer?" Stirk roared, making Enin flinch. He waved his stump at him. "You'd take me to the bastard who stole my hand?"

The horse doctor sank to the bench, perhaps realizing his mistake. Stirk felt his face reddening with anger, his muscles coiling and knotting, and doubted he'd be able to hold himself back.

"But wait," Enin raised his arm, pointed. "Look at where your hand was. Is that the work of someone who is naught but a healer?"

Stirk allowed his gaze to follow the horse doctor's gesture. The smooth skin at the end of his forearm shone dimly in the room's wan light—the scar tissue of a healed wound—but Enin was right; the man who healed his wrist was also responsible for removing his hand. His jaw loosened, but he said nothing.

"The healer took your hand," Enin said, breathless with relief. "He can do more than heal, but the cost of his aid is great, as you already know."

Silence fell in the room, its weight lifted by the nickering of a horse awaiting Enin's attention in the stall beside his workroom. Stirk's mind struggled to work through the horse doctor's offer, but doing so would have taken a while at the best of times. In his life, Bieta did the thinking for both of them while her son did the heavy lifting. They'd been a team from the beginning, just the two of them. He didn't even know who his father was; he suspected a few men as possibilities but with his mother gone, he'd never find out.

His forehead wrinkled and his handless arm fell back to his side. He vaguely noticed the horse doctor's nervousness making him shift his skinny ass on the flat, hard bench but paid the movement little attention. Enin wasn't going anywhere.

The light in the room dimmed as the sun dipped closer to the horizon in the time it took Stirk to decide his course of action. When he did, he blinked rapidly three times to wet his eyes again after staring for so long and trained his gaze on the horse doctor. The big man nodded once.

"Take me to the healer," he said, voice quiet but determined. "His cost'll be met, but it won't be me who'll be payin' it."

VI Trenan - The Search Begins

The streets of the city spread out like strands of a spider's web. Cross streets, laneways, broad avenues, back alleys. With foot traffic, wagons, and horses, tracking someone through city streets proved much more difficult than doing so in the wild. No bent branches to spy, no footprints in loose dirt, no grass pressed flat to denote passage. Their only choice was to inquire of those they encountered whether they'd seen a young woman in a red robe accompanied by another in a Goddess' green smock. Unfortunately for them, the majority of the city's residents mistrusted men in armor and were loath to aid them.

The buildings and atmosphere of the streets changed as they passed from Sunset to Riverside, the conditions shifting from squalor to near-squalor. Thus was the city's Evenside, a stark difference from Midtown, which saw Trenan's birth and rearing, and Morningside, predominantly populated by tradesmen and merchants.

Could Danya be headed toward the other side of the city?

He doubted it. She'd told him the prophecy spoke of Small Gods, but how had she interpreted those words? He raised his eyes skyward, knowing he'd find no pinpricks of light in the late afternoon sky. Those Small Gods wouldn't show their faces until the sun touched the horizon, hiding itself from the world for the night. And how would she reach them if she intended to seek those Small Gods?

The Brotherhood.

The thought of their cult made Trenan suppress a shiver. He'd encountered tales of their doings, but imagined none of them would have reached the princess' ears. Erral and Ishla did everything possible to protect their children from the outside world, and Trenan never spoke of the Brothers to them. She might have heard of them from another source, but he doubted it. The Small Gods of the Green, however, were a different matter. Those legendary creatures reared their heads in most of the bedtime stories told by every wet nurse in the realm.

The Green it is, then.

He stopped at a wide intersection, waiting for a line of wagons to rumble by. Dansil stood beside him.

"Where shall we go, sword master?"

Trenan thought he detected sarcasm attached to the last two words the soldier spoke, but he let it slip by. If he didn't believe the master swordsman lived up to the title because he lacked an arm, he'd one day learn the truth.

"She will head out of the city," he replied.

"Out of the city? Why?'

"She makes for the Green."

Dansil laughed, a braying sound a donkey might have made. Even the wagon trundling past wasn't loud enough to disguise the grating noise and Trenan considered cuffing the man in the side of the head to stop him; he resisted.

"What makes ya think a princess'd be headed for the most dangerous place in the land when she ain't hardly been out of Draekfarren before?"

When the wagon finished clattering past, Trenan started across the avenue, Dansil keeping pace with him. He didn't want to answer the question, at least not with the truth. Dansil wouldn't accept the idea of the scroll and the prophecy. Why should he? Trenan himself doubted its authenticity and—even if it was a true artifact—no proof existed to suggest it referred to Teryk and Danya.

The first-born child.

"She searches for her brother."

A snort. "The prince was last seen dockside. Why the hell would she go to the Green searching for him?"

"She doesn't know where he was." Truthfully, Danya probably still thought the prince dead.

"But why the Green?"

"Never mind. It's a long story." Trenan wished they were ahorse; he'd plant his heels into his steed's side and pull away from the queen's guard and this inane conversation.

"We ain't got nothing but time."

"Horses," the sword master said, changing the subject. "If we are to have any hope of finding her, we need horses."

Dansil stopped in his tracks; it tempted Trenan to carry on walking and leave the other man behind, but he thought better of it, halted, and faced his companion.

"So, you want us to go back after all? Could've said so before we went this extra way."

Trenan shook his head and resumed walking. "We head for the outpost at the edge of the city, on the border of Riverside and Midtown. We can pick up steeds there."

"You're in charge, I guess." Dansil hurried to catch up.

You're in charge, I guess. The words rattled around the inside of Trenan's head, making him clench his hand into a fist and clamp his teeth together. In the past, he'd wondered what made this man grate on his nerves so; he'd realized the obvious disdain Dansil showed toward him for no clear reason provided the cornerstone for his own dislike.

They fell into silence as they traversed the streets, headed for the outpost. At first, they employed trial and error, and got turned about more than once, necessitating they stop and ask for begrudging directions. After a time that dragged on and on, the maze of streets became familiar and the tangled avenues untied themselves before Trenan's eyes. Their feet trod upon streets he'd visited in his youth, running and hiding along them when he was too small to do anything else; later, he strode them as he went to his master's to learn the arts of swordplay or strategy or horsemanship.

Back when I had two arms instead of one.

He couldn't remember the last time he'd been here—didn't care to for more reasons than he'd admit. Once he'd left, he'd never intended to return. Barracks, battlefields, and practice rings became his home, and he'd thrived in them far more than he ever had in Midtown. It was during those days of hard work and training he'd encountered Erral, when the king was not yet a king, and queens and fateful battles still lay in their future.

How different would life be if we never met?

He'd asked himself the question over and over since he sacrificed his arm for his friend, but the answer never changed. Yes, he'd have his arm, and he might have risen through the army's ranks as he had. He liked to think it happened because of his abilities with sword and strategy, but befriending Erral had facilitated the rise. No matter how many times he asked, or how he felt about the things that may have been different, he wouldn't give up the night with Ishla for any of it—the only thing that took the deep hurt from the loss of his arm. Despite the heartache and frustration that followed—the wondering, the hidden desire, the secret love—it remained the defining moment of his life, more so than losing his limb.

Dansil thumped Trenan on the shoulder—purposely harder than necessary, it seemed—the impact pulling the master swordsman from his thoughts. The queen's guard had raised his arm and pointed along the avenue ahead of them.

"Is that what you're talking about?"

Trenan refocused and stared down the thoroughfare, hand held to his forehead to shield the sun from his eyes. A few blocks away, horses tethered outside a building whinnied and shuffled, and sun glinted on occasional slivers of exposed steel. As a child, he'd spent days on end at the outpost, admiring weapons and armor and carefully staying out of the way of the soldiers, the man his mother had told him was his father amongst them, though he knew not which. Back then, the building would have been but a shape in the distance when viewed from the city's edge. Now, buildings and streets had overtaken the farmland that once separated the outpost, many spilled beyond so the outpost no longer served as demarcation of the Horseshoe's leeward boundary.

"Yes, that's it." Trenan lowered his arm back to his side. "The last I heard, Captain Silvius still commanded the outpost. I'm sure he'll see his way to loaning us horses and equipment."

"An old war buddy of yours?"

The swordmaster didn't like the manner in which his companion asked the question; the tone dripped ridicule rather than interest. Had Dansil ever drawn his sword in battle? Judging by the age of him and the station he held, Trenan doubted it.

"You might say that," he replied, choosing once again to ignore the younger man's inexplicable derision. "We've known each other a long while."

They walked the rest of the way in silence and reached the outpost a few minutes later. Several men were gathered by the tethered horses, their voices loud as they engaged in their discussions, laughter occasionally overpowering the conversations. One noticed Trenan and Dansil approaching and stopped speaking mid-sentence. He smacked one of his companions in the shoulder with the back of his hand, drawing the other's attention. A murmur spread through them and the playful arguments and boasts ended; the soldiers snapped to attention. Trenan smiled to himself; he wore nothing to denote his rank or status, but his missing arm made him the most recognizable officer in the king's army.

"As you were," he said upon their approach. None of them relaxed. "Does Captain Silvius still command this outpost?"

"Aye, he does, swordmaster," the man who'd first seen them replied.

"Get him for us," Dansil growled.

The soldier's eyes narrowed as if to ask who this was who'd spoken. Trenan clenched his teeth again, biting back a reprimand. How did Ishla put up with him as part of her guard? He couldn't imagine her enjoying his company. The thought forced him to suppress a disgusted shiver.

"We seek audience with him," Trenan interjected, glancing sideways at Dansil. "If he has the time."

"I'm sure he'll have time for you, sir." The soldier nodded once, then hurried inside. Awkward silence fell as they waited, so Trenan took it upon himself to break it.

"How is business at the outpost these days?"

"Quiet," replied a man with a hawk nose and less hair than a newborn. "Not much happenin' but petty crimes—thievin', gamblin', whorin' and such."

Dansil chortled. "Gamblin' and whorin' ain't really crimes though, are they?"

Before Trenan could decide if he needed to school the soldier regarding the king's stance on those activities outside the crown's whorehouses and gambling establishments, the outpost door swung open and Captain Silvius strode across the threshold. As soon as he spied the master swordsman, a smile crossed his weathered face and he threw his arms wide.

"Trenan, you old war dog. How long has it been?"

"Too many seasons," he replied, accepting the commander's embrace; it included a solid bumping of chests and a slap on the back before quickly releasing him. "You look good. Time has treated you well."

A lie. Silvius appeared to have swallowed a whole pig since Trenan last saw him, and he'd aged beyond the seasons which had passed. The master swordsman wondered if stress caused the changes, or if the deep furrows in his face and spidery veins in his eyes might be the product of too much of the hooch the soldiers concocted in a still out behind the outpost.

"You're a lying bastard, you are, Trenan. But the likes of you doesn't come visit the likes of me just to make me feel pretty. What can I do for you?"

"My companion and I—"

"Dansil," the soldier interrupted.

"Dansil and I—"

"I'm a queen's guard."

Trenan blew a firm breath out through his nostrils and Silvius surveyed his companion. The master swordsman could only imagine the size of the shit-eating grin plastered across the man's face.

"Dansil the queen's guard and I are in need of horses and equipment for a long ride. Rations, too, if you have any to spare."

"The swordmaster and a queen's guard heading off together into the countryside, is it? Never thought I'd see such a thing. Maybe today's the day I should be headed to the king's gambling hall to test my luck."

A forced chuckle spilled from Trenan's lips. "Isn't every day the day for you to be headed to the gambling hall, Silvius?"

"Just so."

The portly soldier headed past the outpost's main entrance, leading them toward the stables. Trenan took up after him but didn't look back for Dansil to follow; more than a good chunk of him hoped he'd stay behind.

"Renner," the commander called over his shoulder. "Gather a tent and bedrolls for these men. Jinton, load saddle bags with all the rations they'll hold, but don't use the good wine. We don't need the swordmaster and his friend wandering the wilds of the kingdom getting drunk and disorderly."

"Dansil," Trenan's companion corrected.

For a moment, the master swordsman considered pointing out they were not friends, but he let the opportunity pass.

They crossed the dusty yard to a squat building with a thatched roof, its double doors thrown wide. Though the interior was dim, Trenan made out the familiar outline of stalls, men moving back and forth; the whickering of horses floated across the open air to his ears. The sight of it flooded him with memories of long days spent swamping out the stalls when he first found his way into the king's militia. To this day, the sickly-sweet aromas of manure and hay cast his thoughts back to this place.

The smell struck him full force as they crossed the threshold into the stables' shadowed interior. Silvius headed down the line of stalls without pausing until he reached the far end.

"You can take these two," he said as he gestured for a stable hand to retrieve saddles and equipment for the horses. "They're not the best of the crop, but they're a damn sight better than walking. Or riding a jackass."

Though I'll be riding with a jackass.

"I'll take that one," Dansil said, indicating the hardier of the two steeds.

Silvius glanced from the queen's guard to Trenan and lifted an eyebrow. "I figured that one for your superior officer."

Dansil snorted at the commander's words and Trenan watched his friend's face harden. He redirected his attention toward the queen's guard and readied to take a step toward him and call him to task for his insubordination. The master swordsman stopped him with a hand on his shoulder.

"That one looks better suited for carrying a fellow Dansil's size," Trenan said. The words tasted of bile, but no point in reprimanding the queen's guard now, not when they'd be forced to spend time in each other's company.

Silvius glanced back to his old friend, a surprised expression creasing his forehead. The swordmaster shook his head minutely, letting the commander know not to worry. The portly soldier stared at him for a moment before nodding once.

"Fine, then. They'll be saddled and ready in no time. For now, come with me to the mess and we'll get a meal into you before you go."

Silvius pushed past Dansil without looking into the man's face; Trenan followed, but saw the wide grin curving across the queen's guard's lips, the deviousness flickering in his eyes.

He wondered if they'd both survive long enough to find the princess.

VII Thorn - Carried Away

The odor of gray clay filled Thorn's nostrils as his cheek pressed against the cold substance and his arms dangled down the giant's back. Normally, such an aroma brought him joy, indicative as it was of the great cliffs beside the sea being in near proximity. Thorn enjoyed sitting on the edge of those cliffs, staring out across the wide ocean and wondering what it would be like to ride upon one of the ships he sometimes saw. But the scent meant something different this time: the clay man carried him away from the cliffs, away from his home and his friend, Horace Seaman.

He let himself hang limp over the golem's shoulder, eyes closed and breath steady as he tried to reclaim the magic he'd spent when the golem laid a finger on Horace Seaman's chest. Thorn wasn't sure why he'd known the touch meant death for his companion; perhaps the power told him, but he was unsure—he wasn't used to how it worked on this side of the veil.

The giant's stride bounced the Small God on his shoulder, making deep breaths difficult as Thorn wondered if his efforts to save his friend had proven successful. Immediately after, he'd sensed the sailor lived, but as the golem and his companion took him farther from the man and the Green, his sense of Horace's well-being dissipated.

He hoped it wasn't because the sailor's life had faded. He'd saved him from the giant's touch, but he couldn't aid him in the water; the sea was a more powerful monster than the beast carrying him could ever hope to be.

Thorn can't save him from everything.

The thought, though true, caused an unfamiliar discomfort in his chest.

To distract himself from worry for his friend—an emotion he'd never imagined he'd experience—Thorn listened to the sounds around him, using them to guess their surroundings, and maybe where the clay man and his companion intended to take him.

The most prevalent sound was the crunch of the

giant's footsteps in dry grass as his strides devoured the ground yards at a time. Beneath that, the quicker, quieter steps of his companion, and the man's heavy breathing as he did his best to keep up with the much larger man of clay. His ragged breath made Thorn realize two things he didn't hear: the giant neither breathed nor possessed a heartbeat. With his ear pressed against the smooth clay back, the Small God wouldn't have missed it.

What sort of creature neither breathes nor has a beating heart?

The answer to the question was obvious: A creature formed of clay.

Thorn remembered how one of his sisters, Ivy, sometimes fashioned the shape of a man out of dried grass bound together, then made him dance for the tribe's amusement. But that figure had been small, and only capable of doing Ivy's bidding as long as she concentrated on the task. When she stopped, the straw man ceased dancing and fell limp to the ground, nothing but a bundle of grass tied with lengths of creepers.

If Ivy made a man as big as the giant, would she have the power to make him dance?

Perhaps. The magic in the Green was immense, concentrated as it was behind the veil, and few channeled it as well as Ivy. But things were different on this side, at least for their kind. He doubted she or any of the others could do it over here, certainly not for such a long time and so seamlessly. Everything about him resembled life.

But what of those who lived here? Was one of them able to perform such a feat?

Horace had never given Thorn reason to suspect he might have the ability to exert such power...or any at all, truthfully. If someone pressed the Small God for the truth, he'd admit his friend had more in common with a child than a man grown—likely why Thorn felt such a connection with him.

His heart ached again, but not just for the sailor; now it ached for Ivy and the others of his kind. Before now, he'd put little thought to them, never doubting he'd find his way back to his home.

The clay man's grip around his legs dispelled his surety.

But who is animating him?

He peered out from between slitted lids at the man struggling to keep up to the giant. Sweat plastered his hair to his forehead, exhaustion tinted his cheeks pink. His lips moved with the effort of breathing, or he might have been speaking to himself.

This does not look like one capable of wielding such power.

"Can we rest, Ves?" the man asked. He raised his head from watching his footing; Thorn closed his eyes. "I'm tired."

The golem responded with a grunt and slowed his pace. The exchange confirmed to Thorn that the fellow trailing behind was not responsible for the golem's movements and actions. If so, and he desired a rest, he'd simply make the creature stop. That meant the clay man was either truly alive or controlled by someone with power beyond Thorn's imagining.

The prospect sent a shudder through his body and the golem tightened his grip around the Small God's legs.

With the giant's pace slowed, his companion's footsteps came closer. With few other options, Thorn opened his eyes again and directed his attention toward the man. At first he didn't notice the Small God's gaze upon him, so Thorn exerted what little influence his body made available. The man's eyes found his and his lips ceased moving.

They stared at each other, the man's exhaustion rendering his expression unreadable. Again, Thorn attempted to draw together the power he'd grown up with coursing through him, but the little he'd just expended left him empty.

"Where are you taking Thorn?"

The man's gaze remained on the Small God, but he didn't answer. His mouth drooped at the corners, but Thorn couldn't be sure if displeasure at his speaking caused it or effort and tiredness. His expression did not suggest he might respond.

"Who are you?"

This time, the man's eyes widened, as though he attempted to use them to communicate with Thorn, but the Small God had not developed an ability to read such things in the people outside the Green. Horace Seaman had not been a man of subtlety, so gave Thorn no opportunity to practice this talent he used so well with the creatures behind the veil. A glance from Father Raven, Ivy's eyebrow crook, the way a dragonfly angled its wings, all spoke to him, but not this man's expression. He had no choice but to press him further.

"What has Thorn done?"

The man pursed his lips and shook his head.

"Why have you taken Thorn from—ahh!"

The giant man of clay squeezed the Small God's legs together firmly enough to grind the bones against one another, sending pain flaring from his knees to his hip. Thorn closed his mouth tight to keep from crying out again. He didn't understand pain, but experiencing it helped him realize the nature of the man's expression.

He tried to warn Thorn.

No more speaking, no more trying to find out where they planned to take him or why, but deep down, Thorn knew the answer. He supposed he had from the moment he met Horace Seaman, the man who rides upon the waves, just like the ancients foretold. Like most of his kind, he'd never thought them more than stories. How could they possibly be true? Small Gods were all but immortal, and no man had ever crossed over into the Green, only washed up on the shore, dead or dying.

But none ever crossed out of the Green, either. Until Thorn.

He allowed his body to go limp again, sagging against the giant's back and letting his gaze fall away from the man following behind them. He continued to sense the man's eyes upon him, but the sensation welling up inside him made him ignore it—another new feeling he hadn't experienced before, nor ever expected to:

Dread.

***

Three hundred eighty-nine. Three hundred ninety. Three hundred ninety-one.

At first, when the small gray man interrupted while he counted his steps, Kuneprius had been unimpressed with losing his place. After the interruption, and seeing how Ves dealt with it, he'd been happy for the distraction. The counting of strides made by a pace forced upon him didn't have the same soothing effect of his usual rituals. How he longed for the kiss of cool water on his face to help him center his thoughts, allow him to be where he needed to be.

He looked up from his feet, lips still moving as he counted silently. The gray man continued lying limp against Ves' back, the color of his flesh lighter than that of the golem. Kuneprius didn't realize the clay used to mold the giant held a brown tinge until seeing the Small God for comparison.

Is he really a Small God?

When he'd happened upon the creature at the shore, Kuneprius knew him to be the one they searched for, though he'd never have expected such a fabled being to be so easily captured. Where was the magic the old stories told of? Where was the power to control, to shape shift, to dominate? If this truly was a Small God from the stories he'd heard in his youth—the one the prophecy said must die—he must be biding his time.

Kuneprius shuddered at the thought. Could it be the small man-like creature simply awaited the right time and place to kill them both? He gulped a mouthful of saliva; the lump in his throat rose and fell as another question occurred to him.

Can a man made of clay be killed?

If not, it left his life as the only one in real danger.

Even after all he'd seen—remorseless killing, no need for rest, a lack of recognition when they spoke—he continued hoping his friend might be buried somewhere within the dun-colored being. Something had to make the thing act as though it were alive, and that something must be a someone.

It has to be Vesisdenperos.

If so, the clay man was a prison holding the friend he'd raised from a babe. He'd dedicated his entire life to protecting and nurturing the boy meant to become the sculptor, all the while having no clue about his friend's true fate. If he'd known, he might have chosen a different path for both of them.

The thing about a prison is there is always a way out.

His eyes narrowed, gaze upon the being who may or may not be a Small God. If he was, and the stories were genuine, he might hold the key to breaking Ves out of his prison. Perhaps he might have a way to get his friend back.

A hesitant smile crept across Kuneprius' lips, and he lowered his chin to keep it from being noticed should the small gray man look up or the golem glance back. Upon seeing his feet again, he realized he'd lost count of his steps. It didn't bring him the same relief as counting while he held his breath, but it was better than nothing.

His smile disappeared as he got back to the task of

tallying his steps and hoping Ves would soon let him rest.

One. Two. Three. Four...

VIII Stirk - The Horseshoe

Stirk glanced up at the dark sky and saw nothing. Black clouds hid the moon and the Small Gods, leaving the world below without light to guide travelers such as himself.

The horse doctor, walking a few paces ahead, took a right down a narrow street, followed by a left onto a wider boulevard. They traversed streets and passed buildings unfamiliar to Stirk. It seemed to him they'd walked long enough to pass through Sunset and into either Waterside or Fishtown, but his nose detected neither of the distinct odors of those parts of the city. With no familiar landmarks, no telltale scents, and no moon or pinpricks of light in the sky—which, truthfully, helped him recognize direction no better than the sun aided him in telling time—the big man was lost and at Enin's mercy.

"How much farther?" he grumbled, the first non-threatening words he'd said to the horse doctor since they left.

"We'll get there when we get there," Enin replied over his shoulder.

Stirk frowned. *What does that mean?*

They passed a man with no legs leaning against a building, his form nothing but a shape in the dark night, a shadow that might not have been real. A dog growled somewhere, a cat screeched. Stirk hurried his pace to catch up to the horse doctor.

"Enin—?"

"Soon. Do you smell it?"

Stirk opened his mouth to say he smelled nothing aside from the stink of manure that followed the gaunt man everywhere, but he shut it instead and took a deep whiff of the night air. His nose detected horse shit first, but other odors mingled with it: fish and, faint beneath it, the sharp tang of the creosote they used on the docks. With those scents, he thought he'd finally placed where they were: in the far corner of Sunset bordering both Waterside and Fishtown.

No wonder I don't recognize nothing.

He'd never been so far from home at night. Both Fishtown and Waterside were places he visited frequently, but he usually snuck in then beat a hasty retreat with items he'd stolen to keep him and his Ma eating because she'd had no visitors willing to pay that week. Even in the daylight, he'd likely not have recognized much. Still, having a sense of their location eased his nerves, if only a little.

They went left twice more, then right. The faint scent of fish grew to a stinking assault on Stirk's nostrils, salty sea water joining it and the odor of the docks. Periodically, he detected another aroma buried beneath the others, a sickly-sweet odor surfacing occasionally as though carried upon a breeze. He didn't recognize it, but neither did he think he wanted to.

At an intersection where three streets came together, Enin stopped. Stirk halted beside him and followed the horse doctor's gaze as the tall man looked first along one street, then the next, and the next. A flash of worry burst inside Stirk.

He doesn't know where to go.

In an instant, he imagined the one-armed soldier and his companion getting away from him. He imagined them on horseback, riding for the setting sun, a cloud of dust kicked up by the hooves of their destriers, and himself with no way to follow. The image brought anger with it, and he spun toward the horse doctor, readying to unleash it upon him.

Down the street to Stirk's right, a movement caught his attention, interrupting him. He faced it, listening to the scrape of something hard dragging on the cracked cobblestone street followed by the squelch of something wet.

"Who's there?" he called, redirecting his ire.

The words had barely left his mouth when the horse doctor's hand touched his arm.

"Quiet," he said, desperate force punctuating the whispered word.

Stirk held his breath and waited. He wiped his sweaty palm on the front of his thigh, the half-moon shaped wounds caused by his fingernails stinging. Enough time passed Stirk needed to release the air from his burning lungs and draw more. Enin spoke right after, as though he'd been waiting for his breath.

"This way."

He spun on his heel and headed down a street away from the noise they'd heard. Stirk hesitated an instant before following and found himself glad they'd chosen not to go the other way. Despite his anger, he decided he didn't want to find out what made those sounds.

They went one more block before taking a right into a narrow alley, wide enough for the two of them to walk abreast if they didn't mind brushing shoulders. Stirk did, so he stayed a pace behind his manure-perfumed guide.

After thirty paces, the alley widened to a courtyard which led to a single storey building with a low, flat roof, no windows, and nothing to set it apart from any other buildings they'd passed on their journey.

"This it?"

"It is."

Stirk stepped past Enin and squinted at the structure,

attempting to find some distinctive feature about it to indicate what and who lay within, but he found nothing. He wasn't certain what he'd expected from a place housing one—perhaps more than one—like the healer who'd taken his hand, but this wasn't it. He'd realized it wouldn't be a palace, especially in this part of the city, but shouldn't they find a hint at what dwelled inside?

"Are you sure this is it?" He faced his guide. "If you've led me..."

The remaining words poised on his tongue teetered for an instant then tumbled down his throat on a gulp of saliva.

The alley lay empty behind him.

"Enin?"

He took a step back toward the alley, stopped.

Where did he go?

He stared along the narrow passage, searching in the night that was dark enough to hide a man's features, but not enough to make him disappear. They'd passed no doors in the alley the horse doctor might have slipped into, nor had he heard telltale footsteps as he made a retreat.

He disappeared.

Stirk's eyes widened. A chill found its way along his spine.

I'm alone.

The muscles in his arms and legs tightened into knots, holding him in place as his gaze darted side to side, up and down. The dark hid all but shapes from him, the buildings transformed to black blocks against the night sky. He shivered. A rustle of cloth behind him halted him mid-breath.

Did Enin get behind me?

The horse doctor couldn't possibly have gotten by him; the man was too tall and gangly, lacking of grace. Knowing this didn't quell Stirk's nerves. Instead, his limbs tightened further until his shoulders ached. His back teeth grated together hard enough he thought he tasted the dust it created.

He inhaled a deep breath through his nose, readying himself to spin around and see who'd crept up behind him. The stink of fish wafting over from Fishtown was near overpowering, but the scent buried beneath it convinced Stirk that following Enin here had been the wrong decision.

Under the pungent aroma of creatures pulled from the sea lurked dirt and rot and death.

With a sudden change of heart, Stirk took off down the alley in the direction the horse doctor must have gone. The thump of his boots pounding the cracked cobbles echoed off stone walls, preventing any other noise from reaching his ears except the hammering of his heart forcing fearful blood through his veins.

At the mouth of the alley, he paused and glanced first one direction, then the other.

Which way?

Something soft slid against stone behind him. He resisted the urge to look back and went in the direction of his arm which still had a hand. His feet tangled and he stumbled, arms flailing. He kept his balance at the expense of a muscle in his groin and labored on, choking down a cry of pain.

Stirk's gait took on an odd cadence as he limped up the block as quickly as the throbbing at the top of his leg allowed. Still unsure which way to go, but knowing he had to get as far from the alley as possible, he rounded the next corner. Sweat ran along his temples, his mouth pulled into a grimace. He hobbled thirty awkward paces down the narrow lane before it widened into a courtyard.

Panic swam through Stirk's head as he gazed at the one-storey building ahead of him, its low, flat roof and lack of windows all too familiar. Gulping a mouthful of frightened saliva, Stirk looked from the structure to the alley behind him, expecting to find the healer fast on his heels.

The alley was empty.

No feet traversed it making the sounds that had sent him fleeing the courtyard that appeared the same as the one in which he now found himself. He dug the knuckle of one hand and the edge of his smooth-skinned stump into his eyes, rubbed hard enough to make light dance in his vision. When he took them away and the sparks faded, both building and alley remained.

How is this possible?

He shook his head. Could it be two identical alleys ended in identical courtyards and buildings? Unlikely, but maybe. He saw no other possibility; at least no others he wanted to consider.

He headed back along the alley, away from the mysterious building. When he reached the adjoining boulevard, he continued straight instead of turning this time, unsure if doing so would carry him home but knowing he didn't want to go back.

In deference to the pain in his leg, Stirk moved more slowly this time, paying attention for noises in the shadows. His feet scraped in dirt and broken stone, his breath wheezed in and out of his lungs, his heart beat hard against his ribs. Darkness wrapped itself around him, giving him the impression the walls on either side of the street bore down on him, closing in.

Stirk craned his head around to peer back along the boulevard. No one behind him but, to his surprise, the buildings had actually closed in. On both sides, blank stone walls set close enough to allow two men to walk abreast if they didn't mind brushing shoulders replaced ones he was sure had had doors and windows when he passed them.

Loose gravel grated beneath Stirk's boots as he

skittered to a stop, a wave of cold crawling over his flesh. Slowly, he faced forward again.

The same courtyard. The same low building.

"No." Stirk shook his head hard. Saliva spilled out of the corner of his mouth and down his chin. "This ain't possible."

He backed away three steps, the pain in his groin flaring as he turned to leave. One step passed beneath him before he halted again.

A blank wall stood not two paces away where the alley had been, blocking his retreat. Stirk blew short, hard breaths out through his nose.

"No. Can't be."

Someone must be playing a trick on him. Despite his fear, he forced himself forward a step and reached out, forgetting the loss of his hand. The stump brushed against stone, its hardness taking away any doubt of its authenticity. Stirk raised his other hand, pushed against the solid, ungiving wall. When it didn't move, he stutter-stepped back two paces.

"How—?"

The chill he'd experienced before returned, but this time it didn't feel like the chill of fear radiating from within. This time, it seemed as though a winter wind blew upon him, coming up from behind.

Stirk stopped and clenched his fist, certain that should he turn around, he'd find someone—something—at his back. He let his lids slide closed; if he didn't look, perhaps it wouldn't exist.

"Stirk."

The voice drew out his name, pulling the single syllable on for the space of half a dozen beats of Stirk's racing heart. His lids snapped open and the wall that had stood before him was gone. Somehow, while his eyes were closed, he'd rotated to face the courtyard, the low building, and the headless woman standing before him.

Stirk's lips quivered. His mouth went dry.

"M...mother?"

The figure might have been a statue for all it moved. The dark outline was undoubtedly a female with a space above her shoulders where her head should have been. Stirk's gaze trailed down the front of her, taking in the familiar shape, the dark stain on her shirt that must have been blood. His appraisal halted when he saw the apparition's head dangling from its grip, fingers laced through graying hair.

The dead eyes stared at him, the minuscule light in the courtyard shining in them. Stirk's lips moved, but no words came out. His knees melted to water and he stumbled, pain from his groin shooting along his leg. If not for the wall at his back to support him, he'd have found himself sprawled out on the ground.

"M...m...m..."

Stirk's eyes refused to move from the severed head, from its stare. His dead mother took a step toward him, then another, closing the distance between them. The head swung back and forth, but its gaze didn't leave his. Another step, another. Stirk slid down the wall until his ass touched the ground.

Dead eyes blinked. Bloodless lips parted.

"Stirk."

The big man threw both arms in front of his face and screamed.

IX Ailyssa - On The Road

The horse's gait lifted Ailyssa's backside up and set it down over and over, each jarring thump inflaming the bruises she'd incurred during her days as a Sister of Jubha Kyna. Each flare of pain reminded her of the men she'd endured and made her appreciate the one sitting on the horse in front of her.

It turned out Juddah was a large man; Ailyssa found herself unable to encircle his waist with both of her arms as she sat behind him. Instead, she hooked her fingers into his overalls, grabbing on so she didn't lose her seat on their steed as they traveled to Juddah's home somewhere near the shore.

Her rescuer stank of grease and sweat, an unpleasant mix wafted over her by the breeze of the horse's movement. She tried inhaling through her mouth instead, but doing so merely set the cloying tang upon her tongue rather than the redolence clinging inside her nose. His stink caused her to breathe short, gulping breaths, and direct her face away in search of fresh night air. With her head cocked to the side, she also used the opportunity to listen for sounds of pursuit from behind them.

She heard nothing but the clip clop of their own horse's hooves.

They'd been riding for a good while, Juddah managing the horse's pace to keep the beast from tiring. The blurred white of Ailyssa's vision remained dim, meaning night still ruled the sky, but she judged sunrise must not be far off. How long before they reached her rescuer's house?

Juddah had spoken little since she released her grip on the windowsill and fell into his arms. He'd caught her as promised and kept her safe from harm but, other than the occasional instruction to hold on or to give warning of low-hanging branches or a tight bend in the road, he'd not let her in on his plan. Whatever it was, it couldn't be worse than her last few days.

Could it?

She leaned away, putting space between herself and Juddah's wide back, his peculiar aroma. The night breeze touched her cheek and she closed her unseeing eyes, allowing it to envelop her, calm her. She inhaled through her nose and scented trees beneath Juddah's greasy sweat, but nothing else. Ailyssa had never been to the sea, where he claimed to live, and didn't know what to expect its smell to resemble or how the ocean might feel on her naked flesh. Warm like a bath? Cold as a river? She wondered how it might look but the thought put an ache in her heart.

I'll never see the ocean. I'll never see anything again.

The horse's gait slowed, its choppy steps bouncing Ailyssa harder against its back and flanks. She gritted her teeth against the pain and gripped tighter to Juddah's overalls, waiting for the horse's pace to smooth out again. The steed halted. Still holding on, Ailyssa leaned away, stretched her neck as if she might see over his shoulder.

"What is it?" she asked.

"Shh," Juddah hissed. "There's a wagon in the road."

Bandits!

Ailyssa's stomach jumped. Every time she thought she'd been rescued from a horrible fate, another one blocked her path. From rapists to brigands. Did the Goddess despise her this much?

Juddah shifted in the saddle, body stiffening with tension. She didn't know if he carried any weapons— she'd detected none at his belt, but his voluminous overalls were baggy enough to hide things beneath. He stood in the stirrups and leaned forward.

"Hmph," he grunted as he sat again. "Stay here."

The big man slid out of his seat, almost pulling Ailyssa along with him. She released her grip and shifted her hands to grab the bottom edge of the hard leather saddle. His boots crunched on the dirt road and a bell jingled mutely, then he whispered to the horse too quietly for her to discern his words. The animal snorted and the scuff of footsteps carrying him away reached her ears.

Footsteps carrying him away and leaving her alone. Again.

***

"I'll be right back," Juddah whispered in the horse's ear, intending the words for the woman, Ailyssa. But the courage to speak directly to her eluded him; despite his intentions, he had difficulty considering her just another addition to his collection.

He put the thoughts from his mind and strode a few paces along the road toward the wagon sitting in a tree's shadow cast by the half-moon. The horse hitched to it caught wind of him and whinnied, but the driver's seat behind it appeared empty. Juddah slowed, moving with care while cursing himself for not bringing a blade from his collection in the barn. Fifteen paces from the wagon, he halted.

"Who's there?" he called. Wind rustled an answer through the trees.

Juddah took another tentative step, stuck his hand in the front of his overalls. His fingers found nothing but the handle of the small, silver bell he'd collected from the bedside table in Ailyssa's room at Jubha Kyna, but he hoped it gave him a threatening enough appearance to throw a scare into whoever might lay in wait in the deep shadows. A second pace forward and he stopped again, squinted. Was that the shape of a man standing behind the wagon?

"What do you want?" Juddah called, raising his voice.

This time, his question prompted a response. The figure hidden in shadow strode to the front, into the moonlight, and stroked the horse's snout. Juddah's thick brows dipped toward the bridge of his nose, meeting in the middle.

"Birk? Is that you, Birk?"

"Hello, Juddah."

He took a step away from the horse, the toe of his boot contacting a rock lying in the road and sending it skittering across the dirt to settle a few paces in front of Juddah. The stocky man watched it come to a stop, then raised his gaze to Birk again, piquant anger flooding his tongue.

"What are you doing here? I told you to stay the fuck away from me."

"No, you told me to keep off your land." He spread his arms and Juddah saw a flash of a white bandage wrapped around one. "This isn't your land, is it?"

Juddah growled in the back of his throat and wished he had a bow or a sling to put an end to this fellow who made it a habit of hanging around his collection. So far as he knew, Birk'd taken nothing—not even the cow Juddah himself liberated from inside the man's own fence—but he sure showed up frequently. Juddah didn't much like that.

A shame Kooj didn't eat him.

"It ain't my land, but here you are anyway, ain't you?"

"Here I am." He took another step.

"Come no closer." Juddah jammed his hand deeper into his overalls, intending a threatening gesture, but the bell hidden within jingled. He cursed himself for his clumsiness.

"Who's your friend?" Birk asked, nodding past him toward Ailyssa.

"Ain't none of your business."

"You're right and, truthfully, I don't care what harlot you've picked up to add to your *collection*."

"She ain't a harlot."

"Yes, of course. She likes you." Birk rubbed the bandage on his arm as though the bite it hid pained him. Juddah smiled to himself. "It's the man I saw digging in your yard I want to talk about."

"Ain't none of your business, either."

"Where did you find him?"

"Birk—"

"Where is he from?"

Juddah's hands balled into fists at his sides and he took a half-step toward the other man. Birk didn't flinch.

"Stay the fuck away from my collection," Juddah grated between clenched teeth. *Or you'll end up part of it.*

"Was he near the shore?" Birk asked, ignoring the stocky man. "Did he come out of the water?"

Juddah set his shoulders, leaned forward, and walked toward the other man again, his pace slow and threatening. Finally, whatever'd given Birk courage let go; he threw up his hands, palms facing outward, and skittered back.

"No need to get angry."

"Leave me and my collection alone."

The space between them lessened and Birk scrambled into the driver's seat, retrieved the reins from the floorboards. The horse nickered and shook its head. Juddah halted short of the wagon, realizing Birk might have a weapon and not wanting to chance getting knifed and losing his latest—and what he figured to be his most prized—addition. Birk yanked the reins and the horse pranced.

"You should be careful what you collect. You never know who else might come searching for it."

He snapped the reins, prompting the horse along the dirt track, the wagon's wheels rumbling in the well-worn ruts. Juddah watched him go for the space of four breaths, wondering what he meant. He released his fists, a frown remaining on his face as he headed back to his horse.

"Juddah?" Ailyssa said as he grabbed the horse's

bridle, intending to walk for a while and let Birk put distance between them. He detected a tremor in her voice.

"Hmm?" he grunted.

"What did he mean, 'your collection'?"

"Nothing. Forget it."

He always expected the Birk fellow'd prove to be trouble.

***

Ailyssa's chin jerked up off her chest and she grabbed the sides of Juddah's overalls to keep from sliding out of her seat. The sensation of falling and confusion about her whereabouts startled her, setting her heart beating hard against her ribs. It passed after a moment as she recalled where she was and everything that had happened.

It gave her no relief.

She rested her cheek against her rescuer despite the unpleasant odor emanating from his body; she craved the stability his presence provided even if her nose could only stand it for a brief time.

When Ailyssa leaned back again, her pulse slowing to normal but the knot of fear in her gut still present, she detected a change in the air temperature, a warming on her cheek.

The sun is rising.

Every day of her life she'd awakened with the sunrise, energized by its warm rays, joy flowing through her at seeing its light transforming dew drops into glimmering diamonds. But today, its light was missing from her eyes and its warmth merely marked the coming of another day in a life filled with fear and apprehension, nothing more.

"Can we stop to rest, Juddah?"

The man didn't answer and Ailyssa thought the clomp of the horse's hooves may have masked her question.

"Juddah?"

"Keep going."

The words floated over his shoulder, more grunt than communication. She fell into silence again, the lead ball of dread in her belly expanding, tightening her chest. Did she make the right decision by leaving Jubha Kyna? Leaving her daughter? She grasped Juddah's overalls tighter, seeking solace from a man with unclear intentions.

They descended a short hill that ended abruptly then rose again. The sudden change in angle jarred their steed's gait and sent a jolt straight to Ailyssa's bladder she hadn't realized was full to the point of bursting. The sensation prompted a squeak in her throat as she clenched the muscles of her lower abdomen.

"Juddah, we must stop."

"I said no."

"But I have to make water."

No response came for the space of three breaths and Ailyssa had conceded she'd have to accept her painful bladder a while longer when Juddah grunted and the horse's direction changed. A moment later, its gait slowed, then stopped.

"Let go," he said.

She did as he asked, switching her grip from his overalls to the edge of the saddle. Experience told her to hold on or she might go off the side of the horse with him when he dismounted.

With a creak of saddle leather and a grunt of effort, Juddah did just that. His feet touched the ground, but Ailyssa heard no crunch of stones and dirt, so she guessed he'd pulled them over to the side of the track.

"Wait here," he said.

His boots swished in grass, the steps carrying him away. If not for the pressure in her belly from the need to empty her bladder, she'd have been fearful at being left alone. Sometimes even fear loses its priority.

Ailyssa squirmed, fingers aching from being hooked around the saddle's hard edge. The steed shuffled its feet, likely bent its head to nibble grass from the road's verge. To distract herself from her need, she wondered about the horse's color, what types of trees stood beside the track. She wondered if Juddah's eyes portrayed him to be a kind man, as she hoped, or something else, as she feared.

She considered who the fellow from the night before had been.

At first, she imagined him a robber lying in wait to steal from them, but Juddah had told her a wagon blocked the road, and she'd heard the clatter of wheels when the fellow left. It seemed unlikely for a thief to use a wagon for his robberies. But his transportation was the least of her concerns—the two men seemed to recognize each other. During their brief, unfriendly conversation, the man had called Juddah by name, and Juddah had used his, too.

Birk.

Why would someone familiar to Juddah stop them in the middle of the night? Why did—

"Come on."

Consumed by her thoughts, Ailyssa hadn't heard him approach, and his words startled her into almost losing control of her water. She faced where the words came from, waiting further instruction. After a hesitation, it came.

"Give me your hand."

She reached out blindly, resisting the urge to grope for him and make it more difficult for him to grab her. Her hand hung in the open air for a few beats of her heart before his thick, callused fingers swallowed hers. He gave her arm a tug to prompt her off the horse and she slid along the steed's flank. Juddah caught her by the waist when she landed, keeping her from losing her balance, but let her go right away.

"There's a spot over here," he said and laid her hand on his arm.

Ailyssa grasped his shirt sleeve, found it stiff with dirt and grime and almost pulled away but made herself hold on. Now she understood where the unpleasant odor originated.

"This way," Juddah said, leading her from the horse, its teeth grating as it chewed.

Her feet brushed through long grass, a sensation that had thrilled her so many times in the past. Today, it meant nothing, gave her no pleasure.

"Who was the man who stopped us last night?"

Juddah didn't answer right away.

"No one. A highwayman. I frightened him off."

"But it sounded as though you knew him."

"I didn't," he blurted.

Ailyssa opened her mouth to inquire further, but stopped herself. She didn't know what his intentions were—this man who had just lied to her—but she couldn't bear the thought of being left to wander the woods alone again if she enraged him. As the Goddess taught, often prudence and forethought go best before boldness.

"Here's a spot for you to do your business."

Wind rustled through leaves overhead and Juddah pulled his arm from her grip. She waited what she estimated enough time for him to remove himself from the vicinity and give her privacy, her ears straining to listen for him moving away amongst the whispering foliage. Satisfied she'd given him enough opportunity, she hiked up the hem of her smock and squatted.

Her water flowed without prompting or encouragement, relief washing through her body and prickling the hairs on her scalp. She leaned forward, chest pressed against her thighs for balance, and closed her eyes, waiting for the voiding of her bladder to end and forcing herself to be grateful for being rescued.

***

Juddah'd never seen a woman piss before.

He watched, fascinated. Any other woman, he'd have ignored the urge to peek at her while she made her water for fear of being caught. But this woman wasn't any other woman—she was a blind woman with no ability to catch him peeping. There was no end to the watching he'd be able to do.

As the thing between his legs that'd prompted him to Jubha Kyna grew and strained against the fabric of his overalls, Juddah decided this might be the best addition to his collection yet.

X Stirk - The Healer

Stirk didn't stop screaming until his voice became too hoarse and his throat too sore to continue. With every breath, every sound, he awaited the cold grip of his mother's dead fingers on his arm, the ghostly rasp of her voice calling his name. She'd come to take him to whatever came after this life, but he was unwilling to go. Without her, he had little to live for, but at least he lived.

Breath panted in and out of his chest as his lungs struggled to recover. Behind his arms, Stirk's eyes squeezed shut, waiting for his fate, but nothing happened. No frigid fingers, no deathly caress, no spectral utterance. As Stirk waited, body unknotting itself the more time passed, he came to realize this was why Enin brought him here. He'd never intended to help him, only to get rid of him once and for all.

The thought flared anger in Stirk's chest. It forced aside some of the fear and he opened his eyes, stared at his forearms for a moment. His gaze found the stump at the end of his arm.

That's Enin's fault, too.

Slowly, he lowered his arms, peering over the top and expecting to discover his dead mother leering down on him, waiting to take him to the neverlands. He didn't believe in them, often thought they were no more than a product of Bieta's imagination, but he didn't want to find out.

The courtyard gradually revealed itself, stretching out before him to the squat building with no windows. His headless mother no longer stood between him and the structure; nothing but dirt separated him from what he'd left the horse doctor's thinking was his destination. As he pushed himself to his feet, he wished to be anywhere else in the Windward Kingdom.

Knees quaking, Stirk started across the courtyard. The solid wall remained behind him, leaving him no choice but to advance to the mysterious building that appeared to follow him no matter where he went. He swallowed hard around a lump in his throat as he crept toward the door, pausing but an arm's length away.

He waited for a time, not moving, afraid to reach out and touch the plain wood door. Since Enin'd brought him here, nothing was as it seemed. If he touched the handle, he might find himself with a python in his grip instead; worse, it may bring about the return of his mother.

But what else am I to do?

Stirk lifted his arm, extended his shaking hand across the space between him and the door, but hesitated before touching it. He flexed his fingers, struggling to keep them from quaking. The air of his held breath burned in his lungs; he let it out between his lips and drew another, hating the tang of fish it brought to his tongue. He clamped his teeth together tight and prepared to reach the rest of the way to the handle when a touch fell on his shoulder.

It startled Stirk so badly, his feet left the dirt when he jumped. He whirled around, swinging wildly as his hand curled itself into a fist, but it found nothing close enough to strike. The momentum spun him, pulling his strained groin and spilling him to the ground in a puff of dust and dirt. His teeth clacked together, jarring his head and setting stars flashing before his eyes.

"Ohh," Stirk groaned, rubbed his jaw.

In the instant of pain and disorientation, he forgot the hand on his shoulder that had surprised him and caused his fall. As he rubbed his chin and flexed the muscles in his jaw, the memory returned and he raised his gaze.

The figure before him wasn't his mother, but the robed silhouette standing in the courtyard was no less unwelcome. Stirk stood, eyes locked on the newcomer, and brushed dirt from his backside.

"Healer," he said, voice low and filled with as much threat as he could muster as he climbed back to his feet.

The apparition didn't respond with either word or movement and Stirk wondered if the cowl hid the same being who'd taken his hand. He lifted his stump, waved it in the air between them hoping to make the healer recognize him.

"Enin brought me here," Stirk said, ashamed of the quake in his voice, noticeable now he strung more than a word or two together. "The horse doctor. He said you might help me."

"Help you what?"

Stirk thought it the same icy voice he'd heard from the healer who removed his hand.

"Seek revenge."

"Revenge? For what and upon whom?"

He hesitated, swallowed. "They killed my mother."

The hood moved as though the head beneath nodded. "I am aware of Bieta's death."

So it is him...it.

"Then you know the men who deserve to die."

"All men deserve to die."

Even in the healer's neither male nor female tone, the words spoken made Stirk gulp hard. The space after the hooded figure's words stretched out too long.

Why did I let Enin bring me here?

"Some men deserve it more than others," he finally responded, attempting to match the ominous nature of the healer's statement but failing, even by his own estimation.

"Perhaps. I presume it is the sword master and his companion of whom you speak."

Stirk nodded. "It is of whom of which I speak."

A sound like dried leaves rattling in the breeze squeezed out from under the hood, and Stirk realized the healer had laughed. Anger flared in him—he hated people laughing at him, even his mother. The big man pulled his shoulders back and pushed out his chest, but the spark quickly extinguished. The healer stood before him, the creature who'd removed his hand with nothing but a touch. He slouched again.

"And the horse doctor," the robed man said, seeming not to have noticed the change in Stirk's attitude.

"Yeah, Enin, too. He gave us up to the one-armed bastard."

"And how should I help? Should I bring an end to their lives?"

Stirk's eyes widened. Revenge might be far easier than he expected. But would it be as satisfying if he didn't kill the horse doctor by wrapping his fingers around the man's throat? Would it fill the void left by

Bieta's death if he didn't open the axeman and watch his bowels spill out on the ground? Would it truly be vengeance if he didn't get to hear the sword master beg for mercy?

Maybe.

"You can do that?"

Another nod beneath the hood. "At great cost."

Stirk's hand folded into a tense fist, the phantom fingers where he now possessed nothing but a stump doing the same. The sensation surprised him and he glanced away from the healer and down at the end of his arm. It still ended in smooth, pink flesh. He sighed.

"No, I'll kill them myself."

"Do you not want to know what cost?"

Stirk shook his head and raised his stump. "I think I got a pretty good idea."

"I suppose you do. What help can I be to you, then?"

The big man pursed his lips, lowered his arm. In his desire for vengeance, he'd put little consideration to the help he'd ask for, didn't know what the healer had the ability to provide. Could he help track them? He supposed, but at what cost? He brushed his hand across the stump at the end of his arm, fingers rubbing the bones of his wrist buried inside.

"Could you..." He hesitated, licked his lips. What if the man wanted his other hand? Without thinking, he snatched it away from the stump and hid it behind his back. "Could you help me find them?"

"Of course."

Stirk shifted from foot to foot, nervous as a child asking his mother for a taste of her milk when she'd forbidden him from having more. He sucked his upper lip into his mouth and clamped it between his teeth. The healer waited. Stirk cleared his throat.

"But what will it cost me?"

The eerie, sexless voice floated out from beneath the

hood again as the figure stood as motionless as if the robe lay upon a stack of rocks positioned in the shape of a man.

"It needn't cost you much. Not if you offer me others to pay."

Stirk squinted one eye. "And how will you help?"

"I will lead you to the men you seek."

"So...you'll come with me?"

"No." The dried leaves chuckle again. "I need not attend you."

"But if you're here, and I'm somewhere else, how'll you know when I need your help?"

"I will be aware. Merely ask and I will set you on the path."

Stirk became aware of sweat in the palm of his hand hidden behind his back. He wiped it on his thigh, unconsciously doing the same with the handless arm. The cloth rubbing against the flesh and the bones pressing into his leg sent a shiver along his spine. Once, his mother had asked the healer's aid, and look what happened without his permission.

He lifted the stump again, pointed it at the healer.

"How can I trust you? How do I know you won't do this again?"

"You have the words I speak to assure you." For the first time, he moved toward Stirk. The big man lowered his arm and tried to step away but found the stone wall at his back. "But perhaps I can give you a token to assuage you."

Movement beneath the healer's robe made the fabric flutter and move, then an arm emerged, extended toward Stirk. He kept his eyes on the darkness hidden under the hood for a moment before moving his gaze to the outstretched hand and the object it offered.

Stirk stared at it for a second before understanding what it was. When he did, his mouth fell open and a half-drawn breath caught on his tongue.

My hand.

It was open, the fingers partially curled but relaxed; healthy-looking pink skin, black hair on the back and on the fingers between the knuckles. Stirk looked from the hand offered by the healer to the one still attached to his other arm, then back again. A matched set.

"Make a fist," the healer said.

Stirk stared at the dark spot under the hood; he'd heard the healer's words but understanding eluded him. He did nothing but gape.

"Make a fist."

After a shuddering breath, Stirk lifted his still-attached hand between himself and the healer, bent his fingers toward his palm. The urge to lash out and strike the robed figure tightened the muscles in his arm, but he held back for fear doing so might be the death of him. The phantom hand curled its fingers along with the other; it may as well have been squeezing his heart.

"Look," the healer urged.

Stirk moved his gaze to the end of his handless arm, hope springing to his chest that the healer had returned it. The hope dissipated when he saw the rounded end of his wrist.

Look at what?

Stirk scowled and raised his eyes, but his gaze caught on the hand the robed figure held out between them. The fingers had curled into a fist.

At first, Stirk refused to believe what he was seeing. He blinked hard, but the fist remained clenched. Slowly, he released the pressure and uncurled his fingers; the severed hand did the same. He wiggled his fingers and the other hand did, too. Stirk's wide-eyed gaze made its way to the darkened hood.

"How...?"

"Take it," the healer urged, pushing the hand toward

Stirk. "A token of our good faith."

Hand shaking, Stirk reached out, hesitating the width of two fingers away from taking it. The fingers of the severed hand waggled in a gesture urging him on. He complied, plucking the appendage from the healer's outstretched palm.

To his surprise, the flesh was warm to the touch, as though blood had never ceased coursing through its veins. Its fingers entwined through the fingers of his other hand, lovers clasping each other, expressing their desire. He fought the urge to burst into tears.

"On whom will you seek revenge first?"

Stirk licked his lips, begrudgingly tore his gaze away from the reunited hands. He stared at the healer for a time, but didn't speak. The reason for his lack of words wasn't because he didn't know which man he wanted to experience his wrath first, but because he needed to collect himself. He cleared his throat before speaking.

"The horse doctor," he said, his voice coming out a rasp despite his efforts.

The healer nodded. "Enin it shall be."

The robed figure moved forward, closing the space between them. This time, Stirk did not shrink way. He stood straighter, pressing his back flat against the stone wall behind him, energy flowing into him from the completeness of the severed hand returned to him.

He tensed when the healer raised an arm, laid a cool palm on the side of Stirk's head. A bolt of pain shot through the big man's temple and he opened his mouth the cry out. Before the sound left his throat, his knees gave out and the world went black.

XI Horace - Along the Shore

If the ol' sailor leaned forward a hair, the tip o' his nose'd've brushed the green wall.

He took great care not to lean forward.

The night'd ended without incident, so long as you didn't count strange sounds comin' outta the forest as incidents. A couple o' times, Horace'd dozed off and caught a little rest. Once, he'd tumbled o'er, his shoulder hittin' against the wall. He'd woken immediately, his sleepy eyes dazzled by emerald lightnin' what he might've found breathtakin' if it didn't scare the same breath from him.

He continued starin' straight ahead. On the other side, the beach stretched away, sand tinted a shade o' green same as the cheeks belongin' to a man what hadn't developed his sea legs, and the rocks transformed to opaque emeralds. Seein' it tempted him, made him think he might just be able to walk on through and head for home, but he knew it weren't a possibility. He couldn't walk through any more'n he could go home.

Not after what I've seen...what I've done.

Farther along the shore, distant but noticeable, he spied the rocky outcropping where the big gray feller'd taken Thorn. Beside it lay the spot where the man what liked to count came near to endin' his life what even the God o' the Deep didn't find a way to put an end to. He'd floated a good distance, as he'd suspected, but they'd been far closer to the Small God's home than they knew.

But we didn't see the shimmery wall from there.

Had Thorn realized how close they'd come? Where were he now?

Horace heaved a sigh and stepped back from the veil, let his chin drop to his chest and his eyes find his feet.

Nobody'd assigned him the job o' takin' care o' the little feller, but somehow everythin' suggested he'd been meant to, and he'd failed. The thought set his chest to achin'; for a god, the little gray man'd been a fine feller.

The ol' sailor closed his eyes and balled his fists. His mind wandered back to the Small God's expression when he'd stolen the britches, his joy at tastin' pig for the first time, how he'd known more 'bout Horace and his life than most anyone else did, and the time he'd made himself appear as a young Rilum Seaman.

Were that why Horace found himself carin' so much for somethin' what not so long ago made him shit his breeches in fear? Because he'd used magic to look like the ol' sailor's son?

Despite standin' on a deserted beach by his lonesome, Horace shook his head. More'n soft feelin's for a boy he ain't seen for season after season caused it. He'd sensed somethin' special 'bout Thorn the minute he'd landed on top o' him. Why else did he about face when given the opportunity to flee? It weren't as though Horace'd chosen not to skedaddle from other things when the chance presented itself. Weren't that partly why he hadn't seen Rilum in so long?

"No," he said, tiltin' his head and openin' his peepers to peer at the shimmery wall again. "I can't let them take him."

A shiver crept along the ol' sailor's arms and made him unclench his fists, but it weren't fear what gave him a shake this time. It were determination.

Horace stepped away from the green veil and pivoted to his right, lookin' down its length to where it disappeared into a thicket o' brush and trees. With a deep inhalation what he meant for givin' him courage but what instead put more o' the sea's taste on his tongue and clenched his throat, he took his first step toward the thicket.

A wind what weren't blowin' a moment before shook the leaves and bristled the whiskers on his cheeks. He hesitated, suddenly aware o' a layer o' sweat on his palms, then took another step. He followed it with another, then a fourth, surprised to find out walkin' here weren't so different from doin' it anywhere else.

Sand and pebbles crunched under his boot heels, each flex o' his foot makin' the too-small footwear pinch. A few more paces and the ol' sailor stood at the verge where the beach ended and the tangle o' brush began. He searched it with his gaze, hesitant to reach out his hand and touch bare flesh to any o' those leaves. Instead, he stuck out his foot, preparin' to toe one o' the thick stalks with it.

And he'd've done it if the thing didn't move away when he tried.

Horace set his foot on the ground, a chill crawlin' up his spine, and this one he'd attribute to the return o' fear. Funny how quick determination can turn on a feller.

The ol' sailor took a step back the way he came, then one to his left, movin' closer to the green wall what separated him from his own world. It might've been a place what'd done its best to kill him, and he were damn near sure it'd disown him if he returned, but at least he knew what kind o' creatures in it wanted to get their teeth into him, and that no bushes'd be shakin' on their own.

Horace sidled up to the veil, stoppin' with his shoulder half a hand's breadth from touchin' it, and peered along its length. It went for ten paces, plain as can be, before disappearin', hidden by trees and bushes. Between where Horace stood and where he stopped bein' able to see his prison's wall, branches and leaves dangled in the space where the wall were as though it weren't even there.

Seein' that gave the ol' sailor a thought.

He eased forward, doin' his best not to get too near the brush, especially with his bare flesh. Not too far away, a long, curved branch o' one o' the bushes hung across the veil, its end danglin' in Horace's world, tauntin' him.

He reached out, gaze fixed upon it until he realized it were outta his reach. He glanced down at his chest, makin' sure he didn't lean into the broad leaves belongin' to the nearest bush. The width o' a finger separated them.

With his bottom lip sucked into his mouth, Horace got up on his toes to stretch farther, leaned forward as far as he dared. His goal remained outta reach. He grunted in his chest, twisted to extend his arm the little bit more it needed. His hand brushed the veil, shooting the verdant energy along its surface, startlin' him.

Horace's feet slipped out from under him.

He toppled face first, eyes and mouth clampin' shut to keep foliage from findin' its way into him. One hand bent back when it hit the ground, jarrin' his wrist and shootin' pain up his arm. His chest hit next, knockin' breath through his tightened lips with a whoosh o' air he might've found funny if it'd happened to someone other'n himself. The broken rib he'd hoped had healed gave him a poke to let him know it hadn't.

Horace lay still a while, eyes closed, chest tight and strugglin' to get him some air. He waited, not sure what to expect—leaves beatin' him? Stalks and creepers wrappin' him up like snakes squeezin' the life from their dinner? A tree uprootin' itself to walk o'er and club him with its thick limbs?

What happened were the one thing he didn't think'd happen: nothin'.

After a short bit, the ol' sailor's air came back. He sucked a breath through his nose, inhalin' the loamy odor o' the forest floor. It were strong enough to hide the sea's briny scent, for which Horace were glad no matter where he found himself lyin'. Even after his chest loosened up and let his lungs do their job, he kept his eyes shut tight, waitin' for somethin' else to happen and not wantin' to see what it'd be.

After a few breaths and a couple o' dozen frightened beats from his heart without leaves beatin', creepers squeezin', or limbs clubbin', Horace pried open his uncooperative lids. His peepers showed him moss and dirt and rocks—everythin' what one might think they'd find on the ground underneath bushes and trees.

The ol' sailor got his arms under him and pushed. A jolt o' pain shot outta his wrist, but it weren't unbearable, so he thought it twisted, not broken. Should've had some relief o'er that, but it'd have to wait. He climbed to his feet, back pressed against the veil for support as green lightnin' spider-webbed out 'round him. To his surprise, he'd fallen into a clear space—leaves all about, but none touchin' him. To his right, less than an arm's length away, were the branch he'd been reachin' for.

Its leaves danglin' on the end on the other side o' the veil moved with the touch o' a gentle wind. On Horace's side, they was dead still.

I'm here now. Might as well find out.

He reached out and touched the wall where the branch protruded through.

Solid.

His brow creasin', Horace's hand did somethin' he didn't mean it to do—grab the piece o' bush what were pokin' through the veil and give it a shake.

The leaves rattled together with an ominous sound. The tremor traveled along the branch and through the wall, shakin' the foliage on the other side, too. Seein' this made shallow goosebumps crawl o'er Horace's forearm. He gripped the stalk tighter, shook harder, its motion unimpeded by the wall what felt same as a slab o' stone to the ol' sailor.

His heart grew in his chest, inflated by the hope this meant he were close to findin' a way outta the green. The swollen organ shriveled again when the branch tore itself from Horace's grasp.

It whipped away as though jerked by an unseen hand, and Horace's now fearful mind wondered if it might've actually been the case. He stumbled backward, leaves brushing his ears and slappin' his back, so he threw his arms up o'er his head and ducked. Elbows first, he blundered toward the sea, hopin' the thick stalk didn't fall across him, seekin' revenge. He imagined creepers reachin' for his ankles, limbs pokin' at him, and didn't stop movin' until sand crunched beneath his feet followed by the splash o' salty water on his boots.

Horace stopped and lowered his arms, gazed back at the tangled brush with his heart beatin' hard against his ribs. The leaves and bushes was motionless, hangin' in the air as though nothin'd happened. The ol' sailor stared at the mess, waitin' for somethin' to happen and promisin' himself he weren't goin' in there again.

***

Enough steps passed beneath Horace's boots that, when he turned 'round to peek back, he no longer had a view o' the green wall.

The sun'd climbed its way high into the sky, o'er its zenith, and begun headin' toward the far horizon. Its warmth prompted sweat to the sailor's brow, under his arms, and along his back, makin' him stop to wipe it away on his sleeve now and then, to keep it from rollin' into his eyes. An achin' rib, a tweaked wrist; he didn't need stingin' peepers, too.

Horace'd walked for the whole day, gaze peekin' first one way then the other, unsure if he should keep his eyes on the ocean to his right what'd tried to kill him more'n once, or the forest to his left what he didn't know the kinds o' things lurkin' beneath its boughs.

One thing he knew for sure: if he could walk right 'round the end o' sunset and make his way to the Leeward Kingdom without settin' foot under them trees, he'd do it.

Gonna be a long walk.

As much as his heart wanted him to do whate'er he could to help poor little Thorn, his head realized there weren't nothin' for him to do, not trapped behind the veil. He had no idea where the big gray feller and the countin' man was plannin' to take him, except it weren't here.

He walked on, thinkin' on the little gray feller. Did he have any o' the magic left he'd used to make himself appear the same as Rilum? Enough to save himself? Horace didn't know, but he thought if they took him farther away from the Green, it'd make Thorn weaker and weaker, maybe even kill him.

He didn't want that happenin'.

While he were walkin' and thinkin', the beach's grains o' sand grew to pebbles, then rocks. By the time the sun'd dropped halfway from its peak toward the sea, the rocks'd become the size o' fists, makin' the footin' precarious and slowin' Horace. He pulled himself from thoughts and regret to take care o' his footin' and noticed there weren't no driftwood scattered along the shore, but somethin' else instead.

Bones.

He crept up on the closest pile o' bones as if it might jump up and run if he made too much noise. They didn't, o' course, and when Horace stood o'er them, he recognized they'd belonged to a fish 'bout the length o' his forearm. Its ribs was translucent and pointy, achin' to find their way into some unsuspectin' diner's throat, and the shape o' its head were like no fish Horace'd ever seen. Besides its odd noggin, he counted too many fins, though not a speck o' scales or flesh were left stuck to none o' them, fins and bones alike.

Horace scratched his stubbled cheek and tilted his head to glare toward the sea.

"What're you up to?"

His words died in the warm, late-day air, swallowed by the wash of surf rolling onto the shore. He narrowed his eyes, suspectin' even the sound comin' from the treacherous ocean might be a lie, then returned his gaze to the bones what used to be a swimmer. His stomach gurgled.

"Too bad the birds already got you," he said. "You might've been tasty."

Saliva washed across his tongue at the thought what made his belly clench and churn. Fish and all the sea's bounty scored low amongst Horace Seaman's favorite foods, despite how much he'd eaten during those seasons with his feet on one deck or another. To him, the flavor o' the briny deep clung to ev'ry bite—a flavor he didn't enjoy havin' on his tongue.

Horace left the bony fish behind, concentratin' on where he needed to place his boots and tryin' to forget the complainin' in his belly.

***

The collections o' bones got more frequent and the creatures what they'd belonged to grew larger as Horace continued his journey toward sunset.

He passed a big fish what might've been one o' them ones what liked to race alongside the ships. The ol' sailor'd always liked watchin' them, usin' them to distract him from starin' out o'er the water with nothin' much to see. He enjoyed the way they swam and the grace and ease with which they leaped outta the water.

Farther along, he found what must've been a seal, because it certainly weren't no fish. Sharp little teeth lined the jaw in its sun-bleached skull but, same as ev'ry other skeleton he passed, not the smallest scrap o' flesh clung to it.

Horace thought it strange the carrion eaters had done such a good job o' pickin' clean the bones when he'd seen not a single livin' creature since he floated across the veil. No birds, no fish, not so much as a crab.

If there ain't nothin' livin' 'round, what be eatin' the dead?

The ol' sailor added the question to the myriad o' others floatin' in his brain search' for answers and findin' none. The biggest of them all were how he'd crossed the wall the one way, but couldn't go back the other. It bubbled to the surface again, stoppin' him in his tracks.

"I were in the water," he said aloud, gaze starin' straight ahead at the sunlight beginnin' to glint a shade o' pink upon the water. "I were in the water when I crossed, but my feet was on the ground when I tried to go back."

Horace spun 'round, fist-sized rocks grating under his foot. The shore stretched away behind him, bleached bones shining in the late day sun, but his eyes found no green shimmerin' wall.

"Fuck me dead," he whispered. "The answer were right there and I left it behind."

He took one step toward where his journey'd started, but stopped. The shadow stretchin' out in front o' him and the pink shine upon the sea made it plain he didn't have time to get back before night claimed the beach. The footin' were too treacherous to walk the shore in the dark.

Horace chewed his bottom lip and squinted, doin' his best to see the emerald veil, but it were invisible to him now; he'd come too far.

"Far enough if I go back and I'm wrong, I'll be dyin'

o' hunger."

He peeked o'er his shoulder toward sunset, then along the beach at the distant gatherin' night.

"Fucked if I do, fucked if I don't." He lifted his hand and banged his flattened palm against the side o' his head. "If you keep thinkin' like Dunal, you might as well lay down and die."

Once upon a time, Horace Seaman might've done exactly that if he found himself lost in the Green. He'd've made dirt in his drawers and fallen to the ground curled up in a ball to await death's tap on the shoulder. But the Horace Seaman who'd've done those things hadn't been spat out by the God o' the Deep, or killed a swabbie to save his own neck, or had a Small God fall on his head. Things'll change a man and, though it might've taken more to change the ol' sailor than it'd've taken for others, change came, nonetheless.

Horace gritted his teeth and faced away from the dark lurkin' behind sunrise's horizon, determined to get farther along the shore before night made him stop. An energy he hadn't had since Thorn'd left him surged through his limbs, urging him on. He thought it might be hope, or courage, but whatever name he put to it, it gave him the strength to keep goin'.

Ten paces later, the ol' sailor encountered the first o' a score o' skeletons what'd once been men. Maybe the idea o' foldin' himself into a ball didn't seem so bad, after all.

XII Stirk - Enin

Stirk crept along the alley, keeping close to the wall to hide in the shadows. At this time of night, there was little danger he'd meet anyone, at least no one sober enough to be a threat or to remember seeing him.

Since even the drunks kept to the wider avenues and avoided the cramped lanes, Stirk decided to approach Enin's shop from the rear. Doing so would be less chancy than striding up to the front door, but he was unsure how he'd recognize the horse doctor's when he reached it. Truthfully, the horse doctor might not be here, but here's where he found himself when he woke, so he had to trust the healer'd be true to his word to show him the path.

The encounter remained fuzzy in his head. He remembered the creature agreeing to help and returning his hand—it resided in a pocket sewn inside the jerkin he wore, its weight bouncing reassuringly against his chest as he walked. Where the jerkin came from or how he'd gotten from the edge of Fishtown to the horse doctor's in Middleton, he had no recollection and didn't care to guess. At least he was in one piece—two, really. He snickered to himself.

The alley stank of piss and refuse, same as the one off which he and Bieta had lived. It took a conscious effort to keep his thoughts from the tiny storeroom and the memories it contained. Instead, he concentrated on the task at hand, thinking about wrapping his fingers around Enin's throat and watching the light of life in his eyes dim and go out.

Another distinct odor added itself to the alley's stench, and Stirk's lips twisted into a lopsided smile when he detected it: horse manure. A horse wouldn't have fit down the cluttered alley, so the scent meant he neared the horse doctor's shop.

"Yer gonna get what's comin' to ya. You'll pay for what happened to my ma."

The words rumbled in his throat, half growl, half whisper. For the first time since he'd seen the axe fall across his mother's neck, Stirk felt a purpose, a reason to live while his mother was dead.

A few more paces farther along the lane, the big man stopped outside a door with two handles allowing the top and bottom portions to open separately. Though he'd never been in the back room of the horse doctor's shop, he recognized the style from the times Bieta sent him to pilfer the stables. They used the same type of doors for horses' stalls.

A grin crept across Stirk's face, but it was short-lived. What should he do next? How should he exact his revenge?

He leaned against the wall outside Enin's shop, back pressed against it as he considered the possibilities. He had no weapon, no rope, no implements of death. Tiredness flooded him and he sank to the ground.

How do I kill him?

The question rattled around his mind, but the exhaustion leeching through his body kept it from finding purchase. In first his fear, then his focus on seeking vengeance, he'd failed to notice the ache in his muscles, the swirling edge of confusion in his brain.

His chin sagged, bounced on his chest; Stirk jerked his head back, blinking rapidly to fend off the threat of sleep. A movement in the pocket of his jerkin caught his attention, clearing his thoughts. He reached inside, where his fingers brushed against fingers. They moved and Stirk nearly yanked away in surprise, but then remembered. He clutched the severed hand and pulled it out of his pocket.

He held it on his outstretched palm, the fingers flexing, then releasing, flexing and releasing. After observing it for a few moments, he realized its pulsations matched the beat of his heart.

"I'm so glad to have you back," he whispered.

For an instant, he considered lifting the hand toward his face, pressing the palm against his cheek the way

Bieta used to caress him when he hurt himself or felt upset. He didn't, though; someone might be watching.

Stirk drew a deep breath through parted lips and let it sigh out again. The hand continued following his heartbeat as he wrapped his thumb around it. The fingers folded closer at the touch, reacting to the stroke of the pad of his thumb on the palm.

With another sigh, Stirk raised his stump, touched the severed end against it. Warmth flowed up his arm.

"Wish you was attached," he murmured, eyelids growing heavy. He concentrated and managed to curl the fingers into a fist, even thinking he sensed the pressure of his nails as they dug in.

His chin drooped again, but this time when it touched his chest, sleep kept it there.

***

Stirk woke with a snort, eyes opening for an instant, then closing tight again when he was surprised by the sun shining in them. Disoriented, he raised his arm to ward it off, his mind reeling as he attempted to discern why he didn't awaken in the converted storeroom at the back of the tanner's.

Because Bieta is dead.

The remembrance started a knot in his throat, but a pain in his side interrupted both memory and emotion. Stirk dropped his arm and looked up to find the horse doctor glaring at him, a pitchfork in his hand and his boot having freshly kicked the big man in the hip.

"What are you doing here?" Enin demanded. He didn't need to sound angry, his expression made it plain, though his eyes held more than a touch of fear, as well.

Stirk tried to speak, but his dry throat gave up nothing more than a croak. He coughed and gave it another go. "Came looking for you."

His gaze moved away from Enin to the end of his own arm where he hoped to find his hand had reattached itself while he slept. It hadn't. The tight skin gleamed in the sunlight and anger seeped back into Stirk's head, forcing sleep out as it took over. He raised his eyes to the horse doctor again.

Enin stared and Stirk realized the gaunt man hadn't expected to see him again. When he left him at the healer's, he'd assumed the robed fiend would finish what he'd started when he took Stirk's hand.

He didn't. Too bad for you.

His brow furrowed and he pushed himself against the wall, using it to leverage himself to his feet. Despite having the pitchfork to keep him at bay, Enin backed away a step.

"You've got to go," the horse doctor said. "You shouldn't be here."

"Shouldn't be here," Stirk echoed. "You figure I shouldn't be here 'cause you thought I'd be dead, like my ma. You though I'd be gone, like my hand."

He raised his arm, waggled the stump at Enin, who fell back another pace, stepping into the doorway to his shop. Stirk's heart jumped as he remembered holding the hand against his empty wrist before he'd dozed off.

Where'd it go?

He couldn't recall returning to its hiding place in his jerkin, but fog still clouded his head. Eyes fixed on the horse doctor, he reached for the pocket, found it spot empty. It must have fallen while he slept but, with a pitchfork aimed at his belly, he didn't dare take the time to search for it.

Its loss meant one more reason to make Enin pay.

Stirk glowered, bared his teeth, and took one step toward the horse doctor hoping to catch him off guard, to scare him. He didn't know the man well but he didn't think he had it in him to kill someone with his own hands—only to set in motion the events leading to their death, like he'd done with Bieta. If he'd misjudged, he'd end up with four holes in his gut and his life leaking out on the ground in a back alley.

He'd estimated correctly; Enin backed through the doorway, sending a half-hearted poke Stirk's direction, meant to frighten, not to injure.

"You'll pay for what happened to my ma."

Not sure how I'll get past your poker.

Enin shook his head and retreated into the makeshift paddock. The horse Stirk had heard in it the night before was gone and fresh hay lay on the floor. Its scent tickled his nose, gave him the urge to sneeze. He switched to breathing through his mouth hoping to avoid doing so.

"Not my fault." Enin's voice quaked.

That's right, horse doctor. Beg for your life.

"You told the one-armed man about us."

"No. I tried to keep them from you."

"Failed pretty badly, didn't ya?"

He backed away and Stirk followed him inside where it was cooler and dimmer. With the sun behind him, he'd be no more than a silhouette in the doorway to Enin's eyes—the perfect opportunity to find his way past the tines of the pitchfork. He feigned a step to the right, then jerked back to the left, but Enin kept the barn tool pointed at him, preventing him from getting closer.

A movement in the dim shadow behind the horse doctor distracted Stirk for an instant, but he kept his eyes on the tall man. When it happened again, he dared a glance. The fresh straw on the floor shifted, stopped, shifted, stopped. Likely a rat or other vermin, but curiosity threatened to consume him, making him nearly forget the threat of the pitchfork pointed at his gut.

Something resembling a large, hairless spider missing three legs scuttled out of the hay. Seeing it made Stirk's heart jump with fear—he loathed spiders—then he recognized it for what it was.

My hand!

It crossed the floor toward Enin on the tips of its fingers. Stirk found it difficult pulling his gaze from its movements, so much like an animal on the prowl, but forced himself to look away lest Enin guess its presence. He let a growl escape his throat, hoping to scare the horse doctor back.

"You have to believe me," the gaunt man said. "I'd never do anything to hurt Bieta. Or you."

"Just 'cause you didn't kill her with your own hands don't mean you're not responsible."

Enin's expression changed; the fear in his eyes loosened and they turned watery. The pitchfork sagged in his grip, the tines drooping toward the floor. Behind him, the hand inched forward, pausing a single pace back of the horse doctor's heel.

"Stirk—"

"My ma's dead. You deserve to join her."

"You don't understand."

"What don't I understand? That if it weren't for you, she'd be alive? And I'd have both hands?"

"You don't understand that I wouldn't hurt you or her because..."

His voice trailed off and his gaze fell away from Stirk's. The big man's heart leapt in his chest for fear he'd notice the hand, but he didn't. Instead, the horse doctor tossed the pitchfork aside and looked back into Stirk's eyes. Tears brimmed his lids; one spilled over and rolled down his cheek.

"I wouldn't hurt you because I'm your father."

Stirk stared at the man, struggling to decipher what he'd said. Somehow, this last time Enin opened his mouth, to Stirk's ears it sounded as though he'd spoken a different language.

"What did you say?"

"I'm your father, Stirk." Enin's face relaxed a little. "Bieta didn't want you to know. It's why I protected you."

Stirk's head swirled. When had the horse doctor ever protected him? And how could he be his father? No, Stirk understood the process that made a man a father, but he didn't know how he never suspected. Stirk had surveyed every man who ever visited his mother, searching for someone with similar features to his own, wondered if each might be the one.

He'd never considered Enin.

"Protected me?" He lifted his handless arm, pointed it at the horse doctor in accusation. The severed hand on the floor behind him scuttled closer. "You call this protecting me?"

"Yes. If we hadn't ensured the prince's life continued, you and Bieta would surely have been killed."

"She was killed," Stirk snapped. "Do you see her standin' here by my side?"

Enin's chin dropped to his chest. "It didn't work out how I'd hoped."

"Damn right it didn't." He took a step toward the horse doctor, jaw clamped tight and hand curled into a fist.

"But I had to try. I had to give you a chance to survive."

"Bieta didn't have no chance."

"I wish I could bring her back." Enin raised his head; dim light gleamed in the wetness on his cheeks. "I wish I could make you safe."

Stirk went to move closer, but hesitated, the horse doctor's tone giving him pause. Was it possible the man told the truth? His eyes narrowed and he surveyed Enin's long, gaunt face, narrow shoulders, his sunken chest. He bore no resemblance to Stirk, and yet he wondered.

Is he my sire?

Under other circumstances, he'd have dismissed the notion. But after so much speculation, and with his mother gone, the prospect of having a father seemed more desirable than ever.

"Are you speakin' the truth?"

Enin nodded fervently. "I am."

"Then why didn't ma tell me? Or you?"

"She begged me not to."

"Why?"

"I don't know. Season after season, I paid the tanner to let you stay in the storeroom of his shop, but Bieta didn't want you to find out. She was a proud woman."

He might tell the truth.

No proof. His lying.

He might be my father.

He's a liar.

Enin must have seen the internal debate playing out across Stirk's face. He reached out a comforting hand and took a long pace forward. During their exchange, neither of them noticed the severed hand make its way to Enin's feet. It grabbed hold of his ankle as he took a second stride, the grip throwing him off balance.

Enin waved his arms in the air, attempting to prevent himself from toppling, but failed. He twisted as he fell, landing with his back to the ground and the pitchfork he'd cast aside. The four points sank deep into his flesh; he gasped a harsh breath through his mouth. He'd barely come to rest before the severed hand scuttled its way up his body faster than one might have imagined it could move.

Stirk stood motionless, gawking.

The fingers wrapped themselves around the horse doctor's windpipe and squeezed; Stirk's other hand mimicked the grip. Enin grasped at it, trying to pry it away, wincing at the pain of the pitchfork sticking him in the back as he did. He pulled at the fingers, but the severed hand's grip proved too tight. His fingernails scratched the back of the hand and Stirk sucked in a quick, pained breath.

Enin directed his gaze toward Stirk, his eyes wide and bulging from the lack of air reaching his lungs. The big man recognized the pleading expression flickering in them amongst panic and fear. For an instant, he considered diving forward, prying the should-be-dead fingers from around his throat, and saving the fellow who claimed to be his sire.

Liar.

Bieta wouldn't have kept it from him. She'd told him he'd never meet his father and, though he'd always watched for the person it might be, just in case, he didn't believe his mother lied to him. The horse doctor, however, feared for his life.

A man'll say anything when he's afraid of dying.

"Stirk," Enin wheezed. He held his hand out toward the big man, fingers splayed in a last, desperate act of begging for mercy and forgiveness.

"Liar."

Stirk crossed his arms, acutely aware of the stump pressing against his chest as the hand that once resided there tightened its grip on the horse doctor's throat. First, the color drained from the man's face, then some returned as his lips turned blue. The arm he held out drooped, his energy draining until it settled onto the fresh hay scattered about the floor.

A spark of hope burned at the back of Stirk's mind, wishing he had a father and Enin might be that man. But the spark was smaller than the fiery rage burning over the death of his mother, so he watched as the blue in the horse doctor's lips spread to his cheeks and his eyes rolled back in his head.

The hand held on a while longer, like it wanted to make sure it had truly extinguished the man's life before releasing its grip and crawling to Stirk like a dog awaiting a reward for a trick well performed.

He picked the hand up, stroked it, stored it in the pocket sewn in the lining of his jerkin, and left the horse doctor's shop determined that, the next time he took a life, he'd use the hand still his own.

XIII Trenan - Bound for Ikkundana

They prompted their horses faster, passing a line of wagons leaving the city along the Sunset Road. A weapons merchant, a spice wagon, an open wain covered by a poorly tied sheet of canvas with fabrics of many colors bulging out from beneath. Three covered wagons accompanied them, each carrying a variety of foodstuffs and supplies as the caravan made its way to the kingdom's many outlying towns to set up market and sell their wares.

As they found their way past the front of the column, Trenan glanced back and wondered if they should have searched the wagons. He slowed his mount, thinking he might go back to do just that, but then changed his mind. No merchants would offer transport to initiates of the Goddess, certainly not one dressed in the red cloak of deadly disease.

The master swordsman put his heels to his steed, urging it to catch up to Dansil. He settled his pace when he did, his mare keeping stride with the bigger gelding the queen's guard had appropriated.

It's just a horse.

But it was more. He'd need to keep a tight rein on the queen's guard or their search for Danya might go seriously astray. He put the thought from his mind for a moment, thinking of the red shroud he'd glimpsed through the crowd when he heard the princess call his name. Might it be a clue where she went?

"Ikkundana," Trenan said, putting voice to his thoughts.

Dansil's head jerked toward the master swordsman. "What did you say?"

"Ikkundana. When I saw the princess and her companion fleeing the square, she was wearing the Goddess' red smock."

"So you think we should risk catching our deaths based on a cloak of crimson cloth? No fucking way."

Trenan's gut knotted and his jaw tightened, but he willed his body to release the tension.

"It's the only clue we have," he said, holding back the verbal lashing he'd rather have given the queen's guard.

"Not much of a clue. We've probably ridden past them already, them being on foot and all."

"Don't underestimate the resourcefulness of your princess. Or the influence of those of the Goddess."

"A disguise is all that was. Why would the Goddess' bitches give a flying turd about the princess and her imaginary quest? Probably she and some street urchin she hooked up with stole them to hide from you."

Dansil stared straight ahead as he spoke, but Trenan saw the corner of his mouth quivering as the queen's guard fought to keep from breaking into a smile. Would he really let his sour feelings for Trenan interfere with their search for Danya and Teryk? He swallowed his anger, but it caught in his throat.

"What would you have us do, then?"

"Hmph," Dansil grunted. "Were it up to me, we'd've returned to Draekfarren with Strylor and your puppy, sent a force of men out to find the whelps while you faced the king's wrath, likely ending up in Dreemskerry like you deserve."

Trenan bit down hard and forced air out through his nostrils. The anger he'd been suppressing grew, its red-hot glow fanned to a flame by Dansil's words. His legs gripped the sides of his steed tighter and his hand instinctively released the reins and moved toward the hilt of the crownsword.

"What is your problem?" the master swordsman demanded. "There need not be others around for you to treat higher ranking officers with respect."

"Respect? You jest. Respect is earned, not given. How can I respect you after what I've seen you do?"

Trenan raised an eyebrow. "What in the king's name are you talking about?"

"Funny you'd use the king's name in that manner, having fucked his wife and all."

The statement caught Trenan by surprise, draining the blood from his face and leaving his cheeks cold. His mouth opened to reply but no words made their way to his tongue.

How could he know?

Was it possible Ishla confided in a guardsman? Or had he overheard her speaking with one of her ladies-in-waiting? Trenan doubted either to be the case. They'd both see dire consequences should their secret become known; it would cost the master swordsman his freedom if Erral felt generous, his life if he didn't.

She wouldn't tell. He's guessing.

When Trenan had no retort, Dansil pivoted in his saddle to face him, putting no effort into concealing the malicious grin contorting his lips. In that instant, the swordmaster understood the queen's guard knew his secret.

"Bet you're wondering how someone like me found out something no one else knows, ain't you?"

"You've lost your mind," Trenan replied, adding steel to his tone, a practice he'd mastered through years of commanding soldiers. "No such thing has ever happened. I should have your tongue from your head for even suggesting it."

"Exactly how I'd expect a guilty man to react, and your conviction might make me doubt my information if I hadn't seen it myself."

"Impossible. There's never been anything to see."

"I was just a pup," Dansil said as though he hadn't heard Trenan, "an adventurous lad exploring the castle late at night, avoiding guards and sneaking to places young lads aren't supposed to go. It's amazing what you find in a castle late at night. Even more amazing who you bump into sneaking out of rooms where they shouldn't ought to be."

Dansil had shifted in his saddle again to face forward as he spoke, continuing his story without looking at Trenan. The master swordsman felt little relief for not having to experience his malevolent smile; he let his hand rest on the pommel of the saddle, a hand's breadth from his weapon.

"Who'd've expected the queen to creep out of the room occupied by the soldier who'd given his arm for the king?"

Trenan's mind drifted back to the night, but not borne on the fond memories and longing with which he usually recalled it. Instead, he remembered the youth who'd knocked on the door, entered without permission. He'd all but forgotten it, dismissed the occurrence from his mind, but now he realized it meant Dansil wasn't guessing.

No use denying it.

"She came to give her thanks, nothing more."

"In the dead of night? I bet she gave her thanks." The queen's guard brayed a harsh laugh. "She gave her thanks and you gave her something else, didn't you?"

"Nothing happened but conversation. She was

pleased I saved her husband and wanted a moment alone to tell me." Trenan hated the way his words sounded: hollow, empty. To him, the truth they attempted to conceal shone through like a beacon in the night.

Dansil again continued as though Trenan hadn't spoken.

"I took a while to realize what you'd given her on that night she gave you her cunny."

Trenan's fingers wrapped around Godsbane's hilt, his eyes narrowed.

"I suppose I might be wrong, but the timing works out too well, don't it?"

He glanced back at Trenan as though he expected the master swordsman to reply. He didn't; he merely met the soldier's look with a glare.

"Seems to me just the right number of seasons passed after that night before the queen gave Erral what he thought his first child. Was surprised the whelp came out with both arms, weren't you?"

"You speak treason," Trenan growled. Blood throbbed in his veins as though threatening to boil. "Forget the tongue in your head, that wretched skull deserves to come off your spine."

Dansil's smile faded, his face went stony. "You'll do nothing of the sort. You don't know who I might've told your secret to. You don't know if I told 'em to spread your secret in the event I don't return from our little foray in search of the royal pains-in-the-ass, do you?"

Trenan recalled seeing Dansil and Strylor sharing hushed words on several occasions, one or the other of them glancing toward him, the conversation stopping when he approached. The opportunity to tell the other man had been there, but had he done so? The swordmaster struggled to remember if Strylor acted differently after any of those hushed exchanges, but he hadn't been watching for it so he couldn't recall; he'd carried an edge of the defiance Dansil displayed right from the start.

"Wonderin' if I'm telling the truth? No way to be sure, I guess."

Trenan released his grip on the sword's hilt and reclaimed his hold on the reins. The queen's guard was most likely lying, but he couldn't take the chance to find out. Trenan didn't care what happened to him; since the moment the axe had separated his arm from his body, he'd made peace with death—wished for it at times—but he couldn't let anything happen that may make things difficult for Ishla.

"You'll behave yourself with me or others'll be finding out about you fucking the queen, understand?"

Trenan didn't reply but continued to glare at his companion. Dansil clicked his tongue against the roof of his mouth and shook his head.

"You're so desperate to find the girl. Is she yours, too?"

"The king's children are the king's children."

"So says you." Dansil laughed and put his heels to his horse, urging the animal to pull farther ahead.

Trenan stared after the queen's guard, letting the gap between them increase. He pursed his lips, wishing to yank Godsbane from its sheath and skewer the bastard on its sharp blade, then leave him bleeding at the side of the path for the crows to feast on his eyes and his innards. But, for the moment, the risk to Ishla was too great. Eventually, though, Trenan would find out if the big soldier's threat held any truth.

And when he did, Dansil would die.

XIV Danya - Out of the City

Danya held her breath and peered through the tiny space between the edge of the canvas and the wooden side of the wain. The multi-colored stacks of fabrics pressing around her made her sweat beneath her armor, but at least she'd been able to shed the thick, red robe. It served its purpose by keeping people away, but it also overheated her and left a rash on her neck where the scratchy material rubbed against her skin.

Although Evalal lay within arm's reach, the wain's cargo silenced any sound she made, leaving Danya in a muted world of creaking boards, rumbling wheels, and a sliver of the world going by. Despite stale air and oppressive heat, getting out of the city and moving toward her goal gave her a measure of comfort.

Even if she was unsure what the goal was or where to find it.

In her heart, she wanted to find her brother. Despite the overwhelming evidence suggesting he may no longer be of this world, she was convinced that if it were true, she'd sense it. They'd always shared a connection she didn't have with anyone else, including their mother. Could the connection have failed her, leaving her to guess her brother's fate at the time she most needed to know it?

She refused to believe it. No sense of danger or despair must mean he remained alive and well.

But where?

He might still be in the city. Or maybe his injuries weren't as grievous as they'd suspected and he'd left, continuing his quest to fulfill the parchment's prophecy.

The firstborn child of the rightful king.

Teryk claimed the title of firstborn child, but was

their father the rightful king? He'd taken the throne by force, so the scroll might refer to someone else. Perhaps they weren't the ones intended to find it. If they'd retrieved it before the intended found it, doing so not only meant they'd put themselves in danger, but the entire world, too.

No, that didn't seem right. She didn't believe things happened without reason. Everyone controls their fates to a degree, within limits. And what of the Mother of Death? She'd been unshakable in her conviction the seed of life required the princess to carry it, and hadn't she rescued it from the cursed garden?

Danya shifted, moving her hand to the pouch tied to her sword belt. She caressed the seed's smooth hardness through the soft doeskin, imagined its color—so dark it appeared black. But it wasn't, for she'd seen many colors hidden in its shell as she'd lain in her bed, staring at it. Out of the darkness, red had whirled across its surface before it darkened again, then blue, or green. Every color had appeared on its lustrous surface. At first, she'd assumed them reflections, but she'd seen purples and oranges, though nothing in her chamber bore those hues. As her fingers rested on the seed, she wondered what color it might be in the blackness within the pouch.

The princess breathed a sigh of stale air and returned her attention to the sliver of the world visible between tarp and wain. During her distraction, a shadow had fallen across it, so she wiggled closer for a better view.

A rider kept pace beside the merchant's wagon, only the horse's rippling muscles visible at first. Then sunlight flashed on metal—armor. Upon seeing it, Danya heard the clank of plate, the muted jingle of mail. Her breath caught in her throat; could they be there because of her? Had she been discovered?

She waited, holding her body rigid without removing her gaze from the armored man. After a half-dozen heartbeats that dragged on much longer, the rider pulled away, passing the merchant and allowing the sun to shine through the gap. She freed her breath, let her tensed muscles relax, when another shadow blocked the light, another rider.

At first, she saw nothing. The sudden shifts from shade to sun and back left her eyes reeling and unable to discern more than a shape. When her vision adjusted, she stared out at the missing arm of a man she knew too well.

Trenan.

Part of her fell into a panic at being found, but welcome relief flooded another part. Her entire life, the master swordsman taught her, supported her, was more of a father to her than the king had time to be. She fought the urge to call out, to throw aside her coverings and reveal herself. Trenan had made it clear he was her father's man, not hers and Teryk's. If he found her, he'd make her go back. What would become of Teryk and his prophecy then?

The sword master's shadow lingered on the side of the wain and Danya envisioned him throwing back the tarp and the cloth hiding her, calling out for his companion. They'd not only force her return to Draekfarren, but they'd also likely execute Evalal for aiding her, the same way she'd seen them end the life of the old woman.

What did she do?

Anger stirred in Danya's gut as she stared at Trenan's side—the only part of him visible to her.

Why did he let it happen?

The ire and disappointment quashed any urge to reach out to her mentor. She suddenly felt she didn't recognize the man riding beside her. The princess' eyes narrowed to slits and she wished for the master swordsman to pass her by. As if he'd read her thoughts,

Trenan put heels to horse and hurried on after his companion. The rage gripping Danya didn't leave with him.

***

Darkness fell, as it often does.

Danya hung back from the others as Evalal slipped a coin into the cloth merchant's hand, one to match the one she'd given him when they first found their way onto his wain. The man nodded his thanks, spoke words the princess didn't hear. Evalal shook her head and then appeared to thank him before offering a shallow bow and returning to the princess.

Like Danya, Evalal had shed her green smock. The younger girl had explained that people held differing opinions of the Goddess and her worshippers, that not everyone held them in esteem. Without mask or vestment, her companion's youthful appearance surprised Danya—slender and unshapely like a boy, but with the face of a girl.

"He has enough coin to keep him quiet for a while," she said as she came to stand beside her companion.

"More coin will loosen his lips, though."

"True, but he'll only be able to say he saw us, not where we went. And he'll less likely say anything, given he aided us. What's the punishment for aiding the royal daughter to flee her home?"

Danya thought of the woman in the square again, her stomach clenching at the memory of the big soldier's axe falling on her neck. "It would cost him his life."

"An item more valuable to him than a few more coins."

The princess swallowed hard to ease her clenched throat and belly, but the stubborn knots in both remained. She didn't understand how the man who raised her let an old woman be put to death, no matter the reason.

"Where do we go now?" she asked.

Evalal shrugged. "The seed will lead us."

Danya narrowed her eyes. "How can a seed—?"

"I'm not sure, but it will."

Danya nodded. "We stay here tonight." She tilted her head toward the inn where the last of the merchants went in through the heavy door. "But I don't know where to go come sunrise."

"You will. The Mother of Death said to trust the seed. And you."

A shiver tremored along Danya's spine, shaking the obstructions from her throat and gut. Not many sunrises ago, she'd been a princess living in a castle, looking for adventure where none existed. Now, unexpectedly, she found herself an adventurer, but she wasn't so sure she wouldn't rather be a princess safe behind guards and stone walls.

She and Evalal started toward the inn, the weight of the seed of life in its pouch bouncing against her thigh.

***

A few of the stars some referred to as Small Gods still twinkled in the sky as Danya and Evalal left the inn. They'd paid for their stay the night before to keep being slowed down in the morn, but they weren't the only ones making an early start; the weapons merchants were already sorting through their wares, blades and armor clanking in the back of their wagon.

Danya glanced sideways at them as she and Evalal passed. The merchants formed an odd team: one tall and slight, the other a monster of a man—wide and stout with thick arms and legs and a thicker-still chest. They checked through the wagon, counting their wares, checking none went astray overnight, though Danya thought she'd seen the bigger fellow sleeping near their goods.

As their feet carried them beyond the tandem, the

taller, skinnier merchant raised his head and cast his gaze in their direction. For an instant, his eyes met Danya's and his expression changed; the princess looked away abruptly, hoping the change did not indicate recognition.

"Is everything all right?" Evalal asked, resting her hand on Danya's forearm.

"Fine," she replied, looking first straight ahead, then up at the last of the fading stars.

The Small Gods of the prophecy?

A vision of the scroll floated into her mind. She pictured it clearly—the yellow of age curling the parchment at the corners, the dark lines of what should have been unfamiliar characters. Even in memory, she read it as if it lay on a table in front of her.

To raise the Small Gods, a Small God must die.

What did it mean? The light of the Small Gods died every morning with the rise of the sun, and they returned every time it set. Did the line refer to the passage of time? Possible, but she doubted it. Why write a prophecy speaking of the fall of mankind and bother to note sunrise and sunset? It made little sense; it meant more.

She narrowed her eyes as they walked, concentrating on select phrases in the stanzas.

A lock with no key. Man from across the sea. A barren mother, a living statue.

The words bordered on gibberish. All locks have keys; nothing but death lay across the sea; a mother couldn't be barren; statues didn't live. If not for the pouch hanging from her belt and the smooth, dark seed it contained, she might have written the entire thing off as fancy, a story made up to entertain someone's child.

No denying the power emanating from within the seed, though. But what to do with it? Where would it take them? She wished she'd thought to ask more of the Mother of Death, but she'd not been alone with her again before they departed. It left her compelled to follow where it lead them.

Another line from the parchment floated to the surface of her mind:

The firstborn child of the rightful king.

Teryk.

Her heart ached for her brother and the urge to abandon their journey threatened to usurp the compulsion put upon her by the Mother of Death. She longed to search for him, hoped to find him alive, but she could no more guess where to begin seeking him than she knew where the seed would take them.

As she mourned Teryk, a final line of the prophecy came to her recollection:

When stars go out, the end is nigh.

Her gaze dropped to the ground to watch her footing as they made their way along the road to who-knew-where, but now she raised it again, directing her eyes skyward.

A washed-out shade of blue crept across the sky in the wake of dawn's gray light. A sliver of panic found its way through her and Danya cast her gaze toward sunset where night still struggled against the rising sun. No pinpricks of light twinkled in the sky and her discomfort widened until she found one. It shone brighter than the others, bright enough to be seen as sunlight took over the world.

Danya stared at it, its presence forcing panic down in her, but not quashing it completely. As she stared, she became dimly aware of the clatter of wagon wheels on hard ground as the merchant caravan began its journey for the day, headed to the next town to separate people from their money.

The last remaining star brightened, a flash of red crossing its surface before it winked out, succumbing to the light of the sun. Danya gasped unconsciously and stopped, a shiver finding its way along her limbs as she stared up at the blank and empty sky.

Should Small Gods rise, man will fall.

XV Stirk - Lost

Without knowing whether to search Evenside or Morningside, Stirk decided to follow the river that separated the two. Trouble was, doing so took him closer to the outskirts of the city where he was less familiar his surroundings. Everything resembled everything else after a while—the buildings, the streets, even the thugs and whores and beggars. Nowhere did he see a single man in armor. No ceegees, no soldiers, no one-armed sword master.

Breathless and hungry, Stirk stopped at the next corner, careful not to tread in a stream of sludge flowing down the cobbles—the result of people emptying their night pots. This part of the Horseshoe stank even worse than Fishtown.

He leaned against the wall, panting from exertion and overheating. Wearing the tight jerkin brought him no joy because it made him too hot, but he needed it for the place it provided for hiding his hand. What might people think if they saw him parading through the streets holding onto his own severed appendage?

The image it brought to mind made him chuckle. Likely some people'd shit themselves; a lot of them practically did when they cast their gaze upon his stump. He shook his head and dragged his arm across his forehead, wiping sweat away before it ran into his eyes. As he finished, he paused, arm still pressed against his head.

Something ain't right.

Unease crept through him, prickling his limbs and constricting his throat. He flared his nostrils, unintentionally drawing in the street's stench, and squeezed a gulp of saliva down his gullet as he lowered his arm.

It's where he touched me.

He raised his hand to the side of his head, hesitating before his fingers made contact. Before wiping away the sweat, nothing'd seemed different than before. Didn't feel any different, things didn't sound different. Could he be mistaken? His hand closed the small distance and confirmed his fear.

He took it. The bastard took my ear.

If pressed, Stirk supposed he'd have admitted to suspecting this'd happened but fooled himself into believing it hadn't by avoiding the issue. He'd refrained from touching his ear until now. He sucked his bottom lip into his mouth, nibbled on it. His fingers traced a circle around the hole left in the side of his head normally disguised by his ear. The surrounding flesh was smooth as the stump at the end of his handless arm.

Will this happen every time I ask him for help?

The thought brought a shiver to Stirk's spine. He lowered his hand, the movement prompting a growl in his belly that startled him at first, making him think an animal had crept up behind him. An instant later, he realized his mistake and rubbed his aching belly with his stump, the missing ear forgotten for the moment.

"Gonna have to do something for you."

He pushed himself away from the wall, stepped over the tiny river of piss and shit and out into the boulevard. The other people on the street gave a wide birth when they saw him, probably fearful of his hungry expression. Stirk couldn't blame them, he was suddenly hungry enough he might have eaten one of them if he thought their flesh'd have the flavor of chicken or cow. He doubted it would. He'd have to find sustenance some other way.

Where there's folk, there's grub.

He chose an arbitrary direction and set out along the cobbles, feet dragging and scuffing. Each door and window he passed begged his attention and he gave it freely, but none of them offered any sign of providing a meal. The stink of excrement disguised any other aromas from his nostrils, made his stomach tighten into painful knots.

A grizzled dog trotted by, its backbone showing through matted fur. The animal's tongue lolled out one side of its mouth and it eyed Stirk with the same hunger others saw in his own eyes. The two passed without incident, predators each letting the other be. When it was past him, a snarl rolled along the street.

Stirk stopped, expecting the dog to have changed its mind and he'd find it crouched ready to spring at him. Instead, it had chosen a crooked man walking ten paces behind him. The man backed away from the dog, waving his gnarled walking stick at the beast. The animal sat back a moment, biding its time and awaiting the best opportunity but when it did approach, the man proved quicker. The end of his stick caught the dog in the side of the head and sent him whimpering away in search of easier prey.

A sliver of anger arose in Stirk's chest at the man's mistreatment of the poor, hungry animal. He took half a step toward the crooked fellow, set on teaching him a helping of manners, but a painful grumble in his gut halted him.

Fuck it. I gotta eat.

He continued down the avenue. The row of squat, misshapen buildings with their off-kilter doors and cracked shutters offered no more promise of a feeding than any of the others he'd passed. He stopped, eyes flitting back and forth along the street. When a moment came when no one looked his direction, he approached the nearest door and rapped on it.

It didn't open, nor did anyone reply from within.

Stirk gripped the handle, took the time to make sure he wasn't being watched, then leaned his weight against the portal. It opened with less effort than he'd expected.

He stumbled across the threshold into a dim room, his grip on the handle aiding him in keeping his feet under him as inertia threw him forward. An instant of panic rushed through his veins until he pushed the door closed and rested his back against it, breathing heavily.

It turned out he needn't have feared. The one-room abode—larger than the storeroom he'd shared with Bieta, but not by much—was empty of people. A bed frame holding up a thin and sagging mattress stood against the wall opposite a fire pit beneath the blackened opening of a chimney. No fire burned in it and the coals appeared cold.

In the middle of the room sat a table and four chairs. Stirk wondered if enough souls lived here to fill the seats. Happening on one man didn't scare him, even two wouldn't be a problem, but four full-grown men might be more than he could handle.

"Better be quick, then."

He stifled a giggle at his own words; given the room's size, being hasty should prove easy. But where to search?

Stirk thought by the fire pit may be a good spot to begin, but as he moved closer to the table, he realized it wasn't empty. Set out in front of each chair were plates with chipped edges and, beside them, wooden forks. It wasn't the settings that held his attention, but the platter sitting smack dab in between the tableware.

More specifically, the chunks of meat perched upon it.

Stirk closed in, squinting at the food in the dim light filtering through the shutters. He couldn't tell what sort of meat it was, but his rumbling belly convinced him it didn't matter. Nor did it matter why four people'd leave it sitting out instead of eating it.

Decision made, he made his way to the table and grabbed a piece of the unidentified meat, held it up under his nose. The odor flared his nostrils, but he'd inhaled worse things that went into his mouth, anyway—things Bieta had assured him would be fine.

'A little extra flavor is all,' her voice said in his head. Still he hesitated, sniffed it again. Under the mild stink of rot, he recognized the aroma of cold chicken. He brought it to his teeth and nibbled at the edge.

The flavor of poultry tinged with mould touched his tongue. He chewed it nearly to paste and swallowed, then waited for a moment. His stomach growled, but nothing more. Stirk took another, larger bite, then another. Not the best food he'd ever eaten, but not the worst either; it didn't take more than those two bites for him to get past the moldiness and give in to his belly's desire to be fed.

He wolfed everything on the platter, leaving behind nothing but picked-clean bones, then hurried out the door and down the street before the residents returned to find him stealing their grub.

***

A stream of liquid shit splashed on the rocky ground and Stirk groaned, his stomach clenching and cramping even as whatever remained within it found its way out. How could there be more? What he hadn't already shit out, he'd done his best to vomit out against a variety of walls during his trek. Didn't seem right anything could be left, yet his body kept finding stuff to expel.

"Shouldn't've eaten that chicken," he grunted between cramps.

He squatted at the edge of a farmer's field with no one around to see as the sun dipped down to touch the silky ends of the tall cornstalks. His gut twisted again and he attempted to push more out of himself, but nothing came this time. He breathed a relieved sigh that another cramp interrupted, then tore a leaf from the nearest stalk of corn and used it to wipe himself.

When he finished, he stood, wobbling as he yanked up his drawers. The knots in his belly prevented him from standing straight and droplets of sweat ran along his nose, down the back of his neck. Stirk let out a groan and paused, hunched over with his elbows on his knees as awaited another stream of puke. He heaved once, twice—nothing came out. Finally, his stomach was empty.

"Should start feelin' better any time now."

He wiped the perspiration from his face and shivered. The shaking had started right before his last bout of diarrhea. No matter how hard he tried, he was unable to control the trembling and quivering, though he was neither cold nor frightened; at least he wasn't until the uncontrollable shivering began.

He did his best to stand and peer over the tops of the corn stalks. Wouldn't be long before the sun'd disappear behind them, leaving the world in darkness and Stirk sick and alone with whatever it hid. If he hadn't already been shivering like a newborn calf, he'd have shuddered at the thought.

He'd never in his life been to the edge of the Horseshoe. What lay beyond was foreign to him, a land of unknown people and unknown dangers. His gaze swept across the cornfield and he wondered how many sets of eyes watched him from behind the cover of those stalks, and to whom or what they belonged.

With a groan, he straightened as far as his cramping belly allowed, which left him hunched over and clutching his gut. He took a wobbling step, but the pain in his midsection knotted and clenched, stopping him. He bent over, trying to relieve the agony, and overbalanced, toppling forward. Mid-fall, he twisted himself to one side so his shoulder took the brunt of the impact instead of his face.

"Oof."

A pained groan followed the expulsion of breath. Stirk lay there, cheek pressed against the dirt, wishing he hadn't eaten the chicken or whatever it actually was he'd found.

The cramp in his gut deepened, curling him into a tighter ball—a groaning, sweating, shivering ball straddling the line between worry it might die and hope it would.

I need the healer.

His good hand touched first the end of his stump, then the spot on his head where he'd once had an ear. Any aid the healer provided would come with a cost. Stirk didn't know what the cost, but a considerable part of him didn't want to find out. The other part was determined to survive and administer the justice Trenan and his companion deserved.

Stirk's stomach gurgled and roiled; he clenched his muscles to keep more liquidy shit from finding its way out and messing the trousers he'd tried so hard to keep from dirtying. Another gurgle, another groan and he needed no more convincing.

"Healer," he panted when the cramp's hold eased enough for him to speak. "Help me."

Agony rolled through him again, along his arms and legs, his back, his chest and head. He squeezed his eyes shut, blocking out the field of corn standing over him like a vulture waiting for him to give up.

I ain't gonna die.

The pain flared in disagreement.

"Argh."

Through it, Stirk detected the rustle of leaves in the cornfield, though his sweat-soaked skin sensed no gust of wind. His eyelids fluttered but didn't open, so he breathed deeply, held the air in his lungs and forced his lids to do his bidding.

The black-robed healer stood at the edge of the field, face hidden beneath the hood.

"You are in need of me, Stirk?"

If he wasn't writhing on the ground in pain, Stirk might've had a coarse and sarcastic word to say for asking a question with such an obvious answer. He nodded instead.

"Here." The healer moved to his side and crouched. "Let me help you up."

He grabbed Stirk by his elbows and jerked him into a sitting position. Stirk's stomach lurched and vomit threatened at the back of his throat. He swallowed hard to keep it down, his head spinning and throbbing, sweat running into his eyes. The world blurred in front of him until he blinked the stinging liquid away.

"Hold on. You'll be better soon."

Stirk stared at the healer, unable to make out a face beneath the cowl despite the man's proximity. Another time, he might have tried harder, may have even reached out and thrown back the hood to see what hid beneath. Even as the thought crossed his mind, his stomach clenched tight with a cramp that sent pain shooting along his limbs.

It held for a time, tightening all his muscles, then faded. Stirk gritted his teeth, waiting for its inevitable return, the muscles in his jaw and neck and shoulders tensed to receive it.

It didn't come.

Slowly, cautiously, he relaxed the tension gripping him. His breathing eased and he became able to sit up straighter. The roiling discomfort in his bowels lessened, the knot in his throat unwound itself and disappeared. He breathed through his nose, inhaling the scent of dirt and corn stalks and his own sweat.

The healer remained before him, clutching his arms.

Stirk nodded. "I feel better," he said and shifted to pull away from the healer's grasp. The robed man's hold grew firmer, tighter. "Let me go."

He became acutely aware of the man's cool flesh on his perspiration-dampened arms, the sweat on his forehead. The healer's grasp tightened further until the two bones in Stirk's forearm rubbed together sending fresh pain along the length of it and into his chest.

"You're hurtin' me. Let go!"

He gazed at the healer's fingers pressing into his skin. Both arms hurt, but the one short a hand was subject to a firmer grip than the other. Stirk pressed his lips together and tried to pull away, but the healer proved too strong for him. Panicking, he had no choice but to watch as the robed man increased his hold further.

He tightened his hold until his fingers sank into Stirk's flesh then through his arm like a warm knife passing through a chunk of lard.

He opened his mouth to scream before realizing he lacked any pain to scream about. A scent like burning meat wafted to his nostrils, but no smoke rose from the growing wound, no blackness singed its edges. The scream stopped before it began, but Stirk's lips remained open.

The healer's fingers passed through flesh, muscle, and bone. In shock at what he saw, Stirk didn't even bother attempting escape as his handless arm detached at the elbow.

When it was free, the healer stood and fell back a step. Unmoving, Stirk gaped at his limb the healer held in his hands.

"My...my arm," he sputtered.

"I told you my help carried a cost, did I not?"

The healer opened the front of his robe, revealing a flash of pale skin as he secreted the arm inside its folds and replaced the flap. The presence of Stirk's detached limb didn't change the shape or hang of the garment; had he not seen the man place it there, he'd never have guessed its presence.

After a short time, Stirk dragged his gaze away from the robed man and gawked at his shortened arm. It ended with the same stretched-looking flesh, smooth and pink, but with the end far closer to his shoulder than it had been a few moments before. He shifted his eyes to the other limb, the one he still had, and saw the red mark left on his forearm where the healer had held onto him. It looked as if hot steel had touched it. He flexed his fingers, feeling no discomfort as he did.

At least he let me keep my hand.

With the realization, he pushed himself up and climbed to his feet. The pain in his gut, the unease in his bowels, the deep ache in his muscles—all were gone as though caused by the arm and exorcised when the healer removed it.

"Will that be all?"

Stirk raised his eyes to the robed man standing before him and nodded. He thought he should say something. Not thank him; he'd rarely thanked anyone in his life, and this seemed a less appropriate time than any other, what with his arm gone. But the man had come when needed, given him relief from an illness that may have been the death of him. Without a hand at the end of it, what good was a forearm, anyway?

The healer strode toward the cornfield, the hem of his robe brushing the ground without disturbing it. The notion he should say something became overpowering, so Stirk gave in and spoke.

"Wait."

The healer stopped, quarter-turned toward Stirk. His position suggested he wanted to hear what the man had to say, perhaps even that he already knew.

"Can you help me find the sword master and the other bastard?"

"Of course, but it will cost."

"I know."

"Are you willing to pay?"

Stirk hesitated. His fingers found first the smooth skin at the side of his head, then the end of his stump. He rubbed the pink flesh, pondered the healer's query. How badly did he want to find them and take revenge for his mother's death?

More than anything.

He thought of her gentle touch, the way she plunged her tongue in and out through the space between her teeth when she was nervous, or when she was thinking, or any time she wasn't speaking or using her mouth for other things. The woman who gave him life, who kept him alive and cared for him for the turning of every season since. She'd been strict occasionally, harsh even, but she never gave cause to doubt her love for him. His gaze flickered between the healer, the stalks of corn, and his shortened arm.

Do I have something to give the healer as payment?

He took a quick inventory of himself and decided he did.

"I'm willin'."

"Then follow me and we will find the men you seek."

The healer strode into the cornfield. Stirk hesitated a moment before following, a sliver of worry creeping into his mind, sending a shiver along his body.

How did it come to this?

He shook his head, dispelling the thought and the doubt, and started after the healer. The setting sun cast long shadows amongst the corn, but he ignored them, staring at the healer's back as he led the way. The tall stalks blurred and ran together, smearing into something unrecognizable.

"Fuckers killed my ma," Stirk said as he kept from looking at what went on around him for fear of losing his nerve. "They've gotta die."

XVI Kuneprius - A Small God?

The Small Gods in the sky twinkled and flashed as they stared down at Kuneprius. Despite his utter exhaustion, sleep eluded him, kept away by the very things unbelievers called stars.

He knew better. Stars didn't judge him for his thoughts and actions the way those Small Gods of old did. To his left shone Ine'vesi, the evenstar, God amongst those who watched from above.

Kuneprius turned his head away, saw the small gray man lying motionless on the ground five arm's lengths from him. Beyond, the hulking silhouette of the golem stood watch at the edge of the forest, gazing along the dirt track lest someone happen upon their hiding spot. Kuneprius shuddered to think what might happen to anyone unlucky enough to be on the road tonight.

Too many people have died already.

The faces of the children by the creek and of the innkeeper refused to take leave of his thoughts—another reason sleep refused to come to him. Guilt burned in his chest that the lives of these innocents had been ripped away from them because of him, his failure to protect them.

He shifted on the uncomfortable ground—a third cause for his sleeplessness, as if he needed more—and grumbled to himself about the clay man's refusal to allow him a night at an inn. Truthfully, he hadn't exactly refused. Kuneprius could have taken a room on his own and left the golem hidden in the forest with Thorn, but he wasn't comfortable leaving them alone. He doubted he'd be able to stop the giant should he want to hurt their prisoner, but he was certain he couldn't if he was elsewhere.

All of this added up to his final discomfort. Not only had several sunrises passed with no access to a bowl of fresh, clean water for him to wash away the sins of his past, the tightness of the woman's blood drying on his cheeks never to be cleansed, but neither had he released his seed in tribute. Though that may have been why he so keenly felt the judging gaze of the Small Gods upon him, concern for the pressure building in his man parts disturbed him more. Not since he became able to produce seed had he gone so long without offering tribute to the gods or, failing to make an offering, satisfied the need later in the day when he was alone with his thoughts of the girl.

His staff stirred and he repositioned himself, rolling onto his side in a way he hoped would discourage it from growing further. This wasn't the time to relieve the pressure; he'd have to find a place come morning, if the clay man allowed him the opportunity.

Ves will understand. He'll make time.

Kuneprius looked to the hulking sentinel positioned by the roadside and wondered for the thousandth time if any vestige of his friend remained within, physical or otherwise. He imagined Vesisdenperos trapped inside, held in a dingy cell with soft, gray walls and dull light filtering in from above. He'd have lost weight, as the golem never ate, so Kuneprius saw his cheeks as sunken, eyes bulging, his ribs and collarbone standing out beneath his pale skin. Clay would clog the space under his fingernails, like when he returned after a day of practice, but the glimmer of joy would be absent from his expression.

With a sigh, Kuneprius diverted his gaze from the golem's' silhouette. Though it was the will of the Small Gods for Ves to be the sculptor, he felt he'd failed in his duty to protect him and wouldn't rest until he'd exhausted every possibility to bring his friend back from wherever he was lost.

The small, gray man breathed steadily beside Kuneprius, drawing his attention. Since the day he'd killed the girl to liberate Vesisdenperos, he'd sworn never to take another life. The children and the barkeep he could do nothing to save as he hadn't realized the golem meant to kill them, but it was different with this creature who called himself Thorn. But the prophecy foretold his fate and it meant Kuneprius would fail at a second vow.

"Where are you taking Thorn?"

The whispered question startled Kuneprius. He hadn't realized the small man's eyes were open, watching him. Noticing his attention, he thought the stare might penetrate his soul.

"I cannot speak with you," he replied, gaze flickering to the golem's back. "I'm sorry."

"He will not hear. Thorn has little power here, but can keep our voices from his ears."

Kuneprius hesitated, torn between his duty to the order and duty to himself. He wanted to talk to this creature, learn about him and his life, but the Brothers would frown upon such a thing should they find out. He shouldn't consider the small gray man a living thing, but a tool to bring about the return of the true Small Gods.

"Please."

The tone in Thorn's voice tugged at Kuneprius' chest. How could he regard this creature who obviously experienced such emotion as a thing? He'd be doing a disservice not only to Thorn by doing so, but to himself, as well.

"Ahem." Kuneprius cleared his throat and eyed the golem for a reaction. The hulk didn't move. He coughed again, louder this time. Still nothing.

His gaze fell back to the prisoner. In the moonlight, his gray skin appeared white and, for a second, Kuneprius might have imagined him a child rather than a being from behind the veil, the key to the Small Gods' return.

"We are meant to bring you to Teva Stavoklis."

Thorn's expression changed. His nose crinkled as though he didn't understand. Kuneprius didn't wait for the small man to ask.

"It is the temple. The seat of power of those who worship the Small Gods."

Thorn's face brightened. "Thorn is a Small God. Horace Seaman said so. Will Thorn see Horace Seaman at this Teva Stavoklis?"

"No, you misunderstand." Kuneprius kept his voice low and glanced often at the golem's back despite Thorn's claim. "We worship those Small Gods."

He raised a finger toward the night sky and Thorn's gaze followed his gesture. He didn't look up himself, didn't expect he'd find those who watch from above smiling on him for having this conversation. Thorn stared up at the dark sky filled with twinkling light for a short time before returning his gaze to Kuneprius.

"The Banished Ones?" he asked, disbelief in his tone. "Who would worship those stricken from our world?"

"Who else is worthy of worship?" Kuneprius asked, struggling to control his voice. "The Goddess who imposes her will without consent? You impostor Small Gods who hide behind the veil? All are weak compared to they who watch from above."

The words spilled form his lips as they'd been preached to him since before he could remember, probably from the time of his rescue from one of the Goddess' caravans the way he'd rescued Vesisdenperos. He'd spoken the words before, and meant them, but he did so with less conviction this time.

"So much in this world is worthy of worship, so many choices." Thorn reached his arm out and swept his hand across in front of himself. "Thorn worships all of this. The ground, the trees, the sky, the air we breathe. It gives us life. Thorn even worships you. Without you being you, Thorn would not be Thorn."

Kuneprius opened his mouth to spew forth more of the gospel of the Small Gods, but the words refused to come out. Thorn's words held an innocence, a joy that stayed his tongue. In the light of the small man's beliefs, the thought of worshipping gods bent on vengeance and destruction suddenly seemed petty and wrong. To avoid speaking sacrilege when those who watch from above might hear, Kuneprius changed the subject.

"If you have the power to keep our voices from Ve...from the clay man's ears, why do you not use this power to escape?"

"Does Thorn need to escape? From what?"

Again, Kuneprius parted his lips, and again the words refused to come. Was it possible the small man didn't realize why they'd taken him? Didn't understand the danger he was in? The expression on Thorn's face shifted, the obvious joy he'd felt talking about what he worshipped disappearing, replaced by concern.

"What is your name?"

Kuneprius knew he shouldn't answer. A man's name contained magic and enchantment, or so High Priest Kristeus preached and taught. What things might a being who may have the power of a Small God be able to do with such knowledge?

"Kuneprius," he replied, cringing at the sound of his voice. He hadn't meant to speak his name, but there it was for their prisoner to claim and use as he saw fit. His muscles tensed as he awaited the consequences for having broken such a simple rule.

"Kuneprius," the gray man repeated, rolling it along his tongue. "Kuneprius. A good name. A powerful name. Did you choose it for yourself?"

Kuneprius shook his head. "It was chosen for me, before I could walk or speak."

Thorn's eyes widened. "There was a time you could not walk or speak?"

The man stared but didn't answer. Thorn's interest passed.

"My name is Thorn, has always been Thorn. Thorn chose it from the time of creation and it will always belong to Thorn." He slid closer, the out-of-place pants he wore scraping the ground. "Now Kuneprius and Thorn are friends, like Thorn and Horace Seaman before. Kuneprius can now trust Thorn, can tell Thorn truths."

Kuneprius stared at the gray man lying on the ground only four arm's lengths away, and Thorn looked back. A moment passed and neither of them spoke; during that time, Kuneprius noticed a lack of need burning in his chest for the first time in days. His body didn't yearn for water to lave his sins, his balls didn't ache to spread his seed. Was this the sort of enchantment Thorn had chosen to cast upon him? He took stock of the rest of himself and found nothing else out of sorts.

"What have you done to me?"

"Thorn has done nothing but offer his friendship."

The corner of Kuneprius' mouth quivered and tilted up despite his not meaning it to. After so many seasons spent amongst the Brothers, he'd only ever considered one person a friend.

He raised his eyes, looked beyond the gray man at the golem standing guard beside the dirt track they'd followed to get here. The clay abomination didn't move, the dark night making it impossible to distinguish him from a statue set at the road's edge. Nothing about him indicated a man within. Kuneprius' chest cinched tight around his heart. He sighed through his nose and returned his gaze to Thorn.

"You are a Small God, aren't you? From the Green."

"That is what Horace Seaman told Thorn. Horace Seaman doesn't lie."

For an instant, Kuneprius considered asking who Horace Seaman was, but he thought better of it. Common sense suggested it to be the man the golem killed when they took the Small God, but why remind Thorn of that now? Still, he wondered how a man and a Small God came to be traveling together outside the veil.

Because the prophecy said it should be so.

"You aren't aware of what is to happen to a Small God who strays from the Green?"

Thorn stared at him, one eye cocked in the manner of raising his brow if he had such things. Kuneprius took it to mean he wasn't aware and was about to explain how dire his situation was when Thorn burst out laughing. He put both hands on his belly and rolled back and forth on the ground. Kuneprius looked up at the golem, worried the outburst might penetrate whatever glamour Thorn had cast, but the clay man didn't move.

The laughter went on longer than Kuneprius expected, causing a coil of discomfort in his gut. Each moment it continued made it more likely the creature who was once his friend Ves would be alerted to their conversation. Then what?

"Shh. Be quiet."

With obvious effort, Thorn calmed himself. The laughter faded to chuckles and then subsided. The gray man wiped mirthful tears away on his forearm and propped himself up on an elbow to study his companion. Kuneprius shot him a scornful look, but it appeared to make no impression on him.

"Kuneprius speaks of the prophecy?"

It shocked Kuneprius that Thorn knew of the scroll hidden in the room without doors where High Priest Kristeus communicated with the Small Gods of the sky. No one but he had ever touched the ancient parchment and the Brothers only knew what they did because Kristeus chose to tell them.

"How did you—?"

"No one believes it. Nothing but a story to scare the newly created into remaining behind the veil."

"So, all of your...kind are aware of the prophecy?"

"Of course. Thorn has read the words supposedly written by the Goddess' own hand."

Kuneprius shook his head. "Impossible. The scroll resides in a chamber at Murtikara. No hands but those of the High Priest have ever touched it since its writing by the death of Ine'vesi, the evenstar."

He raised his eyes skyward as he spoke the Small God's name, searching through overhead boughs to find the bright glow amongst the other, dimmer ones. He'd have said the requisite prayer as well, but another laugh from the gray man interrupted him.

"The parchment gets passed to whoever needs a scare thrown into them. It has been with us since the creation of the Green. Few believe the words contain any truth, no matter where it came from. How can a mother be barren? Or a man survive the God of the Deep, if such a thing exists?"

Thorn's last few words trailed off and something shifted on his face, but Kuneprius' confusion at the gray man's words blurred its meaning from him.

"The prophecy doesn't mention the God of the Deep,

only a man from across the sea. Others were sent for him as we were sent for you."

Thorn seemed not to have heard him, his eyes unfocused and staring as though he saw right through Kuneprius. It made him uncomfortable and he shifted under the Small God's gaze, the worry he might cast an enchantment on him returning. Thorn blinked hard, appearing to clear the miasma blurring his vision, and raised his eyes to Kuneprius'. When he spoke again, his voice was so quiet, Kuneprius had to strain to hear his words.

"Horace Seaman survived meeting the God of the Deep. If the prophecy speaks of him, then the rest must be truth."

Thorn sat up, his head gently moving side to side, eyes widening. Kuneprius knew what the small man's expression meant, but he found no words to speak. He fought the urge to reach out and touch the Small God's arm, to comfort him and attempt to take away his fear. But how could he do so when he caused the fear?

"Kuneprius," Thorn whispered. "You mean to take Thorn to his death."

The man's lips parted, though he didn't know what might emerge from his mouth given the chance. A denial? Words of comfort? The truth?

A movement behind Thorn startled Kuneprius from his thoughts and he didn't get to find out what he might have said.

The golem loomed a pace behind the Small God, forcing everything from his head but for his own fear.

XVII Man From Across the Sea - Kooj

He sat on the dirt floor, elbows resting on knees pulled

up to his chest, head hung, eyes closed.

His mind whirled, struggling to recall anything prior to waking in the barn with sunlight squeezing between its warped and ill-fitting boards. No matter how hard he tried, he saw only water. It enveloped him, splashed over his head, found its way into his mouth and nose. It choked his throat and threatened to fill his lungs.

Water. The sea and nothing more.

He opened his eyes, lifted his chin off his chest and found the sun shining between the boards again. Another sunrise, the second since the man called Jud-dah locked him in the barn with the cow and the dog. At first, he'd worried the dog might make a meal of him if his master stayed away too long, but Kooj had proven himself an excellent ratter—an unusual skill for a canine of his size and ferocity.

Kooj lay on the dirt floor by the door, teeth tearing into the guts of a rat with a body the length of a man's forearm. Droplets of blood glistened on the dog's muzzle and a string of meat hung from the corner of his mouth. The sight disgusted the man but also flooded saliva across his tongue and set his stomach grumbling. He wanted to divert his eyes rather than watch the dog eviscerate the oversized vermin, but hunger pinned his gaze to the spectacle.

The dog tore another strip with a sickening rending of flesh and the man pried his eyes away, shifting them to the pitcher on the floor beside him. He picked it up, raised it to his mouth and tilted it so the last drop slithered along the side toward the lip. It reached the edge and dangled on the cusp, taunting him for an instant before plummeting onto his outstretched tongue.

The single drop proved enough to tease, but not enough to satiate the thirst burning in his throat. Hoping for one more, he shook the pitcher; none came. He threw it across the barn where it thumped on the dirt floor and rolled to a stop against a barrel stuffed with rusted weapons and tools. The man sighed and licked his rough lips, seeking to return moisture to them with a tongue possessing none of its own.

He wiped a frustrated hand across his face and returned his attention to the dog. Kooj had stopped feasting and sat with head tilted and ears pricked. At first, he thought the pitcher hitting the ground had disturbed the canine's meal, but the dog stared off into the air, not at him or at the jug.

He's heard something.

The man jerked in the direction of the dog's stare and listened. The barn creaked, a baby bird twittered in the rafters, his own stomach gurgled. Nothing else. Kooj rose and trotted toward the side of the barn, leaving his feast unattended.

The scent of spilled blood wafted to the man's nose, making his belly gurgle again. He swallowed hard and leaned forward, clambering to hands and knees with a clank of the chain attached to his ankle. A quick glance showed him Kooj standing near the barn's side wall paying him no attention.

Despite the protests in his head, the man's aching gut drove him scuttling across the floor in the direction of the half-eaten vermin lying flayed in front of the door. His stomach growled in hunger and nausea at the thought of it as his hands and knees scuffled through the dirt throwing puffs off dust into the air.

Two body lengths from the rat's corpse, the chain attached to his ankle went taut. He peeked back at it, pulled with a clank, then returned his attention to the dead animal. He lay flat on the dirt floor, stretching out to his fullest, reaching, grasping.

The potential meal, equally tempting and nausea-inducing, lay beyond his fingertips. He strained, reaching further, wiggling his fingers, but to no avail.

Kooj snarled, barked. The man froze, waiting for the dog's jaws to clamp around his outstretched arm, his razor teeth to tear at his flesh as they'd done the rat's.

Instead of biting, the dog barked again and the man jerked his head around to peer over his shoulder. The beast stared at the wall, lips pulled back from savage teeth, a string of saliva tinted pink with rat's blood hanging from its jaws.

The man scuffled back from the canine's food, happy to forgo the stomach-turning meal in exchange for saving his own skin. He climbed to his feet and wiped sticky spit off his lips with his forearm, directed his attention to the wall Kooj stared at. Movement flickered in the space between the boards.

The dog leaped forward a half-step, barking furiously. The man fell into a crouch, squinting against light shining through the gaps to see if it was Jud-dah who'd returned, or someone come to rescue him.

Whoever was outside moved toward the front of the barn, the dark shape blocking the sunlight squeezing between the wall boards in succession as it went. Kooj followed along with it, barking and slathering all the way.

A moment later, the barn door's handle rattled. The dog stalked toward the sound, a growl rumbling in its throat and chest, one paw stepping in the remains of the disemboweled rat, then leaving a bloody print in the dirt with its next step. The handle clattered a second time and the door opened a crack. He glimpsed a hand wrapped in a dirty bandage before Kooj launched himself against the wooden panels.

The dog hit it with a heavy thud, but the fellow outside must have expected the beast's action and leaned against the door to prevent it opening. It moved but the width of a finger.

Kooj fell back to the floor, his furious barking

renewed, muzzle prodding the space between door and frame. He stood on his hind legs, front paws pushing against the wood, and the intruder slammed the door shut.

Movement flickered again, this time headed away from the building. The man watched the silhouette beat a retreat toward the tree line, a dark shape making its way through the grass. Kooj trotted around the inside of the barn, growling and barking, pacing first one direction, then the other. The dog's dark eyes gleamed with what the man might have interpreted as anger and hatred had the beast been human, but it wasn't. It only sought to protect its home.

Or so he thought until the dog directed its attention toward him.

Kooj glared at him, lips still pulled back from his sharp teeth. The dog took one slow step his direction, then another. He backed away a step, arms raised in defense. He cast his gaze around for something to use for protection, cursed himself for having tossed the pitcher out of reach.

The dog took another step and he bent over, grasped the chain binding him in his prison. He looped it once around each hand, unsure what he meant to do with it, and backed up as far as his tether allowed.

Kooj took one more slow step, then launched himself across the barn.

XVIII Ailyssa - Juddah's

The day passed, the sun warming Ailyssa's cheeks. The same sun coaxed sweat on Juddah's back and arms and she did her best to find separation between herself and her rescuer—a difficult task sitting together on horseback. His perspiration dampened the front of her smock despite her attempts.

They stopped once during the day to slake their thirsts at a stream and eat cured meat and hard cheese. She thought to ask him what kind of meat he fed her, but her grumbling stomach preferred not to know. After emptying her bladder—dubious of her privacy—they were back ahorse and continuing their journey.

The comparative chill of night touched the flesh of her arms, the white haze of her blindness changing little as the day's light faded. The rhythm of the horse's gait lulled Ailyssa into a state of semi-consciousness. Whenever her chin sagged toward her chest, she jerked her head back, waking herself for fear if she truly dozed, she'd fall from her perch. Would he stop for her if she did?

Each time a sliver of sleep came, she saw Claris' face, imagined her children, and she'd jerk awake with the pain of regret poking her heart.

At least I'm alive. I couldn't help her if I was dead.

The night passed, like the day before it, and after what felt an impossibly long time in Ailyssa's unseeing world, the sun rose again.

"How much longer before we reach your home?"

"Soon," Juddah grunted in reply and said no more.

Ailyssa knew 'soon' was a relative term, with no clear definition to any but he who spoke it. And so the morning dragged past with but one more stop to eat, drink, and piss. By her reckoning, midday was near when she noticed the change.

Juddah's aroma and the forest's scent disguised it at first, but her nose detected another odor beneath the perfumes of cedar trees and loamy earth; a tang she'd not experienced before. It tickled her nostrils and gave her hope the end of their journey neared, an eventuality her aching thighs and buttocks longed for.

They continued to ride and the day's fragrance changed and changed again. She detected not just the aroma of the forest warmed by the sun's rays, but also the sweetness of drying grass, and a salty bouquet she guessed must be the sea. Excited relief brewed inside her, but she resisted the urge to ask Juddah again if they were near. She'd found him a man of few words and could already guess his vague response.

A short time later, he reined their steed to a stop with an accompanying 'whoa.' A few heartbeats passed before he directed words to his riding companion.

"We're here," he said, shifting his weight.

Ailyssa took the action to mean he intended to dismount, so moved her grip from his coveralls stiff with grease to the edge of the hard leather saddle. He slid off the horse, the heel of his boot bumping her arm. She jerked away from the impact, clutching her forearm, the movement unbalancing her. A fearful hoot escaped her throat as she slid sideways, flailing to regain her hold on the saddle, but she missed. The horse's firm haunches slipped from under her and she braced to hit the ground.

Instead, she fell into Juddah's arms and he caught her for a second time. He held her awkwardly for a moment, the smell of his stale sweat permeating her nostrils and obliterating all others, then he set her down and took a step away.

"Are you all right?"

"Yes, I think so," Ailyssa said rubbing the sore spot on her forearm. Her heart continued fluttering against her ribs, its pace slowing to normal.

"Wait here while I take care of the horse."

Ailyssa nodded and a breeze caressed her as Juddah swept past, then the horse's hooves tapped soft ground. She waited with arms crossed for her rescuer's return, finally inhaling air not tainted by his unwashed flesh.

The salty tang was strong, but smells mingled with it: the grass she'd detected before, the warmth of fresh-turned earth, old manure, and another odor she didn't recognize, a sour fragrance she wasn't sure she wanted to name.

After a short while in which Ailyssa listened to Juddah removing the saddle from their steed, the man returned and the cloud of sweet, stale sweat came with him. He stood close for a few heartbeats, breathing heavily before he spoke.

"Take my arm."

Ailyssa hesitated but then reached out tentatively in her blindness. Her fingers found thick hair on his forearm as he'd rolled up his sleeves while unsaddling the horse. With her hand upon him, he led her away from the spot where she'd dismounted.

Long grass tickled the soles of her feet as they walked. A gentle wind rustled through the blades and made the boards of an unseen structure creak. High above, the cries of gulls reached her ears; she longed to see them wheeling through the sky.

The tall grass grew sparse, then disappeared, and they crossed dirt scattered with rocks. Pebbles pressed into her feet, occasionally causing her pain, but she ignored their bites, concentrating on keeping her worry and fears at bay and counting her steps to distract herself. Juddah didn't speak as he guided her across what she assumed to be his yard, but his lack of verbosity caused no surprise in her; had she counted the words he'd spoken over the course of their journey on her fingers and toes, she'd have a few left over.

The temperature on her cheeks changed, suggesting they'd passed into shadow. Beneath the trees of a forest? The shade cast by a building? The creak of boards coaxed by a breath of wind led her to suspect the latter.

Soon after, they stopped and a door handle rattled, dispelling any question.

"This is where you'll stay," Juddah said. "For now."

The handle rattled again and he stepped back, swinging the door open with a moan that sounded to her more akin to rope rubbing on wood than hinges. Dank air wafted out of the building, redolent of stale hay, fresh manure, and that other, sour odor she'd detected before, but stronger. She forced a smile of thanks on her lips and nodded her head in case Juddah was gazing upon her.

The big man stepped into the doorway, dragging her along with him, but came to a jarring halt and Ailyssa walked into the back of him.

"Kooj?" he said, the word tinted with notes of surprise and distress. "Kooj!"

Juddah shook Ailyssa's grip off his arm and rushed away, leaving her without support, and a wave of vertigo swirled around her. She reached out with the hand she'd used to hold on to her rescuer and found the door frame, a splinter from the aged wood pricking her finger. She stuck the injured digit in her mouth and leaned her shoulder against the lintel, thankful to be steady again as she wondered who or what Kooj was. A heartbeat later, a dog whined in its throat, and she suspected she knew the answer.

"Kooj, what happened?"

Juddah's voice floated from in front and to the right of her, where the dog's cry had come from. The animal whined again.

"Oh, Kooj."

Juddah's feet shuffled and scraped against the dirt floor and, for an instant, no other sounds came. Then the dog cried once more and Juddah spoke.

"You did this," he accused, the words sounding as though he'd spoken them from between clenched teeth.

Ailyssa's unseeing eyes opened in surprise and she

shook her head. How could he think she'd hurt his pet when she hadn't been here?

"You did this and you're gonna pay."

The Goddess Mother cowered against the door frame, an arm raised in front of her face as the man's footsteps tromped across the dirt floor. She didn't realize they headed away from her until she heard the meaty thunk of a fist or foot striking flesh.

Another impact followed by the dog's cry. Was he beating the animal he'd sounded concerned about? Ailyssa lowered her arm, leaned in, listening, appalled. Thump. Thump. Thump.

Amongst the sound of the drubbing, Ailyssa heard the whoosh of breath leaving lungs. The dog whined, its pained expression emanating from a different place than the thud of punches and kicks. She gripped the door frame tight with her fingers, nails digging into wood only a season or two from rotten.

A man moaned.

Ailyssa held her breath. Was it Juddah? Or was someone else in the building?

Another thump. Another thud. A whispered word with a pleading tone; a groan. She realized these last didn't belong to the man who'd rescued her. One more blow fell, then all other sounds became lost to the heavy pant of Juddah's breath.

"Why'd you do it?" he asked between heaving breaths.

No response. After a few heartbeats, the man's footsteps crossed the floor again. They stopped to Ailyssa's right, then shuffled in the dirt. The dog whined, Juddah grunted with effort, and his footsteps resumed, coming closer to her.

Ailyssa shrank away, back pressed against the jamb. Juddah squeezed through the space between her and the other side of the door, fur too thick to be his brushing against her arms and chest. She realized he must be carrying the dog he'd called Kooj. He stopped when he'd pushed past her.

"Get in there," he said, breathless.

A shiver shook its way up Ailyssa's spine and she swallowed hard, but didn't move. She clutched the door frame at her back with both hands like a chunk of driftwood keeping her from drowning.

"Get in the barn!" Juddah bellowed.

Shocked by his sudden ferocity, Ailyssa released her grip on the lintel and stumbled into the building, her bare feet scuffing in the dirt. She parted her lips to ask her rescuer what happened, what she might do to help, but the belabored slam of the door closing cut off her words. The bang made her jump; the thunk of a bar sliding into place, locking her in, followed.

Ailyssa stood facing the door, frightened to turn around and discover what or who he'd left her in the barn with despite—perhaps because of—her inability to see. Outside, Juddah's heavy steps crunched away across the yard, his gait changing as he climbed a short set of wooden steps. His footsteps disappeared, leaving Ailyssa to the silence of the barn.

She closed her eyes and listened. The wind lifted something hanging on the outside wall of the barn and let it drop with a gentle bang. A bird twittered in the eaves overhead. A cow lowed. Ailyssa turned, careful not to make too much noise with her feet, then settled again, waiting. Blood hammered through her veins, making it difficult to detect anything but the pounding of her heart. After a short time, she realized she'd have to take matters into her own hands.

"Hello?"

The word echoed up to the roof and she heard a sound that might have been a cow's tail swatting away a fly, but no other response. The muscles in her jaw twitched, pulling her mouth into a frightened grimace. She took a half-step forward, the sole of her foot dragging along the dirt to prevent her from tripping over anything laid in her path.

"Hello?"

Whether the answering groan was meant as a response or not, it let her know she was not alone. It came from the far side of the room.

"Who's there?"

A long pause, then another moan.

"Are you all right?"

Labored breathing. The bird twittered, the wind sighed.

Ailyssa crouched, then got down on hands and knees. She had no way of knowing what might lay between her and the beaten man, and she didn't want to trip and hurt herself like she did alone in the forest, so she shuffled forward, lifting one hand after the other then placing them carefully, dragging her knees and toes in the dirt. Pebbles and clumps of earth or dried manure skittered across the floor.

"Hello?"

The word squeezed out of her throat choked tight with fear. She understood the chance she was taking reaching out to this stranger locked in a barn, but could it be any worse than relying upon the man who'd put both of them here and beaten the fellow? Her entire life, she'd learned the way of the Goddess, and part of the gospel taught her to offer help and comfort whenever it could be given. Judging by the man's moans, he was in need.

Ailyssa continued across the floor, pausing when she touched cool metal. She ran her fingers along the crude links of the chain, following the end away from the man's groans to find it locked onto a stout spike.

She followed the chain the other way, listening to the quiet clink of metal as her fingers passed along its surface. Her palm touched a muddy spot on the floor—spilt water? Blood? She jerked away, wiping it on the skirt of her smock.

A few more paces and she'd come close enough to make out the breath wheezing in and out of the man's lungs. She hesitated, unsure how to proceed.

"Are you all right?" No response. "I am N'th Ail...I am Ailyssa. I won't hurt you."

A sighing moan answered her, but no words, leaving her to wonder if the mystery stranger could speak. He might have lost his voice as she'd been deprived of her sight. After a sigh of her own, she continued following the chain.

A distance equal to the length of her own arm later, her fingers touched a metal cuff. Her hand slid off it and brushed the man's leg. The white blindness of her vision disappeared, replaced by darkness and vague lines.

Ailyssa gasped and leaned away, hands covering her mouth as the bright haze returned to her eyes. She blinked hard, as though she might clear it. As it had since she woke after her expulsion, it remained.

What happened?

The flash had occurred at the precise moment her fingers touched the stranger. But how could that be possible? The man moaned again, and Ailyssa wondered if he did so in pain or an attempt to communicate.

"I..." She licked her lips, swallowed hard, then whispered: "I won't hurt you."

She reached out with one shaking hand, the other still covering her mouth. Her gut roiled with a nauseating concoction of fear, confusion, and excitement. Warm breath spilled between her fingers. The bird twittered overhead; her hand crossed the space between her and the stranger, came to rest on his ankle beside the metal cuff.

Darkness flashed in her vision again, spinning her

head with vertigo, but she kept her touch on him, wrapping her grip around his ankle to keep from tumbling backward. In the dark, lines formed again, then shapes. Her breath shortened, her heart beat fast.

And she gazed upon the man's face.

XIX Horace - Dead End

Horace hauled himself up the modest boulder, foot slippin' once before he reached the top to sit for a rest.

Thrice the sun'd set, and each time it rose the next mornin', same as always, though the ol' sailor hardly expected it to. Not a single wink o' sleep did he get any o' those nights, so far as he knew. Between the waves rollin' onto the shore and rattlin' the bones what he suspected might belong to men he'd known on the Devil, the wind makin' whispery sounds like voices in the trees, and the painful ache in his belly, sleep were an acquaintance Horace weren't sure he'd ever make again. His body ached for a night o' rest and his gut were tight with hunger, but weren't nothin' to give them but sittin' a spell for the one and suckin' on rocks for the other.

He stretched his neck to peek past the last rock he'd climbed and thought he caught the same glimpse o' movement he'd noticed when he looked before. It were gone again quick as it came; quick enough the ol' sailor weren't sure he'd seen it at all. Might be someone else on the beach, or hunger and lack o' sleep playin' him for a fool. He hoped for the latter but didn't have the sack to find out for sure.

With a sigh a hair's breadth this side o' defeat, Horace glanced 'round. The land had grown up alongside the shore into a reddish-brown wall o' clay. Trees began part way up, their thick trunks sometimes tiltin' as though the ground wanted to give out underneath them and twisted roots stickin' out here and there.

On the other side o' him were the sea, just like the sea always were. The waves'd grown along with the land, no longer rollin' onto the rocky shore but doin' somethin' much closer to crashin'.

Ahead lay the cliff what Horace were makin' for without knowin' why he should.

"Should've gone back the first day when you had the chance." He raised his eyes and looked along the beach but saw nothin' amongst the expanse o' rock. "Now somethin' might be after you. Dummy."

His shoulders rose and fell with a sigh what did nothin' to improve his spirit nor his energy, but he made himself climb to his feet, at any rate. The sea breeze whipped at his sweat-dampened and stinkin' clothes, makin' him teeter atop the boulder and come near topplin' off. He got his balance back, heart poundin' against his ribs, and inched his way down the other side.

Up the next boulder. Pause, glance back. Glimpse somethin' followin', real or imagined, climb down. Up, pause, glance, glimpse, down. Up, pause, glance, glimpse, down.

The muscles in the ol' sailor's thighs ached and burned, knots bore into his calves. His grip slipped climbin' a big rock and he tore a fingernail. The wound left a drop o' blood on ev'ry spot he touched, makin' it easier for his pursuer to follow. Ragged breaths only half-filled his throbbin' chest, leavin' him gaspin' for air by the time he reached the top o' his next climb—the biggest yet. He stopped there, this time without lookin' back.

The sheer cliff loomin' before him made him forget somethin' might be after him. Straight up toward the sky it went, up and up and up. From where he stood, he barely made out the trees at the top, each of them so far off they appeared no more than a blade o' grass.

The cliff protruded out into the sea, its edge full o' jagged rocks on which the waves hurled themselves as though they wished to end their lives. White foam flew up in the air to the height o' twenty men or more. Now he were closer to it, he recognized this bit o' land; he'd seen it from a dozen diff'rent decks each time he'd made the turn. On a map, it'd be labelled the Goddess' Finger, but men aboard ship always called it the Demon's Cock. More'n one boat'd found its death on the jagged rocks.

Horace's heart sank. Even if he weren't far past exhausted, he couldn't've climbed the cliff. Even if the sea weren't poundin' against the fearsome rocks, they was too treacherous for him to traverse. Even if his arms and legs wasn't ready to drop offa his body, the current were too strong for him to swim.

"What do I do now?" he whispered, hoarse voice tremblin'.

Horace shuffled his feet to turn himself 'bout and caught another glimpse between two boulders not too far behind. It appeared dark in color and maybe covered in fur but, same as the other peeks he'd got, he weren't sure if it were true or a trick.

He hung his head, chest heavin' and a throb o' despair pumpin' through his body with ev'ry beat o' his heart. His blood felt heavy, threatenin' to drag him down, and he were tempted to let it, but Thorn's face swam into his mind, kept him from saggin'.

He saw the Small God's wide, flat nose, gray eyes, and grinnin' lips. The little feller tilted his head, then gestured with his chin. The vision in Horace's head and the shivers it gave him felt so real, he had to look to where Thorn indicated.

To his surprise, the ol' sailor spied a narrow trail leadin' up the reddish-brown cliff and disappearin' into the trees. He squinted at it, not trustin' his eyes any more with seein' this than he did 'bout the thing what may or may not be followin' him.

Movement caught Horace's eye and he jerked his head toward it.

Nothin'.

He blinked, thought he saw another flash between two enormous rocks, and it were enough to prompt the ol' sailor offa his boulder and toward the trail.

He sat on the rock and slid on his backside, the hard surface scrapin' his flesh through his breeches, but he hardly noticed. His heart'd started pumpin' energy through him again, givin' him enough to scramble off and keep his feet, push him o'er the next big rock, then 'round the next. He made his way past three more when he found himself standin' at the bottom o' the clay hill, starin' up at the beginnin' o' the forest.

The clay rise weren't so steep as he'd thought, but steep enough for a man without sleep three nights in a row and no food in his belly for as long. He considered if it'd be worth the climb when a chill crawled up his back and he became certain about somethin' creepin' up behind him.

Horace got his feet goin' again, mud churnin' under the soles o' his boots as he blundered his way up the hill. He bent o'er, grabbin' the ground with his hands, usin' them to pull himself up toward the trees—a place he didn't want to head to but didn't know where else to go.

Clay clogged the space under his fingernails by the time he reached the treeline. He grasped the nearest tree, leaving a reddish-brown handprint on its bark, and surveyed the beach below.

He'd climbed higher than he realized and, from where he clung to the leanin' trunk, the light and dark gray boulders scattered across the shore resembled the discarded building blocks of a child too large to imagine.

Horace squinted, searchin' between them for whatev'r'd been followin' him, but he didn't see nothin' but more rocks. A shudderin' breath rattled outta his lungs to signify his relief.

"That's well and good," he spoke aloud, "but what now?"

With a creak of wood and a vague suckin' sound, the tree to which Horace'd affixed his grip leaned farther, readyin' to topple. Its spiderweb roots pulled themselves free o' the ground and the trunk tilted itself toward the beach.

Horace scrambled to get away lest he be dragged back down the hill and dashed on the boulder what'd given a shot to bein' the death o' him. His feet slipped in the clay, spillin' him on his chest as his handhold tumbled. The ol' sailor's boots dug in, pushin' him up and away from the tangled roots reachin' out to grab him and haul him along.

The tree crashed down the hillside, knockin' away chunks o' clay and placin' deep holes in the path Horace'd used to climb up. He dug his fingers in, pullin' hard with his achin' arms, then yanked them outta the ground again as he moved. He grabbed a knot o' creepers what grew where the muddy hill turned to soil and the forest began.

At the last possible moment, he threw himself forward, the chunk o' clay under his feet fallin' away to roll down the steep hill after the tree it'd spent years supportin'. Horace wrapped his arms 'round the trunk o' the next tree, paused long enough to draw a half-breath, then lurched forward again, followin' the narrow trail what led him away from the beach and into the Green what'd always struck naked fear in his heart.

***

Time'd passed, as it had a habit o' doin', but Horace couldn't've guessed how much. The sun still hung in the sky, though the boughs thick with green needles hid it from his view.

After the edge o' the clay hill gave way under his feet and the threat o' bein' dashed on boulders below—not to mention there might've been somethin' after him—he hadn't bothered lookin' back as he fled. Despite their unwillingness, he'd forced his legs to propel him on, grittin' his teeth and ignorin' the burnin', the pain, the agony.

Each one o' them things was better'n endin' up dead. Horace'd been close to dead enough times now to know he preferred livin'.

The tree he stopped beneath struck him as outta place in the forest. Where the rest o' its mates were thick-trunked, tall, rough-barked and full o' needles, this one were stout and wide, with smooth bark and broad leaves.

And fruit hangin' from its limbs.

Horace stared up at the red-skinned bounty, his stomach howlin' and his mouth filled with spit. He'd seen this type o' fruit before, o' course—apples, without a doubt—but he'd nev'r heard o' them growin' in a forest amidst the evergreens. Tempted as he were—and demandin' as his belly'd become at their sight—he didn't even reach out to touch one o' the tasty-lookin' beauties.

"You're standin' in the Green," he mumbled, not fond o' the off-kilter tone in his voice. "You don't wanna be eatin' nothin' what grew in the Green."

His stomach growled loud enough it might've been an animal readyin' to pounce.

"But you gotta eat somethin'."

He rubbed his mouth, the earthy flavor o' the clay stuck under his nails and in the grooves o' his fingers and palms findin' its way to his tongue. Doin' so made him think 'bout the hill and the tree crashin' down it. He turned back to find out if it were still visible.

The path were gone.

Horace stared, concerned, but another groan in his belly suggested this might be an illusion perpetrated upon him by a lack o' sustenance. He faced the out-o'-place tree again, mind and gut battlin' o'er the right thing to do.

"Don't think I can reach, anyways." Rumblin' growl. "But I'll give it a go."

The ol' sailor reached up, stretchin' as far as he could, but it weren't enough. He tried gettin' up on the tips o' his toes, but the knots what'd tied themselves up in his calves weren't havin' none o' that. One o' the tasty-lookin' apples hung no more'n a hand's breadth beyond his reach.

Growl.

"Looks like it ain't gonna happen, my friend. Looks like we—"

The plump fruit fell right into his hand, smackin' his flesh and interruptin' his words.

Startled, Horace lowered his arm and stared at the apple sittin' upon his flattened palm. His mouth filled up to overflowin' with hungry saliva and it tricked his nose into smellin' the scent o' apples baked with cinnamon and cheese what a ship's cook'd made for a treat once many turns o' the seasons ago. He'd never forgot the savory-sweet flavor or the spicy-sweet aroma.

Before enough time'd passed to think 'bout what he were doin', Horace's teeth pierced the tasty fruit's red skin and tore out a chunk o' the white flesh beneath. He chewed hungrily, spit and juice spillin' outta the corner o' his mouth. His belly growled its grudgin' thanks when he swallowed the first mouthful, then he followed it up with another and another. Drops o' juice rolled between his fingers, along the back of his hand and down his palm, leavin' streaks in the reddish-brown clay and dirt caked on his flesh.

He finished the apple, threw the core aside, and reached up for another. It dropped into hand with little effort from him.

By the time he'd finished, eleven cores littered the ground beneath the apple tree and his stomach'd ceased its aching. With his belly satiated, other aches and pains clutched the ol' sailor's muscles, knottin' them, pinchin' them. He put his back against the apple tree's trunk and let himself sink to the ground, tilted himself to the side to pull a juicy apple core out from under his ass, then settled in to stare back where the path what brought him here'd been.

"Gone," he said, his apple juice-lubricated throat doin' a better job'n before. "Gone and ain't no way back to the shore."

Horace stretched out his legs, pressin' them against the ground to relieve the pain twistin' through them. He crossed his arms, rubbin' his hands o'er his achin' elbow joints and shoulders.

Weren't more'n a dozen heartbeats before the ol' sailor's chin dropped onto his chest. The first snore squeezed its way outta his throat as Horace Seaman fell asleep under an apple tree in the land o' the Small Gods.

He slept deep and without dreamin'.

XX Ailyssa - Sight

"I can see."

Ailyssa's gaze flickered from the man's face to the barn's nearest wall lined with barrels stuffed full of rusted tools and weapons, cockeyed shelves stacked with jars and jugs. The sunlight shining through the gaps between wall boards hurt her new-found vision; she directed her attention back to the stranger.

He stared at her, head tilted the way a dog might do in trying to understand its master. One of his eyelids sagged where Juddah's fist or boot had caught him square. Despite the damage done to the man by her rescuer, an unpreventable smile crawled across her face.

"I can see," she said again.

"Why do you speak my language when Jud-dah did not?"

The first words he spoke made little sense to Ailyssa. The smile brought to her lips by the return of her sight faded slightly. She raised one brow to show him she didn't understand his question but he didn't repeat himself.

"What do you mean? Juddah and I speak the same tongue, as do you."

A confused expression creased his forehead, causing him to wince with pain. He shook his head.

"I've been his captive for days and not understood a word spoken until now. How is it possible?"

"You have been his prisoner?"

The man nodded.

In her joy over the return of her vision, she'd forgotten the chain she'd followed across the barn to this man. Sick dread rolled up from Ailyssa's stomach and into her throat with the revelation: her rescuer wasn't a good man out to keep her safe but a letch planning to add her to the collection she'd overheard the thief on the road mention. A collection which included a man chained to the floor. What else did it include? She swallowed hard around the lump clogging her throat.

"How many sunrises have you seen locked in this place?"

Her gaze moved away, finding the rafters above, the cow munching hay in one corner, a heap of bulging sacks in another. He shifted to a sitting position and cried out with pain, pulling her attention back to him.

"You poor man."

She took her hand off his ankle, intending to reach out and offer comfort, but her world went white.

"Oh no."

She dug her knuckles into her eyes, rubbing hard, the pressure sending streaks of green and orange across the blank canvas of her vision. When she removed her hands and opened her lids again, the white haze remained.

"What happened? Why have I gone blind again?"

Her shoulders sagged and tears threatened. If the Goddess wanted to condemn her to a barn as her prison, she might accept it if her vision returned. But to give her a taste of sight then steal it again...could the Goddess be so cruel?

She shook her head, her heart falling into despair. The man shifted again, groaned, but she paid him no attention.

Until his hand found her arm and her sight returned.

Her eyes widened and the man's visage filled her vision, the shape of his face dispelling her anguish. She'd never been so happy to gaze upon anyone in her life.

"It's you," she whispered. "You give me my sight."

"When you took your hand away, I couldn't understand your words. You spoke Jud-dah's foreign language."

Ailyssa continued staring at him. Could this truly be?

"Take your hand away for a few heartbeats, then put it back."

The man nodded. "Speak when I do. Ready?"

"Yes."

He did as she said, removing his touch from her arm, and his face disappeared. The white haze overtook it— not creeping in as a fog falling across the land, but all at once. There, then gone.

"It is true. I can't see you anymore. Please, put your hand back."

For an agonizing time that cast an ache in her bones and felt much longer than it was, the whiteness remained. Panic squeezed Ailyssa's chest; if his touch remained away too long, would it still bring her vision back when it returned?

"Put your hand on me. Please."

His fingers found her arm and his face jumped to life in her vision. For a moment, they stared at each other, neither speaking. Ailyssa's heart fluttered.

Who is this man?

"Did you understand me when I spoke?"

He shook his head, grimaced at the pain it caused. "No, but I do now."

Instinct told her this was against the nature created by the Goddess. But didn't the Goddess create everything? Wasn't She the cause of all?

Ailyssa shuffled closer, careful not to break contact with the man, and fell into his arms.

***

"You're gonna be okay, Kooj." Juddah scratched the thick fur at the dog's neck. "Don't seem nothing is broken. Just a few scratches, but they're gonna heal."

He straightened with a creak of his knees and gripped the small of his back where pain flared, as it did every time he bent over. The dog looked up at him from his stuffed sack bed and thumped the floorboards with his tail.

"Maybe you're making it seem bad so I'll pay you some attention, hey, Kooj? Lucky for both you and him it ain't worse."

Juddah left the dog and crossed to the window facing out into the yard and the barn beyond. He pulled open the shutter and glared at the not-quite-square building.

"Feel bad leaving her in there. She didn't have

nothing to do with you getting hurt." The dog's tail thumped the floor again at the sound of his master's voice. A pang of worry flared in Juddah's gut. "Probably I should get her out before he hurts her, too."

He pushed the shutter closed again and went to the door, the floorboards groaning under his weight. Five or ten of them needed replacing soon; might be a good idea to make the fellow locked in the barn cut him some boards before he ended up in a sack.

"Be right back, Kooj." Juddah opened the door. "I'll bring us company, too."

The thought made the snake between his legs quiver and he stopped on the porch to give it a light rub.

"I might bring company for you, too, fella."

A smile on his face, Juddah bounded down the steps to the yard, the events in the barn left in the past where they belonged. Kooj'd heal and so would the man chained to the floor, then he'd be able to get back to digging Juddah's well and making new floorboards. He'd likely find a few other uses for him, too, before he finished with him.

The breeze coming in off the sea shifted Juddah's long beard, tickled his lips with his own moustache. He smoothed it with one wide hand and paused in front of the barn door. As he reached out to grab the handle, the sea wind died and sounds floated to him from inside the building.

Words.

Juddah's brow crinkled; he leaned into the door, cocking his ear to the wood. Two voices: his and hers, but he couldn't understand what either of them said, the words muted by door and space.

He don't even talk.

Juddah sucked a few long moustache hairs into his mouth, chewed the ends, the bulge that'd been growing in his britches shrinking. He considered bursting in on them, surprising them and carrying Ailyssa back to the house, but sudden uncertainty it'd be the thing to do overtook him. He realized that, if he wanted her to be more than just another piece in his collection, he'd need to treat her differently.

Tiptoeing, Juddah crept to the ocean side of the barn. The sun shone bright on this side and he realized they might notice his shadow passing in front of the gaps between the wall boards, but it'd also be the easiest place to peek in. He stepped over a pile of rotted wood, navigated a tangle of branches. His boots rustled through the tall grass growing up the wall as he found his way to one of the widest gaps.

A chunk of stump he often used for a chopping block rested against the wall in front of the wide gap, preventing him from getting close enough to peep through. He thought about leaning his hands on the wall boards to lean closer, but doing so might make the boards protest and reveal him. Juddah ran his fingers through his beard, pulling at the tangle of hair, pondering how best to handle this.

He rested one hand on his hip, the other remaining buried in his facial hair, scratching an imaginary itch while the sun shone on his back. More words floated out of the barn. Mingled curiosity and anger mashed his lips together and creased his brow. With a creak of his joints, Juddah put a knee on the chopping block, rested a hand beside it, and leaned toward the gap in the wall.

At first, he spied nothing but shadows interspersed with streaks of sunlight. More words reached his ears, and a flutter of movement caught his eye. He directed his attention to it, squinting.

His sight adjusted to the dimness within the building in time to catch Ailyssa, whom he'd risked his life to rescue from the temple at Jubha Kyna—fall into the arms of the bastard he'd found half-drowned on the beach.

Juddah jerked away from the gap, not wanting to watch her betray him, but he overbalanced. His bulk toppled backward off the chopping block, hands clasping at empty air in an attempt to stop his tumble. His ass hit the ground, a rock digging into his fleshy cheek, and he bit his lip rather than cry out. For a time, he sat on the grass, frowning at the side of the barn and fighting to keep from imagining what might be happening within, what they might do to taint his own building.

Vague and distant, he heard Kooj barking, and the sound pulled him out of his angry despair, brought him to his feet. But he didn't leave. Instead, he glared at the building, his fingers curling into fists, the flesh hidden beneath his thick beard hot with emotion. He drew one hand up, arm cocked to lash out at the grayed wood, to direct his anger somewhere, but he stopped. Punching the wall would hurt himself and the board, not to mention alert the lovers that he knew what they were doing.

Juddah lowered his fist. He'd find better ways to punish them for their betrayal, ways that wouldn't abrade his knuckles or damage his barn. With a heavy breath drawn through flared nostrils, Juddah tromped back across the yard toward the porch and poor Kooj lonely within.

"Let them have their fun," he muttered. "And then I'll have mine."

XXI Kuneprius - The Inn

The aroma of cooking meat skipped right past Kuneprius' nose to find its way straight to his aching belly. It growled and gurgled loud enough he worried those within the building might have heard.

They can't hear. They're too busy eating and drinking and being comfortable.

Never had moss-covered stone walls and a thatched roof looked so inviting. After so many nights sleeping on the forest floor followed by as many days traveling with little time for rest, Kuneprius supposed a cave with a few pieces of straw scattered on its floor might appear pleasing. The sight of an inn fairly made him salivate at the prospect of food, ale, and a bed.

He eased back from the edge of the thicket and into the woods. He'd been hesitant to leave the golem alone with Thorn, even only a few paces behind him, but he'd needed to find out what produced the succulent smell so teasing and tempting him.

He broke through a veil of leaves and nearly walked into the clay man's broad chest. The golem—whom he had a more and more difficult time thinking of as his friend Vesisdenperos—didn't so much as flinch. Kuneprius took a step around him to see Thorn seated on a fallen log, elbows on his knees, head in his hands. Over the past few days, his pale gray flesh had faded to off-white and wrinkled in areas like someone who'd stayed too long in his bath. Kuneprius went to the small man and kneeled beside him.

"Thorn? Are you all right?" He reached out toward him, but stopped when he saw his own hand quivering. He curled his fingers into a fist and took it back.

Thorn raised his head. His lids closed and opened with a slow blink and his eyes hunted around until they found Kuneprius. The previous clarity of color and glint of knowledge and understanding he'd seen shining in those eyes had faded almost to the point of disappearing. A wan, strained smile and half a nod were the only response he offered. A pang of regret added to the discomfort in Kuneprius' gut. He stood and faced the golem who hadn't yet moved.

"Ves..." His voice cracked, so he paused, cleared his throat, and began again. "The Small God is dying. Without sustenance and sleep, he won't make it to Murtikara."

The clay man gave no sign he'd heard. Kuneprius glanced at Thorn, who'd replaced his head in his hands, the skin on his arms sagging as though his muscles had become jelly. Seeing him that way—this being who'd at first appeared so vital, so powerful—made Kuneprius forget his hunger and exhaustion, the burning ache in his loins to dispense his seed, the throbbing in his temples at not being able to lave his sins. What troubles were they when compared to this poor fellow wasting away so far from his home?

"Vesisdenperos, my friend." Kuneprius raised his hand, ignoring the tremor along his arm, and rested his fingers on the golem's shoulder. The clay was cool to the touch. "There's an inn the other side of this thicket. They'll have a hot meal for us, a warm bed, and cold ale. Things to refresh me and allow us to travel faster, and to revive the small man, keep him alive until he can fulfill his destiny."

No response. He pressed harder against the golem's shoulder, intending to exert pressure to urge him to reply; his fingers sank into the clay and he jerked them away. The indentations remained for a second before healing itself back to its normal, unblemished state. Kuneprius suppressed a shiver. Did any of his friend remain within this molded man to hear his pleas?

He curled his fingers into his palms, fighting the surge of fury jolting through him, the urge to slam his fist against the abomination. So much anger swirled in his head; he didn't know whether Vesisdenperos being transformed into a mound of soulless clay caused it, or the fact he'd become party to the coming death of a creature who deserved a better fate.

You knew this might be your role when Kristeus appointed you keeper of the sculptor.

Season after season, he'd cared for Vesisdenperos, ensured he was fed, rested, clean, and happy as he learned his craft. Even as the boy went to practice his skill every day, and then the teen, and finally the man, Kuneprius was never sure this day would come. In his understanding, the prophecy hinted at what was to happen, not when. Maybe they'd misinterpreted it. If so, Thorn would die in vain, and he suspected Ves already had. The thought infuriated him, but he forced himself to remain calm, counting his breaths until the tightness in his chest eased enough to let him speak again.

"The prophecy speaks of sacrifice, Ves." He swept his arm toward Thorn seated on the log, his entire body appearing to sag. "This is not sacrifice. This is neglect."

The golem's eyes flickered in the Small God's direction—his only movement or reaction. His head didn't turn, his expression remained unchanged. Hope sparked in Kuneprius and he pressed on.

"One night is all, Ves. I'll tell them my son is sick and we need a room. I'll sneak him in when no one is looking and we'll take our meals in the chamber. We'll leave before sunrise and none will be the wiser."

He fell silent and waited, gaze fixed on the golem's face despite the worry tugging at him to glance at the small man, make sure he was all right. A nightjar sang out from a bough overhead, calling the sun down from the sky; a dull wind stirred the bracken against their knees. The golem stood as still as the statue he so closely resembled while Kuneprius counted the pulse thumping in his ears.

Fifty-five. Fifty-six. Fifty-seven. Fifty—

The clay face relaxed almost imperceptibly and the thing nodded once. It so surprised Kuneprius, his mouth fell open and he remained unmoving for ten more beats of his heart.

Food. A night in a bed. A chance for repentance and tribute.

More importantly, this slim bit of humanity suggested a touch of Vesisdenperos yet survived within the man of clay. The possibility invigorated Kuneprius, pulled him from his trance.

He rushed over to Thorn, kneeled once more beside the Small God, this time not hesitating when he reached out to the gray man. He put a hand on Thorn's shoulder and found his flesh cool and clammy.

"Come, Thorn. Food and rest await us inside."

Thorn raised his chin again, found Kuneprius' eyes more easily this time.

"Food for Thorn?"

"Yes."

"Will Horace Seaman be there?"

"I'm afraid not. Your friend is...gone."

Thorn nodded, then placed his face back in his hands, the sliver of enthusiasm he'd shown disappearing as quickly as it came. Kuneprius' chest ached at seeing the being's natural vigor quashed so completely. He put his hand under Thorn's arm and stood, tugging to make him do the same.

"Come on. Get up and we'll get you fed, watered, and rested."

Thorn rose on shaky legs and Kuneprius noticed the way his ribs showed through his skin. A dark splotch on the Small God's side below his armpit caused him some alarm.

"We need to disguise you," he said, slipping out of his shirt. It left him wearing only his undershirt to cover his own chest, but it would have to do. Without clothing, Thorn would attract unwanted attention.

He draped it across his companion's shoulders and

knew right away it wasn't enough. He yanked the shirt's collar up, pulling it over the small man's head so nothing but his face showed. Better, but he'd still need to be careful and conceal Thorn behind him, keep him hidden from curious eyes.

"Come," he said and took the Small God's arm again. Thorn followed.

As they passed the golem, Kuneprius glanced up at the clay man's face, offered a smile of thanks. The thing that once was his friend Vesisdenperos didn't meet his gaze.

***

The barkeep—a man whose face appeared to have seen the seasons turn only a few times more than Kuneprius had, but whose body looked as though it had lived through a good deal more—raised a brow and craned his neck to see past the new customer. Kuneprius shifted to prevent him from getting a good view of Thorn.

"Sick, you say?"

Kuneprius nodded. "Very ill. Poor tike's cheeks have gone ashen with it."

As he spoke, he struggled to maintain an appropriate expression while his nerves tugged at the corners of his mouth and begged him to dance back and forth, one foot to the other. He resisted, remaining still and keeping the Small God hidden behind him.

"Don't want no sick kid vomiting all over m'room."

"Oh no, not to worry. It's not that sort of sickness."

The barkeep leaned away, crossed his arms in front of his chest. "What sort of sickness is it, then?"

Kuneprius drew a sharp breath between his lips, his brain freezing at the question. What illness poses no danger of vomit?

"He's homesick," he blurted before his better judgement intervened. The only thing to do was to expand and hope for the best. "And weary. And he's hurt his leg."

The barkeep's eyes narrowed. "Not really sick then, is he?"

"I guess not," Kuneprius replied and dipped his hand into the pocket of his breeches. He produced a silver coin and laid it on the bar. "Is this enough for food and lodging? We'll keep to our room and bother no one."

The barkeep lowered his arms, his demeanor shifting with the glint of lantern light shining on the coin. He scooped it up and held it in front of his face, rotating it between his fingers to see both sides.

"More'n enough. Take a table and I'll bring you a couple of plates and tankards of ale."

He turned away from the bar, reaching for the aforementioned goblets, but Kuneprius interrupted.

"No, no. We don't want to be a bother and we'd prefer to take food in our room, if it's all right by you, kind sir."

The barkeep faced them, flicked the coin up in the air with his thumb and caught it. "I think this might be enough for me to bend the rule regardin' food in the rooms. Yours'll be up the stairs, last door to the left."

"Thank you."

Kuneprius crossed the room to the staircase, ushering the Small God ahead of him to keep himself between Thorn and their host.

"I'll have the plates ready when you want 'em," the barkeep called after them. "Be you needin' anything else?"

Kuneprius paused at the bottom of the stairs, peered back over his shoulder. "Is it too much to ask a bowl and a pitcher of clean water? We haven't had opportunity to wash in several days."

"I'll have it for you with your food, if you'd like."

"Yes, fine."

Kuneprius prompted Thorn on and mounted the steps behind him, relief flooding his chest. Things had gone more smoothly than expected.

They paused at the top of the stairs to ensure no one in the hall might see Thorn's pale flesh and unusual appearance. To his relief, it lay empty. He hurried the gray man ahead of him, soles of his bare, gray feet dragging on the wooden floor. Not until they crossed the threshold into the room did Kuneprius realize he'd been holding his breath the entire way.

He closed the door behind them and sighed the air out of his lungs.

The chamber was exactly what he'd expected from a country inn: a single bed, a table, a chamber pot and not much else. It was fine with him, he'd become used to just such accommodations after living in Murtikara for all those turns of the seasons. The problem was, with but one bed, they'd either have to sleep cozy or he'd have to take the floor.

"This will do, won't it, Thorn? Be nice to have a good night's sleep."

The Small God stood in place, swaying somewhat, but otherwise giving no sign he'd heard his roommate speak. Kuneprius pursed his lips. The farther they took him from his home, the worse his condition. If it continued, would he even make it to their destination?

"Can't worry about it now," he murmured aloud as he set his hands on the Small God's bare shoulders.

The faintest sensation of energy emanated from the cool, gray flesh. Thorn turned his head with the intensity and effort of a man moving a heavy object, directing his gaze toward his companion at the touch. A haze clouded his formerly clear and joyful eyes.

"Come," Kuneprius said, exerting light pressure to move him. "Let's get you into bed to rest."

They crossed the room and he pulled back the

tattered blankets covering the thin mattress. A poor excuse for a bed, it turned out.

Better than sleeping on damp ground.

It took an effort to guide Thorn under the blankets. The Small God's arms and legs flopped loosely and he acted as though he didn't understand the concept of a bed. When he finally settled, Kuneprius tucked the covers in around him and stood.

"Now to see if our food is ready. You'd like food, yes?"

Thorn let his head tilt toward him on what passed for a pillow and put great effort into forming his lips into a smile. He didn't achieve what he'd intended and his face ended up contorted in an uncomfortable grimace. Kuneprius' heart ached at the sight.

"I'll be right back. You stay here and wait—"

A knock interrupted his words, startling him. Thorn didn't appear to notice.

"Yes?" Kuneprius called, hoping he wouldn't need to open the door.

"I got you your water," the barkeep's voice replied through the wooden slab. "You want I should bring it in for ya?"

"No, no. That's fine."

He hurried across the room, lifted the latch, and opened the portal a crack. The barkeep stood in front of him, a pitcher in one hand, bowl in the other. He held them up for Kuneprius to see he'd done what he said, his lips tilted in the lopsided smile of a man well-paid for a simple job.

"Where do you want 'em?"

"I'll take them."

He peered back over his shoulder at the Small God in the bed. The blankets covered his bare chest, but his ashen face and wide nose faced the door. Kuneprius swallowed hard and opened it wider, placing his foot to prevent the gap from widening too far. He held his hands out to receive what the barkeep had brought.

The man rotated the empty bowl sideways to fit it through the crack; it got stuck between door and jamb. For a moment, Kuneprius did nothing as the barkeep waited for him to widen the opening and allow him to complete his task.

Kuneprius considered telling him he'd changed his mind and they didn't need the washing supplies, but the thought brought tension to his muscles and limbs. The possibility of yet another day passing without scrubbing away at his sins made his hands shake and his mouth go dry, especially with the opportunity so close.

He shifted his foot back the width of two fingers and the bowl slid through. He took it and immediately switched it to his other hand to receive the pitcher more easily, too. As the barkeep rotated the handle toward him, he tilted his head to see past the edge of door and into the room. Kuneprius leaned, keeping his body between him and the bed, blocking the barkeep's view, he hoped. As soon as the pitcher made it through, he closed the door to only a crack. If doing so in any way offended the man, his expression didn't show it.

"Your meals be ready, too. Should I bring them, too?"

Kuneprius' heart jumped in his chest and he shook his head too hard. Water slopped over the lip of the pitcher and onto his boot.

"No, no. I'll be right down to collect them."

"As you like. They'll be awaitin' ya at the bar."

He stepped back and Kuneprius resisted the urge to slam the door shut.

"Thank you," he said instead, donning a smile he worried might appear false. "I'll be along shortly."

The barkeep nodded but didn't leave, forcing Kuneprius to close the door in his face. The latch clicked into place and he let out a sigh before crossing the room to the small table set against the wall opposite the bed. He placed the bowl on the flat surface and it rocked back and forth on uneven legs. Kuneprius frowned, grasped the edge and tested its stability. Satisfied it would be sturdy enough, he tilted the pitcher until a stream of water splashed into the bottom of the bowl. Just the sound of the cool liquid pattering against the earthenware vessel untied a knot inside him that had been tightening for days.

Despite the relief, he stayed his hand and stopped the flow. As much as he desired to fill the bowl and plunge his face into the water, he couldn't take the chance. If too much time passed before he claimed their meals, he'd find the barkeep knocking again, and a plate of food would necessitate opening the door enough for him to see in.

With a sigh, Kuneprius set the pitcher on the table beside the bowl. He'd waited this long, he could survive a little more time to feed the Small God. His belly growled, reminding him Thorn wasn't the only one in need of feeding.

He went to the door and lifted the latch but hesitated before opening it, overcome with the creeping suspicion he'd find the barkeep waiting in the hall to try for a peek into the room. Kuneprius bit hard on his back teeth and pulled a deep breath in through his nose, then opened the door a crack, moving his eye close.

The space beyond stood empty.

"Be right back," he called over his shoulder and closed the door behind him.

With each step along the hall, and then down the stairs, his belly growled and grumbled. In his concern and worry, he'd forgotten how long it had been since he'd eaten a good meal. For more days than he cared to consider, he'd sustained himself on whatever berries and edible plants he found. None of it satisfied his stomach.

Kuneprius reached the bottom of the stairway and paused. Far more people sat around the tavern than when they arrived; two or three at every table. Conversations competed to be heard, cutlery clattered against plates, flagons thumped on tabletops.

Two women wearing aprons moved amongst the tables, one a slender woman of plain appearance who appeared of similar age to the barkeep, the other a girl who didn't look to have seen the seasons turn more than twelve or thirteen times. Despite her diminutive size, she carried a tray full of ales with the confidence of someone practiced at such a function.

The barkeep's wife and daughter, no doubt.

Kuneprius knew he might be wrong in his assumption, but it mattered not. The elder of the two passed close by, so he stepped off the last stair, headed for the bar where the barkeep had told him he'd find their meals.

"Busy tonight," he commented to the woman.

"Like this most nights," she said in a tone suggesting she had other, more important things to do than talk to him. She glanced at him as they reached the bar. "You the one with the sick boy?"

"I'm afraid I am."

She brushed a loose piece of hair behind her ear. It popped right back out before she lowered her hand.

"I don't got no medicine. Sheela was sick herself not so long ago and we used it up." She nodded toward the younger girl on the other side of the room doling out ales to a table of laughing men. "But if there be anything you need, let me know."

"Thank you, I will."

Two plates appeared on the bar in front of him, and the barkeep waited, his expression expectant. Steam rose from the chunks of meat sharing the pewter surface with roasted potatoes and a piece of cornbread—a better meal than he'd hoped for and his belly gurgled in anticipation. If the tavern hadn't been so busy, the barkeep surely would have heard.

"It looks delicious," Kuneprius said, offering what he presumed he'd been awaiting. The man nodded and smiled his lopsided smile.

"Best meal you're gonna get in these parts." He nodded toward the stairs. "I think your boy'll enjoy it, too. Looks like he needs a good meal."

Saliva flooded Kuneprius' mouth as he stared at the food, his ravaged gut distracting him enough it took a few heartbeats for him to realize what the barkeep said.

Your boy'll enjoy it. Looks like he needs a good meal.

Kuneprius raised his head to find the fellow looking past him and dread filled him. He snatched the two plates off the bar and spun around. Thorn stood at the top of the stairs, swaying as he gazed blankly at the crowded room.

"He don't look good," the woman who may have been the barkeep's wife said. "Kinda...pasty."

"It's...he's fine. Just needs food."

Kuneprius hurried away, weaving between tables and past the tavern's patrons. The closer he got to the stairway, the greater the number of patrons who directed their gazes to the Small God.

"Tho..." Kuneprius stopped himself. What man named his son Thorn? "I told you to stay in bed. You're too sick to be with these people."

He hoped his proclamation of the 'boy's' sickness might deter the room's attention, but it created the opposite effect. More heads turned. Someone gasped upon seeing Thorn, but then Kuneprius reached the stairway, rushed up them as fast as he could make his legs move without spilling precious food from the plates. He halted at the top step, near to eye level with the Small

God.

"I told you to stay in the room," he said through clenched teeth.

Thorn raised his gaze toward Kuneprius, but his eyes caught on the meals in his hands. He licked his lips.

"Come on," Kuneprius said, stepping up and forcing his companion along the hall in front of him. He thought to look back and see just how many of the tavern's patrons had noticed the small man at the top of the stairs, but he resisted; his heart needed no more reason to hammer its way out of his chest.

***

Kuneprius hated wasting water but, in his haste to get out of the tavern and return Thorn to the room, he'd neglected to take the cutlery provided by the barkeep. After getting himself out of bed and traipsing down the hall, the Small God had been too weak to feed himself, so Kuneprius helped him.

It reminded him of Vesisdenperos in his youth and he'd wondered how the golem occupied his time while they were at the inn.

Hopefully doing nothing.

He poured water from the pitcher into the bowl, set the jug aside and dipped his fingertips in, found the liquid cool to the touch. It both comforted him and increased his anxiety; he longed to yank his hands out and plunge his face into the water in their stead, but the greasiness of the meat's juices that had run between his fingers prevented him.

He needed to wash his hands before he could think about washing his sins.

The water's temperature made it difficult to remove the fat, instead spreading it across his skin. He scrubbed harder and quickly realized it was for naught. Hands still in the bowl, he scanned the room, searching for a towel or something to use in place of one.

In the near to empty chamber, the only fabrics in sight were the blanket covering the slumbering Thorn and the threadbare curtain draped in front of the window.

Kuneprius sighed, took his hands from the water, and shook the droplets off over the bowl. Satisfied he'd removed as much of the excess fluid as possible, he gripped the edge of the bowl, carried it to the window, and dumped out the dirty fluid with its oily film. The sound of it splashing on the ground below reached his ears and he cringed; he hadn't peered out to make sure no one stood below. He hoped not, but assumed it to be the case as no curses floated up to the window on the night air.

He dried the bowl with the curtain, removing the last of the greasy smudges from the edges he'd touched, then set it on the floor at his feet. Next, he found the cleanest spot possible on the fabric and used it to scrub the remnants of their meal from his fingers and palms. As he did, he stared out the window. The moon lit the short yard stretching from the inn to the woods beyond, but the forest itself lay in darkness. Kuneprius squinted, trying hard to make out the shape of a large, clay man, but to no avail; darkness prevented him from recognizing one tree from another, so he gave up. Glad to be inside as he was, he missed his friend, despite still being unsure if a part of him yet existed or if he was gone forever.

High in the night sky, Ine'vesi, the evenstar, shone bright; brighter than usual, Kuneprius thought.

Expectant.

Was it possible the Small God—the One Who Watched From Above—knew what had come to pass? Could it be the priest Ine'vesi, banished by the Goddess so long ago, understood the contents of his prophecy had been put into motion making his return imminent?

Kuneprius realized he'd stopped wiping his hands on

the curtain and suddenly felt as though eyes bore into him. He spun around, expecting to catch Thorn observing him, but the gray man lay facing the other direction, his shoulder rising and falling with his sleeping breath. Kuneprius' head snapped back toward the window, instantly finding the evenstar again. It appeared brighter still, more intense.

He took his hands from the curtain and backed away a step, a shiver shaking along his spine.

He's watching me.

Kuneprius stared at the window, the shoddy curtain having fallen across it, blocking out the night sky. Noise from the tavern below floated up through it; the crowd sounded to have gotten rowdier than when he retrieved their food. It made sense—as the night wore on and the patrons consumed more ale, they'd naturally become more raucous. He put the noise from his mind and let his gaze fall on the bowl sitting below the window.

Relief was close, less than a pace away. He knew the respite the simple combination of bowl and water offered him from the world. Despite knowing it was so near, Kuneprius found himself hesitant to approach the window to retrieve the vessel.

Ine'vesi might be watching.

No matter, the relief waiting for him with his ritual couldn't wait. The flesh of his cheeks burned with sin and it was all he could do to keep from clawing it off his head.

He knelt, leaned forward gingerly, reaching out until his fingers brushed the lip of the bowl. His gaze flickered to the window and, for an instant, he thought he saw the glow of the evenstar shining even through the fabric.

He grabbed the bowl's edge and shuffled back, falling onto his buttocks and pushing away from the window with his feet. The light his eye detected faded, the clamor of the bar seeping back into his notice. He sat on the floor for a time, heart beating fast, then shook his head and laughed at himself.

"The priest is nothing but a light in the sky. He can't watch you from there."

Kuneprius laughed again and stood, picking the bowl up from the floor as he did. He went to the table where the pitcher of water sat but amended his path on his way to pass close by Thorn.

As he'd hoped, the Small God had found some peace. He breathed deeply and smoothly, his gray lids closed, his lips parted. Kuneprius took a moment to marvel at the creature he stood over, wishing he'd known him when he still had use of the powers the legends spoke of, that he himself experienced inklings of, despite Thorn's condition.

He might have spent a great deal more time staring at this fantastic being if the burn in his cheeks and the itch in his forehead he'd forgotten with the evenstar's gaze upon him hadn't returned. He raised his shoulder and rubbed one cheek on it, then spun on his heel and hurried across the small room to the tiny table.

It shifted and the ewer clinked against the edge of the bowl as he set it down. Water splashed against the side. The sound it made caused an ache in his chest the way a hungry man might salivate at the aroma of cooking meat.

He could wait no more.

Kuneprius picked up the jug and tilted it over the bowl, fighting the urge to pour it in all at once. If he did, it would spill, wasting precious water. He decanted it slowly, watching the thin stream flow from the lip of the pitcher, savoring the splash it made filling the vessel that would help bring his relief. He poured until the ewer was empty, shaking it to get the last few drops, then set it aside and gripped the edge of the table with both hands.

Lamplight glimmered on the surface of the water,

inviting Kuneprius to plunge his face in, to relieve days of pent up tension and guilt. He cupped his hands, filled them with water, and splashed it on his cheeks. Once. Twice. Three times. He stood over the bowl, droplets plummeting from his nose and chin, and waited, sighing deep breaths in and out of his chest as he counted his heartbeats.

One. Two. Bump-bump, bump-bump. Five. Six. Seven. Eight. Nine. Ten.

On the tenth, he drew one last breath to fill his lungs to capacity, then gripped the edge of the table and leaned forward. Instead of submerging his face all at once, he eased it in, eyes open to watch the water's approach.

The tip of his nose touched first, the coolness of the water instantly easing his discomfort at the path his life had taken. His nose went in, then his chin, brows, and lips. Finally, when his entire face broke the surface, he pushed his head forward until his nose brushed the bottom of the bowl. Water slopped over the sides onto the table, splashing his hands, but he barely noticed. The visage of the woman was already finding its way into his mind.

One. Two. Three. Four. Five.

As her features swam into his vision, staring back at him from the bottom of the bowl, he realized he hadn't been able to call her features to mind since the last opportunity to lave his sins. He'd tried to picture her— mostly at night—with no success.

Eleven. Twelve. Thirteen. Fourteen. Fifteen.

Concern pulled her smooth, young mouth taut, drawing her brows down and tilting her lips into a frown. In truth, this was how he'd seen her face the one time he'd met the woman—the time he'd taken her life—but it was rarely how she appeared to him when he tried to wash away his guilt.

Twenty-eight. Twenty-nine. Thirty. Thirty-one.

185

Normally, she had a smile for him and forgiveness in her eyes. Only in his dreams did she accuse him, blame him. Her expression now concerned him and he concentrated hard enough on changing it he nearly lost count.

Fifty-three. Fifty-four. Fifty-five.

The girl's lips moved, her concern deepening, transforming to another aspect he'd seen the day she died: fear.

His counting ceased. Never had the girl in his vision behaved this way, not when he had control of his mind. When she visited his dreams, she did as she pleased. At times, she blamed him for her death, for the state of the world; at others, he thought she was warning him—the same sense he got from her this time.

Kuneprius blinked her away and pulled his head from the bowl, water dripping off his nose and chin. A knot in his chest made filling his lungs difficult, but he fought through and plunged his face back in, restarting his count.

One. Two. Three.

Her likeness reappeared, the concern it had shown having become panic—the same expression she'd worn at the moment his sword ended her time in this world. The muscles in Kuneprius' jaw tightened and he released air through his nose. The bubbles swirled her image before his eyes but dismissed neither her visage nor the alarm it wore like a mask.

Seventeen. Eighteen. Nineteen.

The creak of a board usurped his attention and the vision of the girl shut her eyes.

Thorn?

Water splashed into his ear and the side of the bowl slammed into his cheek, throwing him off balance. He held onto the table, keeping himself from falling as the bowl and pitcher crashed to the floor, water spilling onto the cracked boards as the earthenware broke into pieces.

Kuneprius gasped a breath into his lungs, coughed out water. He used his forearm to wipe wetness from his face and straightened, anger flaring through him.

"Thorn! What are you—?"

The golem loomed over him, three paces away, the Small God held under his arm. The odor of clay invaded Kuneprius' head as his nostrils flared and his eyes widened with the sudden realization something was desperately wrong.

"What's...?"

His lips continued to move, but the noises they made ceased. The golem's always stern expression bore into him, weighing on him; Thorn looked confused, as might be expected from one ripped from their sleep.

The clay man grabbed Kuneprius by the arm, fingers digging deep into his bicep and sending pain up into his shoulder. A moment of confusion blurred his thinking as the abomination yanked him away, dragging him across the floor toward the door which was open and hanging at an odd angle.

The golem had broken through it without Kuneprius noticing.

How long did he stand in the room watching me?

The thought passed through his mind, but disappeared as other, more pressing questions forced it out.

Where is he taking us?

Why?

They went through the doorway and into the hall before he got his feet moving, relieving some of the pressure of the clay man's grip. The big man's long strides carried them quickly to the top of the stairs.

"What are you doing?" Kuneprius knew the query would go unanswered, but he asked anyway.

As expected, the golem ignored his words and pulled

him down the staircase. Kuneprius directed his attention to his footing, making sure he didn't trip and tumble his way to the bottom. Under the clay man's arm, Thorn made a noise in his throat. Hearing it made him aware of the lack of other sounds emanating from the previously boisterous tavern crowd. Goose bumps crawled along his arms and Kuneprius looked up.

His gaze first took in the Small God, but he saw nothing of Thorn but his legs. Beyond him and the golem's muscled back, he spied the first corpse lying at the bottom of the stairway.

It was the serving girl, the one Kuneprius presumed to be the barkeep's daughter. Her ale-stained white apron was red, her eyes stared toward the ceiling, her body twisted at a grotesque angle. If the golem hadn't been pulling him onward, Kuneprius would have stopped and gawked in horror.

As they reached the bottom of the staircase, he found so much more to be horrified by.

Corpses littered the tavern, some draped across tables, others tangled with chairs or each other, still others leaning forward in their spots as though they'd dozed off after drinking too much ale. Spatters and gouts of blood painted the walls and floor.

Kuneprius gaped. The stench of fresh blood penetrated the odor of clay, the coppery taste of it found his tongue and threatened to gag him. His feet refused to move, scraping on the wooden floorboards as the golem dragged him through the slaughterhouse.

The barkeep's head sat on the bar, tilted to one side and resting on his ear, the body nowhere to be seen. Kuneprius recognized others he'd noted when he came to get food for himself and Thorn, not an unsheathed dagger or inch of bared steel amongst them.

The pieces of the puzzle came together in his mind.

They saw Thorn. Somehow, the golem knew.

His foot caught on an arm no longer attached to a body and he danced away from it, a squeak emanating from his tight throat. They passed the other server—the barkeep's wife—her head twisted around to look behind her at a man torn in two from shoulder to groin; his insides drooped out over his belt.

He killed them all.

"W...why? Why did you do this?"

Fear and despair clenched his throat so tightly it hurt to speak. An unnoticed tear rolled along his cheek. The other man the golem had killed was bad, and the two children worse, but this...

The clay man made no answer, merely continued through the massacre toward the door, pushing corpses and body parts aside whenever they got in his way. His gray feet left red footprints anywhere they touched a clean spot on the floor.

They crossed the threshold into the dark night, passing the splintered door that was the golem's first victim upon entering the inn. He'd torn it from its hinges, shattering its boards and splitting the jamb, the force had been so great. What must the patrons have thought when they saw this monster stride in and begin killing those nearest to him?

"They didn't deserve this, Ves. They did nothing wrong." Tears flowed freely from Kuneprius' eyes, a line of snot trickled from his nose. He craned his neck to look back through the doorway, desperate to see someone left alive. Nothing moved. "They wouldn't have told. They didn't know what they saw."

The golem dragged them across the courtyard toward the trees, as unresponsive and uncaring of his words as always. In that moment, whatever hope he held a sliver of his friend might remain in the monster—that there was any chance of having his dear Vesisdenperos returned to him—vanished.

His body sagged and he allowed the golem to haul him toward the forest, stumbling as he went. Kuneprius raised his head skyward, tears smearing the shining light of the Small Gods into streaks of bright white. The evenstar stood out amongst them, brighter, stronger, intense and powerful. He tried to tear his eyes away, to stop casting his gaze upon the banished priest, but Ine'vesi refused to let him go.

To Kuneprius, it seemed the night laughed.

XXII Juddah – Anger

The sun had begun its downward journey toward the horizon as Kooj snored quiet canine snores on the porch beside Juddah's chair. The dog was recovering nicely from the hurts done it by the man, and Juddah let his hand drop to the scruff of the shaggy beast's neck, dug his fingers into the thick fur.

"Good boy, Kooj," he murmured.

His gaze flickered from his prisoner digging in the yard to the back of the woman's head where she perched on the edge of the steps in front of him. She'd been sitting that way for quite a spell without a word to her rescuer and host. With her elbows on her knees, she leaned forward, facing toward the shoveling man. If Juddah didn't know she was blind, he'd have accused her of staring at the fellow while he worked, something he hated people doing to him. It was a part of why he lived outside town—to keep folk from looking at him.

The well-digger made no more sound than the woman, the day's regular tumult of chirping birds, buzzing insects, and wind stirring the grass broken only by the dog's breathing and the rhythmic scrape of spade moving soil. Juddah had to admit: despite the swollen bruise on the fellow's face, he continued being a good worker. Maybe he'd have to find a few more jobs for him before his time was through.

But that'd mean he'd be around the woman longer.

Juddah's back teeth ground together at the prospect. After seeing her fall into the man's arms, he'd worked hard to keep them apart, but every time they got close, one or the other's hands found its way onto an arm or a shoulder. He'd considered bringing her inside at night, having her share his bed, but hadn't found the courage, so he'd left her in the barn with him.

It made him wonder what they got up to when he wasn't watching.

Better be nothing.

But it wasn't nothing. Whatever they did stopped her talking to him. She'd said but a few words since they arrived from Jubha Kyna; thrice the sun rose without a polite 'hello' or a 'thank you for rescuing me'.

The muscles in Juddah's jaw flexed. He huffed a breath out his nostrils that stirred his moustache hairs, then rubbed absently at his nose, scratching at the tickle it created. His gaze trailed down the back of Ailyssa's neck with its stubble of short brown hair. In the sun's glare, he saw flecks of gray in it he hadn't noticed before, shining like grains of sand on the beach. A line of pink, soft-looking flesh appeared below her hairline, disappearing beneath the collar of her smock.

Juddah licked his lips.

Though he couldn't see it, he knew the smooth skin continued under the plain dress streaked with travel dirt and barn sleeping. Her whole back'd be the same—silky, supple, with a woman's fragrance and the subtle tang of salty perspiration. And the front—

Juddah shifted in his chair at a stirring in his drawers; Kooj lifted his snout off his paws, peered up at his master.

"S'okay, boy," he said breathily. "Go back to sleep."

Ailyssa tilted her head as though listening, but returned to sightlessly watching the well-digger. Juddah let his gaze follow hers.

The man stood in the hole, hidden by the earth and grass from mid-chest down. Sweat shimmered on his bare skin—he'd removed his shirt in search of relief from the afternoon heat—and ropy muscles swelled and flexed beneath his flesh. Watching him, Juddah almost understood why a woman might want to lay with the fellow instead of with him. Young and attractive with taut flesh, he didn't have a protruding belly or hair in all his places.

She's old enough to be his mother.

And he probably doesn't smell of pig fat, neither.

Juddah's lips pressed together tight behind his tangle of facial hair. He imagined how she must run her fingers over his arms and chest, tracing the shape of his sculpted muscles, how she'd put her lips on his, stroke his cheek. Her breath'd shorten into tiny, passionate gasps as his teeth found her neck, his hands went to her—

Juddah jumped up, setting his chair rocking backward near to the point of tipping. It fell back into place with a thud startling Kooj to his feet and making Ailyssa jump. He glared across the yard at the stranger digging his well, choosing to ignore both the dog and the woman. Anger swirled in Juddah's gut, growing and expanding along with the swell inside his breeches.

"What's wrong?" Ailyssa asked, head tilted toward him, blind eyes fixed on a spot too far to the right.

Juddah ground his teeth, unsure for an instant what he meant to do, but another glance at the fellow convinced him.

"Get up," he demanded hooking one hand under the woman's armpit. Before she had the chance to obey, he'd pulled her to her feet.

192

"What—" She stumbled going down the single stair, but he kept her from falling. "What are you doing?"

"Something I should've done in the first place," he growled and pushed her across the yard toward the barn.

"No," she cried, raising her voice. "No, please."

Juddah stared across at the man digging the well; he'd stopped shoveling to watch when he heard the woman's frightened voice. He didn't move to aid her—chained to the stake as always, he'd realized he had no help to offer—but neither did he utter a word. As far as Juddah knew, the fellow couldn't speak at all.

Unless he's alone with her. Don't seem to have any problem with words then.

He threw the barn door open and pushed the woman through. Her feet tangled and she spilled to her knees, more scuffs of brown dirt adding to the mess on her smock. Regret shot through Juddah when she hit the ground, concern he'd hurt her, but it vanished when he caught sight of the bed of straw where he'd spied her falling into the man's arms.

Where they did their dirty deeds.

Juddah seethed, warm blood filling his cheeks beneath his beard, making his face burn with anger and jealousy. He snatched a handful of Ailyssa's smock in his fist and pulled at her.

"Get up."

She clambered to her feet, dragged up by his mighty arm. When she regained her balance, he propelled her toward the wall opposite the shelves of odds-and-ends, jars and jugs, directing her to the rope he used to tether the cow. When they approached it, he allowed her to walk into the wall instead of stopping her. She let out a startled squeal and the sliver of regret flared in his chest; he frowned it back into his gut.

"Hold out your hands," he demanded.

Ailyssa shook her head, pulled away until her

shoulders pressed against the boards. She crossed her arms, hiding her hands.

"Give them to me," he roared, the volume and tone of his voice making her cringe the way he'd hoped.

"Please don't hurt me," she said and uncrossed her shaking arms.

Juddah caught both her wrists in one meaty paw, gripping tight enough he felt the bones rub together. She made a sound in the back of her throat but didn't cry out; he relented on the firmness of his hold and grasped the rope in his free hand, wrapped it three times around her arms and tied off the end. When he finished, he gave the rope a tug to make sure it was secure, then took a step away.

"What did I do, Juddah?" Ailyssa asked.

The hint of a whimper in her voice both satisfied him and shamed him. He swallowed hard, the continuing growth of the bulge in his pants encouraging him.

"You know what you did," he said between clenched teeth. "Now I'm gonna do what I should've done at Jubha Kyna."

His tongue darted across his lips, wetting them, and one hand went to his crotch. He leaned toward Ailyssa, sniffed to inhale her fragrance, but he detected only dirt, his own sweat, and the odor of old manure. His gaze traveled along the front of her, but the way she pressed herself against the wall, arms clenched across her chest, prevented him from seeing even the vague curves the plain smock sometimes allowed him to glimpse.

He reached out, intending to grab her elbows, move them aside, but stopped himself and glanced toward the barrels lined up by the far wall. He could use one of the blades they contained to cut the smock from her; he'd be able to have his way with her, if he wanted. The man remained chained to a stake in the yard, so no one could stop him putting his hands where he desired, his mouth, other parts of him.

His breath shortened to a rough pant and he leaned closer, moving his face near to Ailyssa's. Her unseeing eyes darted, not knowing where to be directed. Fear gleamed on their milky surface, and he recalled the first time he'd gazed upon her face when she'd perched on the edge of the bed at Jubha Kyna.

The muscles in his jaw relaxed. His stiffening staff shrank in his grip.

Nothing had changed. If he allowed her to touch him, she'd still know his body, his private bits. But now, she wouldn't discover them because she wanted to, but because he made her.

Juddah lowered his arm, drew a shuddering breath and let it out, the air moving his whiskers. Ailyssa turned her head away.

"I..."

He meant for more words to follow the one, but they refused to pass his lips. The flush of embarrassment returned to his hidden cheeks and he stumbled back a step, gut knotting at what he'd almost done.

He knew better, more effective ways to relieve his anger, his frustration, his shame.

Turning his back on the cowering woman, he stalked across the barn, threw the door open with a thud, then slammed it shut behind him.

Across the yard, the well-digging man saw him emerge and returned to shoveling. Juddah stomped across the grass toward him.

***

Ailyssa withered against the wall, struggling to keep herself from shaking as her knees went watery and she sank to the dirt floor. She inhaled heavily, using the gulp of manure-and-must-tinged breath to calm her nerves somewhat.

Whatever Juddah intended, whatever she'd done in

his mind to deserve it, had passed. He'd left the barn and, though a thick rope bound her, she was safe.

For now.

She rested against the rough boards, the racing beat of her heart slowing as the baby birds hidden in the rafters returned to their normal twittering after the disturbance. The white haze hid everything from her, but she doubted she could imagine what drove Juddah to drag her into the barn, even if she possessed the ability to see.

From the beginning, she'd sensed a volatility in him and it frightened her, but she ignored it more often than not. Without him, she wouldn't have escaped the awfulness of Jubha Kyna. Instead of the unpleasantry of being kept in a barn, she'd be spending her days beneath stinking farmers who wanted nothing more than to penetrate her despite the loss of her blood. For rescuing her, she owed him a debt.

But at what point would the debt be paid? How long must she put up with this treatment now she had a way to get her sight back and another man to help her?

The thought gave her pause as the last of the fearful tension left her.

What will the Goddess think of me relying on a man again?

She didn't know what to think or feel about the Goddess anymore. After so many turns of the seasons dedicating her life to worship and servitude, she'd have expected things to turn out differently. Sometimes she thought the Matriarch had deserted her, other times she thought this a test.

Sometimes she wondered if the Goddess existed at all.

The sacrilege seeping into her mind shocked her, but the clank of chain and rustle of footsteps in tall grass made her forget.

Juddah's coming back.

***

Moving with purposeful noise, Juddah stopped a horse-length from the man digging his well—too far away for the swing of a spade to reach him. The rage and shame roiling in him threatened to burst through his lips, tensed the muscles in his arms, and curled his hands into fists, but he didn't speak. Hitting the fellow again would help assuage his anger, but also build his shame and delay the digging of the well.

If he let go of control, the man would soon fill a potato sack in the barn, and he didn't want that to happen, not with so much work left for him to do.

Juddah watched as the fellow scooped another spade full of dirt over his shoulder, then stopped upon noticing his captor. Shovel in hand, he met Juddah's gaze, waited.

He'd already discovered many times the man didn't understand his words anyway, so he didn't bother trying. Instead, he made a rough gesture, jerking his thumb to one side and hoping the fellow might understand he wanted him to toss aside the spade. When he didn't, Juddah pointed at the digging tool and gestured again. The fellow looked at his hands gripping the worn, wooden handle, then threw the spade on the pile of fresh-turned earth.

Juddah tugged at his beard, took a step back and waved his hands toward himself, letting the man know he should climb out of the modest hole. He did. Another signal to stay put and Juddah retrieved the key from the bib pocket of his overalls and undid the lock tethering his captive to the steel spike in the ground.

"I had enough of both of you," he grumbled as he straightened, the words intended for himself rather than for the man. "Going to lock you up where you can see her but not touch her."

He walked a wide berth around the stranger, the distance between them enough for the chain to stay taut, then he yanked it to get the fellow moving toward the outbuilding. Having learned his place, he complied.

They crossed the yard, metal links clanking, and Juddah threw open the barn door with a thump. Behind him, Kooj let out a bark from the porch, but he ignored the dog as he swung his arm to urge the well-digger across the threshold.

"Get in there."

The man passed by him close enough for Juddah to smell the tang of sweat digging had brought to his skin. It coaxed a crooked smile to his lips beneath his sagging whiskers.

She ain't gonna enjoy the way you stink, fella.

He entered the barn after him, letting the door swing closed, and Kooj barked again. The woman crouched on the floor with her back to the wall. She swung her sightless gaze toward them as they entered and stared, her milky eyes settling on Juddah despite her inability to see him. He diverted his face, ashamed, his shrunken staff retreating farther.

"Get over there," he said pushing the well-digger by the shoulder.

The man stumbled across the dirt floor, head turned toward the woman cowering against the wall, and Juddah wondered if he wanted to ask if she was hurt. Would he do that if he could speak, or would he be smart enough to hold his tongue?

Juddah gestured with his chin for the prisoner to move toward the far side of the room, giving him space to affix the chain to the stake in the floor. The fellow obeyed and Juddah knelt to lock him in place when Kooj broke into another noisy flurry.

"Damn it, Kooj," he hollered over his shoulder. "Be quiet."

But the dog didn't. The barking spilled off the porch and crossed the yard as the dog's shadow blocked the sun in one gap between wall boards after the next.

"What are you doing, dog?"

Juddah clicked the lock and hurried back to the barn door, not bothering to spare another glance at the stranger he'd found near-dead on the beach or the woman he'd saved from a religious whorehouse. In that moment, nothing mattered more than finding out what was going on with his only friend. He slammed the door and trudged across the yard, following the sound of the dog's constant barks.

"Kooj," he called, heading the direction the dog had gone.

He went three paces and stopped, brow furrowed and the corners of his mouth pulled into a frown. A figure stood at the edge of the forest, one that was becoming all too familiar to Juddah.

"Birk," he whispered.

An instant later, he realized the pesky man had brought friends.

XXIII Man From Across the Sea - Intruders

He sat on the dirt floor, staring across the barn at Ailyssa where a thick rope with fraying strands bound her to the wall. His muscles ached from digging, but the pain in his limbs didn't keep him from finding his way to her side— he knew the chain was too short.

She sagged against the boards, chin drooping toward her chest, and he wished she could peer back at him. When they'd touched, and he'd understood the words she spoke, he experienced something he'd abandoned since finding himself a prisoner with no memory in this barn: he'd found hope.

But hope is fleeting when it bends to the whims of others. Especially men of Jud-dah's ilk.

He inhaled the all-too-familiar scents of old manure and filth, rubbed his bare and aching right shoulder, and crouched, watching the woman. After a moment, she lifted her chin, cocked her head.

Listening.

He did the same, but heard nothing other than the dog's barking. Ailyssa rose, dirt on the front of her shift where her knees had touched the floor. She attempted a step forward, but the rope tied around her wrists stopped her. Two heartbeats later, he detected the sounds of footsteps approaching the door and stood, too.

Sunlight flooded through the doorway as a hand threw the door open and Jud-dah's outline blocked it for an instant, then he hurried across the barn.

"Yewgod a'elp," he said in his unintelligible language. His feet kicked up a cloud of dust as he scuffled along, but not headed for the man; instead, he made for the wall of shelves and barrels. "Goda'elp orweer gunnad eye."

Metal rattled against wood as he wrapped his hands around the hilts of weapons protruding above the edge of a barrel. Jud-dah held them up, examining them, but the dots of rust along the blades and chips out of the edges didn't seem to dissatisfy him. When his captor faced him, he took a step away.

"Here," Jud-dah said and tossed a weapon with a wide, short blade toward him. He jumped back with a rattle of chain as the short sword thumped on the floor. "Pig idup anfallam ee. Yewgoda fitebes idemee ordye."

The bearded man stomped back toward the doorway, leaving his captive to stare after him, confused. His gaze slipped from Jud-dah's back to the sword lying in the dirt, then to Ailyssa. The woman's milky eyes stared after Jud-dah, her mouth twisted in what the man guessed to be fear. Their captor threw another sword—this one longer and heavier—at the woman's feet, startling her. She squealed.

Juddah halted in the doorway.

"Fukmee."

With Kooj's barks echoing across the yard, Jud-dah stalked back toward his well-digger. The prisoner glanced at the weapon lying near his feet, but didn't think he'd be able to reach it before Jud-dah got to him. And if he did, he couldn't be sure he'd know how to use it.

He didn't have to find out.

The bearded captor stopped at the spike driven into the floor, kneeled beside it, a third sword leaning against his thigh as he dug into the pocket of his bib overalls. He pulled out the piece of metal he used to open the contraption holding the chain, but bobbled it in his thick fingers. It hit the floor in a puff of dust.

"Dammit."

He scooped it up with a handful of dirt and fumbled it into the device, rotated it until it clicked. When it did, the chain came free of the spike, then he closed it again, leaving it attached to the last link.

Jud-dah stood and hurried toward the door again, jabbing the tip of his sword in Ailyssa's direction—a gesture, not a threat.

"Untiren cumwi fmee. Yewguna fiter yewgunad eye."

His shape blocked the sun again as he passed through the doorway, then he disappeared. Kooj barked and barked and the man stared at the sunlight shining into the barn in disbelief.

He's freed me.

Another thought followed the first.

Why?

Other thoughts might have followed if not for Ailyssa's words interrupting them. He jerked his gaze away from the sunlight, his eyes taking a moment to adjust as they found her pulling against her bindings, fear and desperation pulling her features taut.

"Pleez," she said. "Pleez undime ee."

The man gave his head a shake, picked the ill-tended sword off the floor, and crossed toward her, chain clanking behind him. When he reached Ailyssa, he put his hand on her arm instead of going straight to the knot holding her.

As soon as his fingers found her, a mist cleared in his brain.

"What's happening," he said, surprised by the words coming from his lips despite knowing to expect them. "What did he say?"

She stared at him, eyes clear, the fear disappearing for an instant, hidden beneath the wonder of seeing again. Distress rushed back in.

"He said you should untie me. He said we have to fight beside him or die."

***

The robed men stalked across the field toward the barn, the tall grass brushing their black robes. Juddah counted enough to take up all of his fingers and thumbs, plus Birk. Even with the man and woman helping him, he wouldn't stand a chance if they wanted a fight.

Why else were they here?

Kooj stood in the middle of the yard, barking himself hoarse, teeth exposed. The noise he made didn't deter the men; they'd come within a dozen paces of the half-dug well.

"Kooj, come," Juddah yelled as he stomped through the tall grass to meet the interlopers. His furry friend had other plans.

The dog shot out like a quarrel from a crossbow,

bounding across the yard and over the would-be well. His four feet touched the ground twice more, muscles beneath his glistening pelt rippling before he launched himself at the closest man.

The dog snarled and snapped his jaws as he flew and, for an instant, Juddah reveled in the thought of Kooj's teeth tearing out the fellow's throat. It would mean the start of a fight, but at least he'd be sure the blood of his enemy soaked the earth.

Before the dog's gaping mouth reached him, the robed man's hand shot out from the long sleeve, grasping Kooj by the neck, plucking him out of the air as though someone tossed him a ball. The dog's growl transformed immediately to a whimper. He scrabbled with his front paws, but the man twisted his wrist and the sharp crack of Kooj's neck snapping stopped Juddah in his tracks.

"No."

He whispered the word, glaring at the fellow holding his limp dog dangling from one hand. Rage exploded in Juddah's chest. He brandished the sword, clenched his teeth hard enough to cause himself pain. Muscles in his forearm strained with the tightening grip on his weapon as he resumed his path toward his adversaries, feet stomping the ground.

The robed fellow responded by tossing Kooj's body at him.

The dog hit the dirt a few arm lengths in front of Juddah and skidded to a stop, tongue lolling between slack jaws, back legs twisted. Juddah halted, stared at Kooj's blank eyes. His hand went limp; the sword fell from his grip and he dropped to his knees.

"Kooj?"

He slipped one hand under the dog's neck, one under his shoulder, and pulled the animal toward him, rested its head on his knees. It swiveled in a way he'd never felt it move.

"It's gonna be okay, Kooj." He ran his hand along the top of the dog's head and down his neck, buried his fingers in his scruff. "Everything's gonna be okay."

It occurred to him it might be wise to take up the sword and defend himself, but the thought got ignored, same as the one that told him he shouldn't cry because Birk'd see him and tell everyone at Krin's tavern. The weapon lay in the dirt, the tears got lost in Juddah's tangled beard.

"Oh, Kooj."

When Juddah next raised his head, the unwanted crying had made Birk and his robe-wearing friends smeared and blurry, but it didn't change the fact they'd formed a rough circle around him. Juddah snorted a wad of snot back into his nose and glared at Birk, despair giving way to anger.

"Where is he?" Birk said. "Where is the man from across the sea?"

Juddah clenched his jaw and shook his head, scanning the grass for where his sword ended up. It lay on the ground to his right, nearer than an arm's-length away but less than a hand's breadth from one of the robed men's bare feet. It might've been the fellow who murdered Kooj, but Juddah didn't know. No matter; he wanted to kill him and stuff him in a sack, whether it was him who'd done it or one of the others.

"Look at me," Birk demanded.

Juddah did, taking in as many of the others as possible. He didn't see a sword or pike amongst them. If they bore no arms, he might beat them, even without help from Ailyssa and the silent man.

Why didn't they come? I saved them when no one else would.

The tears clinging to Juddah's lashes continued to blur Birk's appearance, but he saw the man grasped no weapon in his hand, either. In fact, he held his arm out in front of him, palm stretched open. Juddah thought it a mighty odd gesture.

"Where is he?"

Juddah sniffed hard, pulling his response out of his nose and into the back of his throat, readying to launch it between his lips. But a glow appeared out of nowhere in Birk's open palm, stopping him. He stared at it, unable to move or react as the skinny man moved closer, closer.

Closer until Juddah screamed.

***

With an arm hooked through the man's, Ailyssa rubbed her wrists where the rope had chafed her skin. She stayed close to keep from losing contact with him; if it ceased, her sight would, too.

He peeked around the doorway, shielding her to keep her from seeing what transpired, but it didn't stop her from hearing.

Barking. Snarling.

"Kooj, come!"

Four paws beating the ground. Growl. Whimper. Snap.

The final sound contained something ugly and painful. She realized it wasn't the sound made by a foot stepping on a dry branch, but a living thing. She winced when she heard it.

"Now. Let's go," the man said.

She didn't know his name, because he claimed he had none—or didn't know it either, at least—yet she followed him without question. As she followed Juddah, and Creidra before him, the Goddess before them all.

Will I ever stop following?

Ailyssa adjusted her grip on the sword, the weapon's hilt foreign in her hand. The man stepped out of the doorway, pulling her along behind him, but he didn't head the same direction as Juddah. Instead, he pulled her the opposite way, to the right, toward where she suspected they'd find the sea.

He moved with stealth, the length of chain wrapped around his forearm to prevent it from clanking. His movement forced her to concentrate on her footing to keep up, but she stole a glance over her shoulder.

Juddah knelt in the middle of the yard, Kooj in front of him, the dog's head in his lap. Even from a distance, she understood the snap she'd heard had come from the animal. The barking had ceased immediately after and not resumed. Juddah hung his head over his lost companion, so he didn't notice the group of men creeping up around him.

Ailyssa dragged her feet, attempting to stop her companion, but he continued pulling her along. She yanked her arm away and their connection broke for an instant. White overtook her vision and panic tightened her chest until he grabbed her by the wrist.

"No," she said. He didn't respond. "We can't leave him."

The man stopped and faced her, gaze flickering past her for an instant before finding her eyes.

"He meant to kill me and rape you," he said, his tone angry and desperate. "Who knows why those others are here or what they'll do to us. Do you want to take that chance?"

Ailyssa stared into his face, barely recognizing it from the man whose arms she'd collapsed into in the barn when her sight first returned. His features were hardened, his expression dire. Were all men this changeable? Juddah had been.

Juddah.

The thought of him squeezed her heart. She looked back over her shoulder at the men ringing her rescuer, the man who'd been her captor. The robed men blocked him from her sight except for the side of his face, the dog's hind legs folded over its body. She cringed at what had happened, but her companion was right: if they did this to Kooj, to Juddah, what might they do to her?

She spun away from the scene and allowed the man to lead her past the ramshackle house and into the woods, toward the sound of water. It filled her ears as they moved.

Until Juddah screamed.

XXIV Horace - The Green

Wakefulness arrived with a poundin' skull and a ringin' in his ears what refused to go away.

Horace pulled his tongue from where it stuck to the roof o' his mouth and smacked his lips. The sound it made within his noggin worsened the pain, which prompted a groan outta him, which then put a worse hurtin' in his head. He'd been in this predicament before and understood what it needed to make it stop...more ale.

The ol' sailor pushed himself from prone to sittin', eyes closed tight lest openin' them allowed his eyeballs to jump clear outta his skull. He steadied himself with both hands on what his brain thought should've been a mattress, or a hard floor, but what were plainly dirty ground covered with what felt like needles fallen from some tree. A breeze caressed Horace's cheek, disturbin' his whiskers, and the tiny wind carried realization along with it.

More ale?

Weren't no ale what brought Horace Seaman to this place o' splittin' headache and dry mouth this time. He wished it were so, but things far worse'n too much drinkin' did it.

The ol' sailor pried his eyes open, stuck shut as they

was by more sleep'n he'd had in longer'n he might recall. The lids and lashes came apart and light flooded in, blindin' him and bringin' more pain. He caught a blurry glimpse o' brown and green—leaves and tree trunks, he suspected—then threw his forearm in front o' his face to block it out, not wantin' to see neither the trees nor the light.

His memory returned: the rocky beach, the cliff what collapsed under him, the tasty apples he'd ate before dozin' off.

More'n dozin', judgin' by the sun.

He forced his lids open again, filterin' the sunlight with his grubby shirt-covered forearm until his peepers grew accustomed to the concept o' lettin' in the glare. When they did, he lowered his arm, notin' the brown tree needles stuck to his palm. He brushed them away on his pant leg and turned his attention back to his surroundin's.

Dense foliage encircled the small clear spot o' ground upon which Horace sat. Outta the thick brush grew tall trees with wide trunks, their high boughs blockin' out a part o' the sun's light, but not enough for the sailor's achin' melon. He tilted his head to look up at their height, but his noggin protested so much, he gave up on the attempt.

Don't remember them trees bein' so tall.

He let the thought slide through his throbbin' brain but paid little attention to it. The pasty film on his tongue demanded he pay it more mind; without ale to soothe him, he'd need to find himself some water. It'd do wonders for his mouth and throat and help his poundin' head, too.

Horace straightened his legs and pushed himself to stand. His back creaked, his knees popped, but he got up, stomach lurchin' as he did. A wave o' nausea weakened his knees and threatened to make him lose them apples he'd ate. He steadied himself with a hand restin' against the trunk o' the apple tree as he waited for the feelin' to pass.

Why do I feel like I drank too much? I ain't had ale in...

The thought made his arid mouth go drier still, so he let it fade without bein' completed. He dragged a deep sigh between his lips and puffed it out before haulin' in another chest full o' air. It tasted o' forest: cedar and pine and dirt and moss. Not unpleasant like the flavor o' the hateful sea what always wanted to kill him, but not the fresh, untainted breath he wished to have in his lungs, neither. It'd have to do.

The ol' sailor stayed for a spell, bent at the waist and gaspin' in air until his stomach settled and the ache in his noggin eased up a might. Findin' his balance and sense back, he straightened, movin' like a man what thought his spine might be broken, though he worried most about his head.

His hand remained against the apple tree to keep him steady, its rough and pitted bark bringin' him a sliver o' comfort. He filled his lungs again, this time breathin' in through his nose; about then, things began seemin' odd to him.

The apple tree shouldn't be so rough.

He moved his hand, his fingertips tracin' the deep fissures in the tree's bark on which he steadied himself. His brow creased.

Maybe just got spun 'round.

His gaze crawled across the brush surroundin' him, searchin' for the apple tree, his belly grumblin' now at the possibility o' havin' more o' the tasty fruit despite how they'd made him feel. But he didn't spy it, nor the path what might've led him here.

The path were disappearin' when I sat me down to eat them apples.

The thought were the truth, but it didn't make his worry ease up. In fact, it had the opposite effect. A sense o' dread kindled in his belly, forcin' aside both hunger and nausea. He took his hand away from the steadyin' tree and pivoted in a slow circle, careful not to jar himself and increase the pain throbbin' against the inside o' his forehead.

Evergreen trees surrounded him with not a leafy bough amongst them. Cedars, jack pines, and others he'd heard people what know these sorts o' things call fir, spruce, and hemlock. He knew enough to tell them apart by the shapes o' their needles, but couldn't recall which were which no more'n a man o' the forest would recognize a bowline from a halfhitch.

For sure, none o' them was apple trees.

Disoriented, his head spun. He turned another circle, too fast this time, and the pain swelled inside his skull. Horace groaned and put a hand over one eye, the other half o' his gaze searchin' the ground around him.

Did I walk here in my sleep?

To the best o' his knowledge, he had no such habit. Course, because he'd been asleep when it happened, weren't no way to be sure any more'n bein' certain whether he snored or not. He'd never woken in a place he didn't expect to be, except when he'd taken too much ale, and then it weren't such a surprise. Perhaps havin' spent so many turns o' the seasons sleepin' in a ship's cabin with nowhere to go made it so he wouldn't notice such a thing.

His hurried inspection o' the area offered nothin' he recognized, and no sign o' how he'd got here. No path to follow and no broken branches, torn leaves, nor trampled bits o' earth to suggest a method o' gettin' to this spot.

A shiver rattled Horace's teeth. In the time since Dunal'd put him o'er the side o' the Devil o' the Deep, the ol' sailor'd seen more o' what he'd call magic'n he'd experienced in the rest o' his life. And now he found himself in the Green, where no man should e'er be and no man'd e'er survived to tell the tale.

The pain in Horace's head didn't diminish, but he succeeded in pushin' it from his attention. That is to say, the panic what started in his chest and leeched throughout his body overcame the throbbin' ache behind his forehead and the hunger tearin' at his gut.

A breeze shivered through the brush and the ol' sailor became sure the broad leaves was movin' closer, closin' in around him. Horace's gazed jerked back and forth, then up. Through the boughs hangin' above his head, he made out the glowin' ball o' the sun. Havin' spent near all his life on the decks o' one ship or another, if he knew one thing, it were how to find his way based on the sun's place in the sky.

Horace got his bearin's, determinin' which direction he'd find sunrise and which sunset, but what to do with the knowledge now he possessed it? The Green were an evil and foreign place, somewhere he knew nothin' about and harbored no wish to spend his time. So where to go?

The sea.

More'n once now, the vast ocean'd done its best to end ol' Horace Seaman, but it suddenly seemed more friendly'n a place where he'd find magic and gods only knew what else.

With a chill in his spine and an ache in his noggin, Horace left behind the small clearin', plungin' into the thick brush and pickin' his way windward toward the sea, not a thought in his head about what he'd do when he arrived.

***

Somewhere along the way, Horace'd left the awful throb in his skull behind. He were happy for its absence, but not havin' it to distract him made him notice his thirst and hunger. That and the plain fact he should've found himself at the top o' the cliff leadin' to the shore long ago, yet he stood deeper in the forest'n before.

The sailor stopped and tilted his head back, searchin' through o'erhead branches until he located the sun. When he found it, his lips pressed tight together and his forehead crinkled.

It weren't where it were supposed to be. Again.

Each time he'd directed his peepers skyward to confirm he headed the right direction, he found the ball o' fiery light in a different place than expected. The only explanation were that somethin'd gotten him turned about over and over again, but he didn't believe he'd veered from his path.

Keepin' a straight line walkin' through a forest were harder'n findin' one's way across the water. Atop the sea, no trees nor rocks nor thickets o' bramble blocked your route and made you change course. Mind, weren't no waves wantin' to knock you o'er nor wind and currents pushin' and pullin' you in the forest, neither. Both had their challenges, but Horace fancied himself a good enough navigator he shouldn't't've been this far off track.

The first few times he'd noticed the sun sittin' in a spot where he didn't expect it, he'd corrected his course. After a while, he followed his instincts instead, until now he found himself lost without so much as a hint o' brine in the air.

He stood still as the figurehead mounted to a ship at port, nothin' movin' but for his eyes dartin' back and forth. His breath he held captive in his lungs as he listened to buzzin' insects, the beat o' his own heart, the rustle o' barely noticeable wind in the trees.

A branch snappin'.

Horace whirled toward the sound, heart beatin' faster all o' a sudden. Nothin' to see but trees and brush, branches and leaves and needles, just the same as ev'rywhere else. A bird croaked from the boughs high above, its unfamiliar sound starling the sailor and makin' him jump. He glanced upward and saw nothin', though it cried out again. Wings fluttered, branches bounced, but he caught no glimpse o' the bird. It crawked once more, the noise sounding eerily like a man with no voice attempting to speak the sailor's name, then it went silent.

Horace spent awhile stayin' where he were, his breath doin' its best to keep pace with his racin' heart. The feeble breeze fell away to nothin', but the rattlin' o' tree limbs continued. The ol' sailor walked a tight circle, eyes searchin' through the leaves o' bushes, sweat what weren't there a moment before comin' to his forehead and palms o' his hands.

A noise bigger'n the others came from behind and Horace spun again, expectin' to see the same nothin' he'd found before. In the distance, a thin-trunked tree shook, seemingly by its own accord. Another trembled, closer. The sailor stuttered back a step, feet draggin' in the needle-littered dirt. His legs desperately wanted him to about face and run, but his head told him he couldn't be sure any other place'd be safer for him.

I don't see nothin'. Maybe my peepers are playin'—

A wailin' what didn't sound o' this earth joined the hubbub o' jostlin' branches and the ol' sailor's feet won out o'er his brain.

Horace leaped from his spot like one o' the rats some men on the ships liked to race and bet upon. He plunged though the brush, arms raised to keep branches from pokin' him in the eyes, but he didn't take no time to look back and find the source o' the caterwaulin'. He didn't care what made the racket, preferred not to see it.

His feet throbbed and ached from so long wearin' the boots what pinched them, but he pushed on, fear driving him through tangles o' branches and walls o' leaves. He gave no consideration to what might be on the other side o' them, only cared about gettin' away from whate'er were behind him.

Until he found out what lay ahead.

XXV Dansil - An Unexpected Meeting

By the time the sun prepared to set on the third day, frayed nerves and disappointment made both men grip their reins tighter and eye each other warily.

Every town, every inn and tavern they passed, they stopped to ask if anyone had seen anything unusual: a young woman new to the area, sisters of the Goddess traveling together. At Trenan's insistence, they didn't mention the red robe. No need to—it would come up on its own if it had been seen; if not, mentioning it would only instill unnecessary fear.

"Time to stop for the night," Trenan said as the sky faded toward gray.

"Another fucking wasted day," Dansil grumbled as he reined in his horse and slid out of the saddle. Grumbling appeared to have become the only way the queen's guard chose to communicate; still more than the master swordsman wanted from him.

Trenan followed him off his perch and led his horse to a spot under the boughs of an ancient ash tree. He wrapped the lead around a low hanging branch and the steed lowered its head to nibble at the sparse grass growing at its base.

"It's not much farther to Ikkundana," Trenan said, his back to his companion. When the queen's guard didn't respond, the master swordsman faced him. "Four or five more sunrises should see us there."

Dansil stood beside his horse, the lead hanging loose,

a glare hardening the queen's guard's features. Trenan noted he'd taken his weapon from its riding place tethered to the saddle and hung it from the strap at his back.

"Don't fucking matter how many times the sun rises, we ain't going to find the princess in that disease-ridden death trap."

Trenan took a step in his direction, fighting against training to keep his hand from moving toward Godsbane. As much as he didn't enjoy traveling with Dansil, it was better to have two of them watching for Danya's trail. A fight to the death would help no one, least of all Ishla's daughter.

"What would you have us do then?"

"You know what we'd be doing if I was in command."

"You seem to think you are most of the time. So, what would you do?"

Dansil licked his lips. "I'd take us back to the Horseshoe and get a troop of soldiers. Thirty swinging dicks'd have a better chance of finding the whelps than the two of us."

"Osis will return with men. Erral won't let the search for his children fade."

"The king will more likely send them after you. It's your task to babysit his brats, and you failed."

Heat rose in Trenan's cheeks. He took a breath rather than say what first came to mind.

"I wouldn't feel so safe, were I you, queen's guard. You were the one holding onto our only lead in finding the king's children when he escaped your grasp."

"The idiot knew nothing," Dansil growled.

"So he led us to believe."

"His dead mother was the brains of that operation. Ain't sayin' much." His eyes narrowed and the start of a grin tilted one end of his lips. "Kind of similar to our situation."

Trenan took one more step toward Dansil and the queen's guard tensed, the faint smirk disappearing.

"I remind you who you are talking to."

Dansil snorted. "I know who I'm talking to: a one-armed has-been who'd be nothing if he hadn't sacrificed himself for the king. If you hadn't lost that arm for him, you'd be lucky to be a foot soldier with nothing to say but thank you if I pissed on your boots."

"Why don't you come over here and try it." Trenan's hand edged toward his sword's hilt.

Dansil moved like he wanted to reach for the haft of his axe, but he stopped. He let his arm go slack again and plastered a smile across his face.

"Wouldn't do me no good to kill you, so stop trying to make me. If you're dead, no one will care so much about you fucking the queen. It's better to let the king figure out what to do with you rather'n me."

"Brave words, Dansil." Trenan took his gaze away from the queen's guard, surveyed their surroundings: trees, brush, and not much else. "Brave words from a man alone in the woods with someone with reason to wish him ill."

Trenan turned back to his companion as Dansil's eyes flickered away. In that brief instant, the swordmaster glimpsed a sliver of fear flashing across the queen's guard's face, but a defiant sneer quickly replaced it.

"You wouldn't dare. You better hope I don't get thrown off my horse and bust my neck. Your secret'd come out whether it's your sword doing me in or anything else. Big man shouldn't be threatening me." Dansil approached Trenan until two paces separated them. He leaned toward him and spoke the last words in a whisper: "You should be protecting me."

The queen's guard pushed past, bumping his shoulder against Trenan's as he did. He growled in the back of his throat and watched his companion stride off into the woods, leaving the master swordsman to set up camp alone. The prospect didn't disappoint him.

With Dansil gone from sight, he retrieved the other man's horse, picketing it under the same ash tree as his own steed, then set to lighting a fire. His ire dissipated with the queen's guard's absence.

***

Anger roiled in Dansil's belly as he strode through the woods, stepping over fallen branches and pushing through tangles of brush. He'd hoped getting away from Trenan might calm him, but it had the opposite effect. Each step increased his indignation. He'd worked hard his entire life to become a queen's guard, only to be outranked by a second-rate soldier who attained his position through losing an arm and fucking a woman who didn't belong to him.

How was that fair?

"It ain't fair," Dansil said aloud as he kicked at a clutch of toadstools that had found their way up out of the dirt and through a patch of moss. Their dun heads exploded upon contact with the toe of his boot, spraying chunks through the ferns growing around them. For an instant, he imagined it to be Trenan's head he'd kicked, his pathetic brains pattering against the ferns' leaves. He smiled and laughed, kicked the remaining toadstools he'd missed the first time. The noise he created masked the sound of a footstep behind him and he didn't realize he wasn't alone until the sharp edge of a knife pressed against his throat.

"Don't move or say nothin' or your blood'll paint the ground red."

The words were hoarse and choked, foul breath touched his cheek. Dansil froze, eyes wide. At first, he thought Trenan had followed him, but he soon understood the voice didn't belong to the master swordsman. A brigand, then, lying in wait to rob whoever passed by.

A thief would lurk at the side of the road, not in the middle of the forest.

"What do you want? I have nothing of value."

"You have something I covet: your life."

Dansil swallowed hard and the edge of the knife bit into his flesh. Real or imagined, he felt a drop of blood roll along his neck.

"I don't know you," the queen's guard whispered, taking care not to move lest the blade further open his flesh.

"Yes, you do."

The unseen attacker took the knife from Dansil's throat and pushed his shoulder, forcing him to spin around. Before he could reach for the axe at his back, the point of the blade found the spot under his chin. This time he had no doubt it broke the skin.

The man holding the knife seemed familiar, but he wore a disguise of dirt and old sweat smeared across his face that kept Dansil from recognizing him. With a scowl, he noticed his attacker was missing an ear, an eye, and one arm within a handspan of his shoulder. He tensed, muscles coiled and ready to grab for his axe at the first opportunity.

"Don't be makin' no moves," the disfigured man said. "You won't breathe so well with a hole under your chin."

Dansil raised his hands, showing his palms. "I don't know what I've done to wrong you, but if you tell me, let's see how I can make it right. I have no money here, but at my home—"

"I don't want your fucking money."

"Then what?"

"You killed my mother."

It was as if his words cleared the dirt and snot off his

face, revealing him to Dansil for the first time.

"Stirk?"

A grimace that may have been the man's version of a smile crept across his lips. "Now you know. And you knows what you did. I'm here to kill the man responsible for lopping off my ma's head."

"Bieta," Dansil whispered, his mind working hard to figure a way out of the situation with his life still his own.

"Bieta," Stirk agreed. "You took her life, and now I'm gonna take yours."

"Whoa, hold on. You said you wanted the man responsible for killing her, didn't you? Sorry, Stirk, but that ain't me."

A scowl creased Stirk's brow and the muscles in his arm tightened as though he might lunge forward with the knife. Dansil held his breath.

"I was standing right beside you," the disfigured man seethed. "I watched the axe on your back take her head from her shoulders."

A barely contained sob choked the last few of the man's words, giving Dansil hope he might take advantage of his emotion.

"You're right, Stirk. I'm the one who swung the axe, but I didn't want to." Dansil dabbed his own words with a touch of remorse—enough for him to notice, but not too much to be disbelieved. "I am but a soldier obeying my superior."

"You lie."

"No. You saw him, too. Did you not see him nod, giving me the signal to take your mother's life? If I'd disobeyed, my blood would have spilled, too."

"Why would I care if you lost your life? That's why I'm here."

"Because if I had, you'd be dead, too."

Stirk raised an eyebrow and Dansil saw he was

getting close to saving himself, or buying himself time, at least.

"I let you go."

The expression on Stirk's dirty face shifted to disbelief. For a moment, Dansil expected the disfigured man might burst out laughing.

"The one-armed fella got distracted and I ran away. How is that you letting me go?"

"You think I couldn't have caught you? Thrown a dagger into your back? Killing a man in battle is one thing, but I have no desire to kill unarmed, innocent citizens."

"Innocent?"

Dansil nodded. "We had no proof you brought harm to the prince."

"We didn't." Stirk shook his head hard enough the knife at Dansil's throat moved, too, the tip grating against his flesh. The queen's guard winced and his attacker realized why and edged the dagger away. Dansil breathed a relieved sigh and finally swallowed.

"I know you didn't. That's why I didn't want to kill your ma. Trenan made me."

"The one-armed man."

"Yes. He's the king's confidant and of high rank in the king's army. I have no choice but to obey his commands, and he commanded me to take Bieta's head."

Stirk's eyes flickered side to side in his dirt-masked face and Dansil saw the thought process they expressed. He concentrated on keeping a satisfied grin from his lips.

"You swung the axe, but he ordered you to do it."

Dansil was unsure if it was a question or a statement, but he nodded anyway.

"Then the one-armed man is who I should kill." Stirk glanced over his shoulder, then back at Dansil. He took a step backward. "He's over there? Where you came from?"

"He is."

"Then I'll kill him now." Another step away gave Dansil enough distance between them for him to pluck the axe from his back and cut the man in two before he could react. He didn't.

"Now is not the time."

"Now is the best time."

Dansil shook his head. "Trenan is the most dangerous swordsman in the kingdom. If he has any inkling his life is threatened, you will lose yours."

Stirk stared hard at Dansil. "Why would he think he's in danger?"

"He's camped by the side of a road. Any good soldier treats that like a dangerous situation."

"Then I will wait until morning."

Dansil stepped toward Stirk, aware doing so put himself back in harm's way. The disfigured man tensed.

"Let me help you."

"Why do you want to help me?"

"I have my reasons." He took another step, putting his throat a flick of the wrist away from the tip of the knife. "I've wanted to see Trenan dead for a long time, but there has been naught I could do. You can, with my help."

Stirk's gaze bore into Dansil. His brow twitched, his lips pressed together until the color drained from them. In that instant, the queen's guard saw what his mother had meant to him: she'd led him, made the decisions. All he needed was someone to fill that space.

"You can trust me," Dansil said, inching forward until the knife touched his throat. "I let you live and I want him dead."

A tense moment passed, the near-silent forest pressing in around them like a crowd awaiting the disfigured man's reply. When it stretched on too long,

Dansil worried he might have played his hand wrong, but then Stirk lowered the knife.

"All right. I'll use your help, but if you want to live once the one-armed man is dead, you still need to convince me you're his puppet."

Dansil bit down on his back teeth and swallowed hard at Stirk's choice of words, but he kept himself from reacting. Instead, he nodded his agreement.

Stirk spun around and stalked toward where Dansil had left Trenan, making too much noise as he did.

How did he ever sneak up on me?

The queen's guard hurried after him, grabbing his shoulder to stop him. Stirk whirled, dagger raised, and Dansil faltered back a step.

"Now is not the time," he said. "If you want to kill the kingdom's best swordsman, it will have to be when he least expects it."

"When?"

"When we reach a town. A night at an inn will relax his defenses."

Stirk nodded. "So be it. We'll meet each night at this time. Make sure you're away from him so we can find each other."

"But how—?"

The second half of the question remained in Dansil's mouth, unspoken when the disfigured man disappeared into thin air.

XXVI Kuneprius - Decision

Twenty-seven. Twenty-eight. Twenty-nine...*twenty-nine...twenty-nine.*

Kuneprius cursed under his breath; this had never happened to him. Since the night he rescued

Vesisdenperos from the women of the Goddess, he'd counted—the time he held air captive in his lungs, his steps, his heartbeats, and anything else he could think to count. He did it to calm himself, keep himself grounded, and he suspected he'd reached numbers far higher than most folk imagined existed. He'd never missed one, so why couldn't he remember what came after twenty-nine?

He shook his head, rubbed his eyes with the heels of his palms, removed them quickly. Touching his face reminded him how sins had piled up and piled up, dirtying his cheeks for more days than his foggy mind remembered. How long since he'd tried to wash them away?

Not since the inn. And I didn't wash then, only got wet.

He shuddered at the thought and his step faltered as dead faces sprang to mind. The slaughter at the inn had negated any benefit he received from the water in the bowl and instilled the need to scrub more. A shiver ran up his back; he'd seen enough blood spilled because of him.

Kuneprius drew his tongue across his dry lips and immediately regretted having done so. To him, the coppery flavor of blood resided on his face. The blood of the girl, of the first barkeep, of the two children, and of those who lost their lives because of his carelessness at the inn.

And soon they will taste of the blood of a Small God.

His stomach tied itself in a knot and he thought that, if it had contained food, he'd likely have retched. But too much time had passed since the meal at the inn to worry about such things.

He raised his eyes and stared at the back of the golem walking ahead of him, Thorn thrown over his shoulder like a sack of vegetables being hauled off to market. In the days since the slaughter, he'd often wished his glare was daggers to rid the world of the abomination his friend helped create.

He was merely the sculptor, taken advantage of for his talent with clay. He formed this thing but did nothing to make it a monster.

No doubt remained in Kuneprius' mind that the boy he'd raised to a man was gone, his life sacrificed in the name of an ancient prophecy intended to bring an end to everything. One more death to wash from his flesh, for it was he who brought Vesisdenperos to Kristeus. Had he not, the golem wouldn't exist, all those people would yet live, and the world wouldn't hang on the precipice with the life of an innocent creature from the Green.

Kuneprius inhaled a sigh through his nose; he understood what needed to be done. But how?

He cast his gaze around for the first time in forever and saw farmers' fields on both sides of them, the waving sea of yellow wheat blazing in the midday sun. Not far ahead, the trees began again, their shadows falling across the dirt track upon which they traveled.

Kuneprius blinked. Once, twice...a few more times after that, but he didn't bother counting. The fact they followed a road between fields growing food meant something, but he couldn't figure out what. His sleep- and nourishment-deprived brain spun around its meaning, but refused to find the answer. Instead, he wobbled, struggled to stay on his feet.

I need rest or I cannot go on.

He wondered if the clay man would allow him time for respite or if he'd push on and leave him behind, his strides relentless until he arrived at his destination. Now they had the Small God, the monster had little reason to care about the fate of his mentor.

He curled his fingers into fists, clenched his jaw and winced at the pain both caused his aching muscles.

Despite his discomfort, he pushed his pace faster, determined to catch up.

Determined to fix what he had helped create.

Thorn lay limp over the clay man's shoulder. Kuneprius didn't remember the last time he'd moved, and couldn't be sure he still drew breath. The beat of his heart increased in speed. What if he died before Kristeus sacrificed him? Would those who watch from above remain banished? Or might they return when the Small God of the Green expired, even without flourish or ceremony from the Brothers and the priests?

He didn't want to find out. Maybe he was ultimately responsible for the blood on his hands, but the accursed prophecy set it all in motion. Enough people had died.

I have to stop this.

"Please," he called out, his scratchy voice—unused for days—catching in his throat. "Please, we must rest."

The golem continued his implacable pace without hesitation or any sign he'd heard his companion's plea. Kuneprius sucked his bottom lip into his mouth, chewed on it until his own salty blood flowed onto his tongue. He increased his pace further, closing the distance between himself and the clay monstrosity, the effort sending droplets of sweat cascading from his temples. They passed from the sun beside the farmers' fields into the shade cast by the trees before he caught up.

"Ves." Using his friend's name to reference the brute brought the bitterness of bile to his tongue. "I can't continue without rest and food."

No reaction. Kuneprius moved close enough to reach out and touch the thing's clay flesh if he wanted. The notion repulsed him, but he raised his hand anyway, fingers shaking. Before they brushed the animated mud, he changed his mind and grasped Thorn's wrist instead.

The Small God's flesh was cool to his fingertips and Kuneprius' heart leapt into his throat.

Is it too late?

If so, what did it mean for him? For the world?

Thorn's finger twitched and he raised his chin off the clay monster's back far enough to tilt his face toward Kuneprius. His eyelids opened to slits revealing rheumy eyes. Before doing anything else, his energy flagged and his head fell back against the creature's back.

He's alive. But for how long?

It was a question without answer. The unfamiliar countryside offered no clue how far from Murtikara they might be, nor could he guess how long the poor fellow might last in his state.

I have to take action now.

"Forget about me. It's been days since Tho...the Small God ate. You may have forgotten, but living things need nourishment."

For an instant, Kuneprius thought the abomination's pace slowed but, before he could be sure, his own exhausted feet tangled with each other and he pitched forward. He caught the brunt of the fall with his hands, rocks digging painfully into his palms, but his chest struck the dirt track knocking the air from his lungs.

He lay still, struggling to regain his breath, panic tingling through him that he might not find it. After all he'd been through, to die in the middle of nowhere because he'd taken a fall...

A sliver of air squeaked into his constricted chest. It might have assuaged his fear if the certainty the clay man had left him to his own devices—taking the Small God away to fulfill the prophecy—hadn't replaced it.

Can't think about it now. Have to catch my breath.

He pressed his palms against the ground, the tip of his nose brushing the dirt, and concentrated. Another gulp of air made its way to his lungs, then another, and Kuneprius realized he'd survive the fall. But to what end?

When his breath returned to a resemblance of its norm, Kuneprius rolled onto his side, raised his head to see how far ahead the golem had gotten.

To his surprise, the thing stood facing him not five paces away. It had set Thorn down beside the track where the Small God lay limp. Dark veins showed through his near-white flesh in some places while sickly brown patches covered others. Kuneprius struggled to his hands and knees and dragged himself toward Thorn, ignoring the pain in his hands as he did. Upon reaching the Small God, he brushed dirt and blood from his palms and touched the small man's forehead.

"He needs food," Kuneprius implored. "He won't survive without it."

The golem stared at them with the same unreadable expression its sculpted face always wore. Its visage bore some resemblance to Vesisdenperos, a likeness he hadn't noticed before.

"He's dying."

Kuneprius lifted Thorn's hand and let it drop. It fell back to the ground, but whether it did so because the Small God was unable to hold it up anymore or because he played along, he couldn't say. He suspected the former.

Without a sound, the monster raised its arm and extended a finger, jabbing it toward them, then it turned away and strode into the trees.

It worked.

Leaves trembled and thin trees shook in the golem's wake; Kuneprius watched the signs of the beast's passing until the clay man's gray flesh disappeared amongst them. Its gesture had been an admonishment to stay put, a threat at what he'd do if they didn't, but Kuneprius had no such intention.

For sunrise after sunrise, he'd been unable to scrub the sin from his cheeks and their burden weighed upon him. This was his chance for atonement. His opportunity to set things right. It might cost him his life, but it might save so many others.

Kuneprius grabbed Thorn's arm and pulled him up. The Small God flopped and gave no aid: he wasn't feigning his inability to move.

"Get up."

Thorn's eyelids fluttered. His eyes spun, then settled on his companion and recognition flickered on their milky surface.

"Horace?"

"No, I'm not Horace," Kuneprius said as he draped Thorn's arm across his shoulders and put his around the Small God's waist. "But I will take you to him."

He inhaled a deep breath and pushed hard with his legs, dragging Thorn to his feet. Despite the Small God's diminutive size, he seemed impossibly heavy. Kuneprius faltered under his weight.

"Come on," he said and glanced back over his shoulder at where the golem had disappeared into the trees. No sign of him yet. "I need your help."

Thorn's legs shifted beneath him, taking some of the load off Kuneprius' shoulders, enough to allow him to walk.

"That's better."

He headed into the trees, away from the golem and the dirt track, half-dragging Thorn along with him, counting his stumbling steps as they went.

One. Two. Three...

XXVII Ailyssa - Fleeing

"Can we rest?"

The night hadn't been chilly, but it dragged on. When

was the last time she had a good night's sleep? Her energy-sapped limbs and sagging lids suggested it had been even longer than she might have thought.

Ailyssa followed the nameless man through the forest, their hands joined until the sun rose again. She desired to stop and enjoy the sights—tall trees, glimpses of ocean between their branches, colorful birds she'd never seen before—but he insisted they keep a brisk pace.

At least we're not running anymore.

"Not yet," he replied without casting a backward glance. "They may still follow us."

He hefted the chain he carried wrapped around his shoulder, the links clanking together, the muscles in his arm rippling. Ailyssa stepped over a broken branch lying in her path, careful where she set her tender foot. Why did everyone who rescued her want to hurry?

Why do I always need rescuing?

Similar thoughts had filled her mind through the night as they fled the robed men. Why was it so difficult to find someone to trust? Why did people want so much of her? What did she do to deserve this?

Who is this man leading me into the wilderness?

She wanted it all to be behind her. Olvana seemed so far away, so long ago, but she thought she might do anything to return to its plain walls, to the one place she'd ever felt safe. But had she? From the moment she birthed her first son, she'd worried about being forced out of the order, and it happened. They'd deserted her when she needed them most.

But Olvana's cloistered walls were safer than being pursued through the wilderness, lost with a man without a name. Even Jubha Kyna might be a better choice than the untamed woods and the mysterious men in robes.

They skirted a thicket aromatic of berries hidden amongst the dark green leaves; the bouquet made her stomach rumble. The surrounding trees thinned, giving way to more brush; the remaining trees grew with wide trunks, the forest floor carpeted with moss and fallen needles.

Ailyssa put thoughts of safety from her mind; no finding it here, so why distract herself with it? Instead, she concentrated on appreciating the beauty around her though, for the first time in her life, it wasn't life to the Goddess instilling it in her, but appreciation of her sight.

She looked right, attempting to catch sight of the shimmering sea, but the man had led her deeper into the forest without her notice. Nothing but trees and brush lay both ahead and to the sides. She peered over her shoulder: more trees, more brush.

And a flicker of black.

Ailyssa gasped but kept from making any further sound. She gripped her companion's hand tighter to gain his attention, but he paid her no mind so she squeezed again, made a low, sharp hiss between her lips.

He looked back at her without slowing, one brow raised in question.

"They're behind us," she said, her voice an urgent whisper.

The man slowed, stretched his neck to look past her, then stopped. Ailyssa gazed up into his face, watched his expression change. The urge to spin around and find out what he saw struck her, but she kept herself from doing so. She watched the way his mouth pulled down at the corners, his eyes narrowed, his nostrils flared.

"How can it be?" he whispered.

Finally, curiosity won out and she glanced back to find the robed figures descending on them. Before she got a good view of them, the man pulled her toward him.

He released her hand and the world went white for an instant. Her heart jumped and her breath caught, but then the trees and brush returned as he wrapped his arms around her. The chain looped around his arm pressed uncomfortably against her back.

What's he doing? Shouldn't we run?

The thought got lost as he pulled her tight against his bare chest and his scent filled her nostrils. Mixed with the scents of the forest, the odor of his perspiration added a sharp tang and, beneath it, a musk she recalled from her coupling ceremonies. The smell of a man.

Without thinking, she wrapped her arms around him, hands finding the smooth skin of his back and the muscles tightening beneath it as he gripped her against him. Her mind spun, worry of their pursuers sucked into its movement like a boat ushered into a whirlpool.

She laid her cheek against his chest.

An unfamiliar sensation tingled in the pit of her belly, spilled up into her chest, and down, too. The thrill of it—not unpleasant, anything but unpleasant—surprised her. In all her life, she'd never experienced such a sensation, not from being close to a man. Warmth, tingling, pleasure.

She closed her eyes and images came to her unbidden—men she'd known in coupling ceremonies and at Jubha Kyna. In her mind, they touched her, and the sensation in her midsection grew. Ailyssa licked her lips, opened her eyes, wondered how his skin might taste if she trailed the tip of her tongue across it.

A figure dressed in black jarred her from the unexpected and unfamiliar thoughts.

She glimpsed him beyond the edge of her companion's arm, passing within twenty paces of them. Though the cowl covering his head kept his face from her, she realized he surveyed the forest floor as he walked, searching for signs of their presence. They stood in plain sight, yet he went by without noticing them.

Ailyssa held her breath.

Another robed man passed, this one closer, creeping,

moving with purpose. The only man without a robe and cowl followed him, and Ailyssa understood this to be the fellow who'd stopped her and Juddah on the road from Jubha Kyna.

In one hand he held the end of a thick rope—the same one Juddah had used to bind her arms and hold her fast to the wall of the barn. The rope trailed out behind him, hanging semi-taut between him and the wrists of his prisoner.

Juddah!

One side of his beard was singed to stubble, the small patch of skin visible around it red and blistered. The eye on the same side was swollen shut and ringed by an ugly purple bruise; he limped as he walked.

He drew even with Ailyssa, cocked his head and stared straight at her.

Their gazes met, but no recognition gleamed in his one open eye, only defeat and despair. Blood matted the hair on the other side of his face and his right arm hung limp and useless. His gaze lingered, but she knew he didn't see her. He returned his attention to caring for his footing and a moment later, he was past.

Ailyssa closed her eyes and pressed her cheek tighter against her companion's chest.

***

The susurration of the surf rolling onto the rocky shore grew as the man led her away from the robed men and toward the sea. She'd remained quiet as long as possible.

"How come they didn't see us?"

He didn't respond. She stopped and released his hand, knowing it would throw her back into blindness but trusting him not to leave her. It may be she required his touch for her vision, but he needed her for connection to this world so foreign to him.

The white haze overtook her instantly, like a

weighted curtain dropped in front of a stage. Despite expecting it, the blindness startled her, speeding her heart. What if he decided not to touch her again? Or he thought her more trouble than she was worth and left her to find her way on her own? What if her sight didn't return when her fingers found him again? Panic welled up in Ailyssa's chest and she struggled to suppress it but, a half-dozen fearful heartbeats later, he grasped her hand and dispelled both the fog and the anxiety it brought.

When sight returned, she found him standing in front of her, staring into her eyes. He didn't speak.

"How come they didn't see us?" she asked again. "What did you do?"

He shook his head. "I don't know."

His answer brought a knot to her chest. *How could he not know?*

"But you stopped us. You...you embraced me. You must have known." A phantom of the sensation she'd experienced with his arms encircling her shoulders and her cheek on his chest passed through her.

He shook his head again, squeezed her hand. She wanted to pull away but dreaded the thought of being plunged back into blindness.

"I held you to comfort you," he said. His gaze dropped away. "I thought they'd kill us."

Ailyssa stared. He'd stopped them to await their death, yet their pursuers walked right by them without noticing their presence. How could it be?

"The Goddess," she whispered and raised her eyes toward the sky.

High branches in the tall evergreens waved overhead, blocking her view of the pristine daytime sky, the place she'd always associated with her deity. Nothing in Olvana's teachings said the Goddess lived in the sky, but it made sense to Ailyssa. If she'd banished the Small Gods to the night sky, then the daytime's blue firmament must be the Goddess' domain.

"What did you say?"

She lowered her gaze and their eyes met. She shook her head.

"Nothing. Just..." Her attention flickered skyward again, then back. "Nothing."

The man's expression suggested her answer didn't satisfy him, but he said no more and, rather than inquire further, started out again. Ailyssa allowed herself to be led, glancing up once in a while to glimpse the blue sky peeking between branches.

They hadn't gone far when the trees thinned and the heavens above widened more and more. She hurried her step to walk beside her companion and saw the forest came to an end farther ahead and an expanse of yellow-green grass began. Butterflies flitted amongst the blades, and birds wheeled through the sky overhead, but she paid these only brief attention.

A group of buildings sat in the middle of the field.

Ailyssa's eyes widened. Sunlight gleamed on what might have been fresh white paint on the building's eaves; the grass around the tiny village was cut short and recently tended.

Someone lived here, someone who might help them.

Had she ever seen a town so beautiful?

"We're saved," she said. She looked to her companion, who stood still and tense as a statue, staring toward the group of buildings. She tugged on his arm. "Let's go."

Ailyssa took two paces into the field before her grip slipped from the man's unmoving arm. The sea of grass and the pristine village disappeared with it, dissolving into the white haze, and her steps ceased. Her breath caught and she reached behind her, searching for the man's hand.

"Where are you?"

The need to ask and the nervous tone it brought to her voice sent a lance of anger through her chest. When would she ever stop depending on others?

No response came. He didn't understand her, of course, and couldn't communicate when they weren't touching any more than the world appeared in her vision without him. His fingers brushed hers and the meadow flickered back to life.

"Step back," he said.

Their touch parted again. She stretched her hand out toward where his voice had been, but didn't find him.

"Take my hand." She strived to keep desperation from her voice.

Ailyssa's lips pressed together tight. Why wouldn't he hold onto her while they went to the village and found someone to help them? Their salvation might well lay ahead of them and he was unwilling to go to it.

The white haze wrapped around her, pressing in on top of her. Sighing, she took a cautious step back, then another.

His fingers grasped hers and the grass and buildings returned to her vision. Though she knew—hoped—he wouldn't have deserted her, their appearance was all the sweeter for having disappeared. She held his hand tighter, ensuring her grip wouldn't slip from his, and tugged on his arm to prompt him forward.

"Come on," she said, peering over her shoulder at him.

His head pivoted side to side, refusing.

"We can't."

"Why not?" Ailyssa looked toward the village, longed to accept its invitation to cross the field. "People live there. They might help us."

His head continued shaking. "There is evil."

Ailyssa's brow furrowed, she tilted her head, looked from her companion to the gleaming white buildings and back. Nothing in the white paint or straight lines, nor anything in the stretch of waving blades of grass suggested evil or good or things in between to her. Pure neutrality and detachment, like every other inanimate object. Besides, the Goddess had revealed herself again by protecting them from the robed men; surely she didn't do so to lead them to their doom elsewhere.

Did she?

A shiver trotted its way along Ailyssa's back. Her companion stared past her, ignoring the pleading look in her eyes, his own expression slack. She thought to pull on his hand again, coax him toward this haven, but hesitated as he shook his head.

"What is it?"

He responded with action rather than words as he began walking, following the forest's edge and keeping within sight of the village, but going no closer. Ailyssa let herself be led again, cursing herself for doing so. They went twenty paces before stopping. The man raised his arm, pointed toward the group of buildings.

She followed his gesture. When her gaze fell upon the buildings, her breath caught in her throat.

Wooden walls with faded paint peeling away and the boards beneath weathered to the gray of a stormy day stood where the fresh painted ones had been, tangled ragweed and stunted broom overgrew the pristine lawn leading to the village, and it seemed to grow and expand before her eyes. The wind that had swayed the grass fell still, the heat's oppressive grip pressing on her, bringing sweat to her brow and under her arms. Her gaze darted between the buildings, the weeds, the deserted, neglected appearance so hopeful moments before.

Her eyes fell upon a motionless figure looming at the edge of the hamlet.

With the sun glaring on the land, it was no more than a black silhouette: two arms, two legs, a faceless head.

She couldn't tell if the shape belonged to a male or female, adult or child, but a malevolence gathered around it like a storm cloud. An uncomfortable twinge inserted itself into the bottom of her gut.

"You were right," she whispered and faced her companion. "Something is wrong here. How did you know?"

He shook his head, refusing to meet her gaze, then struck out again, faster than before. They moved into the forest and away from the village with an urgency as though he thought the group of buildings might catch up to them if they tarried.

Ailyssa glanced back before they disappeared into the brush. The walls flickered between newly painted and old and faded, the field of grass grew and disappeared, grew and disappeared. Only the haunted silhouette remained unchanged, unmoving, watching them as they went.

Ailyssa pulled her hand away from her companion's to allow the blank white of her blindness to swallow the mysterious figure.

XXVIII Horace - The Faceless

The too-tight boots skidded in the dirt, leavin' little trails as what lay before him made Horace come to a sudden stop. He held his breath and leaned forward, peerin' through branches and leaves, forgettin' what might've been behind him.

Four o' them gathered around a carcass o' some sort. They'd stripped it beyond recognition, but what kinda thing it might've been were less important than what the hell the things eatin' it was.

Tattered clothin' draped their man-shaped bodies,

some wearin' more'n others. Sickly white skin, long necks, egg-shaped heads with patches o' scraggly hair. Frightenin' enough, them things, but it were their lack o' faces what made the ol' sailor's porthole clench in fear.

He saw nothin' but dents in the eggs where eyes should've been, a lump for a nose, and a ridge what should've been a mouth. Blood smeared this place on each o' them as they used long, claw-like fingers to tear flesh from the carcass and push it against their faces as though they didn't realize they didn't have no mouths. The ol' sailor watched in horror as one tore a chunk off, pressed it to its face, rubbin' and grindin' it until tossin' it aside in clear frustration.

"Fuck me dead," Horace whispered, his voice low enough he barely heard it himself.

One o' the creatures stopped, tilted its head in the sailor's direction. Only then did Horace see the impressions in the side o' them eggs where ears normally was.

Horace's lips pursed to draw a startled breath, but a hand reached around from behind to cover his mouth. Panic shot through his limbs and he jerked, attemptin' to get away, until a second arm encircled his body, pinnin' his arms to his sides. The strong bear hug squeezed hard enough to get across its desperate insistence, but not so much as to hurt. He didn't know who or what grabbed him, but he thought heedin' its advice to stop strugglin' might be his best choice o' actions for the time bein'.

The white thing's egghead remained tilted toward Horace for the space o' more heartbeats than he cared to count. The blood smudged across its non-face gave the creature a grisly smile; its eye dents fixed on the exact spot where the ol' sailor stood captive, but it made no move as though it saw him.

It ain't got no eyes.

He did his best to hold in his air, but the wait dragged

on too long and it forced him to suck some air in through his nose. He did so a quarter breath at a time, fearful o' discoverin' the hand o'er his mouth smelled o' clay. It didn't but, with the white thing starin' at him eyelessly, the lack o' earthy odor didn't ease his trepidation no better.

After far too long, the creature returned its attention to the carcass, its flesh havin' dwindled as the thing's companions tore bits away while the one stared in Horace's direction. It dug its fingers into the animal's belly, pulled out a long string o' innards and ground them into its mouth ridge. Horace gagged against the hand coverin' his mouth.

Whatever held onto him didn't let him go nor even ease its grip. Instead, it began movin' away from the carnage, pullin' the ol' sailor along with it. He gave some consideration to strugglin' but decided stealth were the better choice for now.

Horace moved as careful as the circumstances allowed, but his boots scraped against the ground and leaves and branches rustled at his passin'. The white creatures didn't notice this time, for which he were relieved while wonderin' why.

They backed away until the faceless things disappeared from his sight, then whoever held him let him go. Horace spun around quick, raisin' his fists as though he possessed strength and energy enough to defend himself, but any thought o' doin' so left him when he saw the small gray being what'd been holdin' him.

Thorn?

The Small God must've seen a word bubblin' up toward his mouth, for he pressed a finger to his lips and gestured for the ol' sailor to follow. The horror at seein' the faceless things disappeared as he watched Thorn turn and walk away; relief lightened the weight on his chest.

He's lost his britches.

Horace chuckled silently and followed his friend into the brush, feelin' somewhat safer'n he'd done in some time. In the Green, the Small God'd have his power back, he'd be able to protect the ol' sailor, help him get out from behind the veil.

When he thought they'd gone far enough to be outta earshot o' them creatures what didn't have no ears, Horace decided to find out where Thorn intended on takin' him.

"Where you be leadin' Horace, Thorn?"

The Small God stopped in his tracks as though the sailor's words was rocks what hit him in the back o' the head. He twisted toward Horace, an awe-struck expression raisin' the little feller's brows.

"You know Thorn?"

If the words spoken wasn't enough o' a hint, the voice what came outta the Small God's mouth weren't Thorn's. Surprised, Horace took a step back, inspected his rescuer for the first time and found no man-thing danglin' betwixt its legs. The heat o' embarrassment touched the ol' sailor's cheeks and he diverted his gaze from this obviously-not-Thorn's lady bits.

"Who...who are you?"

"Ivy, sister to Thorn. How could you know Ivy's brother?"

"He fell on me."

Ivy's face contorted and she tilted her head. "How did you get behind the veil for Thorn to fall on you?"

"I weren't. I met Thorn on th'other side. A big, black bird took him o'er."

"Father Raven," Ivy whispered.

"Sounds about right."

She looked toward the ground, eyes flitting as though searchin' for somethin'. Horace used the time to examine her more closely and decided that the missing man-thing were the only difference from one o' them to the other, least far as he remembered. Maybe if they stood side by side, he'd recognize other ways to tell them apart. The Small God raised her gaze and the ol' sailor glanced away again.

"Where did you come from?"

Horace sighed. "It's a long story what starts on a boat—"

"A boat? You ride upon the sea?"

"I guess you might call it that."

"Where is Thorn now?"

Her question brought Horace back to reality; in his fear o'er bein' lost, followed by seein' the faceless things, and then his excitement when he thought he'd found his friend, he'd forgotten what happened to Thorn.

"They got him."

"Who?"

"Some feller I ain't ever seen before. Him and a big fucker made outta clay."

"No." The word came out as no more'n the sound o' breath.

"I tired to stop them, but he—"

"The prophecy," she said, interrupting Horace's guilt. "It is true."

"Prophecy? What're you—"

"Come."

Ivy leapt forward and caught Horace by the wrist, her grip tight. The ol' sailor's bones ground against each other, making him wince as she dragged him away.

"What about them things in the forest?" he asked, craning his neck to look back. Nothin' to spy but trees and brush.

"You are safe from the Faceless while you are with Ivy. They cannot see the folks of the Green."

They hurried through undergrowth and o'er broken off branches faster'n Horace cared to go. Ivy navigated fallen logs, roots and rocks, tree trunks and tangled brush with nimble agility and confidence born o' knowledge. Horace's boots pinched his toes with ev'ry step; he stumbled and blundered, Ivy's grip on his wrist the only thing keepin' him upright more times'n he'd care to've admitted.

They crossed a stream, the Small God's footsteps skimming o'er the surface while the water splashed up and drenched the sailor past his ankles. His breath went short and ragged, but Ivy's pace didn't falter.

She led him up one hill, then down another. O'erhead, the branches first grew more dense, then less, then more again. Birds flitted in the foliage above them, their numbers growing as they went. Horace caught glimpses o' feathers in colors he couldn't've put names to along with the ones he recognized. Birds as big as his head, others as small as his thumb, and ev'ry size in between.

"Where..." He panted. "Where are you taking me?"

His guide neither replied nor slackened her pace. Her footsteps carried an urgency what put a desperation to Horace's thinkin' about his lost friend, added worry to the ol' sailor's chest. No way to know if the little feller still lived, or what might've happened to him if he did, but he figured Ivy knew somethin' about the situation he didn't.

They started up a long hill, the incline increasing as they went, the frequency of trees and brush decreasing as the slope grew. Lookin' up toward the top o' the rise made Horace's thighs ache and brought distress to his lungs. To avoid both, he limited his gaze to the smooth, gray back o' the Small God leadin' him on, or the flock o' birds o' all different kinds wheelin' and squawkin' in the sky.

Horace's legs faltered, his weight draggin' on Ivy enough to slow her pace. She stopped, faced the ol' sailor, and laid her free hand on his head. At first he thought to pull away, partially because he didn't know what she intended, but also because he didn't want her to notice the sweat what'd been drenchin' his brow pretty much since they started out. When her cool flesh touched his warm head, any idea o' avoidin' it flitted away to join the birds.

Refreshin' energy flowed into Horace's head, like a breath o' air bein' blown into a floatation bladder they sometimes used aboard ship. Its sweet touch spread down his neck, through his chest, along his limbs. His fingers tingled with it, the ache left his thighs. It were best when it found its way past his ankles, into his feet and toes. Instead o' the pinched and blistered feelin' his feet'd experienced for what might well've been forever, the soreness melted away, leavin' behind a sensation as though they was soakin' in a cool spring and had been doin' so for quite some time.

Ivy took her hand off his head, but the energizin' force remained.

"Come," she said, her voice calm, even as an unmissable desperation burned in her eyes.

The ol' sailor pushed his legs as fast as he dared, leapin' o'er rocks and stumps like a man many turns o' the seasons younger'n what he really were. He thought he might get used to such a thing, but the anxiety what'd dimmed Ivy's expression kept him from dwellin' on it. Seemed he were safe with her—for now, at least—but Thorn'd still been captured by those what meant him no good.

They reached the top o' the ridge as the pleasant energy fortifyin' Horace dwindled. The fatigue, aches and pains didn't rush back in, but crept back into his muscles, makin' themselves known again little by little. They'd've caused him worry if not for the vast meadow stretchin' out at the foot o' the ridge on which they stood.

Animals filled the grasslands; grazin', frolickin', sleepin'. Ev'ry kinda animal Horace could've imagined lingered on the pasture alongside ones he'd never seen before. He'd've spent some time gawkin' at them if it weren't for the collection o' mud huts gathered together in the center o' the clearin'.

And the scores o' small, gray figures scurryin' about.

XXIX Kuneprius - On the Run

The night pressed in around Kuneprius, a living thing pressing on his chest, insinuating itself into his mind. He struggled to find his breath, his limbs felt carved of rock; he pressed on in spite of it all, dragging Thorn along with him.

The sun had set and risen since they made their escape from the clay abomination. More than once, the fiery ball crossed the sky, more than twice. How many more times, Kuneprius couldn't recall as fear the golem must be catching up to them consumed his mind. Steps, heartbeats, breaths; he counted nothing, nor could he count them if he tried. To him, every branch shaking in the wind, every bush shuddering at an animal's passing, every sound in the forest screamed of the creature getting closer to them. When he found them, their fate— their doom—would be fulfilled.

Since leaving the dirt track, the trees had been unrelenting, then hills added to Kuneprius' effort and his state of utter exhaustion. The high branches hid the Small Gods from view at night, and he was glad not to have to face the judgement of the evenstar, but it also stole his map in the sky. They disguised sunrise and sunset from him, as well, leaving him naught but his internal compass to guide their journey to the Green.

Most of the time, Thorn was little more than comatose. He did what he could to take the weight off his companion's shoulders when he felt strong enough, but he needed rest often. At first, Kuneprius had been hesitant to stop, but it wasn't long before he needed the opportunity to refresh as much or more than the small man. He did his best not to doze, but just this day it had been dark when they sat on the mossy ground to rest against a log, and light the next thing he knew.

"We're lucky he didn't catch us," Kuneprius wheezed as he tugged on Thorn to help him up yet another hill.

Thorn's head nodded, perhaps in response, perhaps because the task of holding it up was too great. Kuneprius turned to gaze at him and saw his eyes hooded, his lips parted as he gasped for breath. The flesh of his cheeks looked as though it had begun melting from his jowls.

"Shouldn't you be getting...better as we near the Green?"

He realized a considerable journey lay ahead of them to reach the Small God's home, but he did his best not to dwell on the distance. If he set his mind to the task ahead, his heart sank and his spirit flagged. The only chance they had to make it was for him to concentrate on reaching the top of the next hill and not allowing himself to think any farther ahead.

The ground rose at a steeper angle than the other hills they'd traversed. Little space showed between tree truck and bush, rock and root, leaving no natural path to follow, forcing him to take care in choosing his footing. The extra effort made his back ache and his thighs burn despite the accidental snatch of sleep he'd gotten. Thorn attempted to aid his rescuer, but his weak knees gave out beneath him frequently, each time he faltered adding to the weight on Kuneprius, threatening to drag him down.

He peered up the hill, its crest tantalizingly near.

We can make it.

His gaze fell back to choosing the proper placement for his steps. With the rough and rocky ground beneath his feet, roots and thorns and twigs, he gave thanks for the first time for the footwear he'd so loathed when they left Murtikara.

Thorn sagged in his grasp and Kuneprius let out a grunt of effort to keep the small man from slipping. Without thinking, he fell to his old habits for comfort and support and resumed counting his steps.

One...three...nineteen...six...

No, no. That's not right.

Ten...fifty-two...thirteen...nine?

He paused, blinked sweat out of his eyes.

What's wrong with me?

He drew a shuddering breath and blew it out between his lips in a huff, raised his eyes back toward the top of the hill. It appeared no closer.

He lifted his foot over a root, past a branch, and set it on a mossy piece of earth.

One.

The other foot left the ground, found a spot atop a flat rock.

Two.

Kuneprius nodded, knowing he'd gotten that much right. Another step.

Three.

Runners and branches clogged the path ahead, so he changed direction, moving to the right.

Four.

This way, another step toward the top available for him, so he stepped forward. He paused, his foot settling into a patch of loam, and waited for the next number to come to him.

It didn't.

His tongue came out and scratched across his dry lips. He held his hand up in front of his face and gazed at his quivering fingers, folding each one into his palm as he counted them.

One. Two. Three. Four...

His thumb remained, sticking skyward by itself. Kuneprius gritted his teeth, concentrating until his head throbbed. The next number refused to come to him, so he unfolded his fingers and gave it another go without success. Again. Again. Five times he tried—he knew because he counted his attempts—but recalling the number for the last digit eluded him.

Frustrated, Kuneprius slapped his hand against his thigh and started out again. Instead of watching his footing, he raised his chin and stared straight ahead at the top of the hill, using his goal to drive him forward, hoping for progress to squash his distress.

He dragged Thorn along beside him, doing his best to protect the Small God, but knowing branches would scratch at his chest and arms as they did his own. The effort transformed his thighs to knots of fiery pain, each step agony. His foot came down half-on, half-off a thick root, twisting his ankle. Kuneprius stumbled forward to compensate, barely staying upright and jarring his back in the process.

By the time the tangle of brush eased nearing the crest of the hill, his entire body had become a mass of knots and cramps and pain. His breaths refused to fill his lungs, leaving them starving for air. With each step, Thorn moaned as though Kuneprius' torments passed along to him through their contact.

Finally, the ground flattened and they reached the hill's apex. Kuneprius had hoped to find the trees and brush cleared on the other side, allowing him to see farther ahead, ideally to spy the glittering sheen of the veil. But more trees and brush, roots and rocks lay ahead, crushing his hopes. The hill descended to a shallow valley, then another began.

Kuneprius intended to set Thorn down gently, but his back refused to bend. A shock of pain shot along his spine and he tumbled forward, twisting to land on his shoulder instead of on the Small God. An involuntary cry spilled from his lips and he clamped his mouth closed around it; if the golem was near, surely it would have heard.

The two of them lay on their backs, the mossy ground soft beneath them as they both labored to find their breath. Kuneprius' lungs protested with each gasp of air, adding their fire to the one burning in his thighs.

He shut his eyes, his fatigued brain setting off colorful fireworks against his lids. Exhaustion settled into him, pushing him deeper into the ground. He considered taking steps to ensure he wasn't sinking into the earth, sucked toward its core, but his body refused to comply. His breathing eased, the pain in his legs and hips and back faded.

The light show dimmed, growing darker and darker until it went black and the pains, the dirt at his back, the Small God at his side, all disappeared.

***

"...end."

The world shook. Kuneprius let out a groan and wondered if he might be dead.

"Friend."

The darkness enveloping him eased and he sensed sunlight falling on his face, filtering through his eyelids. He struggled to open them, but sleep gummed them shut.

"Friend."

The world trembled again, but this time he noticed the hand gripping his shoulder, shaking him. He raised the other arm and wiped it across his mouth, then dug a knuckle into first one eye, then the other. It allowed him to part his lids.

The quality of the light differed from what he remembered it being when last his eyes were open. He blinked, considering this. After a moment, he realized it meant the day was later than it had been. The vague sense he should be concerned by the fact inched into him, but his sleep-fogged brain refused to recall for what reason this should be.

A silhouette leaned over him, its shape odd with ears sticking out to the side. He stared at it, attempting to make out the features of the face on the head.

"Thorn," he said, his voice little more than a croak. Whatever time had passed had dried his throat to a sheet of ancient parchment akin to what the prophecy had been written upon.

The prophecy!

Kuneprius jerked upright, pain exploding through his back as he recalled why he lay on the forest floor with a Small God leaning over him. He remembered the man sculpted of clay pursuing them.

"I fell asleep."

"Yes. Thorn did, too. Here."

The Small God held up a broad leaf in the palms of his hands, the edges folded up so it resembled a bowl. Water covered the bottom of the leafy vessel; not enough to wash Kuneprius' sins, but enough to wet his throat.

He reached out shaking hands to take it from Thorn, but the gray man refused to give it to him. Sticky spit found its way onto Kuneprius' tongue. He licked his lips and anger grew inside him.

Why won't he let me have it?

But his ire extinguished when Thorn extended his arms and held the vessel up to his friend's lips, tilted it toward him. The cool water brought instant relief. He gulped the single mouthful, trying not to spill a drop but, despite his best effort, one escaped the corner of his mouth and rolled down to his chin. Thorn took the leaf away and Kuneprius stuck his tongue out to collect the stray droplet.

"Where did you find water?" he asked; his voice remained but a shadow of its former self.

"Thorn is of the forest and the land and knows how to find water."

Eyes widening, a sensation bloomed in Kuneprius' breast he'd almost forgotten existed: hope.

"You used your magic?" He leaned toward the Small God, ignoring the pain in his back. "Is it returning?"

He shook his head. "No. Thorn finds water without magic." He waved his hand, gesturing about the forest, but it fell to his side before completing the gesture. "Water is everywhere, though sparse today."

The enlivening hope drained away, leaving behind the frustration and dread Kuneprius had become used to over the past days.

"We have to get moving again." He pushed himself to his feet, wincing with the effort. "The golem needs no rest."

Thorn didn't move from where he knelt on the soft moss. Kuneprius drew a deep breath, preparing his aching body for helping the gray man up. The sleep had helped him, as it had helped Kuneprius, but the paleness of his skin and the dark patches upon it remained.

"No, friend. Go. Thorn will stay. It is Thorn the clay man wants."

Kuneprius' head moved back and forth, heavy on his neck. "He'll take you to your death if he finds you."

"And you." Thorn's gaze dipped to the ground in front of him, his words grew quiet. "Clay man killed Horace Seaman. Thorn doesn't want him to kill friend, too."

Kuneprius stepped toward the Small God and

crouched beside him, knees popping. He put his hand on Thorn's shoulder.

"My fate is set. The instant I took you away, my life ended with our capture, as it means an end to yours."

Thorn raised his chin and gazed at his companion. Some of the fog clouding his eyes had lifted, but they still didn't shine the way they had when they first found each other.

"I knew what taking you meant. I cannot stand by and let them take your life, no matter what the reason they do it or what the consequence I must face."

The corner of Thorn's mouth curled; a smile, Kuneprius realized. He squeezed the Small God's shoulder and pushed himself to his feet with a crack of joints, then offered Thorn his hand. He took it and allowed Kuneprius to help him up. They both looked forward, down toward the valley.

"At least it's downhill," Kuneprius said. "Better than that climb."

He gestured back along the hill they'd scaled. From the top, it didn't look as steep as it had as they climbed it. Kuneprius might have stopped to ponder how that could be if not for the trembling of a tree catching his attention. He squinted, hoping to glimpse a mule deer or some other animal as apprehension tingled down his limbs.

The brush shook again and a flash of gray showed between two branches, then disappeared. It didn't have the look of fur.

"We have to go," Kuneprius said, struggling to squash the panic threatening to rage through him.

He grabbed Thorn's elbow and walked backward from the place where they'd dozed allowing the clay abomination the opportunity to catch up to them.

It doesn't need to rest.

Kuneprius put his arm around the Small God's waist

and pointed them both down the hill toward the gully, the next hill, and whatever lay beyond.

***

They'd put several hills behind them by the time the trees thinned. Sweat ran from Kuneprius' forehead and he wiped it away with his free hand, the other supporting the Small God's limp form. He didn't dare peek back for fear of what he might see.

To his surprise, he had more energy and strength than he'd have expected his accidental sleep to give. It remained an effort to carry Thorn—the benefits he'd reaped from their rest were short-lived—but his arms and legs did not threaten to remove themselves from his body as they had before, nor did his heart beat so hard it might escape his chest. He labored to breathe, his muscles ached, but he was confident he'd be able to continue for some while yet.

Exhausted or not, what choice did he have with a murderous statue chasing them?

As they neared the crest of the hill, the trees became sparse, then disappeared completely leaving broom and scrub brush impeding their path. It grew thickly, but not so dense as to slow the invigorated Kuneprius.

Does this energy mean we are nearing Thorn's home?

The Small God dangled in his grip, toes brushing the dirt as his feet did their best to aid his companion, but they came up mostly unsuccessful. If they neared the Green, shouldn't it cause Thorn's power to grow, not his rescuer's?

Step by step, Kuneprius pondered this question, using it to distract himself the way counting his steps might have if the numbers hadn't disappeared from his head. With the top of the hill a few paces away, he realized the answer.

Thorn is using his magic to give me energy.

He'd tried to make Kuneprius save himself and leave him behind, but guilt and dismay prevented him from accepting the Small God's sacrifice. Now he understood Thorn had found a different way to sacrifice himself for him.

But I am responsible. He wouldn't be in this situation if not for me. Why should he care to save me?

He tilted his head to peer at the gray man dangling in his grasp but Thorn's chin drooped to his chest, his energy gone. Kuneprius hefted him, pulling his feet up off the ground, and pushed on, determined to rescue the Small God from his foretold fate.

They reached the hilltop, bursting forth through a tangle of brush onto bare earth. The hill sloped down and away, the path ahead of them clear of trees, broom, and tangled roots. The ground at their feet was stony with patches of moss and grass, but after a short distance, it became grassland. In the dimness of twilight, it appeared near black, but Kuneprius suspected it might be lush green in the daylight.

Like the pasture close to where we found Thorn.

The thought blossomed further as his gaze followed the field to a darker spot on the land. It was large and oddly shaped, and lit here and there.

A village!

Kuneprius stopped in his tracks, staring down the hill at the spots of light his heart knew to be flickering torches, burning lamps, roaring cook fires. The verdant grass at the edge of the trees, the town... this must be near where they'd found Thorn.

We're saved.

The thought filled him with hope and he gave Thorn an excited shake, but the Small God made no response. Kuneprius took two steps forward, beginning the descent, but stopped again.

I don't remember a hill.

He pursed his lips, concentrating. Perhaps they approached from a different direction and he hadn't noticed it the first time they were near this village. If he couldn't remember how to count after all the turns of the seasons he'd done so, it seemed likely his memory had no room for a hill he'd seen once.

Kuneprius sucked a deep breath through his nose, searching for the briny scent of the sea to confirm where they were. His nostrils detected no salt in the air.

The wind blows the wrong direction, that's all.

He took two more steps, glancing skyward. He'd been avoiding eye contact with those who looked down from above, but it was the only other way he knew to approximate their direction and location.

Sometime during the night, while the trees hid the Small Gods from him, a layer of cloud had crept across the sky. The moon was naught but a blur while the evenstar and the others were invisible. Kuneprius froze, his fears confirmed.

Ine'vesi and his priests are angered at what I've done.

He didn't know what the Small Gods would do to him, if they possessed the power to do anything from their place in the sky, but he didn't intend to find out.

They started out again, feet scuffing along the stony ground. Thorn seemed heavier now, as if the judgement of those who looked down from the sky added to his burden. He hiked him up with a grunt, the pain which had mostly disappeared from his back returning, bringing with it a knot in his shoulder blade.

"Come on, Thorn," he muttered.

Grass sprouting between stones became more frequent until his steps whispered through blades rather than scraping across stone. A familiarity of the landscape struck Kuneprius, energizing him with hope they may have stumbled upon the village by the sea while also filling him with dread it might not be.

If it wasn't, where were they? And how would he explain the comatose gray man he dragged along with him?

He slowed his pace, hesitant. Perhaps they'd be better off avoiding civilization. What they found behind the town's walls may be worse than—

Behind them, brush crashed, moved and thrashed by an unseen, unstoppable force. Kuneprius craned his head but saw nothing in the darkness.

He didn't need to see. The sound was enough to remind him the thing trailing them was worse than anything they might encounter in a village. Worse than anything, anywhere.

We can hide amongst the buildings.

Mind made up, Kuneprius forced his pace as fast as possible without throwing himself off balance to tumble to the ground. He thought they might find a cellar, a shed, somewhere the clay monstrosity wouldn't search for them, but the carnage left behind at the inn flashed across his memory. He saw the serving wench's twisted body, the barkeep's severed head sitting upon the bar where he'd spent his life pouring ale for his patrons.

Kuneprius shivered. He didn't want the deaths of these villagers on his hands, but if they sacrificed Thorn and the prophecy proved true, then how many more would die?

One of his knees buckled and he lost his balance, twisting as he went to the ground to keep from falling on top of his charge. As he rolled, he caught a glimpse back up the hill where a clay monster in the shape of a man emerged from a tangle of broom.

Kuneprius' heart jumped up to clog his throat, making it difficult to draw breath, but he clawed his way to his feet. To stop now would surely mean his death.

"Come on," he wheezed grabbing Thorn under his

armpits. "Come on. Please...please."

The Small God found a reserve of energy and pushed with his legs, helping Kuneprius. He hiked him up, back and hips protesting at having to bear the weight yet again, and pointed them toward the flickering lights ahead.

The golem possessed but one speed, he knew. If he outpaced the abomination to the village, it might give them enough time to find a hiding spot before the golem got there. Kuneprius clamped his jaw tight, nostrils flaring with the effort of drawing air into his chest, throat raw with fear.

They drew closer to their goal; the flickering lights brightened. To Kuneprius' mind, the ground shook beneath him with each step the golem took, but he dismissed the thought. Despite the pain shooting through his back, the knots threatening in his calves and thighs, he knew himself to be faster than the monster, that he was leaving it farther behind.

As they came nearer the village, Kuneprius blinked away the sweat stinging his eyes and saw the picketed wall surrounding the town. Like the hill, he hadn't noticed the fence before, but it seemed familiar, nonetheless. Could he have forgotten so much? Hunger and exhaustion played many tricks on a man's mind, he knew.

He pressed on, but doubt nagged at the back of his mind, finding its way through the fear of the golem chasing them down. He was a keeper, tasked with keeping the sculptor safe. His job never included fighting or fleeing, only ensuring meals were eaten, clothing repaired, and sleep allowed in appropriate quantities.

How did I end up here?

To his right, Kuneprius noticed a lighter spot in the wall: an open gate. It meant those who lived within didn't fear attacks from beasts or man, but had they ever seen the likes of the golem?

He amended their path, directing them toward the opening. If he could get himself and Thorn behind the walls, they might survive, but the closer they got, the more the doubt whispering in his ear grew louder, more desperate.

They reached the gate and found no one guarding it. Kuneprius stopped and glanced over his shoulder. Overhead, the clouds parted, allowing the moon to shine through and cast its silvery light over the grassy expanse leading to the hill. Halfway across it, a dark figure followed footstep for footstep in Kuneprius' path.

He dragged his arm across his face, the rough fabric of his shirt chafing his skin as he wiped sweat away, and hauled Thorn over the threshold of the fence and into the village. He inhaled a deep breath filled with the hickory scent of a cook fire, the odor increasing his discomfort with the familiarity of this place. It was as though he'd been here before, but he couldn't think of when in the same way he had difficulty recalling what number came after four.

The moonlight illuminated simple buildings behind the picketing, none of them more than a single storey. They were built of wattle and daub, clay and wood, their roofs thatched, the doors hinged with thick rope. Surely one of them would offer a hiding place from the golem.

Kuneprius redirected them toward the nearest street, intending to find the most stout-looking of the structures, but his pace slowed, a cramp in his right leg and a knot in his shoulder blade hindering him. The pains made it a struggle to keep Thorn from slipping from his grip.

"Please, Thorn. Help me if you can," he pleaded.

"Who is there?"

Kuneprius halted. The man who'd spoken stood directly ahead of them. He wore a cloak dark enough in color to blend him into his background, hiding him from Kuneprius' gaze.

"Help us, please," Kuneprius wheezed. His head felt light, the exhaustion he'd previously experienced returning full-force as Thorn's aid disappeared. His legs trembled and failed him; he went to his knees, arm still supporting the Small God. "Please, there's a—"

"Kuneprius?" The man stepped away from the shadow of the building and into the moonlight. "Is that you, brother?"

How can this man know me?

Kuneprius' eyes narrowed to slits as the robed man approached. He thought to raise his hand, prepare to defend himself, but his body failed him. Thorn slipped out of his grip, the Small God sliding to the ground. Not having to bear the weight gave Kuneprius the impression he might float away, but the opposite happened and he sagged to the dirt beside Thorn.

Kuneprius stared toward the Small God. Thorn's eyes were open, but milky. He couldn't tell whether the gray man saw him or not, but it didn't matter. Soon, the golem would be upon them, making their struggle for nothing. Kuneprius licked his lips and wished he'd said goodbye to Vesisdenperos the last day before the monster who would turn out to be both their killers came to life.

A pair of sandaled feet came into view and the hem of a robe. The man standing by Kuneprius' head knelt, put his hand on his shoulder.

"It's all right, Kuneprius, you're home."

With blood roaring in his ears, Kuneprius thought he'd misheard.

"Home?" he croaked.

"Yes, brother. You've reached Murtikara."

XXX Dansil - Revenge

Thrice the man who'd escaped them appeared to Dansil, and all three times Trenan proved too wary to be caught off-guard. The queen's guard might not agree he was the best swordsman in the kingdom, nor did he like him, but even with only one arm, Trenan was a more dangerous opponent than most men. He didn't think a demented half-wit armed with a knife and missing his nose, half an arm, and various other body parts would fare well without surprise on his side.

The night after the sun set for the fourth time, Dansil found himself in the woods awaiting Stirk as they'd arranged. A sour odor disguised the forest's usual aromas of wood and moss this night—a sign they neared Ikkundana.

The stink of sickness and death.

Dansil swallowed hard to keep his gorge from rising at the thought. He'd never harbored any desire to visit this place, nor come within any distance of it, yet he'd allowed the one-armed fool to drag him here.

"You'll be the death of me if I'm not careful," he growled aloud.

A rustle of leaves at his back startled him and Dansil whirled around, hand reaching for the haft of his axe. The wan moonlight cast the man who'd crept up behind him in silhouette, his shape leaning against the trunk of a tree, torso touching the bark because he had no arm at the shoulder to rest upon. In the dark, Dansil thought Trenan had snuck up behind him. Anger and surprise flashed in him before he realized it was the wrong limb missing for it to be the master swordsman.

"Where'd your arm go?" Dansil nodded toward the limbless shoulder. Last time they'd met, he'd possessed an arm as far as the elbow.

Stirk looked down as though he didn't know what Dansil spoke of. When he raised his head, his expression reflected no surprise. He offered a one-sided shrug.

"There's a cost," he replied, leaving the queen's guard to wonder what he meant.

Stirk stepped away from the tree and moonlight flashed on the edge of the short, sharp blade he held in his remaining hand. He pointed it toward Dansil half-heartedly, his arm threatening to give way under its own mass and the weight of the knife. Dansil considered rushing him and relieving him of the weapon but decided against it; why disarm the man who wanted to kill his enemy?

"Is tonight the night?" Stirk asked. "Or do you have more reason for delay?"

"Tonight must be the night," Dansil replied, the miasma of sickness hanging in the forest flaring his nostrils. "Tomorrow, we arrive in Ikkundana and he will be out of your reach."

"Then lead me to the bastard who killed my mother."

Dansil nodded, goose bumps prickling along his flesh. He told himself anticipation of Trenan's death caused them, not fear of this man who seemed to be decaying and disappearing before his eyes. Why should he be afraid of such a person?

Because it's wise to be afraid of someone with nothing to lose and nothing to live for.

The queen's guard retraced his steps toward the camp where he'd left Trenan and their steeds, more slowly than he'd traveled to meet Stirk. Each footstep he lifted from the ground carefully, placed it gingerly so as to avoid noise that might warn the master swordsman of their coming. Stirk followed along behind, making no more noise than a wraith navigating the fog. He was so quiet, Dansil felt compelled to glance over his shoulder to ensure the man still followed and hadn't lost his nerve.

A sliver of moonlight shone across Stirk's face and the queen's guard noticed he wasn't merely missing his nose; his teeth showed through a hole in one cheek and pink skin shone in the hollow his right eye used to occupy. Dansil glimpsed patches of flesh on his head where hair had been before, but now those spots gleamed red and sore and through two of them he spied the gleam of white bone. He cringed and returned his gaze to the path ahead.

What's happened to this man?

Despite what should have been hindrances, Stirk moved through the brush, making less noise than Dansil himself. He forgot the man's handicaps when, through the trees, he noticed a flicker of light—Trenan had lit a fire.

"We're close," he whispered. Stirk hissed at him to stay quiet.

Dansil slowed his pace, being even more careful of his footing. Trenan wouldn't expect an attack, but he was always on alert, as was any soldier of reasonable skill and experience. The queen's guard inched his hand toward the haft of his axe, at odds over whether he hoped to be involved in the killing or not.

As they approached the clearing Trenan had chosen for them to spend the night, one of the horses nickered and scuffed the ground with a hoof. The sounds drew Trenan's attention and he stood from where he crouched beside the fire, surveyed the area near their mounts. His hand rested on the hilt of his sword as he scanned the woods until his eyes fell on Dansil's approach. The queen's guard gritted his teeth and awaited the master swordsman's reaction to Stirk accompanying him. Instead of pulling his weapon or questioning the other man's presence, Trenan released his grip on the sword hilt, raised his hand in a grudging gesture of welcome.

"Any luck finding game?"

At first, Trenan's question confused Dansil, but then he remembered the lie he'd told to get away and meet Stirk.

How can he not see him?

He resisted the urge to peek back for himself. Stirk must have hidden himself, he realized, but the way the man appeared as if from out of nowhere and disappeared the same way tended to unnerve him.

"No. No game," Dansil said, distracted. "We'll be eating rations tonight."

Trenan's scowling response brewed a familiar ire in the queen's guard's chest. Maybe he shouldn't wait for Stirk to end the bastard; he'd find it much more satisfying to do it himself.

Dansil stepped across the verge from forest to clearing, doing his best to disguise the movement of his hand toward releasing his axe from its harness. Trenan didn't notice, but before he lifted it free, a pressure on his back made his world explode into pain.

***

Without clear reason, Dansil's eyes went wide, his mouth dropped open in an exaggerated caricature of surprise, but it didn't last long. His features twisted and distorted into an expression Trenan recognized as one of extreme pain.

The queen's guard's knees buckled and he slumped to the ground, leaving his attacker standing in plain sight. Trenan's hand leapt to his sword with practiced ease even as his mind whirled. Who was this man? How did he find them? Why kill Dansil?

Before he had the chance to sort through the questions, the man jumped forward, leading with a small knife shining with Dansil's blood. He moved quickly for someone his size and the master swordsman narrowly avoided being pricked. Godsbane hissed from its scabbard and he countered in one fluid motion, but the sharp blade cut nothing but air. The lack of contact Trenan expected threw him off balance and he stumbled, catching himself before he lost his footing. When he spun to face his attacker, he found the clearing empty.

"What the hell?"

He spared a glance for Dansil lying prone on the ground, groaning and trying without success to put pressure on his wound and stem the bleeding. The assassin had placed his knife in the perfect place to be out of reach of its victim and cause the greatest damage and bleeding.

A sound startled Trenan and, out of habit, he jumped back.

The man's knife slid through the night again, nicking the side of the master swordsman's chest, but the armor he'd not yet removed protected him. He took a step away to survey the man, still trying to piece together what was happening.

It was easy to understand why he experienced such difficulty in recognizing his aggressor; the man's face was a mess. A gap where his nose should have been, holes in his cheeks showing crooked teeth beneath, a shimmering pink cavity where an eye had once resided. He possessed but one arm, the other being gone right to the shoulder, the same as Trenan's but the opposite side. The swordmaster imagined the fellow's face without the bits missing and recognition finally dawned.

"Stirk."

The man's mouth twisted into what may have been either smile or snarl; the growl rumbling at the back of his throat suggested the latter. Before Trenan could say more, he lunged again, swinging the dagger in a wide arc destined to open the master swordsman's abdomen and spill his innards on the ground had he not parried the blow.

Trenan countered, but again the man disappeared. This time, he saw it clearly—Stirk faded away as though made of mist.

He shook his head and gritted his teeth. Whatever was going on here, it wasn't natural, and Stirk wasn't doing it on his own. Blade held in front of him, he pivoted on one foot, spinning a tight circle to keep watch for where the man may next appear.

From the corner of his eye, he noticed Dansil's movements had ceased. Was he dead? Could it be too much to hope? He didn't let his attention linger for fear Stirk would reappear, continuing to survey the clearing, examining the shadows thrown by the fire's dancing flames. Nothing but trees and brush and darkness. The blaze crackled and crickets chirped; a quiet, quaking breath issued from Dansil, quashing Trenan's hope the man had expired, but nothing else to see or hear, and it remained so for some time.

The master swordsman stopped moving to concentrate on listening, body tense and ready to defend or attack. A moment later, the scrape of a footstep in dirt behind him made him jump back and spin around, sword cocked.

Stirk waved, but not as a method of attack. He'd lost his balance and pinwheeled his arm to keep from pitching forward onto his face, but was having no luck. The big man hit the ground with a thump hard enough to knock the air from his chest. Trenan stared, discerning what caused the fall when he realized the reason.

Stirk was shy his left leg from the knee down.

Rather than waste time wondering why this might be,

Trenan jumped forward to deliver a killing blow. Stirk cried out and raised his arm in defence, his form already fading. The tip of the crown sword dug into the dirt with a crunch that set the master swordsman's teeth on edge. The noise a blade made cutting flesh and bone always satisfied him, but the sound of good steel being dulled made him queasy.

Every time he disappears, he comes back lacking a body part.

Trenan pulled Godsbane free of the dirt, cleaned the steel on his bedroll and readjusted his grip, waiting for Stirk to reappear. He suppressed a smile threatening to creep across his lips as he wondered what his adversary would be missing this time.

***

Stirk breathed hard, chest heaving as he lay on the ground at the healer's feet. With great effort, he heaved himself onto his elbow and stared up at the hooded man. Sweat ran along his face, stinging the empty eye socket that matched his dead mother's, dripping through the holes in his cheeks so he tasted salt on his tongue.

"Again," Stirk said, voice rasping against his throat.

The healer shook his head. "With what will you pay?"

Stirk tried to chew his bottom lip, but found it gone like his cheeks and eye. Hesitantly, he moved his gaze from the healer and allowed it to travel along his own body. His left arm was but a stump at the shoulder, the remainder of his legs short enough he'd drag his balls on the ground should he stand. An arm, an eye, and whatever might be left inside him—judging by the pain in his gut, the healer had likely already taken a few of those, too.

He returned his attention to the man in the robe. "Heal me so I can take the bastard's life, then you can have mine."

"Tch, tch," the healer clucked from beneath his hood. "Your life is no good to me. It is naught but air and wishes. What can I build with that? What can I repair? Your flesh is all I am interested in. If I give it back to you, then I will not have it. If I give it back to you on the promise it is mine when you kill this man, what happens if you fail and he takes your life? I have less interest in dead flesh than I do in your soul."

Stirk flexed bits of muscle in his face intending to scowl, but the pieces of cheek remaining and the empty spots where once he had lips didn't move. An eye or an arm. How could he kill a man when he had no arms? Or if he couldn't see him? A groan gurgled in his throat.

"Send me back," Stirk growled. "Put me right on top of him, then I don't care what happens."

No point telling the healer what part of him to take; he'd had no say in it before. With an effort, Stirk rolled onto his side, bent his arm, and took the dagger's butt between his teeth. He didn't know if he'd lose his arm or his sight, but this way he'd have the blade no matter what.

As long as he did, he'd have opportunity to stick the bastard Trenan with it.

A familiar pain filled Stirk's body, like his blood heating to near the point of boiling. He closed his eye, not wanting to view the sickening sights that presented themselves when the healer moved him.

A moment later, all sensation disappeared.

***

Trenan stared down at what had once been an imposing man but was now little more than a log. No legs, flesh missing, one eye, no left arm and his right gone at the elbow. He used this foreshortened appendage in an attempt to drag himself across the dirt toward Trenan. The dagger Stirk held in his teeth caused the master swordsman no more concern than if a mosquito buzzed around his head.

Despite the horrific nature of what he gazed upon, he laughed.

"Will you stick me with that? Nod fast and use it to saw my foot from my leg?"

He laughed again and returned Godsbane to its sheath. One step to his right kept him beyond Stirk's pathetic range. The man ceased his scrabbling on the ground and stared up at the master swordsman, eye gleaming with hatred and death. Trenan strode past him and Stirk rolled onto his side, flopping like a fish to reposition himself to follow.

Trenan ignored him, making his way to where Dansil lay in a heap, his blood soaking the dirt beneath him to soggy mud. Before he reached his side, the master swordsman noticed his chest rising and falling with labored breath.

"Damn." Things would be much easier if the queen's guard died here this night.

He knelt beside the man, assessing the situation. The wound was long and jagged and, judging by the amount of blood he'd lost, deep as well, but its location suggested it shouldn't be fatal. At least not unless someone left him to bleed to death.

Trenan sighed and glanced back at the sound of Stirk scraping across the dirt. The man's gaze still bore into him; sweat ran from his forehead and the stump at his elbow was scraped and bleeding, slowing his already snail-like pace. Trenan turned back to Dansil.

The thought of leaving the man behind tempted him but he'd been taught his duty to his fellow soldiers since his first days at the outpost. It may be true no one else could ever suspect what happened here, but Trenan himself would always know. Were the roles reversed, he didn't doubt the queen's guard would leave him to die, but he was not Dansil, and he refused to abandon a soldier in need.

"Damn," he cursed again and grabbed his companion's wrist, pulled him to a sitting position.

The queen's guard's dead weight proved difficult to get up onto his shoulder, but Trenan accomplished the task. Enough life had passed with a single arm, he'd figured out how to overcome such challenges. He shifted to settle his load properly, then turned, intending to take Dansil to his horse, strap him to the saddle and dress his wound, but found Stirk nearly at his feet, the man's neck stretched out as he stared up at the master swordsman. The dagger he'd held in his teeth lay in the dirt a body's length behind him and the gleam of hatred in his eye had faded to something else.

"I see you made good progress," Trenan commented as he stepped around the man.

Stirk fell onto his side, reached out with his shortened arm, the scraped and raw end brushing Trenan's foot. The master swordsman paused, staring at his one-time adversary, and kicked the stump away. Stirk collapsed with an expulsion of breath.

"You can't leave me this way," he croaked.

Trenan raised an eyebrow but didn't reply. He glared down at the man, feeling far more revulsion than pity.

"Kill me," Stirk begged. "Don't leave me to the forest creatures or—"

"Mercy? You ask me for mercy? Look at you. You sacrificed your body for an opportunity to take my life, and now you ask mercy from the man you intended to kill?"

If Stirk had lips and cheeks, the expression his face contorted into might have been one of sadness, or perhaps pleading. Tears welled in his eye, but both only furthered Trenan's anger.

"Please."

The master swordsman turned his back on Stirk,

ignoring the man's pleas as he strode across the clearing to the waiting horses.

***

It took a surprisingly short time for the one-armed man to dress his companion's wounds and lash him into the saddle. That task completed, he struck the half-set camp, mounted his own horse, and led the wounded man away into the night.

Stirk continued begging for the man to kill him as they rode away but stopped when his raw and ragged throat gave out. After that, he settled for watching, hoping Trenan would find compassion in his heart and return to end this pitiful existence.

It's my fault I'm here. My choice.

The two horses disappeared into the darkness, leaving Stirk alone with the night sounds of the forest. His gaze darted from tree to tree, examining each shadow, expecting to spy red eyes and bared teeth amongst them. His heart beat faster in his chest, cool sweat formed on his brow and ran into his eye, stinging it. He blinked hard to clear it and, when his lid opened, the robed figure standing over him startled him. His fright became relief when he realized it was the healer come to end his misery.

"Is that truly what you think? That I will release you from the miserable prison you created for yourself?"

Stirk opened his mouth to speak, though he didn't know what he might have said. It didn't matter as his throat failed to produce words.

The healer kneeled beside him, put a hand on Stirk's shoulder. An unpleasant sensation started where he touched, a tingling that increased until it became painful, like fine thorns dragged across his flesh. It spread through the remainder of his body; he felt it in phantom limbs and missing skin. The discomfort brought him hope for the end of his life.

"Tch, tch. I told you I have no use for dead flesh. Nor your soul. No, Stirk, I have other plans for you."

Pain grew in Stirk's chest, and the world grew darker. He tried to close his eye, but it refused. Vertigo gripped him, agony enveloped him, then the world exploded.

XXXI Teryk - Storm

The act of gripping the handle of a mop and drawing it back and forth across the deck brought blisters to the tops of Teryk's palms within an hour of the first time he held it. They didn't burst until the second day, and it took a couple more sunrises after that before the pain they caused diminished to a reasonable level. His shoulders ached, his knuckles hurt, the muscles in his chest and back wound themselves into knots. Each night when he set his head on the skinny pillow Ash had provided along with a threadbare blanket, he fell asleep faster than he could have imagined.

Learning to use a sword and spear, being instructed in the ways of fighting for a few hours a day was one thing, but spending almost every waking minute working from the time the sun rose until it set again was something completely different.

The mop splashed in the bucket, slopping brown water over the side and onto the deck.

"Careful," Ash said. "Just makin' more work for yourself."

Teryk leaned on the wooden handle and wiped an arm across his forehead. Doing so stung, and he knew that, if he caught sight of himself in a looking glass, he'd find his face red from his time in the sun. He looked up at the clear sky, licked his lips and wondered if they'd be able to have a break to get a mouthful of water soon. Lowering his eyes, he spied a bank of dark clouds on the far horizon; perhaps they'd bring rain and relief from the heat.

Will I have to swab the deck in the rain?

His hands smarted at the idea and he wondered if he'd have been better off telling the captain his true identity. No sooner did the thought enter his mind than another followed.

The firstborn child of the rightful king.

Blisters and aches and pains or not, the kingdom needed saving. Despite his misgivings and the torture of prolonged labor, he had to trust the prophecy to lead him on the path he was meant to follow.

Everything has a reason.

Teryk flopped the mop head onto the deck and dragged it back and forth more enthusiastically, the wet wood glistening in the sun. He threw himself into the work, invigorated by the knowledge his life had a purpose, pondering where this voyage might lead him, when he realized Ash had spoken to him.

"What?" Teryk asked, leaning on the mop again.

The cabin boy looked at him with one eye closed against the glare of the sun, his shoulder length brown hair tussled to the point of being knotted.

"I said you ain't spent much time 'board a ship, have ya?"

Teryk stifled a laugh; the way Ash affected the lilt of the older sailors amused him. He'd heard the boy speak without dropping letters and with proper words instead of slang—mostly when he was tired or talking to himself and didn't realize anyone else heard him—but Ash insisted on adopting their way of speaking to feel more a part of the crew. Here was a lad who seemed to know where his life would lead him.

"No, I haven't," Teryk admitted. "Only once, when I'd seen fewer turns of the seasons than you have."

"Thought so. You ain't got much in the way o' sea

legs."

The prince glanced at his legs, an image of red crab appendages flashing through his mind. He knew it wasn't what Ash meant, but it amused him, anyway.

"I guess one short trip on the Devil of the Deep isn't enough for me to earn them."

"The Devil, was it? That be quite a co-in...co-in.... That's kinda weird."

"Weird?" Teryk raised an eyebrow. "What's weird?"

"The Whalebone be asea in search o' the Devil."

"In search of? You mean the Devil of the Deep is missing?"

Ash nodded, a grave expression pulling the corners of his mouth into a frown. Teryk rubbed his cheek, palm brushing against the sparse stubble he supposed made him look more sailor than prince.

"I didn't think that ship could sink."

"Didn't say she sank," Ash replied.

"No, I guess you didn't." Teryk dunked the mop in the bucket again, swished it around in the water. "What do you suppose happened?"

"No way o' knowin' lest we find her. Maybe the crew got fed up and took a cruise to the land across the sea."

Teryk stopped with the mop pulled half out of the bucket, water streaming from its strands onto the deck. The speed of his heartbeat jumped and he had to consciously keep his voice from shaking. "Isn't the land across the sea a myth?"

"Bah," Ash scoffed. "I s'pose you think the man what lives on the moon and the fairy who takes your lost teeth are myths, too."

Teryk did, but he didn't say so. Instead, he took the cabin boy's comment to mean he believed it real.

"Have you ever been there?"

"To the moon?"

The prince laughed a false laugh in attempt to hide his excitement. "No, to the land across the sea."

Ash's expression shifted. He stared at Teryk as though he'd spoken without moving his mouth, or like his head had gone missing. His face didn't change until he finally shook his head.

"Course not. No one's ever been there. Strayin' out to sea means death in the jaws of the God o' the Deep." Ash looked away and his voice grew quiet. "Prob'ly what happened to the crew o' the Devil."

Teryk stared at his companion, barely noticing the wind rising, cooling and drying the sweat on his face. They stayed that way until a footstep drew their attention. A man with a scar on his cheek and his beard trimmed to a point glared at them, hands on his hips. Teryk had seen the man before but hadn't spoken to him in his brief time on the Whalebone. He'd learned he was appropriately named for the path his life had taken: Seaman. Rilum Seaman.

"Get to work, ya lazy layabouts. Deck needs t'be swabbed afore the storm hits." He tilted his head back and to the left; Teryk's gaze followed.

The wind had risen further, pushing the clouds from the horizon closer. A gray haze blurred the space between sky and sea; Teryk recognized it as sheets of rain. Beside him, Ash dunked his mop.

"Yes, father. It'll be done."

Rilum grunted, glared at Teryk, then spun on his boot heel and left them to their work as he likely headed off to harass another crew member into doing their job faster.

The prince resumed mopping, eyes still on the dark gray billows of cloud as they closed the distance toward the ship. Overhead, the sails billowed and snapped in the rising wind and men clambered up rope ladders and masts to do whatever they needed to do to contain and protect them.

"I didn't realize Rilum's your father," Teryk commented, turning his attention back to the job at hand.

"He doesn't like it when I call him that."

"He's sort of—"

"Grumpy?"

Teryk smiled but Ash wasn't looking at him to see it.

"Not the word I was thinking of, but yes: grumpy."

"He has good reason to be." Ash's sailor speak had vanished.

"Why is that?"

"My grandfather was part of the crew of the Devil."

The first drop of rain spattered on Teryk's forehead and he raised his eyes skyward. The sun and the blue of the firmament were gone, hidden behind angry, boiling clouds. Teryk stared, surprised at how quickly the storm overtook them.

***

The storm fell upon the Whalebone like a hungry beast upon its prey. Wind whipped the sails as men worked frantically to tame them and stow them. Anything not lashed down shifted and moved as the growing waves tossed the ship around; Teryk's mop bucket had slid across the deck until it hit a coil of rope, tipped over and rolled away. Rain pelted his face hard enough to sting.

"Get ye below," Rilum Seaman yelled as he hurried by, his beard dripping rain from its tip. "Lash the cargo afore we lose it all."

Ash snagged Teryk's sleeve and pulled him toward the hatch. The ship's motion sent them both reeling, but Ash's sea legs kept him upright and his grip helped the prince remain the same. They weaved their way across the deck, wind howling through ropes, sails snapping, wood creaking. A huge wave crashed against the side of the ship, sending spray over the wale and splashing on the deck.

"Hurry," Ash shouted, throwing the hatch open.

Teryk did, blinking away the water streaming out of his hair and into his eyes as he scrambled down the ladder. Ash came close after him, pulling the hatch shut behind him, throwing them into darkness. The prince wiped rain from his face, relieved to be out of the weather, but keeping his footing here proved no easier than above, so he gripped the nearest rung for balance. In the dark, he heard Ash take a lantern from where it hung on the wall and light it. Flickering light sprang to life, casting writhing shadows across the sailors' bunks.

"Come on."

Ash dragged Teryk from his safe haven, through the crew's quarters, and to the ladder leading to the main hold. The narrow confines of the crew deck lent their passage more stability, but the violent ocean still threw the ship about. Teryk banged his leg against one bunk or another more than once.

The cabin boy handed the lantern to the prince and descended the next ladder first. Teryk waited until he completed his descent before passing the lamp down, then followed, moving deliberately, careful of his grip. At the bottom, he found Ash staring at the dim hold, a grim look on his face. Teryk followed his gaze.

The hold was a shambles. Crates had toppled, one striking a barrel and splitting it open to spill the pickles within onto the floor. The items already lashed down strained against their bindings as the boat pitched with the will of the waves. The prince wondered how they'd restrain the cargo without it crushing them.

"Get a rope," Ash demanded.

One hung on the wall by the ladder, so Teryk took a step toward it, reaching to retrieve it when he stopped, foot splashing in water. He lowered his eyes and saw enough to come to the top of the sole of his boot. A shiver crawled up his spine, only partially brought on by the wet clothes clinging to his skin.

"Ash."

The water moved with the pitch of the ship, making it impossible to tell where it came from. It might be the brine spilled along with the pickles they preserved, but it seemed far too much liquid to be the case.

"Get the rope, Taylor. Hurry."

"Look at this, Ash." He grasped the cabin boy's sleeve, wet cloth squelching between his fingers, and pulled him closer. The lantern's light glistened on the wet deck. Ash stared, eyes widening.

"We're taking on water."

"What do we do? Should we get someone?"

"No time. We have to find it and stop it."

Teryk nodded, a fearful lump in his throat. If he'd told the truth when they found him, he wouldn't be here now. He'd likely be in the practice yard, sparring with Trenan—if his father and mother hadn't locked him in his chamber for leaving Draekfarren.

The cabin boy moved away from the ladder and Teryk followed, taking advantage of the light cast by the lantern. His eyes scanned back and forth across the deck until Ash struck him in the arm to get his attention.

"Not the floor. There's another deck below. It'd have to be filled for water to come through the floorboards. Check the sides."

Teryk nodded, embarrassed by his mistake, but the effort of keeping his feet as the ship churned beneath them relieved him of the discomfort. They moved through the hold, wary of shifting crates and of pickles under foot. The noise of the storm was less here than on the crew deck, making communication easier.

"Anything?" Ash asked.

"No."

The cabin boy slid a crate aside and checked behind it

while Teryk continued on. A few paces ahead, the lantern's light found the hatch leading to the lowest deck: closed and bolted, the fastener rattling with the ship's movement. Teryk moved closer, squinting to see in the dim illumination.

Water ran from the narrow space between hatch and floor.

The prince gulped hard, his saliva tangy and acidic. A wave sent him reeling into a crate, striking his knee against the wood and sending a bolt of pain along his leg. He grabbed the edge of the box to steady himself, raised his gaze to make sure he'd seen what he thought he'd seen.

The volume of water seeping through the hatch had increased.

"Ash."

The cabin boy didn't respond, so Teryk shouted.

"Ash!"

The light cast upon the door brightened as Ash moved closer. He held the lantern out with one hand while using the other to support himself on crates and barrels. Teryk looked back at him and, for an instant, the way the storm threw the boy around and swung the lantern in his grasp brought nausea to the prince's gut. The change in Ash's expression made him forget it.

"No," the cabin boy whispered. "It can't be."

Teryk looked from Ash to the hatch then back. In that instant, he recognized panic in the cabin boy's face and saw him as the boy he truly was, not the sailor he'd viewed him as. The prince realized he'd have to jump to action or they'd continue staring at the water leaking through the hatch until it filled the hold and drowned them.

He stumbled across the deck and grabbed Ash's arm, pulling him back toward the ladder. As they did, the ship lurched and they lost their footing. Teryk fell against a crate, jarring his shoulder, and Ash went down behind him. The lantern slipped from his grasp, crashing against the floor and shattering the glass. The flame extinguished, throwing them into darkness.

The panic Teryk had seen on Ash's face gripped him now, tightening his limbs to blocks of wood. He knew he should find his feet, fumble his way to the ladder and back up to higher decks. Someone needed to be told, something needed to be done, but he couldn't move.

Boom.

Crates and barrels rattled in the dark and the deck shuddered beneath them.

"What was that?" Teryk's voice quaked, but he didn't care.

"I don't know."

Ash was closer than he'd expected, so it startled him when the cabin boy's hand grasped his ankle. Water splashed as he pulled himself closer and the two of them used each other to find their way to their feet.

Boom.

The sound again, and the rattles and shudder, but this time accompanied by the rending of wood and the splash and rush of water.

"We've struck something. We have to warn everyone."

Teryk felt Ash move away, leaving him alone in the dark as the ship pitched and the sea rushed in. Panic gripped his heart and, for a moment, he didn't move. Couldn't move. The cabin boy's hand reached out in the darkness and grasped the front of the prince's shirt, forcing him into action.

Ash was up the ladder and onto the crew deck, Teryk halfway up behind him when the ship was struck a third time.

Boom. Crack.

The sound hurried Teryk's pace. He dragged himself

the rest of the way up the rungs and crawled along the crew deck, using the ends of the bunks to guide him, the low center of gravity to keep him from being thrown about. The noise of the storm increased, blocking the sounds of Ash finding his way ahead of him.

They reached the ladder and Ash scurried up, Teryk right at the cabin boy's heels, waiting as he pulled the rope to release the hatch's clasp. Ash pushed the portal open and a wave of sea water rushed down upon them.

Teryk grasped the rungs tight and turned his head, barely keeping the salty sea out of his mouth and nose. Above, the force of the wave loosened Ash's grip on the rungs. The cabin boy's weight landed on Teryk's head and shoulders, but he maintained his hold and his presence kept Ash from falling all the way back to the deck below. The prince grunted with effort as the cabin boy struggled to regain his grip; when he did, the weight upon him first eased, then disappeared.

Ash scrambled up and out through the hatch. Teryk paused to catch his breath, then followed. His head emerged through the opening and salty spray slapped his face, the roar of the wind in the masts and ropes and the crash of waves against the hull assaulted his ears. Lightning flashed and thunder added its throaty growl to the cacophony.

Teryk gaped. He'd never in his life seen a storm like this.

Ash's hand fell on his shoulder, his fingers gripping the prince's shirt, urging him up and out. The cabin boy's urgency snapped Teryk back to reality and he hauled himself out through the opening.

"Shut the hatch," Ash shouted, wind whipping his hair into his face. "Enough water down there already."

Teryk complied, then followed the cabin boy. The ship bucked and pitched under his feet and it was all he could do to keep from falling. Ash took off toward the upper deck, presumably in search of his father, his practiced sea legs giving him little advantage over Teryk in the heaving sea.

One step passed beneath the prince's feet before the ship's gyrations got the better of him and he toppled over, landing hard on the wet deck. He spread his arms and legs, sprawling and keeping himself from rolling or sliding across the ship. Panting, he remained for a few seconds, gathering his energy and his courage, though he had trouble finding either. Another wave washed over him as he lay there and he spat salt water from his mouth before drawing himself up to his hands and knees.

Teryk saw that Ash had made it halfway to the stairs leading to the upper deck, his progress hindered by the sea throwing him back and forth in a cockeyed path to his goal. He admired the way the cabin boy kept his feet under him in such awful conditions. It gave him courage and hope they might survive.

Hard rain pelted Teryk's cheeks as he clambered to his feet. Another wave hit and he wondered if that was what they'd heard on the lower deck. He bent at the waist, one hand on the edge of the hatch to keep from falling over, and looked up to the side of the ship.

The wave approaching them was taller than a building, perhaps as high as the Pillars of Life before they'd fallen. Teryk stared, saltwater stinging his eyes, then jerked his gaze away to see if his friend made it to the stairway. He hadn't.

"Ash!" Teryk screamed, but the wind stole his voice and threw it out to the raging sea.

He let go of the hatch and lurched across the deck after the cabin boy, stealing a glance at the approaching wave. Its height dwarfed the ship.

The shouts of crew men swirled with the howl of the wind, but Teryk didn't know who cried out or what they said. He focused on the cabin boy ahead of him. It didn't seem Ash had noticed the monster wave bearing down on them; he continued lurching toward the stairs.

Teryk's foot caught on a coil of rope washed from its proper spot and unspooled to lay across the deck like a snake waiting to snare him. He fell hard, striking his elbows and shooting pain along his arms.

"Ash!"

He stretched out his hand toward the cabin boy struggling ahead of him as though he might reach him, catch him by the arm and keep him safe. At the last second, Teryk saw Ash turn his head and glimpse the wave before it crashed into the ship.

The force of it picked the cabin boy up and tossed him like a child's doll made of rags. Panic seized Teryk for the boy's safety, but then water filled his mouth. It plucked him from the deck, rolled him over, threw him. Salty seawater grated against his eyes, his lungs pined over the thought of never taking another breath.

Teryk's world was naught but water. He thrashed with his arms and legs, remembering the last time he'd been underwater—when he got pinned beneath the gate and would have drowned if not for his sister freeing him.

Danya.

In the time since he'd regained consciousness, he'd focused so much on his shipboard tasks and his role in the prophecy, he'd barely given her a thought. Now his heart ached that they'd parted; he'd never see her again.

The sea spun and rolled Teryk until up and down became distant memories. Distress filled his chest, begging him to draw breath, but there was no air to be had. If he gave in, his death would be a certainty instead of the likelihood it already was.

The tossing lasted so long, he was sure he'd gone over the side, destined to perish in the sea, when his back struck something hard. He reached out and his fingers found purchase. He grasped with one hand, brought the other to it and held on, recognizing it as his only chance for life.

A moment later, the water disappeared. Teryk fell to the deck, coughing and hacking to empty his lungs and throat. The sea streamed from his mouth and nose and he blinked to clear his vision, found himself holding onto the railing of the stairs leading to the upper deck. The wave had washed him from one end of the ship to the other.

"Ash?"

He used the railing to pull himself to his feet, cast his gaze around the deck. He saw sailors righting themselves after having been thrown about like himself. Some were already on their feet and helping others or getting back to the tasks in need of their attention.

As far as Teryk saw, the cabin boy was not amongst them.

"Ash?"

He relinquished his grip on the railing and stumbled across the deck toward the wale. On his way, he passed Rilum Seaman—Ash's father. He'd struck his head and blood poured from the wound as another of the crew helped him. Teryk thought about telling him Ash had disappeared, asking him to help find the cabin boy, but his eyes appeared unfocused and bleary; he'd be no help in his condition.

The prince reached the side of the ship without losing his balance, gripped the edge and looked out across the heaving sea. Waves rose and fell, undulating in great swells that sometimes hid the cloud-filled sky and other times held the Whalebone up above the rest of the world. Teryk realized that, if the wave washed Ash overboard, there was little chance—

He glimpsed something as the ship rose on a swell that stretched as high as the mainsail. An arm waved and Teryk was sure it was Ash, then they dipped back into a trough between waves and he vanished. Desperate, the prince searched for some way to help his friend, a line to throw him. He looked down to his feet and found the rope responsible for tripping him up—likely saving him from being washed overboard himself—lying nearby.

Teryk snatched it off the deck and ran it through his hands until he reached the end. He tied it to the rail and looped it into his fists as the ship rose on another swell. Legs spread wide to keep his balance, he looked back to the sea, searching for his friend, ready to throw him the rope and drag him aboard.

He saw no sign of the cabin boy this time. What he did see made the coils slip from his fingers.

Wide head, long neck, sharp teeth.

The God of the Deep.

XXXII Ailyssa - The Veil

A green glow crept into the sky above the tops of the trees, like a sunset gone awry. They amended their path, heading for the eerie light, though Ailyssa felt uncertain it was the best course of action. So far, the nameless man's instincts had proven correct, so she followed without comment despite the twinge of foreboding gripping her chest.

The glow neither brightened nor dimmed as they moved toward it. Instead, it climbed higher and higher into the sky, appearing to separate the twilight creeping in from behind them from the daylight still stretching out ahead.

The land they'd traversed since leaving the transforming village rose and fell, the ground undulating with hills. They found themselves alternately in dales filled with shadow and air cooled by the shade of tall trees, then atop crests bathed in the warm rays of the sun. Ailyssa wished to take the time to enjoy both, but the strange figure they'd seen watching them from the village left her unsettled, wary, frightened. It had been too far away for her to discern who it was, but she didn't need to know; to her mind, its presence exuded danger.

As they approached the green glow, the land flattened again, allowing Ailyssa the opportunity to survey the path they'd taken and convince herself the strange figure hadn't followed them. She spied nothing but forest and hills; a shudder trembled through her shoulders.

"Look. It reaches to the ground."

The nameless man raised his hand, pointed ahead of them. Ailyssa did as he said and glimpsed flashes of green fire between the trunks of the trees. She didn't understand what might cause such a thing, but it didn't fill her with dread the way the shadowy figure at the village did.

The man quickened his pace, pulling her along with him. The glow pulsed and wavered in the waning light of approaching twilight, brightening and dimming in steady rhythm as though a heart beat within it. Seeing it made Ailyssa forget the ominous silhouette, the weird village; even Jubha Kyna and her banishment from Olvana left her, replaced by a sense of awe.

"What do you think it is?" she asked breathlessly as they approached the green wall.

"A barrier of some sort."

Ailyssa tilted her head back to survey the shimmering wall's full height. It was impossible to say how high it climbed; from her vantage point on the ground, it appeared to reach all the way to the sky.

"I don't understand," she said, directing her attention to her companion.

He didn't appear to hear as he stared at the green curtain, eyes wide and mouth gaping. A trance-like state had overtaken him, drawing him toward the barrier and blocking out the rest of the world. Ailyssa understood—she felt drawn to it as well—but caution kept her from giving into it.

"Stop," she said, grabbing his wrist with her free hand.

He tried to keep walking, but she dug her feet into the ground. For a moment, she thought he'd drag her along behind him, heels cutting deep furrows into the dirt, but her weight pulled him from the trance. He stopped and faced her.

"We don't know what it is," Ailyssa said.

The man blinked twice and shook his head, regarded the shimmering wall briefly before returning his attention to her. When he did, his eyes had cleared.

"I couldn't stop," he said, letting his gaze drop. "It was like something within the glow beckoned me."

"We should take care."

He nodded and they took up walking again, amending their path to travel parallel to the barrier rather than heading toward it. Only ten paces separated them from it, but its attraction diminished. They walked in silence until it occurred to Ailyssa that she didn't know where they'd go and assumed her companion didn't either. She parted her lips to ask when he broke the quiet before she had the chance.

"Look," he said, pointing again.

This time he gestured skyward. Ailyssa lifted her gaze, looking where he indicated, and noticed an unusual cluster of clouds on the horizon. In the distance, the cloud was broad, but as it came closer to them, it narrowed until it ended in a point.

Ailyssa narrowed her eyes, staring at the apex of the cloud. A movement at the front of it drew the vapor across the sky behind. She took a few heartbeats to realize what it was.

"A bird!"

Cloud puffed out behind it with each flap of its wings and Ailyssa stared, open-mouthed. She'd seen nothing like it before. They watched it come closer until it passed overhead. The trail of cloud it left spread out above them, butting up against the green wall on one side, its expansion halted, but expanding across the sky on the other. She attempted to continue watching the bird, but the cloudy trail left in its wake obscured it, so she turned her attention to the cloud swirling against the barrier high above.

"Come with me," she said, tugging on the nameless man's hand. "But avert your eyes from the wall."

He followed without hesitation, the sensation of leading swelling her heart. As they crossed the space toward the shimmering green barrier, anticipation grew in her, an unexpected excitement. The wall tugged at her as before, but not with such insistence that she couldn't resist it if she chose.

When they'd come within arm's reach, she stopped and glanced back at her companion. He'd directed his eyes toward the ground to avoid gazing at the barrier as she'd told him. He halted when she did.

The green light, brighter with the clouds blotting out the near-twilight sky, pulsed and faded, pulsed and faded. After watching it for a few breaths, Ailyssa realized the rhythm of the glow matched the beat of her own heart; whether her heart kept pace with the wall's pulsations, or the wall duplicated hers, she didn't know. Either way, realizing it dried up all the saliva in her mouth.

"What are you doing?" her companion asked.

"I want to find out if it's as solid as it seems."

Why did she say that? She'd never intended to touch the green glow, only to examine it more closely. Yet the words came from her lips and she found herself lifting her arm, reaching toward the strange light.

Her fingertips brushed its surface and bolts of verdant lightning crackled across it without making a sound. It was warm and smooth and the effect her touch created caused no pain or discomfort. She drew her hand away and the wall's reaction ceased. When she touched it again, it returned.

"Amazing," she said, breathless.

This time when she removed her touch, she noticed movement on the other side. Startled, she stepped away, back pressing against her companion. Her heart beat faster, the pulse of the light keeping pace until she found what drew her attention.

On the other side of the barrier opposite her stood a deer, different from any deer she'd seen before. It resembled the size and shape of any she'd encountered—most of which had been dead, brought to Olvana by hunters and sold to them for food—but this one sported only a single, straight horn jutting from the center of its head. It bore no sign of fights or accidents that might have caused the loss of others, no stumps where they should have been, just the lone antler. The animal stared back at her with as much surprise and wonder in its gaze as she imagined must be in hers.

"Look," she said, gripping the nameless man's hand.

He did as she continued holding onto him, squeezing, hoping to keep him from being lost in a trance again. He raised his arm. At first, she thought him reaching for the wall and her heart leapt with concern. A shock of lightning sprinted across the barrier along with it, but he was gesturing beyond the strange deer.

"There are others."

She looked past the animal. On the other side of the wall, the forest grew thick with tree trunks and brush, having been allowed to flourish when someone had cleared the forest away where they stood. On a fallen log behind the deer sat a rabbit with floppy ears and a wiggling nose, but it was the size of a pig. Birds perched in the boughs of the trees, too. She counted at least five different varieties, each notable by their colorful plumage and none of them like any she'd ever seen. Every bird and animal stared back as though as curious about them as they were about the animals.

Ailyssa shivered.

"Perhaps we should keep moving."

From the corner of her eye, she glimpsed the man nodding. An instant later, he started out and she went with him, keeping herself between him and the green wall. Try as she might to keep her gaze from the forest on the far side, the barrier compelled her to raise her eyes from watching her footsteps and glance beyond it as they walked. She found the deer loping along with them, and birds following, flitting from branch to branch.

"Where are we going?" she asked, more to distract herself from the animals than because she expected him to have an answer.

"Eventually, we'll find a town. A real town."

The thought brought her both hope and fear. Though the sun had risen several times since they escaped Juddah's barn, they couldn't be sure their pursuers gave up the chase, so it would do them well to find somewhere to hide. But Ailyssa had had little luck when accepting help from strangers; first Creidra took her to Jubha Kyna to become the plaything of men, then Juddah locked her in his barn, intending to keep her as his own. She had no choice but to trust the nameless man whose touch gave her sight, but she doubted her ability to believe anyone else genuinely wanted to aid her. Sometimes, she wasn't sure her companion did.

The deer following them on her right halted, its attention diverted from the two people to something ahead. It backed away one step at a time, then turned tail and ran, bounding through brush and over moss-covered logs. Hesitantly, Ailyssa looked ahead, searching for what frightened the one-horned animal.

It took little effort to differentiate the large creature from the dense forest.

Thick, black hair covered its massive form while its head—larger than a man's—sported a blunt snout and short, rounded ears. It stood on all fours, head tilted back as though listening or scenting the wind. Ailyssa pulled on her companion's hand, dragging him to a stop.

"What is—?"

She put her finger to his lips to keep him from speaking and attracting the creature's attention, then pointed. When he sighted the beast, the nameless man's demeanor didn't change. Instead of acting fearful, as Ailyssa felt, he coaxed her onward. After three steps, the animal caught wind of them.

It reared, standing on its back legs, the top of its head two arm's lengths higher than the nameless man's. The beast's lips parted, revealing sharp teeth designed for rending flesh. It waved its gigantic paws and its mouth opened in what should have been an ear-splitting roar but which Ailyssa and her companion couldn't hear.

"The barrier may be as much to keep them in as to keep us out," the nameless man said.

Ailyssa swallowed. Assuming the wall had it trapped on the other side did little to ease her fear of its pointed teeth and dangerous claws.

It is good to be afraid of such things. Goddess made them fearful looking for a reason.

When the animal realized they didn't react to its warning, it dropped back to all four feet and moved toward the green wall, its bulk heaving side to side with each step. Ailyssa pulled herself closer to the nameless man, gaining small comfort in the touch of his chest against her shoulder, but the beast stopped short of the barrier, not close enough to brush against it.

"See? It knows better."

Ailyssa nodded and sighed a relieved breath as they walked again. From the corner of her eye, she saw the beast lumbering along beside them, picking its way over fallen trees and around thick brush while the path on their side remained clear. After a short while, she convinced herself to forget the animal, directing her attention instead to the clouds blotting out the sky.

Approaching twilight painted the blanket of cloud covering the world in shades of gray, with darkness and night soon to follow. The green wall looked to hold back the clouds as effectively as it kept Ailyssa out and the forest creatures in.

Can anything pass the wall?

A fat raindrop plopped on Ailyssa's shoulder, a few others pattered against leaves and grass. The thought of being caught out in the rain should have dulled her spirit, but Ailyssa had always enjoyed whatever the Goddess' world offered: sun, rain, wind, night. It all reminded her how good it was to be alive. Despite everything that had happened—the heartache and hardships she'd endured— the drops felt splendid on her cheeks.

The wind rose, playing through her short hair and she resisted the urge to close her eyes, enjoy how the elements touched her. A jagged bolt of lightning shot across the sky, startling a gasp out of her. The nameless man squeezed her hand tighter, as though he thought she feared the lightning rather than being surprised by it. His action at once made her feel an indebtedness to him and a loathing he should assume she needed his protection. If it wouldn't have thrown her into blindness, she'd have pulled her hand away from his comforting gesture.

The space of five heartbeats later, thunder rumbled through the world. This time, since she prepared herself for it, she giggled at the sound. The rain increased; not enough to drench them, but enough the drops couldn't be avoided. She tilted her head back and allowed them to caress her cheek, to cool her skin.

Her companion halted and Ailyssa walked into him, bumping her nose on his shoulder and sending painful stars flashing across her vision.

"Hey. What are you—?"

She raised her head and saw the robed figures emerging from the edge of the forest.

The nameless man's body tensed, his head jerked side to side, searching for an escape route. Ailyssa looked too and found other figures had crept up behind them, surrounding them, cutting off any path. The last to show himself was the one who wore no robe and led Juddah by the length of frayed rope.

Ailyssa gasped when she spied her one-time rescuer/captor. Even with night descending upon them, she recognized his swollen face, his shoulders sagging with fatigue and defeat. His feet dragged as he was led toward them; he looked like a dead man who didn't realize his time was done.

"Well, well, Juddah," the man leading him said, "it appears you've done more work for me and the brothers than we might have hoped."

The nameless man ushered Ailyssa behind him and backed away as the robed men formed a semicircle around them, penning them in with their backs to the glowing green wall. Distress at needing to be protected once again flitted through her, but the fear of what these men might do to them quashed it at once.

"Not only have you brought us the man from across the sea, as the prophecy said," he continued, "but it seems you have also led us to the barren mother."

Rain cascaded down Ailyssa's cheeks, dripped from her chin, found its way under her collar and down her back, but she noticed none of it. The term the man used in describing her—barren mother—cut into her as if he'd plunged a knife between her ribs. Her companion continued backing them away from the robed men and she wondered if he could do anything to keep them from harm.

Ailyssa sensed the barrier close behind them. She glanced over her shoulder and saw it fewer than two paces from her, rain droplets striking it and sending spiderwebs of fine, green lightning crawling across its surface. She set her feet and pushed back against her companion, letting him know they'd gone as far as space allowed. He stopped, planted his feet, braced himself.

A smile crept across the face of the man leading Juddah. It smacked of satisfaction, Ailyssa thought, like the grin of someone who'd worked a long time for something, finally achieving it. Lightning filled the sky again, the light flashing in his eyes as though fire burned within them. For the first time in her life, Ailyssa considered true evil might exist in the world.

"Take them," the man commanded.

The semicircle drew closer around them, leaving their leader where he stood, the smile making a home upon his lips. Ailyssa's gaze flitted from one to the next. She saw no weapons in their hands, but suspected it didn't matter; they could still do them harm.

Thunder rolled, the rumble building and folding over on itself until it became a roar.

"No!"

The word was all but lost in the booming thunder, but it caught Ailyssa's attention, for neither she nor her companion uttered it. Everything moved so fast afterward, she struggled to recognize what happened.

Juddah jumped forward, his sudden and unexpected movement catching his captor off-guard. The thick rope slipped from his grasp and the big man hurled himself with surprising energy into the nearest robed fellow. His bulk lifted the stranger into the air and sent him toppling to the ground before Juddah threw himself at the next.

Half of the robed men turned their attention to the escaped prisoner while the others closed the distance to Ailyssa and her companion. The nameless man jerked away, pushing her back. She gasped as the barrier pressed against her spine. The man without a robe shouted, Juddah growled, energy crackled through the air; another robed figure reached for her companion, a dim light emanating from the sleeve of his robe.

Green light engulfed her vision and a hiss like rushing water filled Ailyssa's head. It lasted for only a moment, but in that moment, she watched one of the robed men grab Juddah by the head and twist his neck hard. He crumpled to the ground.

First, the sounds disappeared, followed by the world itself. Ailyssa fell, landing hard enough to knock the air out of her lungs. Her companion's touch drifted away and the forest returned to nothing but featureless white haze as she lay on her back struggling to find her breath. When it returned, she gasped air into her chest, filling her lungs. Panic filled her chest along with it.

A wide leaf touched her cheek and she jerked away, startled, wiping at the spot with the back of her hand. Only then did she realize the rain had stopped. She froze, fighting to control her breath and ignore the pounding of her heart in her ears. Instead of the sound of a fight, she heard the gentle rustle of leaves stirred by a light wind, the chirrup of crickets singing in the night. The odors were different, too: wood and moss and loam, the scents of the forest.

I've passed through the barrier.

With the realization, she identified another fragrance amongst the aromas of the woods, this one not as pleasant: the musty odor of a wet thing not given the opportunity to properly dry.

Ailyssa held her breath as a branch snapped under the weight of a footstep. Her mind, unhindered by sight, brought a clear picture of the black beast with the small ears and sharp teeth to her, speeding the beat of her heart.

A deep rumbling disturbed the forest's sounds, but this wasn't the complaint of thunder. The noise rolled in the throat of a great, black animal rooting through the brush in search of her.

***

Juddah didn't know where the energy came from to yank the rope out of his captor's hands; blind rage, perhaps. A memory of Kooj's twisted corpse flashed through his mind at the sight of the robed men approaching two more of his possessions, and he snapped, unable to accept that these prizes should suffer the same fate as his beloved dog.

He sprang forward, launching himself in to the nearest of the 'brothers,' knocking him from his feet. The element of surprise on his side for a fraction of a moment longer, he knocked over a second of the dangerous men before a third grabbed his arm. Juddah did his best to jerk away, intending to go back after Birk who'd been holding the rope; Birk who dogged him season after season; Birk who was to blame for Kooj's death and everything bad that ever happened to Juddah—he understood that now. The man had stalked him, used him, and now was the time for him to pay.

He made it one step toward his goal before a robed man grabbed Juddah's head in both hands, the grip tight enough his eyeballs bulged in their sockets, causing the swollen one to shoot agony through his head and along his neck. The pain ceased as the man twisted Juddah's head, a popping sound filling his ears. His aggressor let go and Juddah intended to stop himself from falling to the ground, but found his body refused to respond to his wishes.

As he tumbled, gray crept in at the edges of his vision. Through it he saw the man he'd discovered lying on the shore push the woman from Jubha Kyna—Ailyssa, her name is Ailyssa—through the green glowing wall, hopefully to safety.

By the time Juddah hit the ground, life had left his body.

XXXIII Horace - Small Gods

By the time they reached the bottom o' the ridge and grass were brushin' the legs o' his breeches, exhaustion and fatigue'd returned to Horace with the force o' a fourth season squall. He considered askin' the Small God for more o' whatever she'd given him before, but doubted his voice'd work the way he meant it to. His legs became short stone pillars, barely capable o' bendin' and movin'. His lungs refused to fill themselves more'n half full and his muscles cried out for the air they was supposed to supply. Ivy were fairly draggin' him along behind her when she let go her hold on his wrist.

Horace tumbled to the ground, twistin' himself at the last second to land on his shoulder instead o' his face. He lay on his side for a bit, wishin' to spend some time enjoyin' the rest. Since he couldn't, he pushed himself to his elbows, arms what had nothin' to do with walkin' givin' him as much discomfort as his legs.

The Small God were sprintin' across the field, her skinny legs a blur. Animals raised their heads as she passed, but none o' them seemed disturbed by her presence or her hurry. As soon as she'd gone by, each beast returned to whatever they'd been doin'.

A grunt made its way up from Horace's chest and forced itself out between his lips as the ol' sailor struggled to his feet. Them heavy legs didn't wanna help out, and he tumbled back to the ground at first. He sighed and gave it another go, pushin' himself up to hands and knees. He crawled toward the mud huts, draggin' his feet in the grass, stainin' the knees o' his filthy britches. The length o' three men'd passed beneath him when the big cat sauntered into his path.

He'd not seen an animal like this before, bein' a seafarin' man as he were, but he'd heard tell o' such creatures. What the stories'd said didn't give him no confidence it wouldn't eat him.

Muscle rippled under the cat's tawny coat. Its long tail flicked side to side like a thing with its own life. The beast stared at him, movin' as though it thought to be sneakin' up on him. Horace froze, more sweat burstin' on his brow and a sudden and urgent need to piss makin' itself known.

The big cat licked its lips.

Horace gulped hard and forced his uncooperative limbs into reversin' course. His hands and knees scuffled through the grass; a rock dug into his palm, causin' him to draw a sharp breath, but he forgot it as the beast took to stalkin' his direction.

It means to make me its lunch.

Were this why Ivy brought him here? She must be blamin' him for losin' her brother, and bein' consumed by the animal slinkin' toward him were his punishment. How could it be he'd survived a watery god for the same life to get ended by a land animal's teeth?

Scufflin', cursin', and quakin' in fear o' his life, Horace drug himself back the way Ivy'd brought him, but the big cat picked up its pace. Its quick feet and easy stride ate up the ground the way the cat'd eat him up when it got to him. The ol' sailor's arm and legs gave out under him, pitchin' him to the ground; he strained his neck to keep his chin outta the dirt.

So, this is it. This is the end.

He let out a sigh and pulled his arms up 'round his head. He didn't imagine doin' so'd stop the big cat's jaws from splittin' his skull and snackin' on his brain, but he figured he needed to do somethin'. His muscles clamped tight, tyin' themselves into fearful knots for the very last time.

I'm sorry I didn't take better care o' you, Thorn. And sorry, Rilum, I weren't a better dad to you.

The quiet pad o' the cat's paws drew close; for him to detect them steps, Horace estimated the beast must be damn close. The sailor gritted his teeth, preparin' for the death blow, whether it came by tooth or claw.

Nothin' happened.

"Fuck me dead."

The words escaped his lips despite his not wantin' to speak lest it'd anger the big cat. It didn't. Instead, someone laughed; tittered'd be a better description. A quiet rumblin' joined in with them snickers.

Horace relaxed his muscles and took his arms away from his face. He didn't remember doin' it, but he found he'd closed his eyes, too. He opened them slowly, prayin' he'd see nothin' but grass close by him and mud huts in the distance.

The cat sat on the grass a bit more'n an arm's length away. Seein' it so close made a drop o' piss squeeze outta Horace against his will, but he kept his bladder from releasin' any more, partially because Ivy stood beside the beast, fingers scratchin' the fur between its pointed ears. The rumblin' came from the animal, a response to the Small God's touch. All around behind her and to both sides, other gray men and women gathered.

"This is the one Ivy told about," she said. "The sailor

from the prophecy."

Horace shook his head, tryin' to get them to understand he knew nothin' o' no prophecy and, even if he did, weren't no way it mentioned him.

"The prophecy is not real," one standin' off to Ivy's right said. "A story to keep our kind from escaping the veil."

Many of the others nodded or mumbled their agreement. In fact, as Horace glanced about them gathered around, it appeared none but Ivy wasn't agreein'.

"But my brother Thorn escaped. The sailor saw him on the other side of the veil, as the prophecy foretold."

"Ha!" scoffed a gray feller what stood taller'n the others—not by much, but enough to be noticeable. Weren't much way but height to tell them apart, with not even a heap o' difference in that from one to the next. "Ivy believes...this?"

The taller feller gestured in Horace's direction and the ol' sailor felt a twinge o' annoyance at his choice o' words. He didn't know Horace, nor nothin' about him; he'd ne'er done anythin' to deserve bein' called a 'this'.

"I saw him," Horace piped up as he pushed himself up to his knees. "Fact, he fell outta the sky, right on toppa me."

No titterin' in response this time. A wave o' laughter rippled from one Small God to the next and the next until they belly-laughed at him. All o' them except Ivy. A grave look'd settled on her face.

"You should not laugh. Why should this human lie to us?"

A diff'rent feller than what first spoke stepped forward. Horace knew it to be a feller due to the man-thing danglin' betwixt his legs, but this Small God stood shorter than the first, and broader, too. Weren't no belly on him, but he were wider at the shoulders and hips;

even his face and head was diff'rent from the others. The laughin' ceased as though this one'd given a silent command. Ev'ryone waited for him to speak, Horace included.

"This...man...should not be in our land."

"But Thorn—"

The broad feller raised his hand and Ivy stopped speakin'. Her chin drooped toward her chest and she lowered her eyes from his gaze.

"Sky understands Ivy misses her brother, but this is not the first time Thorn has gone off alone." He shook his head and, for an instant, Horace thought he spied a smile flit across his lips, but then it disappeared and he doubted what he'd seen. "Because Thorn went exploring does not mean the sky will crash down upon us."

Horace directed his attention from the broad feller what called himself Sky to Ivy. The muscles in her jaw bunched up as if she wanted to say somethin' but forced her mouth closed to keep from doin' so. The ol' sailor didn't like the way it made her look; Thorn'd been so happy-go-lucky, it seemed wrong the weight o' the world pressed down on his sister.

"The prophecy is a story, as Branch spoke, and our land is no place for those other than our own kind. Ivy knows that. Every man who ever set foot behind the veil became Faceless."

Faceless.

The word brought a picture o' the creatures to Horace's mind, blood smeared across their smooth, white faces as they attempted to feed themselves. He swallowed hard.

They once were men?

Knowin' that brought a boatload o' questions and icy fear. How did they get here? Where were their faces? What made them that way?

Did the Small Gods take their faces?

Horace's gaze darted from one gray face to another; the tall feller called Branch leered at him with what the ol' sailor thought were somethin' like hunger burnin' in his eyes. Sweat ran along Horace's temple onto his cheek. Suddenly, it seemed havin' his skull cracked open by the big cat might've been preferable to what might happen to him now.

"But Thorn—" Ivy's voice trailed off as she raised her head to meet Sky's gaze.

"Thorn will be fine and will likely return soon," he said, his tone softer, soothing. It hardened when his gaze found Horace again. "Ivy must take the man away from here."

Thorn's sister didn't respond with words, simply nodded once and closed the distance between herself and the sailor. The big cat stayed behind, its golden eyes watchin' as Ivy put her hand under Horace's armpit and helped him to his feet. The energy she'd given him before flowed from her touch again, allowin' him to hold himself up without fallin' on his face. Gave him vigor, but not courage; it seemed to him a hideous fate awaited him.

Many of the gray people was leavin', headin' toward the mud huts from where they'd come. Sky remained, and Branch and a few others, watchin' as Ivy led Horace away across the meadow and up the hill leadin' to the ridge.

Toward them Faceless.

***

They walked for a long time without speakin'; long enough the sun dipped down outta the sky, showin' Horace which direction were Sunset. They wasn't headin' that way as shadows crept their way through the forest. Ivy kept her hand on his the whole time, her energy keepin' his legs movin' toward his fate.

Though it appeared they followed a similar path to

what they'd taken to arrive at the clearin'—they'd need to, to get back to them Faceless fiends where he suspected she meant to take him—Horace didn't find anythin' familiar in their surroundin's. Not recognizin' anythin' and not knowin' what lay ahead for him filled his chest with dread the way Ivy's touch put energy in his limbs. The ol' sailor drew a deep sigh in through his nose, expectin' to pick up the scents o' carrion and death but findin' only foresty odors. He'd never expected it'd happen, but his heart ached to smell the sharp tang o' oiled boards and brine upon the wind.

Least I knew what to expect with my feet on a ship's deck.

"Are you gonna take my face?"

Ivy quit walkin', but Horace carried on for two paces; her touch left his arm, makin' thick and gooey fatigue ooze back into his limbs. He had no choice but to halt, too, or he'd end up with his nose in the mossy forest floor.

"Ivy will do nothing to hurt you, sailor. Why would you think that?"

"Because o' what the broad feller said. You're to get rid o' me and all the men what comes to the Green turn into one o' them Faceless we saw."

She closed the short distance between them and Horace resisted the urge to back away, mostly because he didn't think his legs'd hold him up if he tried to move. He tensed as her hand returned to his arm.

"It is not Ivy and her kind who take the faces of men, but the Green, as you call it, sailor."

"Seaman," he corrected. "I be called Horace Seaman."

"Is that what Ivy's brother Thorn called you? Horace Seaman?"

"Yes."

The ol' sailor thought of the small, gray feller, his

joyous way o' bein', his love o' the world around him. What had become o' Thorn?

"Then Ivy will call you Horace Seaman, too."

She began walkin' again, pullin' him along with her.

"If you ain't gonna take my face, then what are you doin' with me?"

"The prophecy must be fulfilled."

Horace shook his head, but it did nothin' to clear the foggy confusion what were sneakin' into it. "Your friends said there weren't no prophecy."

"Sky does not believe it, but that does not mean it is not truth."

As they walked, a stiff wind picked up, rattlin' leaves and branches. Had he been on his own, the racket would've frightened Horace for what might be lurkin' in the gatherin' darkness, their movements hidden by the gustin' wind. Rememberin' how them Faceless couldn't see Ivy helped him put some o' the fear aside. Some, not all.

"So you believe it."

"Ivy does, Horace Seaman. A Small God missing and a man who rides upon the sea. Both are in the prophecy. Does Horace see it cannot be a coincidence?"

He shook his head again. "Can't be me. I'm nothin' more'n a man what spent too many turns o' the seasons standin' on one deck or another when I'd rather've been anywhere else."

"Be that as it may, Horace is the sailor who met the Small God escaped from behind the veil. There can be no other."

He didn't respond at first. Were it possible he might be the feller mentioned in a prophecy? Seemed unlikely. He weren't ever anythin' but a less'n average man and it weren't likely he'd be anythin' but. What could he do what'd make him part o' some prophecy? The ol' sailor tilted his head skyward and saw the wind'd blown a bank o' clouds in, hidin' the moon and the stars from sight and throwin' the world into deeper darkness. He shivered.

"If you ain't makin' me into one o' them Faceless, then where are you takin' me?"

"Horace's arrival means the barren mother and the seed of life must be near."

"My mother be long dead."

"Not Horace's. The barren mother."

"What's that s'posed to mean?"

"Ivy does not know. The prophecy suggests sailor, seed, and mother must come together for there to be any hope."

Hope?

Horace tried to speak, but his voice came out as nothin' but a croak. He cleared his throat and gave it another go.

"What'm I to do with this seed and mother?"

"The prophecy does not explain. Horace will know when the time comes, as Ivy knew what to do when Horace showed up."

"And what happens if I don't?"

"Then all will perish."

She spoke the words matter-o'-factly, as though she hadn't just proclaimed the end o' life. Horace gulped back a flood o' spit what threatened to overflow his mouth, its taste acidy with fear and dread.

They walked on in silence, the ol' sailor's mind racin'.

How can I save anyone when I can't keep myself outta trouble?

Through the trees, he saw a greenish glow against the backdrop o' scuddin' clouds. They was gettin' close to the veil what he'd crossed while floatin' in the water but what he hadn't been able to get through here on the land. Why take him there? Even Thorn'd needed to use Father

Raven to go o'er it because nothin' were goin' through it.

Horace's eyes went wide. Were Ivy goin' to make him fly o'er it with a bird? If that be the case, then the world were gonna end because Horace Seaman weren't gonna fall from the sky the way Thorn'd done.

He peered up through the swayin' branches at the clouds swirlin' o'erhead; the wind stopped all o'a sudden. The leaves and limbs fell silent along with any other sound the forest might've been makin'. Ivy stopped walkin' and looked up, too, leavin' Horace's own breath and the beat o' his heart the only sounds in his ears. The world seemed to be waitin', and Horace had no choice but to wait with it. After a bit, he could bear it no longer.

"What—?"

Thunder boomed, startlin' him, and the wind whipped back to life, stronger'n before. Trees bent and flexed with its force and Horace suspected he might have to hold onto Ivy to keep her from blowin' away. He moved closer to her, grabbin' her hand when she spoke one word what sent a shiver along his spine.

"Thorn."

Ivy still held her gaze skyward, so he did the same, lookin' up in time to see a streak o' light, but not like no lightnin' he'd seen in many a storm. This streak o' light trailed out behind a ball o' fire what hurtled toward the ground.

Ivy ran.

XXXIV Kuneprius - Teva Stavoklis

The rumble of wagon wheels on hard ground became monotonous background noise soon after they left

Murtikara. No one spoke aloud their destination, but the others knew, and Kuneprius suspected.

Teva Stavoklis.

When he'd first climbed into the covered wagon, his inclination was to peer out the side, both to see where they were going and to locate what the brothers had done with Thorn. He soon proved incapable of either as exhaustion leeched through his bones and muscles, bearing Kuneprius to the wagon's floorboards and smothering him with sleep.

Despite his desperate need for rest, nightmares disrupted his repose. Faces of the dead stared back at him in the dark, their penetrating gazes accusing him of their deaths. The first innkeeper, the children by the creek, the serving girls and patrons of the last inn; their dead eyes glared at him, condemned him.

The young woman from the caravan all those seasons ago visited him, too. She smiled when she saw him, the glint in her eyes hinting at something Kuneprius longed for in secret but would never know. But the mirth on her lips melted away, leaving a scowl in its wake, then pain, and finally blood.

Kuneprius jerked in his sleep, moaned, but the nightmare wasn't done with him. One more remained to lay blame at his feet.

Thorn.

The gray man strode into his dream, full of smiles and enthusiasm and vigor. A nod of his head brought light to the darkness. He waved his hand and flowers bloomed. He danced in a circle and birds of many colors took to the sky.

Such beauty; a welcome relief to Kuneprius' sleep after the stench of blood and death had permeated it. But the respite proved short-lived. The flowers wilted, the birds fell to earth, and the sky dimmed to night. Thorn's energy faded with the light, his shoulders drooped with the dying flowers.

And the evenstar shone overhead.

Ine'vesi glowed brighter than Kuneprius had ever seen, the intensity of the evenstar a palpable thing. It bombarded Thorn, its heat making his flesh sag on his limbs like wax melting from a taper. Ine'vesi's glare drove the Small God to his knees, head hung forward in defeat.

Kuneprius himself appeared next, walking into the scene with a measured gait. He'd never watched himself like this in a dream, observing as though he were someone else.

Light flashed on an object in his hand: a long knife with a curve to it and a wicked edge. He stopped behind the kneeling Thorn, stared at the Small God for a time before raising his hands skyward and throwing his head back in a gesture of reverence to the priest in the sky. In front of him, Thorn trembled but did nothing to protect himself. He merely kneeled in his place, ready to accept his fate.

Dream Kuneprius lowered his arms, faced the Small God. He placed one hand on Thorn's forehead, tilted his head back, and brought the blade to his throat, his expression blank, unreadable. His arm jerked and the knife's edge opened Thorn's throat, sending bright red blood fountaining into the air.

Kuneprius woke with a gasp, the tang of musty canvas on his tongue, and sat upright fast enough to send a jolt of pain through his back. His gaze flickered around the inside of the covered wagon, lit from the outside by the sun, but found nothing except the same coils of rope and boxes of supplies he'd seen when sleep overtook him.

How long did I sleep?

The hard ground clattered by under the wooden wheels, the solid axle transferring every bump and rut through the boards beneath him, rattling Kuneprius' teeth. He panted through his nose, trying to regain a sense of well-being as sweat cooled on his brow. No surprise to him, the calm he yearned for eluded him, leaving him to wonder if he'd ever experience comfort again.

And if he ever truly had.

When the beating of his heart slowed to a reasonable pace, Kuneprius rubbed his eyes with his knuckles, wiped his forehead on his sleeve. The fabric of the robe the Brothers gave him to replace his filthy clothes with was rougher than his shirt had been. Despite having lived most of his life in such a robe, he missed the softer touch of the shirt. He flexed the toes of his bare feet, expecting to relish the lack of footwear but finding he missed the manner in which the boots had contained his feet.

It's not the clothing and footwear I miss.

The rumbling in the floorboards smoothed out. The sensation of movement continued, but the rattle and clatter disappeared and Kuneprius' teeth ceased juddering in his mouth. He stretched out, reaching for the canvas covering the wagon to pull it aside and see what had changed, but his knotted muscles prevented him, and he found himself with his cheek pressed to the floor once again.

He lay on his front, listening, trying to vanquish the last remnants of the nightmare clinging to his mind. All those he'd seen were dead, and he blamed himself for their deaths, but what about Thorn? What did the horrendous end to his dream mean?

Is he dead?

If so, the Brothers wouldn't be going to Teva Stavoklis. But what if they weren't? It occurred to him Thorn may have died and they'd taken Kuneprius as part of a caravan making its way back to the Green to kidnap another Small God.

He shuddered and forced himself to sit again. Outside, the sounds of water came to his ears; horses' hooves splashed in it, wooden wheels shushed through it. It should have made sense, but sorting through it proved impossible. The sound meant something, but what?

He closed his eyes, imagining the procession making its way through water. Across a creek or river? Through a swamp or bog? Neither seemed right. The path was too smooth, the sound continuing too long.

Moving more slowly this time to protect his fatigued body, Kuneprius inched his way to the side of the wagon. He rested and drew three long breaths before reaching out and lifting the edge of the yellowed canvas, peeking through the opening.

Water.

It stretched on as far as his vision. No one walked beside the wagon, no other horse or wain traveled at his side. Not trees, no rocks, no land. Water and nothing else.

With the canvas pulled aside, the briny scent of the sea found its way to Kuneprius' nose. He inhaled, the scent reminding him of the shore where they'd found Thorn. But that wasn't where they were. They rode atop the water without sinking, which meant only one thing.

This was the inland sea he gazed upon, a body of water he'd never seen. The sun sparkled and glinted on its gentle waves, each of them dispersing a horse-length from the wagon. Kuneprius opened the canvas wider and leaned out, ignoring the pain it brought.

In front of his position, a line of wagons and wains stretched on toward a watery horizon with no apparent end. He struggled his body into a different position to look back. A similar procession of vehicles followed his wagon, but behind them he saw the shore of the

Windward Kingdom. No road led to the water's edge through the driftwood and stony expanse leading to it, yet the caravan had passed and now traversed the fabled water bridge. None but the Brothers knew how to locate it, for it led to their most holy of places: Teva Stavoklis.

Two thoughts occurred to Kuneprius, the first bringing with it a sliver of hope.

Thorn is alive.

The second followed quickly behind, quashing hope with dread.

Alive to be sacrificed.

Kuneprius slouched back inside the wagon, the canvas falling into place to block the sun and the briny odor of the sea. He hugged his knees to his chest, pressed his face against his legs and allowed despair to take him.

***

Improbably, sleep found Kuneprius again, and the rest of the voyage passed while he was unaware of it doing so. When he awoke to the canvas separating him from the outside world being thrown aside, the day had finished and night had come. Darkness filled the wagon and the muted rush of water greeted his ears. Where the covering lay open, the light of a torch flickered across the face of the man looking in. He recognized Brother Ianix, a man ten turns of the seasons his senior, whom he'd known his entire life.

I've known most of the Brothers my whole life.

Where once he experienced comfort amongst these men, a sense of family and belonging, Kuneprius now suspected his life had been a lie, nothing more than a result of being in the wrong place at the wrong time. A child of the wrong mother. Where would he be now had a woman not of the order of the Goddess birthed him? Might he have had a normal life?

"It is time, Kuneprius."

Brother Ianix pulled the canvas open wider, gestured for him to make his way out, but he hesitated.

"Time for what?"

Ianix chose not to reply; they both knew the answer.

"High Priest Kristeus awaits you. Everyone awaits you."

Ianix offered his hand, but Kuneprius didn't take it at first. The urge to crawl away and curl himself up in the farthest corner of the wagon tugged at him, but it would do him no good. If Kristeus wanted him, nothing could hide him from the High Priest's will.

The offered hand remained, patiently waiting, so Kuneprius took it. Brother Ianix gave a gentle tug, pulling him to his feet while steadying him. He'd set a short ladder against the side of the wagon, an act Kuneprius might have seen as an insult at another time, but was glad of while his body ached and complained with every movement.

As he emerged, the muted rush of water he'd heard within grew to a dull roar. A briny tang filled the air and a cool mist touched his face; he licked it from his lips and tasted the salt of the sea.

Brother Ianix's hand remained on Kuneprius' elbow and the man smiled at him. His eyes shone with an adoration and respect he'd never seen in them the times they'd shared the mess hall or the prayer room. The expression made him tremble.

"Come."

Ianix pulled at his elbow, guiding him away from the wagon. The closed space behind the canvas had given him a measure of safety, if the comfort he desired eluded him. Now, outside it, the immensity of his surroundings left him awe struck.

The roar of water emanated from everywhere at once as a circular water wall rose around them. The darkness made it difficult to tell where it ended and the sky began, the only demarcation between the two being the twinkling of the Small Gods staring down from above. Kuneprius diverted his gaze from them, afraid of their judgement.

This is why Kristeus wants me. I'm to be punished for my actions...my sins.

He gulped hard and scuffled his feet, attempting to stop Brother Ianix from dragging him toward the ornate temple filling the center of the opening in the sea. His legs were yet too weak to halt him.

The temple was a wonder of a kind Kuneprius had never seen. A spire rose skyward, its domed roof topped by a slender needle at least as tall as two men. Though the darkness dulled its sheen, he thought both roof and adornment might be fashioned of gold, an incredible expense equalled by the skill needed to create it. A moat surrounded it, the water filling it drawn from the walls of sea encircling this amazing location. From what he understood, this place of worship and tribute had stood since before the Goddess banished the Small Gods, making it as old or older than Draekfarren castle, as old as history itself.

As they approached the building along a stone bridge wide enough to accommodate two wagons abreast with room to spare, Kuneprius peered over the edge at the water below. It swirled and eddied, black in the darkness, but the sheen of the Small Gods reflecting on its surface hinted at its flow. What he realized shocked him.

The water moves away from the temple, not toward it.

His gaze followed the water's course, drawing his eye to the wall of the sea protecting the temple. At first, he thought of nothing but how it was possible for the wagons to find their way down here. The water wall stood taller than the temple's spire, taller than any tree or building Kuneprius had ever seen, perhaps as tall as some mountains.

Then he realized it did not cascade down from the Inland Sea above, but flowed upward, away from the temple, as if called to the sky by the evenstar himself.

Kuneprius blinked hard, thinking it a trick played on his eyes by lingering exhaustion, but the water continued its course, defying the laws of nature and finding its way up and up and up.

Brother Ianix led him through an arched doorway as wide as the stone bridge, and the spectacle disappeared from sight to be replaced by another wonder.

No walls separated one part of the temple's interior from another. Instead, it was a single great room. In Kuneprius' estimation, the distance from the entrance to the far end measured as much as the lengths of two hundred horses, with its width equal in size. Stones of many colors made up the floor, their shapes similar to each other but different enough he suspected viewing the colorful floor from overhead would reveal a pattern or depiction, and he wondered what it might be.

Brother Ianix continued leading Kuneprius across the great room toward a group of robed Brothers gathered in a circle. Though he knew he should pay attention to them because they would decide his fate, curiosity drew his eyes upward to the ceiling, searching for a viewing gallery from which to observe the floor's design.

He forgot his search when he realized the temple's great room lay open to the sky.

But what of the spire and its needle?

Astounded, Kuneprius thought he might be mistaken; perhaps an accomplished artist had painted a likeness of the night sky on the inside. It took but brief observation for him to note the way the Small Gods twinkled; Ine'vesi stood out amongst them, glowering down on him. He forgot the ceiling's anomaly, the evenstar's judging glare forcing his awareness back to the fate awaiting him.

He peered ahead over Brother Ianix's shoulder as they neared the circle of Brothers. Kuneprius couldn't see into the ring, but one thing stood out above their heads.

The clay head of the golem.

A shuddering breath found its way into Kuneprius' chest and he averted his gaze to his feet, bare toes visible in the black sandals. It took great effort to control his breathing, which wanted to shorten to fearful pants, but he forced his lungs to fill before he released the air again, attempting to use the technique to keep fear from overpowering him. If the golem stood within the circle, then it made sense the man who'd controlled him would be there, too, the man waiting to call Kuneprius before the Small Gods to be judged and sentenced: High Priest Kristeus.

A thumping startled him and it took a moment to recognize the sound of his heart beating in his ears. Without thinking, he counted the beats.

One. Two. Three.

He glanced up and saw they'd almost reached the circle, looked back down to his feet. His heart raced.

Seveneightnineteneleven...

Not so long ago, he'd have been pleased to remember his numbers, but not now. For every heartbeat he counted, he lent the number to each person left dead in their wake. Each beat he noted brought him one closer to his last.

Brother Ianix slowed and stopped, squeezed his elbow. When Kuneprius looked up in response, Ianix nodded toward the circle. He didn't want to look, but couldn't stop himself.

The Brothers closest to them had stepped aside, transforming the ring into a horseshoe, at the center of which stood Kristeus, dwarfed by the clay abomination standing at his side. The High Priest stared toward Kuneprius, a smile on his lips, but the golem glared past him, through him, the dead, blank eyes giving no hint they saw anything. Seeing the monstrosity again brought a shudder across his shoulders. He diverted his gaze to the altar in front of them, its sight making him forget the clay abomination.

The altar seemed out of place in the huge, elaborate room. Instead of being made of marble or gold, jewels or jade as befitted the temple, it was fashioned of plain stone and rotting wood, held together by clay and lengths of hemp rope. The materials used to build it meant nothing when Kuneprius saw Thorn bound and gagged on top of it.

He stood at the edge of the horseshoe, refusing to move despite Ianix's prompting at his elbow. His head moved back and forth slightly, denying this was happening.

"All hail Kuneprius," Kristeus intoned, breaking the silence. His clear, loud voice startled Kuneprius as it bounced and echoed from wall to wall. "Our Brother, the savior of the Small Gods."

Thorn didn't move. The gray man's chest rose and fell as tough he still drew breath, but the motion was slight. Concern for the Small God so gripped Kuneprius, it took a moment for the High Priest's words to penetrate his consciousness. When they did, he raised his eyes, looked from priest to golem and back, unsure he'd heard what he thought he heard.

"S...savior?" His lips trembled as he spoke. He'd thought nothing could be worse than facing punishment from the brotherhood and the Small Gods. Could he have been wrong?

"Come." Kristeus gestured for Kuneprius to enter the horseshoe, but he didn't move. "You are a favored son of those who watch from the sky. Come take your place at my side."

Brother Ianix prompted him more forcefully and his still tired legs could resist no longer. He stumbled forward a step and would have fallen if not for the hands on either side catching him under the arms and holding him up. The two helpful Brothers at the mouth of the horseshoe took him from Ianix and led him toward the altar, the High Priest, the monster. Kuneprius shook his head and resisted, sandals scraping the floor.

"No, I—"

"You helped bring this..." Kristeus waved a hand at Thorn, "this thing to us. Your efforts have provided the fodder we need to fulfill the prophecy and restore the evenstar and his brethren to their rightful places as rulers of this world. Hail Kuneprius!"

"Hail!"

The voices of the Brothers combined as one, the immensity of the room multiplying their enthusiasm to the point of deafening. Kuneprius winced, both at the volume assaulting his ears as well as at what they thought he'd done.

The two helping him brought him to stand between the High Priest and the golem before returning to their spots. They left him close enough to Thorn he could have reached out and stroked the Small God's forehead, wiped stale sweat from his ashen brow. He raised a shaking arm, intending to do just that, but stopped himself when the clay man's heavy hand came to rest on his shoulder. Kuneprius let his arm fall back to his side.

"The God Ine'vesi has whispered in my ear," Kristeus said, directing his words not to Kuneprius alone, but to the entire group. "He is pleased with you, Kuneprius, and wants to honor you."

The words registered, but he didn't move his gaze from Thorn. Being closer confirmed the Small God still lived; his chest drew shallow breaths; his flesh, though pale, radiated warmth; his eyelids fluttered but remained shut.

Wake up, Thorn. Wake up and use your magic. Save us both.

Kristeus had gone silent and, for an instant, Kuneprius feared he might have pleaded aloud. His eyes flickered away from the Small God to the robed men but none of them gaped at him as though he'd committed sacrilege of the highest order. He drew a breath, the stink of clay strong in his nostrils.

Everything remained silent and Kuneprius wondered if they expected him to speak. Did they want him to display his gratitude? What if he didn't?

A sound broke the silence, at once foreign and familiar—the scrape of steel on hard leather. He raised his gaze from Thorn, directed it toward Kristeus.

The High Priest held a knife in his hands, the grip resting on one palm, the end of the curved blade on the other. Light glinted on the polished metal, hinting at ancient words inscribed in the blade, words few in the world spoke or understood.

Mesmerized, Kuneprius stared at the torchlight dancing on the steel like fireflies flitting through a summer night. Seeing the weapon tightened the muscles in his jaw, made him want to flee no matter what the consequences, but he was powerless to so much as look away.

The knife from my dream.

Kristeus extended his arms, moving the weapon closer to Kuneprius. The air in the room became thick; too thick for him to draw enough breath to satisfy his struggling lungs. His mouth went dry and he gulped a sticky ball down his throat with a click.

"The evenstar told me the honor of raising the Small Gods belongs to you, Kuneprius. You are the reason their feet will again grace the ground of our world."

Sweat formed on his brow and Kuneprius shook his head, slowly at first, then with more urgency. The golem's grip tightened on his shoulder, rubbing the bones together and twisting the tendons. He grimaced, grunted in his throat, and raised his hand to accept the offering.

Only he and the abomination knew the truth.

When he accepted the knife, the golem's grip eased enough Kuneprius no longer wanted to cry out, but not so much as to allow him to flee. The weight of the dagger surprised him. He turned it in his hands, examining the fine quality of the blade with its delicate inscription despite his wish to throw it away. With his fingers touching the weapon, it seemed natural he should wrap them around the grip. He sifted it one hand to the other, nicking the side of his finger with the edge.

Blood sprang to the surface, as though it had been awaiting the opportunity. He watched a droplet roll down his finger into his palm, following the lines, blossoming across his hand.

My life line is filled with blood.

A chant began on Kristeus' lips, the words whispered but familiar. One of the Brothers took up the mantra, making the whisper into a murmur. Another joined in, then another. They all knew the incantation—Kuneprius included—though none among them other than Kristeus understood their meaning. Since they were all children who'd seen only enough seasons turn to learn to speak, they'd practiced the words taught by the priests.

The Brothers' voices united, increasing exponentially until the chant filled the room, floating up toward the sky and the Small Gods trapped in the night. Their words vibrated in Kuneprius as he watched another drop of blood run down his finger, his palm, his wrist. The first plummeted to the floor, landing on a green stone.

One.

More followed.

Two. Three.

How high would he count before he could no longer do so? Each morning, when he held his breath and laved his sins in a bowl of water, he knew what numbers he'd reach before having to stop and remove his face, draw breath again. But how many drops before the end came, relieving him of his sins and his life?

Six. Seven.

"Now is the time, Kuneprius," Kristeus said, breaking away from the chant as the others continued. "Fulfill the prophecy and return the Small Gods to their rightful place."

The incantation shuddered along Kuneprius' bones, gripped his muscles. He had no choice but to relinquish control and watch as his hand raised the knife in the air. His lips moved, forming the same words spoken by the others, the words he'd repeated over and over and over again.

His mind wanted to stop this, but it no longer had dominion over his body. The chanted words enveloped him, permeated his skin, forced his arm skyward. The dagger shook in his grasp as he resisted. His gaze fell on the Small God.

And Thorn opened his eyes.

***

Thorn's eyelids fluttered and opened. Dark sky dotted with pinpricks of light hung above him, a rush of water filled his ears. Hard, smooth stone pressed against his back, cooling his fevered flesh and bringing him a comfort he hadn't felt in many sunrises.

He blinked, inhaled. An unfamiliar odor mingled with the tang of sea water and the dusty scent of old stone.

Where is Thorn?

His eyelids slid closed once more as he concentrated

on sounds and smells. The aches and pains in his muscles and joints distracted him, but he centered his focus, shifting it first to listening. After a few seconds, he noticed a repetitive sound beneath the rush of water: many voices joined together, chanting. This puzzle piece showed him what the unfamiliar odor was, too. The sweat of many men. He recognized it because his friend Horace Seaman smelled of it whenever he went too long without washing.

"Horace?" Thorn's voice came out a croaking whisper to which no one responded. Did his friend hear him?

When Thorn opened his eyes this time, the world blurred. The stars became fuzzy streaks of light across a black canvas. He attempted to move his head, see who gathered around him, but the pain it caused in his neck was too great, so he settled for directing his gaze to his right.

A man stood beside him, both arms raised as though appealing to the sky. Thorn's vision remained blurred, but there was a familiarity to the fellow, the shape of his face.

"Is it you, Horace? Thorn is happy to see you again."

The voices surrounding him grew louder, the chanting more distinct, speaking the words of a language Thorn had not heard in a long time. He thought that, if he had his wits, he'd be able to decipher them, but both his wits and the words' meaning eluded him.

He blinked again and the fuzziness of his vision cleared. The features of the man standing beside him became visible, as did the shapes of the hooded men gathered in a circle around them. Thorn felt an instant of disappointment it wasn't the friend he thought it was, but it was still a friend.

"Not Horace," he said on a sigh. "But Thorn's other friend."

The man's face contorted, twisting into an expression of agony and despair. The chanting grew in volume, overpowering the rush of water.

"I'm sorry." The words squeaked out of the man's throat. "I'm so sorry."

"Do not be sorry, friend." Thorn forced a smile onto his lips in spite of the discomfort in his body. "Thorn will be fine."

The man's eyes closed, his mouth opened expelling an anguished cry, his shoulders shuddered. Light flashed on metal and the knife he'd been holding aloft came down. Its point tore through Thorn's flesh, through his chest, not stopping until it chipped the stone of the altar beneath him.

Thorn gasped and his gaze jerked back to the sky. A dark silhouette crossed in front of the stars, its wide wings blocking them out as it passed. Somehow, even in the darkness, he saw the bird's colors and the storm clouds it left in its wake.

"Stormbird," he whispered, his mind returning to the day he'd tried to use the creature to escape from behind the veil and inadvertently let it get away. In a lifetime stretching back in time for so many turns of the seasons, that day seemed so long ago.

Despite the pain and the sensation of his life draining from him, Thorn smiled. How could he not? Hadn't his long life been a thing filled with beauty and wonder? In the last short while, he'd flown with birds and eaten with men, he'd seen and done things no Small God had done since they took refuge behind the veil.

"It was a good life, Stormbird" he said as the bird passed out of sight leaving a night sky full of clouds behind.

He saw the first drops of rain plummeting toward him a few heartbeats before it spattered on his flesh, cooling it. He knew they'd be the last thing he'd experience, the last things to touch his skin, so he savored them. He filled his chest with one last breath, paused, then released it with a satisfied sigh. His vision dimmed, but before it faded to black, he saw the first of the streaks of light break through the Stormbird's clouds.

ABOUT THE AUTHOR

Bruce Blake lives on Vancouver Island in British Columbia, Canada. When pressing issues like shovelling snow and building igloos don't take up his spare time, Bruce can be found taking the dog sled to the nearest coffee shop to work on his short stories and novels.

Actually, Victoria, B.C. is only a couple hours north of Seattle, Wash., where more rain is seen than snow. Since snow isn't really a pressing issue, Bruce spends more time trying to remember to leave the "u" out of words like "colour" and "neighbour" then he does shovelling. The father of two, Bruce was once the trophy husband of burlesque diva...not so much anymore, but they remain friends.

Bruce has been writing since grade school but it wasn't until the mid-2000's he set his sights on becoming a full-time writer. Since then, his first short story, "Another Man's Shoes" was published in the Winter 2008 edition of _Cemetery Moon_, another short, "Yardwork", was made into a podcast in Oct., 2011 by _Pseudopod_. Since then, he has concentrated on writing novels, publishing the Khirro's Journey trilogy (Blood of the King, Spirit of the King, and Heart of the King), three books in the ongoing Icarus Fell urban fantasy series (On Unfaithful Wings, All Who Wander are Lost, and Secrets of the Hanged Man), and the Books of the Small Gods series (When Shadows Fall, The Darkness Comes, And Night Descends, When Ravens Call, The Twilight Fades, and And Kingdoms End). Bruce has many more projects simmering on the back burner, so stay tuned.

Blood of the King (Khirro's Journey Book 1)

A kingdom torn by war. A curse whispered by dying lips. A hero born against his will.

Khirro never wanted to be anything more than the farmer he was born to be, but a Shaman's curse binds him to the fallen king and his life changes forever.

Driven by the Shaman's dying words, Khirro's journey pits him against an army of the dead, sends him through haunted lands, and thrusts him into the jaws of beasts he wouldn't have believed existed. In one hand he carries the Shaman's enchanted sword, a weapon he can barely use; in the other he holds a vial of the king's blood, the hope of the kingdom. His destination: the Necromancer's keep in the cursed land of Lakesh. Only the mysterious outlaw magician can raise the king from the dead to save them all from the undead invasion, but can Khirro live long enough to deliver the vial?

Can a coward save a kingdom?

"Blood of the King is a masterpiece. It is as close to perfection as I would consider a book to be."- Ella Medler, author of *Blood is Heavier*

"Blake has a knack for bringing you into the story"

"Mr. Blake's writing is masterful and clear, he draws you into his story and when it's finished you feel like you're leaving an old friend."

On Unfaithful Wings (Icarus Fell #1)

To some, death is the end; to others, a beginning. To Icarus Fell, it should have been a relief from a life gone seriously awry.

But death had other plans.

Icarus doesn't believe that the man awaiting him when he wakes up in a cheap motel room is really the archangel Michael, or that God's right hand wants him to help souls on their way to Heaven. Icarus doesn't believe there's a Heaven, so why should they want his help?

But the man claiming to be the archangel tempts him with an offer he can't ignore--harvest enough souls and get back the life he wished he'd had.

It seems Icarus has nothing to lose, until he botches a harvest and the soul that went to Hell instead of Heaven comes back to make him pay by threatening to take away the life he hoped to win back.

To save the wife and son he already lost once, Icarus will have to become the man he never was. Somehow, he will have to learn to believe.

"The next book in this series cannot come out soon enough for this reader. Not just my favorite Kindle book of the year, but one of my favorite books ever."

"I loved this book."

"Bruce Blake's On Unfaithful Wings is a great urban fantasy novel. I love good character development in a story's protagonist and Blake nails it with Icarus Fell. I found myself rooting for him from the get-go and laughing out loud at some of his observations."

"On Unfaithful Wings was an impressive first novel. All of the characters were interesting and engaging, but in particular the main character and his struggle to reconcile with his new identity/job. This is one of those stories that stays with me long after I read it and I'll be on the lookout for more from this author."